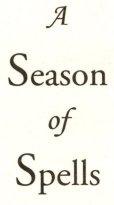

A
Season
of
Spells

A
Season
of
Spells

SYLVIA HUNTER

Allison & Busby Limited
12 Fitzroy Mews
London W1T 6DW
allisonandbusby.com

First published in 2016.
This edition published in Great Britain by Allison & Busby in 2017.

Copyright © 2016 by Sylvia Izzo Hunter
Maps © Cortney Skinner

A CIP catalogue record for this book is available from
the British Library.

10 9 8 7 6 5 4 3 2 1

ISBN 978-0-7490-2039-2

Typeset in 11/16 pt Adobe Garamond Pro by
Allison & Busby Ltd.

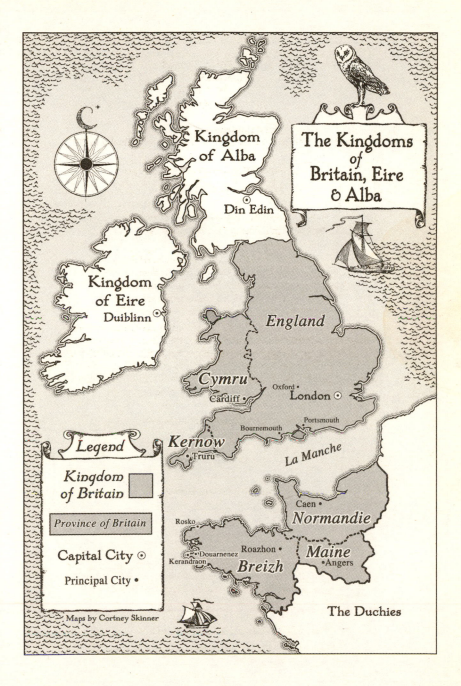

Kingdom
of Alba

Din Edin

The Kingdoms
of
Britain, Eire
& Alba

Kingdom
of Eire
Duiblinn

England

Cymru
Cardiff • Oxford • London ⊙

Portsmouth
Bournemouth

Kernow
• Truru La Manche

Legend

Kingdom
of Britain

Province of Britain

Capital City ⊙

Principal City •

Rosko

Caen •

Normandie

Roazhon •
Kerandraon • Douarnenez Maine
Breizh • Angers

Maps by Cortney Skinner The Duchies

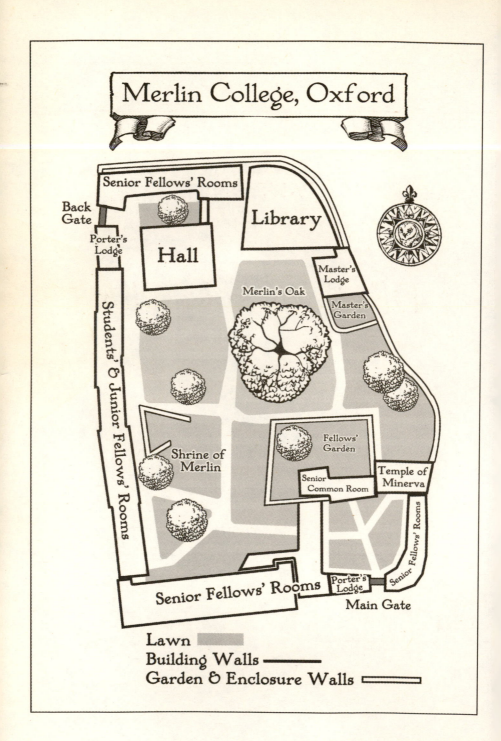

Merlin College, Oxford

Senior Fellows' Rooms

Back Gate

Porter's Lodge

Hall

Library

Master's Lodge

Master's Garden

Merlin's Oak

Students' & Junior Fellows' Rooms

Shrine of Merlin

Fellows' Garden

Senior Common Room

Temple of Minerva

Senior Fellows' Rooms

Senior Fellows' Rooms

Porter's Lodge

Main Gate

Lawn
Building Walls
Garden & Enclosure Walls

PART ONE

Din Edin to London

CHAPTER I

In Which Sophie and Gray Depart on a Journey, and Gwendolen Loses a Wager

'Well, Magistra?' said Gray.

The small flock of new graduates broke apart, smiling and laughing, and Sophie Marshall emerged from it to look up at her husband. He was beaming all over his kind, honest face, and when she stepped towards him, holding out her hand for him to shake by way of congratulation – for they had not met since before the day's long ceremonials – he laughed aloud and swept her into a fierce, albeit chaste, embrace.

Sophie's friends hooted and applauded.

'Where next?' Gray said, when Sophie had her feet under her once more. 'Have you some grand festivity to attend, Magistra, to which I may escort you?'

Sophie tilted her head, laughing up at him, and – trusting to the confusion of motion and noise that surrounded them – said, 'I had hoped that a handsome Doctor of Practical Magick might give me his arm as far as Quarry Close. And after that . . .'

Astonishing, she thought, with an inward grin, that being nearly six years married, she still could make him blush.

'Sophie!' cried a voice behind her. 'Gray!'

Sophie turned on her heel to find her friends (and Gray's colleagues) Mór MacRury, Rory MacCrimmon, and Sorcha

MacAngus, together with Lucia MacNeill – it was she who had been calling them – elbowing their way through the crowd.

A new round of back-slapping and embracing ensued, after which Mór said brightly, 'We shall see you both at the bonfire this evening, I hope?'

Sophie and Gray exchanged a lingering glance; Sophie, for her part, was calculating the hours remaining until dusk, and finding the number sufficient.

'Of course,' she said, turning a general smile upon her friends. 'We should not dream of missing it.'

Then she caught Gray's right hand in her left, and they began making their farewells.

The succeeding fortnight was lost to a mad welter of preparations for departure. In May, Lucia MacNeill – heiress to the chieftain's seat of Alba, and, if all unfolded as planned, soon to be Sophie's sister-in-law – was to journey to London to meet her future husband and the rest of Britain's royal family. Gray and Sophie, in her capacity as Princess Royal, were to travel south as part of Lucia's retinue, and there remain until after her marriage to Prince Roland, so that Sophie might serve her friend as guide and interpreter of London society.

It was not, in truth, a prospect which Sophie greatly relished; not only was she, in her own estimation, very ill-equipped to be anyone's guide to that circle of society in which Lucia MacNeill must be expected to move, but the task must bring her into prolonged and frequent contact with her stepmother, Queen Edwina, a circumstance unlikely to occasion joy to either. Lucia *was* her friend, however, and might very well have need of a sympathetic ear in the course of her sojourn in Britain. And of course she wished very much to see her sister Joanna, and Gray's sister Jenny, and Jenny's growing family.

The Marshalls' immediate plans, in any case, had thus been determined for them; but it remained to decide – or, perhaps, to discover – what they were to do with themselves thereafter. Were they to return to Din Edin and their work at the University, or even a permanent home in Alba? To Oxford, in hopes that a second sojourn there might be more successful than the first? To London, or to the house in Breizh which had belonged to Sophie's stepfather, Appius Callender, and now was Gray's? All these possibilities had been the subject of six months' intermittent and inconclusive debate.

The packing-up of their small house in Quarry Close, therefore – their home, and a very happy one but for the dramatic disruptions of their first spring in Din Edin, for the past three years – had something of the character of a magistrate's court, each object in it being interrogated as to its possible fate, should any of a variety of futures come to pass.

'Gray,' said Sophie one morning, for example, 'I have found that three-volume work on botanical magicks by Niall MacNeill, which you spoke of returning to Lachlan Ruadh MacDougall. Shall I set them aside for him?'

Gray, on hands and knees with his head and shoulders inside a cupboard, sat back on his heels, thrust one dusty hand through his equally dusty hair, and said, 'Yes – no – I must just read once more through the chapter on Niall MacNeill's experiments with wild celery; he claims to have used it to prevent a rival of his from executing a shape-shift, and Rory and I have been meaning to put his method to the test—'

'Absolutely not!' Sophie exclaimed, hugging the books to her chest and taking a step backwards. 'Of all the absurdly dangerous—'

She closed her eyes briefly – counted ten in Latin, then in Gaelic – invented a compromise which might put off the real

11

decision to another day. 'If I copy out the chapter for you, in my very best hand,' she said, 'so that you may have the necessary information to hand when next you and Rory find yourselves at leisure to conduct hazardous experiments, may I then return the books to Lachlan MacDougall?'

Gray sneezed; Sophie extracted her handkerchief from her sleeve and handed it to him.

'Very well,' he said, when he had finished with the handkerchief. 'I thank you, *cariad*.'

'You may thank me,' said Sophie firmly, 'by finishing with that cupboard, and making a start upon the one under the stairs; and by remembering that we shall be living out of our trunks and valises for the foreseeable future, and must consider their contents accordingly.'

She reflected a little guiltily on the contents of her own trunks, and went upstairs to agonise once more over the ratio of commonplace books to gowns and bonnets.

Their methods, in other words, were not conducive to either speed or efficiency, and Donella MacHutcheon, the daily woman who had had the care and feeding of Sophie and Gray since their arrival in Din Edin, exclaimed in despair at their manner of going on. When the day of departure arrived, however, it found the Marshalls' affairs sufficiently in order that they might oversee the strapping-up of their trunks and ascend into Lucia MacNeill's carriage with a reasonably clear conscience – though still with no clear notion of what, beyond the journey itself, their future might hold.

Lucia MacNeill studied her friends as they settled themselves, side by side, on the opposite *banc* of the carriage. Sophie was rather pink in the face, and Gray patting the pockets of his coat as though searching for something, or (perhaps more likely) reassuring himself that he had not left some item of importance behind. They looked, in fact, nearly as unsettled and anxious as Lucia felt – not at all a reassuring beginning.

Lucia clasped her gloved hands tightly together and looked out of the window at the narrow row-houses of Quarry Close, crowded together like herring in a barrel. She tried to imagine the Sophie who lived here – who so matter-of-factly presided over her creaky dining-table and cramped kitchen, who existed in a perpetual semi-disorder of half-read books and half-finished essays and ongoing academic debates – as the Princess Edith Augusta Sophia, only daughter of Henry of Britain; and, as usual, failed.

The carriage quickly left Quarry Close behind, and soon enough was joined by its companions: the equipage carrying Lucia's cousin Sìleas Barra MacNeill and her husband, Oscar MacConnachie, envoy to the British Court; and Lucia's personal squadron of her father's household guard, mounted and travelling as outriders, together with Sophie's guardsmen. Not all of Lucia's guardsmen were, in fact, men; she expected some degree of trouble on that score, but had determined that she must begin as she meant to go on, which was not by compromising either her troops' esprit de corps (a pretty phrase *en français* which she had learnt from Gray Marshall) or her own safety for the sake of her betrothed husband's sensibilities. Compromises there must be, of course, but if he was to be her consort, he must take some things in stride.

Despite the crowds assembled to see Lucia off, which impeded the progress of their convoy to a quite extraordinary degree, they had nearly left Din Edin behind by the time Sophie said, in an uncharacteristically hesitant tone, 'You shall not be away so very long, after all.'

Lucia turned from the window. 'I beg your pardon?'

Sophie's brow was crumpled in concern. 'You have been looking

13

out at Din Edin as though you half expected never to see it again,' she said. 'But if all goes well, you shall be coming back in a few months' time, with Roland; and if it does not . . .'

If it does not, I shall be coming back very soon indeed, with my tail between my legs like a dog who has lost her sheep.

But there was no need to give voice to such a melancholic thought.

'Yes,' said Lucia instead, attempting cheerfulness. 'Very true. Now, I shall be your guide to the country round about, so long as we are in Alba; but once we are over the Wall, you must return the favour, and tell me all about everything we see, so that I shall not be entirely ignorant when we reach London.'

'Not that necklace,' said Joanna.

'Why not?' said Gwendolen. Though her tone demanded justifications, her fingers were already reaching for the clasp.

'Why not?' echoed Joanna's niece Agatha, watching them dress for Lady Lisle's ball from her perch on the end of Joanna's bed.

'It spoils the line of the décolleté, just there,' said Joanna, pointing. She turned back to her dressing-table and rummaged in her jewel-case, finally laying hands on what she wanted: a twisted string of round beads, smooth amethyst and faceted violet glass, and the matching set of ear-drops, a gift from Jenny for her fifteenth birthday.

'Sit down,' she said, turning again. 'You are entirely too tall.'

Gwendolen smirked and folded herself gracefully into Joanna's abandoned chair.

In this way, Joanna's face appeared directly above hers in the dressing-glass as Joanna fastened the amethysts about her slim throat and adjusted their set on her collar-bones, and side by side when Joanna bent, out of Agatha's line of sight, to kiss the curve of Gwendolen's left ear.

'Perfect,' Joanna pronounced, straightening up again with both hands resting on Gwendolen's shoulders.

As Gwendolen reached for the ear-drops, their eyes met in the mirror – cheeks flushed, eyes shining – and they shared a secret, promising grin.

'Aunty Gwen!' said Agatha. 'Do you suppose Mr Trenoweth will ask you for the first two dances?'

Gwendolen's smile went rather fixed. 'I suppose he may, duckling,' she said. 'He must ask someone, presumably, though I do not know why he should ask me in particular.'

She turned her head this way and that, examining the effect of the ivory rosebuds in her dark hair.

'Oh, but *I* know why!' Agatha crowed. She had got her feet under her, and scrambled up to stand on the bed's low footboard, clinging to the bedpost with one arm – imagining, Joanna knew, that she was a sailor standing lookout up aloft. 'Mr Trenoweth's sister is Lady Lewes, and she came to call upon Mama once, and said that she hoped he might ask you to marry him! . . . But I do not know what Mama said about it,' she added, now sounding rather cross, 'because Rozena found me and made me come out from under the sofa, and so I did not hear any more.'

Joanna (who knew exactly what Jenny had said, and to whom, and why) stifled a chuckle at her disgruntled tone; but her mirth died away as, out of the corner of her eye, she caught a glimpse of Gwendolen's face.

'I think I hear Rozena calling you, Captain Agatha,' she said. 'Run away now, and we shall be sure to come and see you before we go.'

Agatha clambered down the end of the bed with what she fondly imagined to be a nautical cry and slipped out of the room, closing the door firmly behind her.

When the sound of her running footsteps had faded, Joanna caught Gwendolen's hands in hers, turned her away from the looking-glass, and peered up into her eyes. 'None of that,' she said firmly. 'We have had all of this out before, and you know that Jenny is with us and not against us.'

Gwendolen briefly squeezed her eyes tight shut, then opened them again and sighed. 'Yes,' she said. 'I do know it, Jo.'

'And Mr Trenoweth has not been making a nuisance of himself?' Joanna said.

Another sigh. 'No, not particularly. He is a perfectly unobjectionable young man, you know, now that he has set his matrimonial sights elsewhere.'

'I am glad to hear it,' said Joanna. 'Now, before we go downstairs—'

The words began what had become a sort of ritual between them, for occasions of this kind, when they should both be spending most of the evening dancing with other people. Gwendolen continued it by casting an approving eye over the tiny pink roses in Joanna's hair, her garnet earrings, her new gown of rose-pink satin, the silver buckles decorating her dancing-slippers; Joanna returned her glance for glance, enjoying the blush that spread prettily over Gwendolen's sharp cheekbones as she grew conscious of being admired.

Joanna tipped her face up towards her friend's, and for just a moment lost herself in the press of Gwen's lips upon her own – so familiar now, yet always half unexpected, always astonishing. Her hands found Gwen's hips, her waist; crept up her spine to press her closer.

'You look very lovely,' said Gwendolen, drawing back at last, too soon.

'And so do you,' said Joanna. 'As you know very well.'

Gwendolen, being taller, held out her arm – bent at the elbow,

16

as a gentleman does for a lady – and when Joanna tucked her hand under it, pressed it close against her ribs. 'Shall we go, Miss Callender?' she asked.

'Certainly, Miss Pryce,' said Joanna, matching her light, untroubled tone; and, moving as regally as either of them knew how, they swept out of her bedroom, along the corridor, and up the stairs to the nursery, to bid farewell to Captain Agatha as promised.

Joanna was afterwards to look back on the beginning of that summer as a sort of idyll – no different on the surface from the years that preceded it, but bathed in a rosy glow of affection, freed (to some degree, at any rate) from the shadow of their shared but always unspoken anxiety by Jenny's explicit promise to entertain no offers of marriage for either of them, no matter how apparently eligible. Less than a month before Lucia MacNeill's anticipated arrival in London to make the acquaintance of her betrothed, the ladies of the royal household were consumed with preparations, and the Kergabet ladies with them; but though the endless talking-over of tedious minutiae sometimes frustrated and bored Joanna and Gwendolen almost past bearing, they had only to meet one another's eyes, and the tedium gave way to relief and occasional jubilation.

All too soon, however, a hired carriage deposited Mrs Edmond Marshall in Grosvenor Square to disturb the peace of its occupants. Ostensibly her purpose was to be of use to her daughter – presently expecting her third child – but Joanna rather suspected her of a desire to *make* use of Jenny, or at any rate of Jenny's connexions. Or perhaps, if one were being charitable, Mrs Marshall might simply (in common with half the kingdom, to judge by the influx of persons into London at present) have been possessed of a desire to gawk at Lucia MacNeill of Alba.

At any rate, there was nothing to be done but to make Jenny's mama welcome, and to keep her – so far as possible – from fretting Jenny into a state of misery. It was a task in which Joanna was grateful, this time, to have Gwendolen's assistance.

'I tell you,' she said, low, as they stood on the steps of Lord Kergabet's house, watching two footmen assist their visitor's descent from her equipage, 'Mrs Marshall the elder is the most tiresome woman I have met in the whole of my life.'

'Oh, come, Jo!' said Gwendolen, grinning behind one hand. 'Did you not travel the whole way to Din Edin with Lady MacConnachie, and live to fight another day?'

Eight days later, Joanna and Gwendolen sat pressed close together on the window-seat in Joanna's bedroom, listening to the rain.

'I did not think anything could be more tiresome than a long journey with Lady MacConnachie,' said Gwen, after a moment, 'but now that I have spent fully a se'nnight in the same house with Lady Kergabet's mama, I must admit that you were quite right.'

She reached for her reticule, rummaged in it briefly, and handed over two silver coins.

Joanna took them from her with a triumphant grin; but her conscience smote her, and, sighing, she handed them back and folded Gwen's fingers gently around them.

'I ought not to have taken your wager,' she said. 'I knew how it would be, for she stayed here a month entire when Agatha was born, and drove Jenny nearly to distraction; she was not nearly so horrid when you met her here before, being so pleased to have a grandson at last. It would not be fair of me to take your coin.'

'Well, then, I ought not to have wagered!' said Gwen, laughing. 'We cannot be everlastingly going back on our word to one another, Jo, only because one of us occasionally makes an idiotic bet; and I assure you that I should not let you off if our positions were reversed.'

Joanna considered this. Then a thought struck her, and – feeling greatly daring, for it was full day, though pouring with rain, and this window plainly visible from the square below – she said, 'Very well; I decline to accept your coin, but you may pay your wager in kisses instead.'

Gwen gave her a long, stern look, then drew the curtains and did so.

CHAPTER II

In Which Mrs Edmond Marshall Is Inexplicable, and Sophie Conceives an Idea

Sophie and Gray parted from Lucia at their last halt before reaching London, she to travel in Oscar MacConnachie's carriage to the Royal Palace, and they to continue to Lord Kergabet's house in Grosvenor Square. Lucia had been brought up from infancy in the knowledge that she might one day be named her father's heir, and was as well versed in the concealment of private trepidation as anyone of Sophie's acquaintance; whether her composure were real or assumed, therefore, was almost impossible to determine, but Sophie knew very well that she herself, in Lucia's place, would have been quaking in her sturdy calfskin boots.

'Do you suppose . . .' she began, peering through the window of their carriage as the other receded into the distance – then, changing tacks, 'It will all go off very smoothly, I am sure. Oscar MacConnachie knows what he is about.'

Gray chuckled – showing, Sophie could not help thinking, rather less care than he ought for the well-being of their friend – and said, 'I notice you do not say the same of Sìleas Barra MacNeill.'

Sophie waved this away impatiently. 'Of course I do not,' she said. 'Nobody *could,* you know – though she is all very well in her own sphere, of course, and she is Lucia's cousin, which Lucia may find comforting. I hope it may be so, at all events.' She grimaced, keeping her face turned away from Gray's so that he should not see it. 'I should not have been averse to having Cousin Maëlle to protect me, when first I went to stay with *my* mother-in-law.'

Gray's chuckle this time was low and rather bitter. 'Nor I,' he said. 'You do remember, I hope, *cariad*, that we may well be staying with her on this occasion also, in a manner of speaking.'

'I remember,' Sophie sighed. 'Of course I remember. But at any rate we shall be in Jenny's house; it is not quite the same as actually living under your parents' roof.'

They spoke thereafter of anything and everything but the Marshalls of Glascoombe, and spent a good deal of time pointing out to one another scenes and landmarks which they had had no sight of since their last visit to London – on the occasion of Prince Edward's wedding, nearly two years past. As an attempt to take their minds off the coming ordeal, it was (at least in Sophie's case) an abject failure. But at any rate, she reflected, they should not waste this last precious sliver of private conversation in dredging up past hurts and irritations.

The household which assembled to greet them had been translated from the house in Carrington-street to a much larger and more imposing one in Grosvenor Square, more befitting the dignity of Lord Kergabet's present position on His Majesty's Privy Council; and not only Joanna and Gwendolen Pryce but also Gray's mother joined Jenny, her children, and their nursery-maid in the silver-papered hall where Treveur and his minions were attempting to divest the newcomers of their travelling-cloaks and hats.

Jenny had written to warn them that she expected a maternal visitation at some point during the summer; his mother's presence, therefore, did not startle Gray – until she approached him, beaming, and put up her face to be kissed.

21

'Mama,' he said, nonplussed. He kissed her cheek, and when he unbent his neck again was further startled to see her turning to greet Sophie with even greater effusiveness.

Over their heads, Gray met Jenny's eyes, as full of bafflement as his own thoughts. Sophie and his mother had avoided coming to blows during their first and only sojourn in the same house, but only just, and according to Jenny and Joanna, Mrs Marshall the elder habitually referred to Sophie as *that girl* and had more than once dropped dark hints about love-spells. What could possibly be behind this sudden change of heart, if such it was? Gray knew not whether he ought to feel wary or relieved, and instead of indulging himself in either, turned his attention to his niece and nephew, and submitted to being climbed upon, as though he had been a tree.

'Your mama seems friendlier,' said Sophie, meaning, *She appears to detest me less than formerly.* She tugged at the bedclothes; Gray grumbled good-naturedly but ceded her a further hand's breadth of coverlet. 'Perhaps time – or absence – has reconciled her to your unfortunate choice of bride.'

Gray, tucked up behind her, shifted slightly so as to kiss the top of her left ear. 'I hope she may be sincere, *cariad*, for your sake,' he said – meaning, she suspected, *I hope she may be sincere, but I should be surprised to find her so.* Or perhaps this was only the effect of her own deep caution with respect to her mother-in-law.

'And she mentioned to me after dinner,' Sophie went on, 'that your brother Alan went up to Oxford in the autumn, at last, and is reading alchymy at Plato College! Does not that sound as though he were turning out rather better than you feared?'

'It does,' said Gray. 'For which I thank all the gods, for I have not the least idea to which of them thanks may be owed in this case. Now, why should she have told you that, I wonder?'

'Gray.' Sophie's attempt at a reproachful tone ran afoul of a strong urge to laugh, and Gray kissed her ear again, and drew her closer. She wriggled round to face him, laid a hand on his cheek, and said seriously, 'If your mama is inclined to be conciliating, love, I do not mean to look a gift horse in the mouth.'

'Of course you do not,' said Gray, with a fond smile just visible in the cool glow of the magelights they had called to light them to bed. 'And may it so continue.'

Sophie drew breath to ask him what he meant; he tilted his head and kissed her, however, and she forgot her question entirely.

The Marshalls of Din Edin were not by nature early risers, but the arrival at their door of morning tea, heralded as of old by Daisy's quiet knock – together with a suite of morning noises quite different from those of Quarry Close, or of a country inn-yard – brought them down to breakfast at an hour which even Jenny, surely, could not consider excessively late.

Mrs Marshall, it appeared, was yet abed, and though neither was so ill-judged as to say anything about it, Sophie did not think she was imagining the look of relief that crossed Gray's face, mirroring her own feelings, upon finding his mother absent from the breakfast-table.

The conversation was at first general and perfectly ordinary, but partook of an ease and candour which had been altogether absent from the dinner-table on the previous afternoon. Mr Fowler soon afterwards appeared, and by degrees the conversation took a more political turn: first to a dispatch from one of Lord Kergabet's agents in the Duchies, which reported that the local lord was recruiting foot-soldiers on behalf of some unknown person improbably styled Imperator Gallia, or Emperor of Gaul, which occasioned much discussion and not a little scoffing; and then, by way of the

Marshalls' impressions of Lucia's state of mind when last seen, to the Kergabet household's latest news of Roland.

'Prince Roland,' said Miss Pryce unexpectedly, 'hopes that Lucia MacNeill's conversation may be more lively than her letters.'

'Does he,' said Sophie, frowning. What could this signify?

Mrs Marshall's arrival in the breakfast-room necessitated a change of subject – which (fortunately or unfortunately) she herself provided, by turning to Sophie with an expectant expression and announcing, 'You must tell us all about Din Edin, and the Alban princess.'

Lord Kergabet and Mr Fowler exchanged a look, and rapidly though very civilly took their leave.

'Graham is a most unsatisfactory correspondent,' Mrs Marshall continued, oblivious. 'Though I suppose there cannot be very much to relate, when all of one's time is spent amongst piles of dusty books! Now that you are come back, however, I hope you may be able to persuade him to put them aside, and go out into society from time to time, so as to make the best of your visit.'

'Mama,' said Jenny, in a tone of gentle reproof which Mrs Marshall entirely ignored.

Gray said nothing. Sophie swallowed her outrage, reminding herself that her mother-in-law, for sound political reasons, did not and could not know the true tale of their first year in Din Edin, nor understand how near she had come to losing her second son for good and all.

'I believe, ma'am,' she said, when she felt able once more to speak without fatally offending her listener, 'we may expect to enjoy a good deal more society during Lucia MacNeill's visit than ever in our lives before; and I assure you,' she added with a smile, 'that I shall be more than satisfied to return to my dusty books at the end of it.'

She had meant it as a rebuff, if a gentle one; Mrs Marshall, however, seemed not to hear it as such, for she said, 'Tell me, my dear, is it true that the Alban princess walks about Din Edin unescorted, and plays at being a student?'

Gray's head rose sharply, his eyes narrowing. 'Lucia MacNeill does not play at anything she does, Mama,' he said. 'She is not a student at present, but she is certainly a scholar – a very fine one, indeed, and every bit as clever as Sophie.' This, Sophie knew, was among the highest compliments of which Gray was capable. 'It is quite as usual in Alba for clever young ladies to take up University places, as for clever young men to do so.'

'Which is just as it ought to be, *I* think,' said Joanna stoutly, and Miss Pryce, after a cautious glance at Jenny, said, 'I quite agree.'

'And she does not walk about Din Edin unescorted,' said Sophie, before any of them could go on, or Mrs Marshall present some retort. 'She has guardsmen lurking in the shadows, always, just as I have.'

'Have you, indeed?' Mrs Marshall looked about the breakfast-room (quite empty of royal guardsmen), her eyebrows pointedly raised. 'They must be past masters of concealment, I conclude?'

'Of course I can have no possible need of a bodyguard in Jenny's house, ma'am,' said Sophie. *If I swallow any more outrage, I shall have a dreadful bellyache.*

By now every eye had turned to see how Jenny would bear her mother's insult to her hospitality; Mrs Marshall seemed to recognise at last exactly what she had said, and how it was likely to be understood. Flustered and wrong-footed, she tittered – a startling sound from a woman of her age and dignity – and in an entirely transparent attempt to turn the conversation said, 'Genevieve, my love, you are eating no more than a sparrow! I hope you are not unwell? In your condition—'

'No, Mama,' said Jenny patiently; 'I am quite well; I was down to breakfast an hour ago and have eaten all I can hold, I assure you.'

After a further quarter-hour of limping conversation, consisting mostly in ingratiating questions from Mrs Marshall, and in less and less patient answers on the part of everybody else, Joanna and Miss Pryce (who had increasingly been exchanging covert looks of amusement and exasperation) excused themselves from the breakfast-table and went away. Mrs Marshall frowned after them; Sophie, on the contrary, rather wondered at their not having fled sooner.

As always during visits to London, and irrespective of her role as shepherd or chaperone to Lucia MacNeill, one of Sophie's tasks was to mend fences with her father.

She therefore found herself occupying an idle hour in the library of the Royal Palace, in the interval before the family dinner, so called, to which she (but not Gray) had been summoned; and it was here that she found it – tucked almost invisibly between two quarto volumes, its leather binding faded and its endpapers badly foxed. *A Dove amongst the Peacocks,* the title-page read; *Being the Tale of the Founding of Lady Morgan College, Oxon.*

She had forgotten until this moment the astonishment, the fascination, with which she had pored over this volume, when first she discovered it amongst her mother's books; the wondering, bubbling joy, to learn that such a place – a college for the education of women, founded by a clever Cymric heiress hundreds of years ago – existed, and to imagine that she might one day aspire to a place there; the falling of her heart when Mama told her, her eyes soft with regret, that in fact it had closed its doors two centuries before.

This copy of the book bore a variety of scuff-marks and several illegible annotations in ink, but no cataloguer's mark or number; very possibly, no one but Sophie knew of its existence here.

'Gray,' she said, 'see what I have found—'

Then she recalled that Gray was not here, was at this moment no doubt eating his dinner in Grosvenor Square, and scowled ferociously at the bookcase before her.

She laughed at herself, if a little crossly – *I am justly served, for thinking Gray impossibly absent-minded!* – and sat down to examine her find.

The volume was more or less as she remembered it, insofar as she remembered it at all – which was odd, considered rationally; in general she had an excellent memory for books, yet the contents of this one seemed to have slipped sidewise from her mind whilst her attention was elsewhere. The frontispiece, an engraved view of the College buildings with the central dome of Minerva's shrine, caught her gaze, familiar-strange – like and not like the buildings themselves, glimpsed behind the ivy-covered outer wall on the far bank of the Cherwell in Sophie's Oxford days, always at the periphery of her attention, never reaching its centre.

She had first seen that derelict dome, those overgrown walls, from the window of a hired carriage on a rainy autumn day. The sight had gripped her with a sorrow so profound as to steal her breath – the memory of it, lost till now, returned in force, and she let the book fall on the table, struggling to draw breath around the sudden tightness in her chest.

And she had had another thought – had wished, had *yearned* to restore that dead place to vivid life – and Joanna had said—

'Mother Goddess,' Sophie breathed, as the vice-grip on her lungs began to ebb.

—Joanna had said, *Perhaps you may do so, when you are a princess again.*

'How could I have forgot such a thing?' she spoke aloud now, only for the reassurance of hearing her own voice – which, to her immense relief, sounded absolutely as usual. 'How could I live two years in Oxford, and never once—'

She stopped, arrested open-mouthed by another vivid recollection: an evening stroll over the Cherwell bridge, the fragrant Midsummer-tide twilight, her hand tucked through Gray's elbow, faint splashing and young men's voices singing and calling to one another from below, and the dome of Minerva catching the light of the setting sun, and Gray's voice, thoughtful: 'What a place it must have been, in its day!'

And again the press of sorrow and loss, the yearning to see the gate flung open and the halls and quads filled with scholars once more.

There is a pattern here, Sophie thought. *There is, there must be – but, by the gods, I cannot see its shape.*

Now that the idea had caught hold of her once more, however, it was easy to succumb to its persuasion. There had been a college for women in Oxford once; why should there not be again? Sophie's namesake and distant quasi forebear, the Princess Edith Augusta, had been one of its patrons, as well as a student there; why should Sophie not fill the same role?

The Princess Edith, it was true, in her capacity as co-Regent for her brother Edward, had had access to powers and resources which Sophie had not; true, too, that to assume the mantle of patronage in respect of a living, thriving institution was one thing, and to rebuild it from what might well be literal rubble, entirely another. *But if it could be done . . . If* I *might be the one to do it . . .*

The steward's knock upon the library door startled her out of her thoughts, and half out of her seat; but by the time it was followed by the man himself, she had regained some of her composure.

'If you would be so good as to join Her Majesty in the small reception room, ma'am,' he said, with a nicely judged bow.

'Of course,' said Sophie.

She tucked the book into her reticule – no one would miss it, she reasoned, and she should return it upon a subsequent visit, of which there were bound to be many – and followed him out of the room, making notes in her mind as to the possible means of proceeding.

Point the first: search the remainder of the Palace library for further published works.

Point the second: gain entry to the Archives, and find whether any unpublished documents exist which might shed light upon the problem.

Point the third—

Point the third: how did I come to forget something so very much worth remembering . . . ?

But now, at this moment, there were her father and her brother Ned to be reassured as to her well-being, and Delphine's shy raptures over the child she was expecting; young Harry to be regaled with tales of life in Alba, and Roland to be talked out of his nerves; and Queen Edwina – with her seemingly unbreakable habit of addressing Sophie as 'Edith' – to be borne with cheerfully.

But when next I have leisure for my own pursuits . . .

CHAPTER III

In Which Lucia Meets Her Match

On the morning of her third day in London, Lucia MacNeill, daughter of Donald MacNeill, holder of a graduate degree in practical magick and heiress to the chieftain's seat of Alba, stood in her borrowed bedchamber – truly alone for almost the first time since leaving Din Edin – and gazed disconsolately at her reflection in a tall cheval-glass.

She could not fault her appearance; her unruly curls were smoothed and tamed into a knot low on her neck, and her simply but exquisitely cut sea-green gown made the most of her slim figure and of the colour of her eyes. She looked, in short, as much like a suitable successor to her father as she was ever like to do. She adopted a grave expression, suitable for affairs of state – then turned away abruptly, hands clenched and lips pressed tight together, when it threatened to dissolve into either giggles or tears.

The last leg of Lucia's journey to London had been made in the sole company of her cousin Sìleas Barra MacNeill and Sìleas's husband, Oscar MacConnachie, to whom – thanks to the latter's status as Donald MacNeill's envoy to the British Court – had fallen the duty of introducing Lucia therein. Sìleas was a kindly and motherly companion, for whose presence Lucia (who had lost her own mother at the age of ten) was duly grateful; she was also, alas, a rather tedious one, for her mind ran solidly in a very few tracks and could not be jolted out of them. And she was at present waiting just outside the door, and very likely fretting over Lucia's odd behaviour.

'You are the heiress to the chieftain's seat of Alba,' Lucia said aloud, sternly, as she turned back to the glass. She stood straighter. 'Confirmed by the clan chieftains in full council, with the blessings of Brìghde and of the Cailleach. If the prospect of ruling a kingdom does not alarm you, why should you so dread meeting your mother-in-law?'

Dread it she did, but there was nothing to be gained by delaying the inevitable. Lucia smoothed her hands down her skirts one last time and went out to meet her fate.

Queen Edwina, it transpired, could scarcely have appeared less frightening: a small, plump, smiling woman, blue-eyed and golden-haired, who rose to welcome Lucia with every appearance of genuine pleasure at her arrival. She addressed Sìleas Barra MacNeill as *Lady MacConnachie*, which Lucia recognised after a heartbeat's frozen confusion as the appropriate British form of address for Oscar MacConnachie's wife.

A lovingly polished welcome-cup – bright gold on its inner surface, and finely etched without, prominently bearing the Tudor rose – stood ready to hand, half filled with a deep red wine. The Queen took up the cup; drank deeply from it, holding Lucia's gaze; and, passing it into Lucia's hand, spoke the blessing in formal Latin: 'My welcome to this house, Lucia MacNeill of Alba, and to this kingdom.'

Lucia accepted the cup. 'I thank you for this welcome,' she replied, in the same tongue. 'May the gods smile on you, on this house and on this kingdom, and all who dwell here.'

The wine was much too sweet for her taste, but she did not like to appear less than enthusiastic (or, worse, to seem suspicious), and so drank deeply nonetheless.

The formal ritual thus accomplished, Queen Edwina rose a-tiptoe to kiss Lucia on both cheeks, and bestowed upon her a beaming smile that creased her bright eyes nearly shut.

Lucia's English and Français were not so fluent as she might have wished, her lessons with Sophie Marshall having dwindled in frequency as she grew increasingly occupied with her father's affairs; but she rallied herself to return this unexpected gesture, making her best and most grateful curtsey to the Queen and saying hesitantly in English, 'I am so very glad to make your acquaintance at last, Your Majesty.'

Queen Edwina smiled even more widely and clapped her small white hands in childlike delight – reminding Lucia inescapably of Sophie, though otherwise the two could not have been more unlike. 'How clever you are, my dear! However do you contrive to speak so naturally, when you must have learnt from books?'

'Oh! I did not learn from books,' said Lucia; 'Sophie taught me.'

'Of course.' The Queen's welcoming smile grew a little fixed, and her warm voice a little cooler. 'Yes, I understood you to be already acquainted with the Princess Edith.'

Rattled, Lucia cast a pleading glance at her cousin: *I have put my foot in some rabbit-hole, but which?* Sìleas, however, either did not or chose not to understand her difficulty.

In any event their private audience was at an end, it seemed, for a liveried servant now opened a door opposite the one through which Lucia had entered the room, admitting a veritable parade of ladies. Lucia at first set about learning all their faces, but gave up the attempt when a familiar face and form leapt out at her from the mass of strangers, and Sophie's voice cried, 'Lucia MacNeill! Come here at once, and let me see you.'

'Sophie!' said Lucia, delighted and relieved, as Sophie (contradicting her own instructions) ran forward to embrace her, as eagerly as though they had been parted for months instead of days. At once she regretted it – ought she not to have said *Your Royal Highness*? – and cast a glance over Sophie's shoulder to see how this relatively intimate greeting might have been received.

Queen Edwina, indeed, wore a slightly pinched expression; whatever had been Lucia's earlier transgression, it appeared she had now compounded it.

'Never mind,' said Sophie, speaking in Gaelic, and very low, into Lucia's ear. 'It is only that she does not like me, because I am my mother's daughter; I did warn you, you know. I shall endeavour to prevent my unfortunate shadow from falling too heavily upon you.'

Before Lucia could express either protest or acquiescence, Sophie was returning her to the care of Queen Edwina, with a graceful curtsey and a pretty, altogether un-Sophie-like apology for stealing her away.

The rest of the introductions went rather better. Sophie's uncharacteristic deference to her stepmother continued, though Lucia strongly suspected her of storing up sharp remarks for some later, more private conversation. Lucia made the acquaintance of Prince Edward's pretty, diffident young wife, and if the Princess Delphine was no longer quite so blushing and bashful as Sophie had once described her, she certainly did not accord with Lucia's notion of a future Queen. On the other hand, she was very evidently doing her part to ensure the continuance of the royal line.

Next came Lady Lisle, who seemed genuinely delighted to make Lucia's acquaintance and genuinely to have nothing else to say for herself; Lady Kergabet, wife of King Henry's chief advisor and, Lucia recalled just in time to avoid abject humiliation, already familiar to her as Sophie's much-admired sister-in-law Jenny; Madame de Courcy, with whose husband – the British envoy to Alba – Lucia had already a long and sometimes very surprising acquaintance; the elderly Lady Craven, and the humblingly elegant Madame de Mayenne, and at least a dozen more. Lucia smiled at them all, and thanked them for their kind welcome, and tried not to feel as though all of them but Sophie were studying her like some exotic insect under glass.

Was it her imagination that beneath the warm, sometimes almost effusive welcomes there lurked a note of anxious apprehension?

She was not to be introduced to Prince Roland himself until the following day, a proceeding which seemed less idiotic now than when Sìleas had explained it to her this morning. By tomorrow, one might hope – with this first ordeal behind her – she should have had a proper night's sleep, and a long talk with Sophie, and should have got her feet under her once more.

The next afternoon, Sophie and Joanna stood side by side, a little apart from Jenny and Delphine, and watched Roland advance towards Lucia MacNeill. Lucia herself was accompanied only by her cousins, Sìleas Barra MacNeill and Oscar MacConnachie, and appeared to Sophie to be regretting the women-at-arms of her personal guard, whom she had left behind in her temporary quarters in the Queen's wing of the Royal Palace. She was entirely calm and composed, her hands steady, her red-gold hair impeccably dressed, and smiling in welcome; but to Sophie the composure seemed just slightly too stiff, the smile just slightly too symmetrical.

Roland, on the other hand, looked so straightforwardly nervous that Sophie felt quite sorry for him.

'Lady Lucia,' said the Queen, 'allow me to present His Royal Highness, Prince Roland Edric Augustus.'

Roland made an elegant leg, spoiling his performance very slightly by glancing up at Sophie and Joanna as he raised his head, and by going rather pink in the face. It made him look rather younger than his seventeen years – which was a pity, as he already seemed so young beside his poised and elegant betrothed.

'Roland: Lady Lucia MacNeill, heiress to the chieftain's seat of Alba.'

Lucia's deep curtsey was flawless – to Sophie's secret relief, for Lucia had practised it on her endlessly, first in the sitting-room of the house in Quarry Close, and more lately behind closed and guarded doors in her Palace quarters, persisting long after Sophie's assurances that she had mastered it. ('It is not that I am afraid of doing it wrongly,' she had explained; 'I am afraid of forgetting where I am, and putting out my hand instead, as I should do at home.' Sophie could not deny that this was a risk, having done the same thing herself half a dozen times at least.)

Smiling benignantly upon her son and his betrothed, the Queen collected the rest of the party and withdrew, so that the Prince and his bride-to-be might converse in relative privacy.

Everyone with whom Lucia was at all acquainted retreated to the far end of the Queen's elegant sitting-room, leaving her alone with Prince Roland and a silent, impassive pair of Royal Guardsmen; and Lucia, accustomed to debating learned mages and giving orders to her father's generals, could think of absolutely nothing to say. She forced herself to stop staring down at her folded hands, to raise her head and meet Roland's gaze with a smile; and at once was glad that she had done so, for he seemed equally ill at ease.

'Y-you are very like your portrait,' said Roland at last, producing a nervous half smile. His pleasant tenor voice was slightly husky, by nature or by circumstance it was impossible to say. Did he sing as beautifully as his sister?

'Am I? You are not much like yours,' Lucia said, startled by this last thought into perhaps too much honesty. 'I suppose you have grown up since then.'

Roland's pink cheeks grew pinker. 'I have grown nearly four inches,' he conceded. His hands gripped the knees of his fine buckskin breeches. Like his mother, he spoke in Latin; had he yet made any efforts towards learning Gaelic, or must Lucia begin at the beginning? Ought she to try out her English or her Français? Or might that make the conversation more awkward, rather than less?

It was maddening to know herself capable of mustering and leading an armed expedition to a distant corner of her own kingdom, of understanding Alban law and administering justice as her father's deputy, and yet freeze in agonised indecision over such a trivial question.

'Have you been out riding?' she enquired at last, still in Latin. 'You are dressed for it, I think?'

He looked down at the buckskins, at his tall polished boots, as though surprised to see them. 'I-I-I meant to go out later in the day,' he said. 'Before dinner. You are fond of riding, are you not, Lady Lucia?'

'Lucia, please,' she said, laughing a little, for Roland had been so addressing her for some time in his letters. 'I am, yes. I have had no opportunity since arriving in London, but I hope I shall do so; Joanna Callender tells me that she and her friend Gwendolen Pryce are in the habit of riding in the park every morning before breakfast – I am not perfectly sure which park she meant – and perhaps I may be able to join them on some of those excursions.'

'Miss Callender is a thorough horsewoman,' Roland said. 'Though I wish she would not insist on riding astride.'

'Whyever not?' said Lucia, baffled.

Roland blinked at her. 'Why, because – because it is not proper for a lady,' he said.

When in Rome, Lucia reminded herself, and smiled. 'In Britain, perhaps,' she said mildly, 'but in Alba I assure you it is accounted entirely proper.'

'Ah – I – of course,' Roland said, his cheeks flushing up once more. 'I meant no offence! I have been endeavouring to learn your customs, as you know; but Oscar MacConnachie is not much interested in riding, and Lady MacConnachie still less.'

'Sìleas Barra MacNeill is no horsewoman at all,' she acknowledged, and noted with approval that though Roland had referred to her cousin in the British manner, he was not confused by Lucia's using her Alban name.

A second long pause followed, in which Lucia cudgelled her brains in search of something to say. She had once hoped that they might become sufficiently acquainted through the exchange of letters as to make this meeting more reunion than halting introduction; but her correspondence with Roland had begun very formally and continued stilted and awkward, and she had concluded that if friendship and intimacy were ever to grow between them, it could not be by that means.

But this alliance was for the good of Alba; her father and she, with their most trusted advisors, had debated for more than a year how best to play their hand – *her* hand – and had their choice not already paid off handsomely, in the bride-gifts which had helped save her people from starvation? In the friendship between Sophie and herself which had, quite literally, helped to heal Alba's ills?

And no matter how fraught and fragile their kinship, surely no brother of Sophie's could be entirely uncongenial?

Perhaps Roland too had been thinking of Sophie, for just as the excruciating silence was threatening to stretch past breaking, he said, 'Sophie has been trying to make me promise to study at the University, when – when I come to Din Edin.'

Lucia concealed a rueful smile at this evidence that he had as much difficulty as herself in speaking aloud the words *when we are married.*

'You do not much like the notion, I collect?'

Roland's full lips quirked. 'I am not stupid,' he said – Lucia thought frantically back over her words; had she suggested that she thought him so? – 'but I am no scholar. I do not see how anyone should choose a stack of dusty books telling how mages took their tea in my great-grandfather's time, over a fast gallop through the deer-park on a fine day.'

Then his cheeks grew pink again, and his bright blue gaze slid away from hers, as he grew conscious of the oblique insult in his words.

'You are a man after my brother's heart,' said Lucia, entirely without thought; 'I predict that the two of you will get on famously.'

'I hope we shall be good friends,' Roland said, and now he smiled shyly, 'as I have been with my own brothers.' After a moment he added, in what seemed a corresponding burst of honesty, 'Mostly.'

The recognition struck Lucia, all unwelcome: it was not Sophie, at all, whom Roland put her in mind of, but her own fourteen-year-old brother, Duncan.

'I am sure you shall,' she said, returning the smile to cover her unease. 'And I hope you may change your opinion of the University, when once you have made its acquaintance. If dusty books are not so much to your taste, perhaps you may follow in Sophie's footsteps in the School of Practical Magick. The University is a famous place for making friends, you know.'

Roland looked thoughtful. 'I suppose it must be,' he said slowly; and then, in a confiding rush, 'My brother Harry is wild to study magick at Merlin College, when he is old enough. I wish he may persuade my father to let him go; but it is not at all the done thing, you see, as it is in Alba. Jo – Miss Callender went to school when she was younger, in Kemper, and she is forever telling Harry stories of her escapades. I am sure that most of them are her own invention, but,' he concluded, rather wistful, 'I think perhaps I should have liked to go to school with a crowd of other boys – besides my brothers, that is.'

A brief but painful sympathy gripped Lucia, for the little boy Roland had once been – though considering that little boy's doting mama, his panoply of playthings and carefully vetted tutors, the small army of servants undoubtedly devoted to his needs and wishes, made her sympathy recede somewhat. Nevertheless—

'Miss Callender is a good friend of yours, I suppose?' she said, before the strong temptation to say, *We shall not let our children be lonely, as you were*, could quite overcome her better judgement.

'Yes,' said Roland. 'That is – she is Sophie's sister, and a sort of assistant to Sieur Germain de Kergabet – oh, but you will know all of that already, for you met Miss Callender in Din Edin, did you not? – and of course you will have heard how all of us first became acquainted—'

'I have not, in fact,' said Lucia, taking pity on him, 'but I hope you may tell me of it, another time?' For Sophie never would consent to tell her that tale, and Lucia continued desperately curious. 'Oh! And I have brought you something.'

Roland's eyes brightened, like – alas, yes, *exactly* like – Duncan's on being offered some treat.

Lucia opened her reticule, extracted the small, flat parcel, carefully wrapped in fine linen dyed scarlet, and handed it across to Roland; their fingertips brushed, for just a moment, and he ducked his head. *We shall never make a diplomat of you at this rate, Your Royal Highness.*

He turned the parcel about in his hands – strong hands, with a horseman's calluses; Lucia spied a scraped knuckle on the right hand, and a spot of ink on the left – before carefully tugging on one end of the bow-knot. The wrapping fell away, and Roland studied the slim codex thus revealed, whose title, stamped in gold leaf upon the front board, he perhaps did not recognise as meaning *Poems of the Inner Isles*.

'You are fond of poetry, I know,' said Lucia, abruptly shy. 'It occurred to me that you might wish to become better acquainted with some of the poetry of Alba. And,' she added, 'that verses might make your study of Gaelic a less onerous task. I . . . I have not much patience for poetry myself; I enlisted the aid of my cousin Ciaran Barra MacNeill, who is my father's serjeant-at-arms and a great collector of poems, to guide my choice.'

Roland drew one index finger along the book's spine. 'I thank you,' he said, looking up at Lucia, 'very much indeed. This is a most thoughtful gift, Lady – that is, Lucia. I . . . May I hope for your assistance in translating it?'

He looked as doubtful, hopeful, and off-balance as she felt, and, perversely, Lucia took heart from the knowledge that they both were equally at sea.

'I should like that very much,' she said.

They smiled at one another, faces half-turned; the silence now seemed more hopeful than otherwise. Before either of them could make any further overture, however, Queen Edwina came bustling back again to observe their progress, and to exclaim at and fuss over Lucia's gift in a manner which made Roland blush furiously and Lucia wish she had left the accursèd book in Din Edin, and the moment dissolved once more into awkward, limping conversation.

'I understand that Lucia MacNeill has invited you to take tea with her in her rooms?' said Queen Edwina.

'Yes, ma'am,' said Sophie.

The Queen nodded. 'You may do so,' she said, as though Sophie had been asking her permission, or seeking her approval. 'And then, of course, you must speak with Roland; and afterwards—'

'Am I to be a go-between, then?' said Sophie, daring to interrupt. 'Or a spy? I must tell you, ma'am, that I have no great liking for either notion.'

Her stepmother regarded her steadily. 'Roland admires you,' she said (she did not add, *the gods alone know why*, though Sophie could hear the sentiment hovering unspoken), 'and Lucia MacNeill, I am told, considers you an intimate friend; hence His Majesty's request that you act as a guide and companion to her whilst she remains in London. All that your father and I ask of you, Edith, is that you refrain from encouraging either of them to . . . to seek out objections.'

'Sophie,' said Sophie firmly.

Queen Edwina blinked. 'I beg your pardon?'

'My name is Sophie, ma'am. Not Edith.'

'Your name is Edith Augusta Sophia,' said Queen Edwina, in a tone which suggested she was exercising patience in speaking to a small child, or a simpleton.

'So it is,' Sophie acknowledged, 'but *I* am Sophie.' It seemed a foolish thing to insist upon – but if so, surely the Queen's own insistence upon *Edith* was no better?

Queen Edwina frowned; before she could reply, however, Sophie drew a steadying breath and said, 'I should like us to be friends, ma'am, so far as circumstances permit. And my friends have always called me Sophie.'

It was a gamble; and, like many another such, it failed.

'You must not think me ungrateful for the care and affection you have bestowed upon my sons,' said the Queen, 'but surely you cannot imagine that anything resembling true friendship can subsist between us.' Her small, soft hands – entirely free of calluses and ink-stains – smoothed down her figured muslin skirts; then she raised her eyes again to Sophie's face and, perhaps misinterpreting her expression, added in a kinder tone, 'You need not fear that I wish you any ill, Edith.'

With some effort, Sophie refrained from wincing. *She has no power over you that you do not grant her yourself.* 'No, ma'am,' she said.

'Your father may rely on you, then, I trust, to carry out his wishes with respect to Roland and Lucia MacNeill?'

Sophie hesitated before replying, uneasy in the extreme. But if she had only to avoid *encouraging* either of them to object to the other . . .

'Yes, ma'am,' she said at last.

The Queen gave a brisk nod of satisfaction. 'You may go,' she said, gracious in victory; and Sophie, after a nonplussed moment, made her escape.

Lucia MacNeill received her with a quite astonishing enthusiasm, considering that they had last met less than a fortnight since. Having sent one of her attendants to procure the makings of tea, she then banished them all to the sitting-room and poured tea for Sophie in her bedchamber – an awkward makeshift, certainly, but no more so than many an impromptu meal they had shared in Din Edin, in the years since their bizarre joint venture on the Ross of Mull had made Lucia an intimate of the Marshalls' tiny house in Quarry Close, and Sophie a regular visitor to Castle Hill.

'May I ask you a question, Sophie?' she said.

'Of course,' said Sophie, accepting her cup of tea.

Lucia poured for herself; looked down at the delicate cup and saucer in her hands, then up at Sophie; and at last said, 'Tell me truly, what is there between Roland and your sister Joanna?'

Sophie, astonished, paused with her teacup halfway between saucer and lips. 'They were the best of friends, once,' she said, 'though there was some coolness on Roland's part, I understand, when he learnt of her part in arranging his betrothal – behind his back, as he saw it.'

'Hmm,' said Lucia. 'Yes, perhaps that may explain . . .'

They sipped their tea, both frowning in thought.

An old and half-forgotten notion occurred to Sophie – oblique complaints, a letter impatiently tossed aside – and she added, 'I have a theory that at one time Roland fancied himself in love with Joanna, a fancy in which she of course could not encourage him.'

'Oh!' Lucia's fine arched brows rose, and her lips twisted in a rueful little grimace. 'Yes, certainly your sister must have found such advances most unwelcome.'

'It is only a theory of mine, as I said,' said Sophie, wishing that she had not said anything at all. 'I may be quite wrong – though it does account for several remarks of Roland's, and one or two of Joanna's, which at the time I could not at all make out. But even if it was not all my own fancy, Lucia, it was years ago.'

'Indeed,' said Lucia. 'But in any case, it is not as though Joanna were on the hunt for a husband.'

Sophie blinked. It was true that Joanna seemed remarkably uninterested in marriage, matchmaking, and young men generally, though the Kergabets' extensive acquaintance must include – at least from the pragmatic and determinedly unsentimental perspective which Joanna appeared to have adopted for herself – many very eligible candidates. Sophie had not much expected her sister to fall desperately in love, but it seemed reasonable to suppose that she should prefer an establishment of her own to a perpetual dependence upon one or other of her relations; and, Joanna's personal fortunes being what they were, a good marriage was undoubtedly the best means of achieving that goal. But then, Joanna had political ambitions, which very few potential husbands were likely to encourage; and besides—

'She is very young to be thinking of marriage,' said Sophie.

'She is older than Roland,' Lucia pointed out, 'who certainly is *very* young to be anyone's husband, but no one else seems much

43

inclined to object on that account. And *you* had been married nearly two years at her age, by my reckoning.'

'I had,' said Sophie, frowning at *no one else* as much as at the remarks that had followed it, 'and you know my thoughts upon that subject.'

'In any case, that is not what I meant,' said Lucia. Sipping her tea, she regarded Sophie sidelong, as though attempting to gauge the effect of her words in advance of speaking them. 'I meant – well – Gwendolen Pryce, you know.'

'What of her?' said Sophie.

Her thorough bafflement must have shown in her face, for Lucia's eyes widened and she said, sounding almost dismayed, 'Oh! Sophie, you cannot mean – do you tell me that you did not *know?*'

'Lucia MacNeill.' Sophie deposited her teacup very precisely on the corner of Lucia's dressing-table and clasped her hands together in her lap. 'You are my dear friend, and very nearly my sister, and I am enormously fond of you; but if you do not cease talking in riddles—'

Lucia had the grace to look abashed, and hastily said, 'Your sister, I believe, is not seeking the companionship of a husband because she has already a companion who suits her better.'

In itself, this did not much clarify things; but in the context of Lucia's previous remarks upon the subject of Gwendolen Pryce . . .

'Oh,' said Sophie, feeling thoroughly at sea. 'I . . . I had not considered that possibility.'

It had not escaped her notice, of course, that amongst the ladies of her father's court there were some whose eyes alighted with appreciation and affection not upon any gentleman, but upon one another; and, for that matter, Mór MacRury, one of her closest female friends in Din Edin – and once Lucia's tutor – shared with a lady lecturer in Astronomy both her lodgings and a companionship which looked to Sophie very like a happy marriage.

The notion of Joanna's being likewise companioned had never crossed her mind. But the moment she began to consider it, the fragments of observation fell into place – the constant presence of *Gwendolen says* in Joanna's letters; the small half smiles, the chaste but affectionate touches to shoulder or elbow; the tone-deaf Joanna's apparent pleasure in sitting by the pianoforte whilst Miss Pryce played and sang; the two dark heads bent close together over a book – and she said, 'I am a fool.'

'Sophie?' said Lucia, hesitant now. 'You are not . . . distressed by this news?'

Sophie looked up sharply. 'No!' she said. 'That is . . . yes; if there is indeed so strong an attachment between my sister and her friend, I am very much distressed that Joanna should not have trusted me with the knowledge of it. But as to the nature of that attachment: no, certainly not.'

'No,' Lucia repeated. 'No, of course you would not be, in that way. But, Sophie, I should not have said anything about it to you, had I for a moment suspected that you did not know already.'

No, Sophie reflected: Lucia, so much more the diplomat than herself, would have refrained from even such delicate hinting as she had first engaged in, had she not supposed Sophie already in the secret.

'You must not blame yourself,' she said. 'I cannot think how I failed to see it. And I understand, of course, why Joanna and Miss Pryce should wish to be discreet; but I cannot understand – but never mind, Lucia! What else did you and Roland talk of, then?'

'Of riding, a little,' said Lucia. 'And poetry, and Gaelic, and—' She stopped abruptly, and for whatever she had been about to say substituted, 'this and that.' A small, sardonic smile, then: 'I fear I shall be forced to cultivate a taste for romantical poetry, or your brother will have nothing to do with me.'

'Roland is perhaps too much inclined to be romantical,' said Sophie, 'but he is not a fool – though I cannot deny that he is a very young man, with some of the follies thereof. And now you are here, and have begun to be properly acquainted, I am sure he cannot fail to appreciate his good fortune.'

Lucia smiled tightly and sipped her tea. 'I do wish,' she said, returning cup to saucer, 'that your younger brother did not remind me quite so much of my own.'

Sophie winced. 'Lucia . . .'

'Will you make me a promise, Sophie?' Lucia set down her teacup altogether and gazed earnestly into Sophie's eyes.

'Of course,' said Sophie at once.

Lucia's eyes narrowed in something like amusement, and it occurred to Sophie belatedly that perhaps she ought to set more hedges round her promises to foreign heiresses, allies or not.

'I know you have been appointed my keeper and nursemaid,' said Lucia, 'and if I must have some such person, I am grateful that it should be you. But, as you are my friend, Sophie, will you promise to tell me the truth, always? Even when it may be unpalatable or inconvenient?'

'Of course,' Sophie repeated. So little for Lucia to ask of her, after all. 'Yes, of course.' She held out her right hand, Alban-fashion, and Lucia clasped it; and after a long moment's thought she said, 'I swear upon the blood we have mingled and the magick we have shared, to give you the truth as I understand it, so long as I shall live and remember.'

There was nothing particularly arcane about such an oath; but nonetheless Sophie felt something shiver through her, like a distant echo of that long-ago sharing of magick. By Lucia's pensive, grave expression, she had felt it too.

'Thank you,' she said solemnly, and waited a long moment before releasing Sophie's hand.

* * *

Sophie had no particular wish to speak to Roland at once; her head was spinning with new facts and with evidence dramatically realigned, and she wanted nothing so much as a quiet hour to put her thoughts in order. But Queen Edwina had made it very clear that a conversation with Roland was expected of her; and as between Roland and his mother, the choice was evident. Sophie, accordingly, went looking for her brother.

She found him wandering about in the shrubbery and persuaded him to sit with her upon a bench in the rose-garden. Taking a leaf from Joanna's book, she did not attempt subtlety but asked him outright: 'What think you of Lucia MacNeill, now that you have seen her for yourself?'

Roland looked down at his feet – rotated his left ankle, broken last summer in a fall from the saddle – rose from the bench, tugged a wilted rose off its stem, and began pulling it to pieces.

'I do not understand her,' he said at last, his tone skirting the line between forlorn and merely petulant. 'We have been corresponding for the best part of two years, and now we have met at last, and still I know next to nothing of her heart. She is always wanting to talk of some book or other – of politics, or magick, or of tactics and strategy – what sort of young lady prefers talk of politics to talk of love?'

'The sort, I imagine,' said Sophie dryly, 'who has been brought up to rule a kingdom.'

She rose to her feet, approached her brother (a little warily, for he was now grown taller than herself), and, gently removing the abused rose-leaves from his fingers, drew him back to sit with her once more upon the stone bench.

'Ned was brought up to rule a kingdom,' he said mulishly, 'and it has not prevented him from making sheep's eyes at Delphine whenever they are in the same room together, or from sitting in the garden with her, reading minstrel-tales aloud.'

47

Sophie refrained from pointing out that this speech had a strong flavour of Joanna Callender about it.

'I am sorry that Lucia should not have made a better first impression,' she said.

'That is not what I said,' Roland protested. The petulant tone was quite gone, and he looked genuinely astonished and not a little dismayed. 'Not at all. Only . . . Sophie, I had not the least notion what to say to her! It was bad enough when we were a kingdom apart, and writing letters to one another – I had time then to read the difficult passages over, and study how I might reply—'

'You mean, I suppose,' said Sophie, 'that you do not feel sufficiently clever to carry on an ordinary conversation with an educated woman, and that you fear being accounted her inferior – no – you fear that you will *not* be accounted her superior?'

Roland stared at her a long moment, before at last one corner of his mouth quirked – their father to the life – and he said, 'I take your point, Magistra.'

Sophie kissed his cheek and patted him on the shoulder, in her best elder-sisterly manner – which Ned, Roland, and Harry seemed able to take seriously, though Joanna (who knew her much better) never had.

'I am sure you will manage it,' she said.

CHAPTER IV

In Which Sophie
Attempts a Reconciliation

'Horns of Herne!' said Joanna, at breakfast some days later, looking up from a letter which had been waiting by her plate when she and Miss Pryce came in from their morning ride.

'Language, Jo!' said Miss Pryce. It was no very loverlike speech, to be sure; but Sophie, who had been watching Joanna and her friend closely since her conversation with Lucia, recognised the same half-exasperated, half-affectionate tone in which she herself occasionally spoke to Gray. *How in Hades did I never see it before?*

Hoping for some reply from the Oxford friends to whom she had dispatched requests to investigate their personal or College libraries and map-rooms for materials relating to the history of Lady Morgan College, Sophie herself had again been disappointed – which only increased her interest in everyone else's correspondence. She craned her neck to see the direction on Joanna's letter, and her eyebrows flew up as she recognised the hand. 'From Amelia?' she said, astonished; a letter to either herself or Joanna from their elder sister, still resident in the house in Breizh where all of them had grown up, was a rarity indeed. 'Truly this is a day of wonders and portents! What does she say?'

'That she and Lady Maëlle are coming to London,' said Joanna, still in the same tone of astonished dismay; and – continuing over Sophie's involuntary *What!* – 'at once. And it is worse even than that, because the

49

letter was mis-sent to Carrington-street, and is nearly a fortnight old.'

Jenny sat up straighter, winced, and laid one hand on her belly, just now beginning to round out. 'We ought to have expected it, I dare say,' she said. 'Half the kingdom is coming to London at present, the better to catch a glimpse of Lucia MacNeill.'

'This must have been a very hasty decision, however,' said Sophie, frowning, 'unless, I suppose, other letters have also gone astray.'

And that was odd, too; in fact, the more she considered this odd turn of events, the odder it grew. Amelia was not, it was true, the most faithful of correspondents, but it was not like her to forget Joanna's direction altogether.

'Does she give an address in London?' Jenny enquired, in a tone which tried very hard to be neutral, and nearly succeeded.

Joanna returned her attention to Amelia's letter, and presently said, 'Yes.'

Jenny's covert expression of relief was erased almost at once by Joanna's reading out the address in question, which proved to be that of a hotel almost equally unsuited to Lady Maëlle's elevated station and to her limited means.

'I shall have to invite them to stay, of course,' she said. 'Apart from anything else, I should never live down the stain on my reputation otherwise. But, Vesta preserve us! Where am I to put them? The South Room and the Lilac Room are not likely to be finished for another month, and the plasterers have left the Rose Room in such a state . . . !'

Joanna, Miss Pryce, and Sophie – the only other occupants of the breakfast-room at present – exchanged a look.

'If Gwen and I were to share her room, Jenny,' said Joanna after a moment, 'you might give mine to Lady Maëlle, as it is the largest, and the Little North Room to Amelia.'

'That is generous of you,' said Jenny – looking, however, not at Joanna but at Miss Pryce. 'What say you, my dear?'

Miss Pryce met Jenny's gaze steadily. 'Certainly,' she said. 'I have not the least objection. Indeed, I should be happy to offer my room in place of Joanna's, but, as she says, hers is the larger.'

'That will appeal to Lady Maëlle's sense of her own consequence,' Sophie agreed. *Jenny does not know, of course*, she thought, bemused by the entire exchange. *Or . . . does she?*

'I think, however,' said Jenny, acknowledging Sophie's remark with a brief, mischievous glint of her hazel eyes, 'I shall pander a little to your sister's consequence, also, by shifting Mr Fowler into the Little North Room, and giving her the Kingfisher.'

She nodded decisively, then rose from her chair and sailed out of the room, presumably to send an invitation to Lady Maëlle de Morbihan and Miss Amelia Callender in care of Bracquart's Hotel.

Not for three days after the belated arrival of Miss Callender's letter, and the swift dispatch of Jenny's invitation, was any further word of the travellers from Breizh received in Grosvenor Square. It came in the form of a note – written, in Lady Maëlle's small, austere hand, on ivory-coloured writing-paper engraved with the elegant *B* of Bracquart's Hotel – which, upon being opened and read, caused Jenny to press her lips together and close her eyes.

Gray could not help rather wishing that Sophie's imperious cousin might persist in maintaining her independence, for the sake of poor Jenny's nerves. On the other hand, Joanna had regaled him and Sophie (over tea in the nursery, on the nursery-maid's half-day) with the tale of Lady Maëlle's last encounter with his mother, and he could not entirely suppress a competing wish to see what might happen this time.

Jenny's next invitation seemingly produced a change of heart, and on the following afternoon Lord Kergabet's carriage was dispatched to retrieve the two ladies from their temporary lodgings and bring them to Grosvenor Square.

The household, or most of it (Mrs Marshall having sniffed about *country manners* and resolutely kept her seat in the morning-room), assembled on the front steps to greet the newcomers. Standing close beside Gray, her hand gripping his behind the curtain of her skirts and his coat-tails, Sophie fairly hummed with anxious anticipation – and, as Gaël Roche opened the door of the carriage and unfolded the steps, with the thrum of sympathetic magick through the bond that connected her to Gray.

Lady Maëlle, he saw, was still as stout and straight-backed as ever, if rather more grey; the young servant who descended from the barouche box, where she had been conducting an animated conversation in Brezhoneg with Gaël, he recognised as the erstwhile Callender Hall housemaid Katell, now presumably acting in the capacity of lady's maid. Miss Callender, on the other hand, Gray should scarcely have known out of context, for the plump rose-and-golden prettiness he remembered, the tendency to look down her nose at all the world, had bloomed into a true and quiet beauty.

'Amelia!' Sophie exclaimed. 'How well you look!'

Miss Callender's composure cracked very slightly, Gray fancied, at the unfeigned enthusiasm in her stepsister's voice; but it was for a moment only. 'Your Royal Highness,' she said, making a graceful curtsey.

Sophie, hands outstretched in glad greeting, faltered and went very still. 'Amelia,' she repeated, in a doubtful tone, 'what—'

Miss Callender was spared from any immediate necessity of explaining herself, however, by Lady Maëlle's holding out her arms to Sophie, and by Sophie's flinging herself joyfully into them.

Gray said, 'How do you do, Miss Callender?'

Her lovely damask-rose face flushed a little, and she looked down, smoothing her skirts with hands grown suddenly restive. 'I am well, I thank you, Mr Marshall,' she said. 'And . . . and yourself?'

'Gray, what are you about?' said Sophie, laughing. 'Come and make your bow to Cousin Maëlle.'

He turned to them, meaning to do so, but Lady Maëlle forestalled him by approaching with both hands outstretched to clasp his own. 'How do you do, my dear?' she said, smiling so warmly and maternally at him that he blinked in surprise and almost stammered his answering 'Very well indeed; and yourself?'

'I am glad to hear it,' said Lady Maëlle, smiling. 'I fear your wife is a most frustrating correspondent; her letters tell me all about the books she is reading, and the price of butter and eggs in Din Edin, and nothing whatsoever about herself. And Joanna is grown shockingly neglectful, since she became such fast friends with this Miss Pryce of hers – Miss Pryce will be that tall, dark girl, I suppose—?'

'Yes,' said Gray. This sunny, confiding iteration of Lady Maëlle had begun to unnerve him rather, and he was not sorry when a summons from Jenny recalled them both to the duties of welcomes and introductions.

For the most part, the moves of the dance were not difficult to predict: Miss Callender and Miss Pryce, all complaisant smiles to one another's faces, could be seen eyeing each other sidelong whilst each was conversing with somebody else; Joanna and her eldest sister executed a cautious embrace, each looking as though she were remembering every cutting remark she had ever made to the other. Katell was quickly swept up by the laughing Breizhek grooms, and as quickly rescued from their attentions by Mrs Treveur, who sent Gaël and Loïc away to their work with fond exasperation.

Sophie, having been so thoroughly rebuffed, made no further attempt at conversation with her stepsister, and instead tucked her arm through her cousin's and bent her head to speak rapidly and unceasingly in her ear, pausing only to permit the occasional small gust of laughter.

As they passed into the house – and now at last Gray understood

53

his mother's refusal to leave the morning-room, for of course she should have had to cede precedence not only to Jenny but also to Lady Maëlle – Miss Callender lingered a little, looking up at the grand facade of Jenny's house with an expression curiously both wistful and disapproving.

'After you, Miss Callender,' said Gray, for he could not leave her standing in the street alone (even so salubrious a street as the west side of Grosvenor Square). She started a little, turned her head so that her bonnet-brim hid her face, and preceded him obligingly enough up the steps and through the front door.

'I should not have known Amelia again,' Gray confessed, as Sophie and he were dressing for dinner, 'had I seen her in some other place.'

Sophie looked at him with narrowed eyes, her head upon one side. 'She is much prettier than she used to be,' she said. 'But she has forgot how to smile.'

'Yes,' said Gray, 'but that is not what I meant, exactly; she was never much given to smiling at me in any case. No; the difference is . . . Well, perhaps it is only that she has grown older, while we were not by to see it.'

'Well! If that is so, we must hope she has grown wiser, also,' said Sophie darkly, 'and will not fall prey to unscrupulous persons.'

'What sort of—' Gray began, but Sophie flapped one hand at him.

'It is an old tale,' she said, 'and I shall not tell it to you whilst we are under the same roof with Amelia; that, I think, she could not forgive me, Princess Royal or no, and I should not blame her.'

Amelia, it appeared, had taken up music again. When the ladies removed to the drawing-room after dinner, she eyed the pianoforte with eager interest – poorly concealed – and upon Jenny's sitting down upon a sofa, drew near and asked in a low voice whether she might be permitted the use of it; and when, permission granted, she sat down to play, her performance was recognisably much better than Sophie's remembrance of it.

Sophie too, insofar as the other demands upon her time permitted, had been renewing her acquaintance with Jenny's pianoforte, so different from the scuffed and battered (though always meticulously tuned) third-hand instrument that had graced the tiny front room of the house in Quarry Close. Might Amelia's renewed interest in this once-shared pursuit open the way to some manner of reconciliation?

Certainly Sophie's efforts in that direction thus far had not enjoyed much success. Enquiries after the health of tenant farmers and half-remembered neighbours in Breizh had been answered in a reproving tone which reminded Sophie, more pointedly than mere words could have done, that she might at any time have come to see them for herself, and had not. Offers of excursions to see the sights of London were politely but firmly declined, and attempts by either party to interest the other in her pet topic – in Sophie's case, her new-found (or renewed) fascination with Lady Morgan College and its history; in Amelia's, the London season – tended to disintegrate with alarming rapidity into childish squabbling.

On one warm, close evening, astonishingly free of engagements and scented with the roses Mrs Treveur had set in silver bowls all over the house, Sophie extracted from her music-case the collection of (mostly Alban) songs which she had learnt and painstakingly transcribed during her years in Din Edin, and, turning to Gray, said, 'What song shall we have tonight, love?'

'"Fear a' Bhàta",' said Gray at once.

'Are you sure?' Sophie cast a doubtful glance at Lady Maëlle, at Amelia. But Gray nodded, and, reasoning that, of all those present, only they two had enough Gaelic to appreciate the melancholy import of the lyrics, she shook out her fingers, arranged her music on the rack, and began to play – and, for the first time since coming back to London, to sing.

She scrupulously suppressed the magick that tried to weave itself into her song; nevertheless, by the final verse, Amelia had laid down her fancy-work and drifted close to the pianoforte, studying the hand-notated music over Sophie's shoulder.

'You sing so beautifully,' she said, low, when Sophie lifted her fingers from the keys, and – astonishingly – settled herself on the bench beside Sophie, so close that their elbows touched. 'I had forgot how you used to sing, when we were small. Until you stopped.'

With enormous effort, Sophie contrived not to gape at her. 'I never stopped,' she said, after a long moment. 'I sang to Joanna, always. But out in the park, and in the fields, because the Professor forbade it. Or had you forgotten that, also?'

Amelia flinched – pressed her lips together – turned away. Then she stood abruptly, retreated to the sofa, and seated herself a careful distance from Joanna and Miss Pryce, who had their heads bent together over a book, and took no notice of her.

Sophie's stomach churned with a sickly stew of guilt and grief and half-forgotten anger, and she could not think how to apologise.

They met again the next morning across the breakfast-table, and Sophie put down her knife and fork and took her courage in both hands.

'Amelia,' she said.

Amelia looked up.

'I am sorry,' said Sophie. 'For what I said to you last night.' She tamped down her reflexive annoyance at Amelia's expression of surprise. 'It is not your fault that the Professor so detested the cuckoo in his nest, and encouraged you to detest me likewise. And when you paid me a compliment, I ought not to have thrown it back in your face.'

Amelia blinked, and for what seemed a very long time said nothing.

At last she looked down at her plate, then up again at Sophie, and said, 'I was always so very jealous of you.'

'Of *me*?' said Sophie, incredulous. 'Because I was not permitted to go to school, or to read the books I wished to read, or to—'

'Because Mama loved you so.' Amelia's words cut across hers like ice cracking. 'You, and no one else in the world – certainly not her *other* daughters.' She laughed; her laughter sounded as though it hurt her. 'Of course I see now why she could not love *me*. I ought to have known, even then.'

Tears stung Sophie's eyes. *What has become of the world, that I should have cause to weep for Amelia?*

'It was not because you were not hers,' she said, and swallowed against the lump in her throat. 'It was nothing to do with you, at all – with either of you.'

'Do you think I did not know it?' Amelia demanded, in a sort of harsh half whisper. 'Papa and she were entirely unsuited to one another, and ought never to have married; and she could not love either of us, because we were his children.'

Unsuited. Sophie hesitated in an agony of doubt: to tell Amelia, or not to tell her, that her beloved papa had repeatedly forced himself on Sophie's mother? *Mother Goddess, did he do the same to Amelia's mother? No, surely not.* But the thought niggled, and Sophie could not bring herself to inflict it upon Amelia.

'Mama may not have loved you or Jo as she loved me,' she said at last, 'but she loved you well enough to take thought for your safety, and seek to spare you pain.'

'I do not see how,' said Amelia, frowning; too late, Sophie recalled that Amelia did not know the truth of her stepmother's death – had never read, in Queen Laora's last letter to her beloved cousin, the words, *I weep to think of my girls left in his power.*

It was not an explanation which could be given in a quarter-hour's time, over breakfast; and, indeed, Sophie had not the least idea where to begin, nor whether she had any right to tell her mother's secrets.

'You may ask Cousin Maëlle, if you doubt me,' she said instead. 'She knew Mama far longer and better than I.'

Amelia was tearing a bread-roll into tiny pieces, and resolutely not raising her eyes from her busily working hands. Sophie watched this process to its natural conclusion – the sight was oddly hypnotic – as she collected her thoughts.

'We were none of us very well served by our childhood, I think,' she said at last. 'But it does not follow that we must carry our hurts like stored-up treasures all our lives. We were good friends, once, Amelia, as well as sisters; might we not try to be friends again?'

Or, at the least, to lay down our arms and cease to be sworn enemies?

'We might have gone on being friends, if you had not turned Joanna against me,' said Amelia – not accusingly, but as though stating a settled fact; and before Sophie could draw breath to object, 'And driven off every suitor I ever had, for now I do not suppose I am likely to have any more; and if you had not the power to turn me out of my own home—'

'Catharine Amelia Callender.'

Amelia's litany of accusations cut off abruptly, giving way to a silent, furious glare.

Sophie swallowed hard. *If that is how she sees things, I wonder that she should have been willing to come within a hundred miles of me.*

'You may believe whatever you wish about Joanna,' she said, 'and I freely confess that I once kept watch whilst she put half a dozen frogs in Walter Mandeville's bed, because by that time we both of us knew better than to attempt to tell you of his improper advances to the housemaids.'

She overrode Amelia's squeak of outrage, for she had one last thing to say: 'But I have never had any intention of turning you out of that house, Amelia, and never shall have; you may think what you like of me, but you must never think *that*. You shall always have a home there, if you wish it.'

Then, not waiting to see or hear Amelia's reaction to this, Sophie pushed back her chair from the table, stood, and left the room, abandoning her unfinished breakfast; the sight of it made her stomach churn.

She strode blindly along this corridor, down that staircase, and when at length she came back to full awareness of her surroundings, she found herself in the small park at the centre of the square, standing before a stone bench not unlike the one on which she had sat with Gray and Jenny, long ago, when her life was just beginning to unravel. The sun was shining, and the scents of chamomile and clover, box and elm and chestnut, rose up around her like a blessing – as though Hegemone, goddess of plants and growing things, had led her here to soothe away her irritation of spirits.

Sophie shook her head and chuckled wanly. What a notion! Yet the warm sun and the scents of green things growing were already beginning to loosen the knot of old guilt and new hurt that had gathered beneath her ribs, so that she felt able to breathe again, and even perhaps to think.

Lady Maëlle found her there, nearly an hour later, still wrestling with her conscience.

'Your mama loved gardens,' she said, settling herself beside Sophie on the sun-warmed bench, 'even your stepfather's gardens, for all that she grew to loathe the man himself. A garden is its own creature, you know; we may say to ourselves, *This belongs to me*, but in truth a garden belongs only to itself, and to the gods.'

'I always loved the Professor's gardens, also,' Sophie admitted. 'They seemed quite a different world from the house itself. And they were always full of beautiful things – even in winter – and of hiding-places.'

'Indeed,' said Lady Maëlle, with a small, enigmatic smile. 'And what makes you hide amongst the oak and the ash and the bonny ivy-tree today, *ma petite?*'

For the oak, and the ash, and the bonny ivy-tree / They flourish at home in my own country, Sophie's mind supplied, catching at the quotation and fleshing out the melody of the Border-country song. She waved it away impatiently.

'Amelia,' she said, looking down at her feet. 'All of my attempts to make friends with her seem to run aground in the same way. Now she has accused me of turning Joanna against her – she believes I mean to turn her out to starve—'

Lady Maëlle startled her anew by curling one arm about her and drawing Sophie's head down to rest against her shoulder. 'You must give her time,' she said, shifting into Brezhoneg, 'and a little space to think.'

'Time?' Sophie demanded. She sat up straight. 'Space? She has scarce set eyes on me these past five years!'

'Perhaps,' Lady Maëlle said gently, 'you might consider the matter from Amelia's point of view. Suppose that rather than having been hurt yet again by a stepfather who had long and openly resented your existence, by the use he attempted to make of you, you had been betrayed by the father whom you loved wholeheartedly, believing yourself beloved in return.'

'Oh,' said Sophie, in a very small voice. Of course she had believed herself to be considering Amelia's feelings – why else offer her the use of the house which she so loved? – but evidently to much less purpose than she had supposed.

'And suppose further,' Lady Maëlle went on, 'that rather than emerging from your trials possessed of a powerful magickal talent, a doting husband and devoted friends, a royal title, and an unlooked-for opportunity to attain the education you have long dreamt of, you had found yourself branded the child of a traitor, almost friendless and without prospects, through no fault of your own—'

'If I could give the house and the gardens and all of it to Amelia and Joanna, I should have done it long ago, and gladly!' Sophie interrupted, unable to keep silent any longer. 'I did not ask to be given it – Gray did not ask – but he consented to it, only because we should then be able to offer them a home there! . . . And you, of course, ma'am,' she added.

Lady Maëlle inclined her head with a wry smile. 'And I thank you both for that kindness,' she said. 'But I am well accustomed to depending upon the hospitality of others; and you must consider, too, that I left Callender Hall a servant, and returned to it as myself. Your sister Amelia was its mistress once; to expect gratitude for your generosity in making her a perpetual guest in the house which she expected that she – or at any rate her husband – should one day inherit, was perhaps unreasonable.'

'I have never asked for Amelia's gratitude, either,' said Sophie tightly, 'or anyone else's. She is perfectly free to consider herself mistress of, of *that house,* if she likes—'

'But she is not mistress of it, truly, nor ever shall be,' said Lady Maëlle, gently, 'though she loves every room of it, whilst you cannot bear even to speak its name. And Amelia knows it, if you do not.'

'What is it you wish me to *do,* Cousin Maëlle?' Sophie's demand sounded, to her own ears, mortifyingly like an infant's pleading.

'Think on it, child,' said Lady Maëlle.

Then she kissed Sophie's unresisting cheek and took herself away.

CHAPTER V

In Which Amelia Is Inscrutable, and Lucia Hears a Tale

'*Jenny*,' *said Sophie* hesitantly – this conversation had seemed much more advisable in the abstract, turned over and over in the back of her mind whilst the most of her attention was occupied with Amelia, than it did now, in the flesh – 'has either Joanna or Miss Pryce any thought of marrying, do you suppose?'

Jenny, blessedly calm, looked up from the letter she was composing, put down her pen, and gave Sophie a measuring look.

'I should not think so,' she said at last; and after another long moment, 'Why do you ask?'

'Joanna is my sister,' said Sophie – not unreasonably, she felt.

'But Miss Pryce is not,' said Jenny. 'For that matter, Joanna's being your sister is a perfectly sound reason for asking *her* what plans she may have for the future, but it is no reason at all to ask *me*.'

There followed a long and increasingly uncomfortable silence, which Jenny made no move to assist Sophie in breaking; and at length Sophie said, 'I only – they are both of them handsome and clever, and if they have not much fortune between them, they have at least the great advantage of your patronage; I expected them both to be besieged with suitors, and yet it is no such thing. And,' she added, 'as Jo is a ward of the Crown until she marries, I should have expected her to be looking about her in search of some independence, if for no other reason.'

'Sophie,' said Jenny firmly, 'if I believed Joanna's life to be in jeopardy, I should not hesitate to divulge any confidence of hers which might assist in saving it. As things stand, however, I can only repeat that whatever questions you may have about your sister's plans, you must ask her yourself.'

'Yes, of course,' said Sophie, in a chastened tone, and bent her head to her sewing.

All the same, she reflected, *I have my answer: Jenny knows something about Jo and Miss Pryce, which she considers none of my affair.*

She was not altogether pleased to have so provoked Jenny, for whom she felt enormous affection and esteem; but short of asking Joanna outright, *Does Jenny know?*, this had seemed the best means of mapping out the territory.

In any case, Joanna and Miss Pryce – allowing for the dampening presence of Mrs Edmond Marshall – seemed well contented; Amelia, on the other hand, did not.

'Amelia is hiding something,' Sophie announced, almost before the door had closed behind her.

They had been in London only a fortnight, and already Gray was growing weary of the daily tensions of living in Jenny's house not only with Sophie, Joanna, and Miss Callender, but with his mother and all the various persons whom she had also contrived to antagonise, and beginning to think longingly of Din Edin – of Oxford – even, almost, of Glascoombe in Kernow, which at least offered one set the less of familial grudges to navigate.

Had Sophie not been bound to her shepherding of Lucia MacNeill more or less by royal command, he should have been urging an end to the visit several days since; he had even, for the first time, begun to consider begging the hospitality of the Royal Palace – though, knowing Sophie's opinion upon that subject, he had not yet dared mention it to her.

'Oh?' he said now, turning. 'Why do you say so?'

Sophie seated herself at the dressing-table and began pulling the pins from her hair. 'She had a letter this morning at breakfast,' she said, 'which must have given her some sort of shock, for she turned very pale; do you not recall Cousin Maëlle's asking her whether she was quite well?'

'Vaguely,' said Gray, from within the folds of the shirt which he was pulling off over his head. 'I confess that your sister Amelia was occupying very little of my attention at the time, as Mr Fowler was telling me—'

There was a brisk knock upon the door; Gray hastily struggled back into his shirt as Sophie called, '*Quo vadis?*'

The door-handle turned, the door opened a few inches, and Joanna's face peered round its edge. 'May I come in?' she enquired – rather belatedly, in Gray's view.

'Come in or go away, as you like,' said Sophie, 'but in either case, do shut the door, Jo.'

Joanna opened the door, stepped through it, and closed it again behind her; Sophie dropped the last hairpin on the table-top and took up her hairbrush.

'Let me,' said Gray. She half turned towards him, holding out the brush; he took it from her, but, out of sight of Joanna, indulged himself by running his free hand through the silky mass of her hair before setting to work.

Joanna folded herself into the armchair onto which Gray had recently flung his coat, tucking up her bare feet beneath the hem of her dressing-gown.

'Sophie,' she said, 'what ails Amelia, do you suppose?'

64

'I have been asking myself the same question,' said Sophie. She repeated the tale of the letter for the benefit of Joanna, who had come in too late from her morning's ride to see its arrival for herself, and concluded: 'She would not say what was in the letter, nor who had sent it. And I cannot blame her – she is not a child, and her correspondence is her own business! – but there was something in her face, and her voice – I do not know Amelia so well now as I once did, but I should have sworn that she was truly frightened.'

Gray's hands stilled. 'Frightened,' he repeated. 'Now, what could frighten the indomitable Miss Callender?'

'Gray,' said Sophie severely, meeting his gaze in the glass with her eyebrows drawn together. 'I am entirely serious; I beg you will not make fun.'

'I was not making fun,' he protested, startled. 'Why should you think so?'

Sophie twisted round to look at him straight on; from the armchair, Joanna regarded him with a deeply sceptical expression.

'Truly,' he said. 'Have I never told you how much your sister alarmed me, when first I came to Breizh? The proud and elegant Miss Callender, undisputed mistress of all she surveyed, very evidently finding fault with my very existence, and liable to report my least misdeed to the Professor at once! I was never so much relieved as when she determined me to be of no consequence, and ceased to pay me any attention.'

As he spoke, an expression of disbelief had spread over Sophie's face; now she rose to her feet and hopped nimbly up to stand upon the seat of her chair, so as to lay her hands on Gray's shoulders and smile down at him – a small, rueful smile. He wrapped one arm about her to steady her.

'I was eaten up with jealousy,' Sophie said, after a moment – very softly, for his ears alone – 'though I do not think I understood it at the time. All the young men I had ever met paid court to Amelia, you see, and I had never begrudged her their attentions; but for some reason I could not bear that you should be like them.'

'"For some reason", aye,' Gray agreed solemnly. 'I see. Come down from there, my green-eyed goose.'

'Now,' he said, when Sophie had resumed her seat, and he his brushing, 'my question stands: who, or what, might she be frightened of? I do not suppose you chanced to catch a glimpse of the letter, or of its direction?'

'I did not,' Sophie admitted. 'We were placed across from each other, as you may recall' – Gray had no particular recollection of anyone's placement at the breakfast-table, apart from his own, but did not like to say so – 'but I did see the envelope for just a moment, and it bore no frank.'

'An express?' said Gray, surprised. He had finished brushing out Sophie's hair, and was braiding it into a long plait. How his brothers would jeer at him! And how comfortable to discover that he no longer cared what either of them thought. 'Or delivered by hand?'

'I have not the least idea,' said Sophie, 'though we should have heard an express arrive, I think, as the breakfast-room overlooks the square.'

Gray considered this. 'It does not seem very likely that Amelia should take any of us into her confidence,' he said, tying off the plait, 'but surely if something were very much amiss, she would confide in Lady Maëlle? Or,' he added more confidently, 'Lady Maëlle would find it out.'

'That is what *I* should do,' said Joanna – not, perhaps, an entirely accurate assessment – 'but only the gods know how Amelia may proceed.'

'What I cannot understand,' said Sophie, 'is why they should be here at all. Amelia has never once set foot in London since the Professor's trial, to my certain knowledge; no one could suppose that she had any wish to see me, or to see you, Jo – so why, then, should she choose to come here *now*, when you and I are both to spend all the summer in Town, as we have never done since that year?'

'Half the kingdom has come to London to see Lucia MacNeill,' said Gray, not unreasonably. 'Might not Lady Maëlle have wished to do the same, and brought your sister along with her?'

'Oh, but it was Amelia's notion to come,' said Joanna. 'Katell told me – she was a whole fortnight persuading Cousin Maëlle to make the journey.'

'Was she, indeed?' Sophie pounced on this admission. 'But why on *earth* . . . What did Katell say, exactly?'

'I hardly know,' said Joanna, which was not precisely true. 'It was a perfectly ordinary conversation, Sophie, not an interrogation. She said . . .' She tilted her head back and closed her eyes briefly, casting her mind back. She could not, *would* not repeat everything Katell had told her. 'Amelia complained of the utter lack of eligible young men in the neighbourhood of Cal—of your house,' she said at last, 'or so Katell told me, and said that if she were not to die a miserable spinster, living on sufferance in someone else's home—'

Gray winced, and Sophie said (speaking under her breath, but not so inaudibly as she perhaps supposed), 'How *dare* she!'

'—she must have a season in London, as she ought to have had when she was my age, so that she might have some opportunity of marrying, even if she cannot hope to marry well.'

'I must say,' said Gray, with a thoughtful frown, 'that does not seem a likely tactic to succeed with Lady Maëlle.'

'Oh! No, it did not succeed at all,' said Joanna. 'I only mention it because it shows that Amelia cannot have been thinking clearly; she knows Cousin Maëlle as well as either of us – better now, perhaps – and she may not be exceptionally clever, but she is not *stupid.* No; she persuaded her, according to Katell, by other means entirely – appeals to her better nature, and reasoned arguments, and on at least one occasion, tears. But—'

She paused, biting back the words, *But I have seen Amelia set her cap at many a young man, and this . . . is something else entirely.*

'I do not pretend to any expertise in the matter,' said Gray, slow and thoughtful, 'but it seems me that if your sister is come here in order to hunt for a husband, she is going about it in a very odd manner indeed.'

Sophie hummed, not quite in agreement, and frowned at her reflection in the mirror. 'I *do* think something is amiss,' she said; and after a moment, more cheerfully, 'but I do not suppose much harm can come to Amelia, whilst she is living in this house.'

The following morning, however, when Miss Callender appeared in the breakfast-room (of which Gray and Sophie had hitherto been in sole possession), looking pale and shadow-eyed and strung tight with some unspecified anxiety, Sophie startled all three of them by exclaiming, 'Amelia, what is the matter? My dear, you look very ill – is there nothing we can do to help you?'

Miss Callender looked properly gobsmacked and, for just a moment, as though she were considering telling Sophie her troubles. But the moment passed, and she gathered her considerable dignity tight about her and said, 'I did not sleep well; I believe I have a little cold. It is nothing of consequence.'

Then she sat down at the table, helped herself to scones and apricot jam, and rang for a fresh pot of tea.

A tense near-silence prevailed in the breakfast-room until Treveur came in with the tea, at which point Sophie, still looking rather shaken, excused herself and fled.

Gray took a deep breath. 'Miss Callender,' he said, and then –

for they were close kin now, in a way – amended, 'Amelia, if ever Sophie or I may be of any help—'

'You are very kind,' she said evenly. 'I assure you, there is not the slightest need.'

She took a last sip from her cup, replaced it silently and precisely in its saucer, and rose from the table. 'Good morning, Mr Marshall,' she said, and left the breakfast-room.

Kindly but comprehensively rebuffed – the rebuff entirely expected, the kindness an unprecedented gift – Gray finished his breakfast in thoughtful silence.

Sophie is quite right: something is much amiss here.

The Princess Delphine was fond of walking in the gardens of the Royal Palace, and Prince Edward equally fond of indulging his wife. As, not for the first time, Lucia, Sophie, Roland, and Joanna all agreed that they had rather be out of doors than not, the excursion diffidently proposed by Delphine quickly became a general enterprise.

This afternoon their path took them through the inner gardens, towards the main fountain and the slope down towards the river, where, not twenty feet from the steep-cut bank, could be seen a large, oddly-shaped green . . . thing.

'What is that?' enquired Lucia, pointing – not only because she was curious, but because a silence had fallen, and if she could not think of anything to say she could at any rate provoke one of her companions to do so.

'The maze!' said Joanna. 'Has no one told you of it, Lucia?'

No one had; whilst Edward and Delphine fell gradually farther and farther behind them, therefore, Joanna and Roland (with occasional interjections from Sophie) regaled Lucia with the somewhat baroque history of the Palace maze.

It had been commissioned, Joanna explained, by Roland and Sophie's distant ancestor, the seventh King Henry, and designed by an ancestor of Madame de Courcy, wife of the British ambassador in Din Edin.

'He was raised to the peerage for his pains,' said Joanna, 'but was later executed because one of Henry the Great's mistresses lost herself in it.'

'What became of her?' asked Lucia. It must have been something dire – though had not Henry the Great famously had several of his numerous wives beheaded? 'Did she . . . starve to death, or—'

'No,' said Joanna thoughtfully, 'though that would make a far better tale.'

Roland stifled a snort of laughter behind his hand, and strode off to hurry Edward and Delphine along.

Sophie, however, frowned at her sister and said, 'Jo, how can you?' in a tone of genuine reproach.

'She did not starve to death,' said Joanna to Lucia, ignoring both of them, 'but she wandered for some hours before she was missed, well after the sun went down; and when one of the gardeners found her and brought her out, she was raving of disembodied voices whispering in her ears, cold hands clutching at her in the darkness, wailing and sobbing from thin air.'

Sophie shivered.

'Shades?' said Lucia doubtfully. 'Or someone playing a very unpleasant joke?'

'It might have been either, for all I know of the circumstances,' said Joanna, shrugging, 'or something else entirely. Some drug or poison, perhaps, which induced hallucinations. No one has ever discovered what, exactly, befell her in the maze, but she continued persuaded that the maze was haunted by the shades of those who had perished in it – which, so far as I know, no one ever has. She refused to remain any longer at court, and in the end – after Madame de Courcy's ancestor was beheaded over the affair – the King arranged a marriage for her, and she retired to a life of utter obscurity on her husband's country estate. She lived to a ripe old age, but never recanted her tale.'

They pondered this in silence, accompanied by the gentle plashing of the fountain.

'A pity she did not know a finding-spell to bring her safely back to the fountain,' said Lucia at last.

'It would not have helped her,' said Sophie. 'The maze is not only yew-trees; it is woven through with spells to dampen findings and summonings. Like an interdiction, you know, but more specific. It is one of the tasks of the Court mages to maintain the spells. Though, I suppose,' she added thoughtfully, 'it may not always have been so. I wonder – were the dampening-spells worked on the seedling trees, to grow with them, or were they added later? Perhaps the maze was not thought difficult enough without them? Do you suppose . . .'

'You must both have walked the maze, I suppose?' said Lucia, in an attempt to reel in Sophie's wandering attention. 'Perhaps you might show me the route.'

'I have walked it many times,' said Joanna, 'and—' She broke off abruptly, and began again with, 'But Sophie and I are expected in Grosvenor Square this evening, and I fear we have already overstayed our time.'

Sophie, glancing up to gauge the angle of the sun, seemed about to object; Joanna trod on her toes, however, and she subsided. Lucia pretended not to have seen any of this.

'In any case,' Joanna continued cheerfully, 'Roland knows the maze better than either of us.'

Lucia eyed Roland, who appeared to have given up his brother and sister-in-law as a lost cause and was making his way back towards

71

the fountain, and turned this notion over in her mind. Joanna was transparently throwing them together; but was it because she believed Roland might welcome such an excursion, or simply from a sense of her duty to promote this match?

Less thinking, Lucia MacNeill, and more acting in your own interests.

'I shall ask him,' she said.

She carefully did not look at Sophie, for she was remembering their conversation of a few days past, during one of Queen Edwina's soirées.

'How does Roland go on in his Gaelic lessons?' Sophie had inquired.

'Very well indeed,' said Lucia, 'when—' She caught back the words *when he can be bothered about them*, and instead said, 'when he can find the time to study.'

Sophie had not been at all taken in. 'He is young yet,' she had said quietly, slipping into Gaelic.

And Lucia, gritting her teeth: 'That is very plain.'

'Lucia, Roland admires you, and thinks you very clever and rather formidable. He is half afraid to speak to you on any serious subject, lest he say something which will lower your opinion of him beyond repair—'

'Sophie.' Lucia closed her eyes. 'Tell me truly, is Roland in love with someone else?'

'Why should you suppose such a thing?'

'You made me a promise, Sophie,' said Lucia, as gently as she could manage. If what she suspected were indeed so, she must find some way of conveying to him – without giving offence – that so long as he upheld his end of their bargain, he might do as he liked besides; but all depended on accurate intelligence.

'So I did; and I have no notion of breaking it. You suppose me deeper in my brother's confidences than I have ever been. I believe . . .' Sophie paused, gazing at nothing in particular, before continuing: 'I believe he had persuaded himself in love with . . . with some idea of you, constructed from your portrait and perhaps your letters, and from his own imagination—'

'And I am nothing like the Lucia MacNeill of Roland's imagination,' said Lucia. 'Well, I am sorry to disappoint him, but, for the matter of that, it was never my intention to promise myself to a man who prefers poetry to statecraft.'

Sophie turned back to her. 'Do you mean to cry off, then?'

'"Cry off"?' Lucia repeated the English phrase – she recognised the words, but what did they mean together?

'Put an end to your betrothal,' said Sophie, reverting to Gaelic; and, while Lucia was still gaping at her, 'I know you are empowered to do so, irrespective of your father's wishes; even had I not known it before, I received separate lectures on the subject from my father, my stepmother, and Joanna, all of whom apparently feared that I might encourage you to seek happiness elsewhere.'

'Sophie, what has *happiness* to do with it?' Of course, one had rather be happy than not, all else being equal; but could even so romantical a person as Sophie have so profoundly mistaken Lucia's point?

Now it was Sophie's turn to gape, though almost at once she smoothed her face into stillness. 'It is all I wish for either of you,' she said, low. 'For any of those I love.'

Lucia had drawn a deep breath, then – released it – squared her shoulders. They could have only a few more stolen moments in this quiet corner, before they were winkled out and borne off to be displayed to Her Majesty's guests.

'I did not mention this because I resent Roland's affection for any other person,' she said. 'I do not wish him unhappy – or myself, either – but, Sophie, you must know that my father and yours, in agreeing to this match, were not acting to secure any one individual's happiness but in the best interests of their kingdoms, of their people. Our people. To throw such considerations away—'

Sophie, when well and in control of her magick, was more adept at keeping her feelings from showing on her face than anyone else Lucia had ever met, her own famously unflappable father included. To one who knew her well, however, that inscrutable expression was itself a signal of danger ahead: Sophie would not trouble to conceal her state of mind so thoroughly unless there were something of great import to conceal.

They had eyed each other for a long, fraught moment, until Lucia's own words came back to her and she understood what she had just said, and to whom.

'I am my father's heir, Sophie,' she said, very gently, 'and this marriage was my own idea as much as his. My case is not at all the same as your mother's, or yours.'

Sophie's expression had relaxed slightly, so that she looked merely cautious, rather than frozen like a fox caught by lantern-light. 'I . . . No, I suppose not,' she conceded, and the topic had mercifully been dropped.

Now, fetching out a smile for Roland as he came within speaking distance, Lucia felt uncomfortably under scrutiny – if Sophie and Joanna meant to go back to Grosvenor Square, why could they not go at once?

'Our thanks for a charming afternoon,' said Joanna, winking impishly at Lucia. She clasped Lucia's hand and stretched on tiptoe to press a sisterly kiss to Roland's cheek; then, almost before Sophie had made her own farewells, took her sister by the hand and towed her away across the lawn.

PART TWO

London

CHAPTER VI

In Which Lucia and Roland
Make a Discovery

Edward and Delphine were nearly within earshot now, at last; they appeared to be gazing lovingly into one another's eyes and no doubt were cooing endearments, a performance which Lucia did not greatly care to witness yet again. She looked at Roland, and back at the maze.

Her curiosity had been pricked by the others' tales; the sun was growing warm, and the maze would provide some shade; and as between exploring a maze and watching Edward and Delphine make sheep's eyes at one another . . .

'You must have walked the maze many times, I suppose?' she said, striking out towards it, though without quickening her pace.

'Of course,' said Roland.

He smiled at her, suddenly, briefly; so unexpected was it that she could not help grinning back.

'Once,' he said, 'Ned and Harry and I so lost ourselves in it that by the time the undergardeners found us and brought us out, we had missed our dinner. We had never seen Nurse so cross – I suppose she must have been frightened out of her wits, not only of our coming to real harm, but of the consequences to herself – and she forbade us to step even one foot into the maze. Of course after *that*, we could not rest until we had conquered it.'

'Of course not,' Lucia agreed. Roland darted his eyes at her, dubious: did he suspect her of making sport of him? 'I quite understand the necessity,' she said. 'My cousin Morag MacNeill and I once climbed to the top of Arthur's Seat on a moonless night, only to prove her elder brother wrong, for he said that we should be too frightened to do it.'

'And were you?' said Roland.

She had his ear now, plainly, for good or ill.

'Quite terrified,' she said cheerfully. 'Either one of us alone, I dare say, could not have got past the castle gate in broad daylight. We egged each other on, however, and when the sun rose, there we were, asleep like puppies in the lee of a boulder on the top of the hill. We had meant to go back straight away, you see, so that we should not be missed, but from Castle Hill to the top of Arthur's Seat is a very long walk for a child of ten; and there comes a point, it appears, when exhaustion overcomes terror, even in the dead of night.'

Roland produced an admiring whistle, then cleared his throat self-consciously.

'And you?' said Lucia. They were standing very near the entrance to the maze now, and much better that he should be thinking of his own past deeds – or misdeeds – than of hers. 'What came of your clandestine explorations?'

A fleeting grin; another sideways glance. 'Ned's tutor set him the tale of Theseus and the Labyrinth,' said Roland. 'I rather suspect him of doing it on purpose. And we begged a ball of twine from the kitchens—'

'Oh!' exclaimed Lucia, who had been studying her Ovid, at Sophie's instigation. 'The Minotaur, and Ariadne and her thread!'

'Yes, exactly,' said Roland.

Lucia studied his profile; he was smiling now, truly – the deep, slow-blooming smile that dimpled his cheeks and narrowed his eyes to gleaming slits, fringed by honey-gold lashes. He was rather appealing, in point of fact, when he smiled.

'Harry and I were all for rolling up the twine again on our way out,' he said, 'once we had found the centre at last, and could prove we had been there. But Ned had thought it through – Ned is not so quick a thinker as some, you know, but there is not a more methodical fellow in the kingdom, I am sure! – and he said, "If we do that, we may not be able to find our way in the next time."'

'That is so,' said Lucia, interested by this view of Edward-as-strategist. She glanced up; Edward and Delphine would hear them in a moment, always supposing they had any attention to spare from one another.

'So instead,' Roland continued, oblivious, 'he made us go over and over the path until we knew it cold, and leave signs which no one else would recognise – just in case; and *then* we rolled up the twine and gave it back to the kitchen-maids. Some of the signs are there still.'

That was encouragement, surely?

'Will you show me?' said Lucia. 'That is, if you are not sworn to secrecy.'

Roland blinked – glanced again over his shoulder at his brother and sister-in-law, still some yards away – looked at Lucia.

Then he turned on his heel, cupped his hands around his mouth, and called, 'Ned! Delphine!'

They raised their heads; Edward shaded his eyes with his free hand and quickened his pace.

'We are going into the maze,' said Roland, when they drew near enough for speech: not a question but a firm statement of fact.

Prince Edward's eyes lit – a tiny spark, but a spark nonetheless – and he said, 'I have not been into the maze for . . . It must be years! Delphine, we must go with them; you shall like it of all things, I am sure.'

Delphine did not look as though she expected to like it; she pressed closer to Edward's side and in a small voice said, 'Is it not . . . Are there not unquiet shades within? Ought we to disturb them?'

'That is only a tale, Delphine,' Roland scoffed. So dismissive was his tone that Lucia, though she agreed with him entirely and found Delphine rather trying at the best of times, winced a little; Edward's glare could have melted steel.

'You need not go in if you do not like it,' said Edward, kindly (no one, thought Lucia, would guess that he was only a year Delphine's elder), 'but there is no truth in those tales that the maze is haunted, I promise you. And Roland and I know the way very well; we shall not lose ourselves.'

'I . . . I had really rather not,' said Delphine. Was she actually shivering? 'Ned, I am a little cold; may we not go indoors now?'

Roland and Lucia, for the moment utterly in sympathy with one another, exchanged a look of disbelief: was Delphine sickening for something, that she should feel a chill in the sun-warmed, almost breezeless Palace gardens?

Edward looked anxiously down at his wife, and up at his brother. 'Of course,' he said, but doubt edged his tone. 'But, Roland, it does not seem to me proper that you and Lady Lucia should be wandering the maze unaccompanied. Perhaps you may put off your excursion for another day.'

Lucia, who had been studying Delphine, did not at once appreciate Edward's objection; when its implication dawned, she rolled her eyes (which made him wince) and said, 'Edward, I give you my word of honour that we shall behave with the utmost propriety.'

'Indeed, Ned,' Roland added, though Lucia remarked that he took care not to look at her, 'you ought not to judge others by your own habits. Good morning, Delphine; I hope you may soon be quite recovered.'

And with courtly ceremony he turned aside, neatly snubbing his elder brother, and bowed Lucia ahead of him into the maze.

The yew hedges that made up the walls of the maze were carefully pruned and shaped to prevent them growing together overhead, but so high were the walls that the moment of entering the maze felt to Lucia like passing from broad day into twilight. She paused to look about her, trying whether she could guess which was the correct turning to take or spot the first of the signs left by Roland and his brothers.

'I yield,' she said at last, finding that she could do neither. 'I am in your hands, my lord; lead on!'

She spoke half in jest – an appeal both to Roland's self-consequence and to the sly, mischievous sense of humour which she could nearly always see lurking beneath his armour of princely dignity – and was delighted to see him take up her small challenge.

'There,' he said, and stepped across the path to thrust one hand into the hedge straight ahead of him – a blank wall facing the entrance, which curved away on either side.

Lucia stepped up beside him.

Feeling about inside the hedge, Roland frowned, then rose a-tiptoe to explore farther up; and at last said, 'Ha! Yes, here we are. The hedge has grown up more than I expected, since I last sought out the marks – I do not need them for myself, you know. We cut them near to the ground, so that Harry should be able to find them.'

He smiled fondly, shaking his head, and Lucia's mouth curved in a fond smile of her own: Harry topped both his elder brothers by half a head now, and she liked Roland the better for not resenting it.

'Had we better cut the marks anew, lower down?' she said. 'For . . . for Ned's children to discover, one day?'

Roland turned from the hedge (his hand still buried in the

foliage, his arm still stretched above his head) and in the dimness his eyes glinted at her. 'Ned's children must find their own way into the maze,' he said. 'It will do them good. But we shall cut the marks again for their own sake,' he added, his teasing tone gone abruptly sober, 'in memory of the boys we were, and to make our own memories for—' He looked away from her.

'For our own children,' said Lucia quietly, touching his free hand, soft and quick, with her fingers.

Roland's boot-heels came down again with a quiet *thump*, and he dropped his arm and turned fully to face her. 'Lucia,' he said, low. He reached for her hands, and she let him take them, hoping against hope that he should not be intending to descend once more into poetry.

And he did not; but what he did say was very nearly as bad: 'Lucia, tell me – can you – shall you ever be able to love me?'

Lucia shut her eyes briefly to keep from rolling them. 'I like you very much, by times,' she said honestly. *When you do not insist on speaking to me of love, and reading romantical poetry at me.* 'Many a happy marriage has been built on less solid foundations. Can we not let that suffice for the moment?'

Roland sighed, plainly disappointed. He did not drop her hands, however, or turn and stalk away in high dudgeon; Lucia therefore considered her plea to have met with some success.

'Will you show me your marks?' she said, after a moment, tilting her head up towards the hedge-wall.

Roland nodded, and let go of one of her hands in order to guide the other. She, too, had to stretch up onto her toes, but her searching fingers soon found what they sought beneath the foliage: a scar in the curved surface of the yew-bark, smooth where the shingled outer layer had been stripped away, in the shape of the letter *W.*

'Because we first turn west?' she asked, coming back down to her heels.

'Yes, exactly,' said Roland. 'Now . . .'

He rummaged in his coat pockets and brought out an elaborately adorned pocket-knife.

'Oh!' said Lucia.

Roland – in the act of crouching down to look for a suitable space of bark near to the ground – looked up at her with his brows drawn together in bafflement. 'What is it?' he said.

'I expected magick,' she explained, half apologetic and fearing lest he should take offence. 'I had forgotten, I suppose, how young you and your brothers were, at the time of this adventure.'

'We were very young,' said Roland, slowly and thoughtfully, 'but I own I had not considered the possibility, even now. I blame my tutors,' he added, his wry grin flashing momentarily, 'for they have been telling me since first I learnt to call light that relying too far upon one's magick carries as much danger as failing to learn to control it. But now that I do think upon it – if the marks were made by magick, one could find them by magick, is that not so?'

Lucia, crouching down beside him, nodded. 'Whether that confers a benefit or a disadvantage depends, I suppose, upon your purposes,' she said. 'One could make a mark which can *only* be found by magick, but if one were minded to use magick to defeat a maze, there are easier ways of doing so.'

Roland chuckled. 'I was for having Ned use a finding-spell to bring us to the centre,' he admitted. 'I should have used one myself, had I been capable of it at the time. Ned would have no part of it, however – it would be cheating, he said, and would prove nothing but that he could work a finding, which everyone knew already – and of course he was quite right. We learnt afterwards,' he added, just as Lucia was about to repeat Sophie's remarks upon the nature of the maze, 'that the whole of the thing is spelled against finding- and summoning-spells. I am glad we did not know it at the time, however, for it was a comfort to Harry to think that should we lose ourselves after all, there was only Ned's favourite finding-spell between us and rescue.'

A comfort to Harry, indeed, thought Lucia, with an inward smile.

'One of my tutors was a scout in my father's guard,' she said, 'and had been a forester in his youth, before he became a guardsman.' She reached into the hedge at elbow height and felt about for a trunk or a large branch to suit her purpose. 'It was his doing that Morag MacNeill and I were able to carry out our hare-brained scheme, though I never told anyone so, for fear he might be punished for encouraging me in reckless behaviour, which he had never done. He taught me—'

The pads of her fingers brushed over a smooth, broad curve where the outer bark had sloughed off itself, and she curved her palm over it and let it rest there.

'These trees are not like the trees I knew as a child,' she said. 'They are tame trees' – Roland raised his eyebrows; Lucia ignored him – 'and belong to the world of men as much as to their own. But perhaps they may still remember their ancestors . . .'

She reached inwards for her magick – the power she had been born with, twined together with that of Clan MacNeill and of Alba itself, invested in her as her father's heir – and with the scarlet-and-gold thread of it in her hand, reached outwards to find the spirit of the tree under her palm. For a long moment, nothing stirred; but at last she felt (saw, heard: to describe in the language of the physical senses the sensations of using magick was an enterprise that continually defeated her) the thread of sweet green light that was the yew-tree's pulsing lifeblood, faint and distant and tasting of iron as well as of leaf-mould and wood, and gently tangled her magick into it.

But the tree was not *her* tree – the ground from which it grew was not her ground, and her own was far away.

Lucia let the magick go and drew her hand away, surprised to find that she was breathing hard and perspiration beading on her forehead.

'It is not my tree,' she said, answering Roland's worried expression. 'It will not mark itself for me, as the trees of Alba would do.'

Roland studied her – studied the yew-hedge – laid his hand alongside hers against the smooth under-bark.

Acting on instinct above all (though later she would see the parallels with events in an ancient yew-grove on the Ross of Mull), Lucia caught his other hand in hers and sent another tendril of her magick questing cautiously towards his.

'Mother Goddess!' said Roland, low and reverent. 'I did not know – is it always – *Oh.*'

And now, under their two hands, drawn out by the calling of Roland's magick to the tree's, the mark took shape, rising out of the bark – embossed upon it, rather than incised into it, but otherwise echoing the original in every particular.

Roland blinked hard, shaking his head like a dog coming in out of the rain. When he turned to Lucia, his eyes were alight with something like awe.

'It called to me,' he said wonderingly. 'The tree – or all of the trees – it called to me. Not – it – it *knew* me. How can such a thing be?'

He had turned away from her again, and was running his fingertips over the raised *W*, peering through the branches. He raised his other hand and almost absently muttered, '*Adeste luces*'; a globe of magelight, no larger than a gooseberry, bobbed into existence in the air above his palm, then floated into the yew-hedge.

'It is exactly like,' he said. 'And yet the tree made it – or I thought it did.'

Now he sat back on his heels, frowning at Lucia. 'This is an astonishing thing,' he said, 'yet you do not seem even mildly surprised. Does none of this' – he waved a hand, and the magelight described a drunken tumble inside the hedge – 'seem at all out of the ordinary to you?'

Lucia shrugged. 'If I am astonished at anything,' she said, 'it is – well – your astonishment. Though of course there are Albans aplenty who know nothing of such magicks, and understand still less. Not every father would have his child taught by a man who speaks to the trees.'

She smiled – a peace-offering of sorts – and climbed to her feet. Roland returned the smile, but when Lucia extended a hand to him to pull him to his feet, his eyebrows rose in astonishment and instead of taking it, he scrambled upright and offered her his arm.

I have put my foot wrong again, thought Lucia, a little despairingly, as she allowed Roland to tuck her hand up under his elbow. *I suppose I ought not to have implied that I am as strong as he is.*

But all the same, Roland had looked at her with wonder in his eyes – had smiled at her – was guiding her through the maze now, with his hand warm over hers, and pointing out each turning where a mark might be renewed – was talking of magick, and of gardens and labyrinths, and not of poetry or of love – and all of this, despite her repeated missteps, felt like the beginnings of victory.

'The way is not so difficult, you see,' said Roland, pausing at what must be the final turning.

They had been a long time in the maze, through stopping so often to renew the little Princes' way-finding marks; the sun, sinking towards the western horizon, had dipped below the barrier of the high yew-hedges, making the path through the maze dimmer than ever. It might have been gloomy, but Lucia did not find it so; the trees knew Roland, welcomed him, as the woods of Alba had always known and welcomed her, if more sedately, and if they did not yet know her, she could imagine the possibility of their coming to do so.

She had chosen her guide well, though for what undoubtedly were, from the trees' point of view, entirely the wrong reasons.

They rounded the last turning, and the high, close hedge-walls fell away.

'*Cailleach mór!*' breathed Lucia, staring around her.

'It is something to see, indeed,' said Roland; and if he sounded very slightly smug, who could blame him?

They stood in a great three-sided clearing, carpeted with chamomile, clover, and creeping thyme, so that every step smelt of sunshine. In its centre stood a weathered sundial, whose brass gnomon was green with age, and whose foot seemed to grow up from amongst the thyme-stems like a great stone toadstool. In each corner was ensconced a small, well-tended shrine, and along each wall a low stone bench grown over with thyme, and over the whole fell a profound and listening silence. The air was so still that Lucia almost hesitated to breathe, for fear of disturbing it – yet bright and alive with expectation.

'Hegemone,' Roland murmured, gesturing to the buxom figure atop the nearest shrine, whose feet, like the sundial's, were hidden by vines twining about her legs and up her uplifted arms. 'She who watches over growing things. Apollo and Diana, sun and moon.' Two figures: a man who held a harp, a woman with a bow. *Your goddesses may be handy with a sword or a bow; but your women, almost never. Why is that, I wonder?*

'And Minerva,' said Roland, nodding at the last shrine.

Lucia peered at it across the clearing – or was it a grove? – and slipping her arm out of Roland's, took a few hesitant steps towards it, skirting the sundial.

'That is an owl,' she said last. 'An owl who sits upon a helmet, and holds a sword in his claws.'

'Yes,' said Roland. 'Minerva's sacred bird – her sword – her helm.' He paused, looking from Lucia to the owl-shrine and back again, and at last said doubtfully, 'You will not like to make an offering, I suppose. I shall do so, however, if you have no objection?'

'Objection?' said Lucia, bewildered. 'What objection could I possibly have to your making offerings to your own gods in your own garden?'

'Well,' said Roland. He looked at his boots. 'They are not your gods, I know; and I have heard that in Alba, the gods of Britain are . . . not well regarded.'

Lucia sighed. 'Alba resisted the great legions of Rome,' she said, 'when Britain did not; there are still far too many Albans who cannot, or will not, regard their gods with anything but suspicion.' This was something of an understatement, as Roland must be aware. 'It is not all the gods of Britain whom such persons so resent, you understand, but only those who are also gods of Rome. But in any case, Roland, I should never ask you to disavow your gods! No matter how much an altar to Minerva or Apollo in the Castle may irritate the priests of the Cailleach.'

She paused, turning this notion over in her mind, and added, 'In fact, now I think on it, I believe that may be rather an advantage than otherwise.'

Roland looked up at last, brows furrowed, to gauge whether this were a serious suggestion; and before Lucia knew what had happened, they were laughing together.

Roland began searching his pockets. The much smaller pockets of Lucia's worked muslin gown producing nothing of interest, she hunted through her reticule and at length extracted a long blue-black feather which she had picked up in the course of their walk; a copper ring in the shape of two snakes, a gift from

Sìleas which, however, fit none of Lucia's fingers; and a linen handkerchief embroidered with the lion of Alba.

'Will any of these do?' she enquired diffidently, holding out her hands to Roland. 'Or I suppose chamomile-flowers, or clover—'

'One of the secrets of the maze,' said Roland, 'is that any offering you make here, you must bring in with you from the outside. I had not the least notion of going into the maze today, however, and so—'

He had been rummaging in an inner pocket of his coat, and now withdrew from it a folded paper. This he unfolded, and read through with an expression of chagrin growing upon his face. 'No,' he said – to himself rather than to her, Lucia judged – and tucked it away again.

Eventually he discovered a pen in one pocket and a silver coin in another, which he appeared to consider satisfactory. 'But may I have the crow's feather?' he said, and smiled at Lucia when she gave it to him.

Roland knelt at the shrine of Apollo and Diana, and laid the silver coin upon the tiny altar before the twin figures of the gods. His prayer was silent, or at any rate was spoken too softly to be intelligible; Lucia was glad of it, though she could not entirely suppress a flicker of curiosity. At the end of it, however, he bowed to the altar and spoke aloud the same formula she had by now heard used more than once in more public forms of worship: '*Do ut des.*'

I give, that you may give in return.

The pen was offered to Minerva ('It was made from an owl's feather,' Roland explained; 'Sophie's pens are all made so, and she brought some as a gift for Harry'), and the crow's feather to Hegemone. Having finished this third offering, Roland rose to his feet and said, 'Shall we rest here a little? These benches are more comfortable to sit on than they look, I promise you.'

Lucia let him steer her towards the bench that separated

Minerva's shrine from that of Apollo and Diana, and perched on one end of it whilst Roland settled himself on the other, his knees angled towards her own. The bench was not a long one, and they were closer together than Lucia had been prepared for, though not perhaps so close as Roland had meant.

'It is very beautiful,' she said. 'Is it true, the tale of the old King's mistress who heard the shades of dead men and women howling for vengeance, and had to be sent away?'

Roland's eyebrows shot up, and he let out a bark of incredulous laughter. 'You must not believe every tale Joanna Callender tells you,' he said.

'Is it not true then?'

'It is certainly true that she left court,' said Roland. 'There are records of the King's gifts of property and so on in the Archives, or so I am given to understand. And that Henry the Great had the fellow who designed the maze – he must have been an old man by then, if the walls were grown high enough to lose oneself in! – beheaded. Henry the Great was always beheading people, however,' he added, with a glinting smile which made him look, for just an instant, like a fair-haired, blue-eyed Sophie, though they resembled one another so little in any other respect. 'It need not mean that any of the rest is true. I have certainly never seen or heard anything of the kind, nor has anyone else, that I know of.'

Lucia hummed thoughtfully. As between Roland and Joanna, which was the more likely to have the true tale? Roland, who had lived all his life at court, had certainly the better opportunity to gather information; but he seemed to catch at facts and rumours haphazardly as they floated by him, whereas Joanna went after them like a hunting-dog on the scent.

'It has occurred to me,' she said, 'that perhaps it was the trees she heard, without knowing it.'

Roland's eyes widened. 'Indeed,' he said. 'I had not thought of that.'

They sat in silence a long moment – a more comfortable silence than was usual between them, for which Lucia was briefly grateful; until it occurred to her that the rustling of leaves all about her had no breeze to go with it.

'The trees,' she said, very softly. 'The trees are speaking to us – to you, I mean. What do they say?'

Roland, who had been looking about him (in search of a breeze to explain the noise?), turned to her wide-eyed. 'I have not the least idea,' he said.

Lucia considered, her eyes closed, her ears pricked to catch at the least possibility of meaning in the sounds about them.

Put out your hand, she was about to say, when upon opening her eyes she saw that Roland had already thought it; on his feet again, he had stepped close to the nearest hedge-wall and was reaching in. Lucia, forgetting entirely her resolution to conduct herself in a manner becoming a lady of King Henry's court, drew her knees up to her chest, braced her boot-heels on the edge of the bench, and, wrapping her arms about her shins, settled down with her chin upon one knee to observe him.

The moment dragged on, and the shadows lengthened; above the hedge-walls there appeared the upper edges of a flame-and-crimson sunset, and its alchymy turned Roland's fair hair to burnished gold.

Roland stood with both hands in the hedge, one foot braced behind him and his head tilted in rapt attention. He ought to have looked absurd in such an attitude; in fact, however (thought Lucia to herself), he might have been one of his kingdom's several mischievous gods, caught in the act of emerging from the trees to tempt some unsuspecting mortal maiden.

It was a disconcerting thought – but not, in the circumstances, unwelcome. She turned it over in her mind – tried to imagine kissing him, as she had kissed several of the cousins who had been her childhood playmates, and found the notion not altogether unappealing – but all too soon was brought up short by a vivid impression of Roland's resemblance to her brother, Duncan.

At last – just as Lucia was growing truly anxious, and weighing the consequences of making some attempt to gain his attention – Roland let out a shuddering sigh, and pulled his hands out of the foliage to scrub them through his hair.

Lucia scrambled to her feet as he turned away from the hedge, still gripping fistfuls of curls on either side of his head. He raised his head and found himself face-to-face with Lucia across the stone bench; though she had scarcely altered her position since first sitting down, he seemed genuinely astonished by her presence.

He was swaying on his feet; alarmed, she darted forward and caught him by both elbows.

'Sit down,' she said, keeping her tone level, 'and tell me what you heard.'

Roland resisted briefly, but his body, it seemed, conceded what his mind would not, and before long his knees folded him obediently into a seat on the bench.

He turned his face to hers, and – an unprecedented intimacy – brought one hand up to cup her cheek. 'Lucia,' he said, and smiled dreamily.

Lucia blinked. Her cheek was warm where he had touched it; the same hand, his left, came down to rest over hers in her lap, and reflexively she turned her hand over to clasp his, palm to palm.

'The trees,' she prompted again, to cover her confusion but also because she was desperately curious. 'What did they say to you?'

'I did not understand above half of it,' said Roland, still in that alarmingly dreamy tone. 'But they are not so tame as you think.'

His hand in Lucia's trembled. It was all the warning she had before his eyes rolled up and he tumbled sideways off the bench, dead to the world.

For the space of four heartbeats Lucia sat frozen in shock. But not for nothing had Ceana MacGregor trained her, and Donald MacNeill chosen her as his heir; by the time the fifth battered at her ribs and thudded in her ears, she was up and moving.

'Magick shock,' she said aloud in Gaelic, as she knelt at Roland's shoulder and felt for a pulse at his throat. Yes, there it was – quicker by half than it ought to be, as her own certainly was, but strong and steady. 'You are badly magick-shocked, Roland, and what am I to do for you?' She gently straightened his limbs, turned him onto his left side so that he should not choke to death if he should happen to be sick, and, lacking anything that might serve as a pillow, settled his head in her lap.

'We are at the centre of this maze, and I have got nothing to feed you or to warm you with, and how are we to get out again, with you in such a state? And what were you thinking, to be doing . . . whatever it is you have been doing?' Her left hand was in his hair, Lucia discovered; it was very soft. 'Has no one taught you to know your limits? To say true, Highness, I have met half-grown children with more sense. Though of course I have also met your sister, Sophie, who, as you may know, thinks nothing of—'

Roland stirred and muttered something unintelligible.

'Roland,' said Lucia, more gently, carding her fingers through the tumbled curls, and craning her neck in an effort to see his face properly without jostling him; and, shifting into Latin, 'Roland, can you hear me?'

By way of reply, he groaned softly and curled forward a little, as

93

though he were attempting to roll himself into a ball like a hedgehog but could not quite manage it.

'Are you hurt anywhere?' Lucia enquired.

Roland managed a sort of negatory hum.

'Has anything of this kind ever happened to you before?'

'Nnnn.' His shoulders shifted as he planted one hand flat on the creeping thyme and attempted to lever himself upright.

'Lie down, if you please,' said Lucia with some asperity; and, in response to his inarticulate noise of protest, 'I have been magick-shocked before, Roland, if you have not, and I had rather you did not fall over again before we have had time to determine what we ought to do.'

He subsided at last, and rolled his head so as to peer up at her. His face was ashen, his eyes nearly all pupil. Had he struck his head in falling? He blinked slowly – attempting, Lucia supposed, to bring her into focus – and the shade of a smile passed across his face, sweet and sad.

Lucia laid one hand along his cheek and was taken aback by the fierce tenderness that briefly swamped her thoughts when he turned minutely into her touch – just as Duncan had, as a motherless small boy, ten years and more ago, and yet . . . altogether not.

'Is there some way of summoning help from here?' she said. 'A signal of some kind, in case of emergencies?'

'Mmm,' said Roland. His eyelids drooped, then rose again, revealing pupils still blown wide. 'Signal, yes. Shan't use it . . . I sh'd never live it down.'

'Roland, we must have help of some sort to make our way out,' said Lucia, patiently. 'You are in no condition to walk so far, and as we had not the foresight to bring a picnic supper into the maze with us, there is not much to be done for you until we *are* out, except rest; there is nothing to eat here, but thyme-leaves and chamomile flowers, neither of which is much to the purpose. And I am not of a size to carry you, even if I were quite sure of the way, which I regret to say that I am not.'

Roland frowned. 'But . . . marks,' he said. 'On the trees, marks.'

Would he remember, later, the things he had done and said in this misfortunate hour? Lucia rather hoped not, for the sake of his pride. She had never seen magick shock manifest in precisely this way – had she not known better, she might have supposed Roland deep in his cups – but then, it took some people oddly.

'You marked the way, yes,' she agreed, 'but the marks are not easily found, if one does not know where to look, and I do not know where to look so well as you do.'

Roland was struggling to sit up again, and this time Lucia, conceding the battle in hopes of winning the day, helped him to do so. He leant heavily upon her supporting arms, and did not resist when she tightened them about his waist and shoulders.

They sat thus, Roland folded awkwardly into Lucia's encircling arms, as the sun sank below the horizon and the stars began to prick the dark fabric of the sky.

The principal means of treating a person suffering from magick shock was to keep him warm, feed him well – preferably on cold meat, hard cheese, and strong tea with plenty of milk and honey – and put him to bed to sleep off its effects. Lucia had, as she had told Roland, been the sufferer herself on more than one occasion, as she grew towards mastering her talent, and she did not for a moment believe that Roland had never before been affected likewise. More importantly, however, so often had she been called upon to cope with the consequences of someone else's magickal miscalculations, that the necessary steps were by now a matter of instinct. To know – to *feel* – what was needed, and to be prevented by circumstance from providing it, made her twitch with frustration. No food was to be had; she dared not call fire, for nothing here could be spared to burn; and though the day had been so warm, night was coming on and a chill mist creeping in from off the river.

Had she only had her mother's knife with her, and a flame or some spirits with which to clean it, she might, in this extremity, have attempted the spell which, as a mage of Clan MacNeill, she had been taught on her sixteenth birthday – a sharing of magick through the sharing of blood; she had used this spell only twice in her life, but as it had ultimately saved not only several persons' lives but also her father's kingdom, she felt reasonably confident in its efficacy. But the knife, in its sheath embroidered with scarlet lions rampant, was tucked away safely in a locked dispatch-box in her bedroom, and thus was no good to anyone.

After this, thought Lucia bitterly, *I shall carry it with me everywhere, whatever Father may say about it.*

What she could provide (and it was little enough) was light, and the warmth of her own body in the gathering chill, and a firm encouragement to rest; and these she was engaged in supplying – her back pressed painfully against one end of the stone bench, both arms wound tight about Roland's rib cage, and his head heavy on her shoulder – when a distinctly human set of noises caught her ear, and resolved themselves into footfalls, a haphazard rustling of leaves, and someone calling, 'Prince Roland! Lady Lucia!'

CHAPTER VII

In Which the Crown Prince Effects a Rescue

Roland reacted to the sounds of his rescuers only with a groan of weary irritation. Lucia, on the contrary, would have leapt to her feet with cries of joy, had she not been restrained by the limp weight of Roland's body in her arms.

Instead she laid her hands over his ears, drew in a deep breath, and bellowed, 'Here! We are here, by the shrine of Hegemone.'

The footfalls accelerated, and after a moment a small crowd of persons – nearly all of them Royal Guardsmen – tumbled out into the central clearing. At the head of the column was Prince Edward; pink-faced with exertion, he paused with hands on knees to catch his breath and look about him. Upon catching sight of Lucia and Roland, he straightened at once and said sharply, 'What ails him? Is he hurt?'

'He is magick-shocked,' said Lucia, 'and I had nothing to feed him, else we should have been out of the maze again by now, I expect. I suppose you have not brought us anything to eat?'

Edward had crossed the clearing now, and was crouched on his heels beside Lucia, peering into his brother's tallow-pale face. 'Magick-shocked?' he echoed, raising his eyes to Lucia's. 'How comes this?'

'It is a long tale,' said Lucia, 'and not a simple one, and I should be happy to tell it to you, Edward, at some other time; but at present—'

'At present, we have more pressing concerns,' Edward agreed. He laid his palm against Roland's forehead, then his cheek; lifted one eyelid, and frowned at whatever he saw beneath it. Then he was on his feet again, organising his small troop.

The trees were rustling anew, more frantically than before, though there was still no breeze to speak of, but Edward seemed not to remark it.

Lucia was grateful for his sensible, practical approach to the present predicament, however.

'What is the hour?' she enquired. It was very nearly full night now, which at this time of the year made it late indeed; they must have been missed hours ago, surely, and what in the world had everyone supposed them to be doing all this while?

'I have not the least idea,' said Edward, absently. He stretched out an expectant hand to one of the guardsmen. 'Reynolds, your flask, if you please – no, not *that* one – the brandy.'

Reynolds hesitated, frozen in the act of unshipping his *cantine*; Edward's expression grew thunderous. 'Mars and Mithras!' he hissed. 'Now, man, at once, and a plague upon your scruples.'

Reynolds fished a smaller flask out of a pocket and presented it to Edward with a muttered *My lord*. To Lucia's surprise, Edward turned at once to pass it into her hand.

Lucia was not at all convinced of the wisdom of applying neat spirits to a case of magick shock, but Roland had now six strong men to help extricate him from the consequences of his folly, which must soon put him in the way of receiving proper care; meanwhile, a sip or two of brandy could not greatly harm him.

It did not greatly help him, either, she judged, when she had trickled a little of the brandy between his lips; he sputtered a little, and opened his eyes only briefly before subsiding once more into near insensibility.

'Before all else,' said Lucia, looking up at Edward, 'we must get him indoors and well wrapped up. It is fortunate that the night is not colder, but—'

'Hughes – Gagnon – with me,' said Edward, turning away.

Lucia forbore to comment: Edward might be as rude as he liked to her, she decided, so long as he was helping her to help Roland.

Hughes and Gagnon – who proved to be the two largest of the small troop of guardsmen – stepped smartly forward and made a carrying-chair of their clasped arms, into which Edward (disdaining the assistance which Lucia tried to offer him) lifted his brother. Roland's head lolled against Gagnon's broad shoulder; his eyes opened again and focused for a moment on Lucia's magelight, floating now just above her head.

'*Fove quod est frigidum*,' he said distinctly – *warm what is chilled*; it was a quotation from something she had heard before, and heard in an accent very like Roland's, but she could not for the moment call the source to mind – then closed his eyes and slumped once more against Gagnon.

'Yes, Roland,' said Lucia, noting with annoyance the hint of a catch in her voice. *Well, Roland is not the only one who is feeling the chill.* 'We certainly shall.'

She stepped in front of Hughes to take Roland's hand in hers; it was like touching a tree-branch covered in ice. 'Your coat,' she said sharply to Edward. 'At once.'

He was peeling it off already, and as quickly helped her to drape it about Roland's broader shoulders and tuck it round his frigid hands.

'Now, let us go from here at once,' said Lucia, 'if not sooner.'

Edward led them out of the maze, as he had led his search party into it, and Lucia was surprised to find that the journey took very little time.

'I assure you, Lady Lucia,' said Prince Edward, a little stiffly, as they strode across the lawn towards the Palace, 'that my guardsmen are all entirely discreet; you need not fear that any breath of impropriety will—'

'What impropriety can you be talking of?' Lucia demanded, indignant. She did not care if the others heard her. 'Your brother was suffering from magick shock, and as I had not the means at hand to provide any other curative, I did the only thing I could do, which was to keep him warm. I do not see what impropriety could possibly attach to any action of mine – or of Roland's, either,' she added.

'Nonetheless—'

'Nonetheless, what?' Lucia's patience, already worn thin by lack of food and by the evening's events, was rapidly shredding. 'If I did not know better, Edward Tudor, I should suspect you of believing that I ought to have let your brother freeze to death for the sake of your precious *propriety*.'

To his credit, Edward looked honestly appalled at this suggestion. 'Of course not,' he said, in quite a different tone. 'No, never that.'

'Well, then,' said Lucia. Relenting in the face of his evident dismay, she patted his arm in a sisterly manner and said kindly, 'I should be quite as frantic and irrational as you were, if such a thing were to befall my small brother. Fortunately, however, Duncan is not so much given to outrageous escapades as I was at his age.'

Edward looked at her sideways, eyebrows raised.

'Come now, brother dear,' said Lucia, attempting a rallying tone. 'Did you imagine that my father chose me as his heir for my biddable temper and my lack of adventurous spirit?'

Edward looked, in fact, as though he had never thought of asking such a question in the whole course of his life – and perhaps, thought Lucia, he never had.

After all, poor Edward had been heir to his father's kingdom from the moment of his birth, whether he liked it or not.

Whatever else it might be, King Henry's palace was well supplied with talented healers and with very good cooks, both of them, it seemed, ready to hand at a moment's notice. Almost before the rescue-party had reached the staircase that would take them up to Roland's rooms, a plump little man in healer's robes was trundling down to meet them, issuing orders to his apprentice for conveyance to the kitchens.

Lucia answered the healer's questions – his name, she contrived to learn, was Henri Vauquelin – as best she could as they all went up the stairs and along the corridors, and in this way crossed the threshold of Roland's rooms with the rest.

Whilst the healer and his apprentice were peeling Roland out of his damp clothing and tucking him up in bed, Lucia busied herself in the adjoining sitting-room, tidying into neat symmetrical stacks the books scattered on the table and plumping the cushions on the silk-upholstered settees and the one heavy, slightly battered armchair which, she judged, was Roland's favourite seat. She would not be ruled by the threat of idle talk, but nor was she eager to court it by lurking in Roland's bedroom whilst he was being undressed.

When the apprentice healer emerged with an armful of discarded clothing, however, she straightened from her by now fruitlessly repetitive cushion-plumping and, with a nod to him, passed back through the doorway, equally without fanfare and without the slightest attempt at subterfuge.

Look as though you believe in your right to be where you are, her father had once told her, *and the great majority of persons will never think to question you.*

But Queen Edwina and Prince Edward, it seemed, did not live

101

by this maxim, for the former looked outraged, while the latter came forward at once to intercept her.

'You must be very tired,' he said – kindly, but firmly. 'Let me ring for someone to escort you to your own rooms—'

'I had much rather stay here,' said Lucia. 'I should not be easy in my mind otherwise, not knowing how Roland does.'

'Your devotion to Roland's well-being does you credit, my dear,' said the Queen. 'You must see, however, that it would be quite improper.'

Lucia did not say, *Roland and I were alone in the maze for hours; what can it matter now?* She did not ask what acts of impropriety Edward or his mother imagined might take place between Roland and herself whilst he lay half dead from magick shock; she did not say, *If you truly believe me capable of taking advantage of a man in such a condition, I wonder that you should have allowed me within ten leagues of your blue-eyed boy.*

Instead, for Roland's sake (for in truth she was growing very fond of him, if not in precisely the way he wished her to be) and for the sake of avoiding a diplomatic incident, she swallowed back all of these thoughts, produced an innocent and complaisant smile, and said, 'I shall do very well here, I assure you. Surely there can be no impropriety in a young lady's watching by her betrothed husband's sick-bed, in full view of two healers and a pair of guardsmen?'

'That is not the point,' said Edward – but almost absently, as he glanced aside at Henri Vauquelin, who presently was clasping Roland's wrist and frowning.

Whatever other faults she might find with Edward, Lucia did not doubt that he loved his brothers. He was, she judged, eager to conclude the present debate so that he might return to personally superintending Roland's care.

Surreptitiously, Lucia planted her feet, lest the aforesaid

guardsmen be called upon to remove her bodily; they were larger and stronger than herself, but she should at least not do their work for them. All the same, she rather wondered at her own vehemence. Her growing fondness notwithstanding, until now it had never for a moment occurred to her to resist being parted from Roland – *Am I a child, holding tight to my doll only because the nursery-maid threatens to take it away?*

'My dear Lucia,' Queen Edwina began, 'I must insist—'

'Lady Lucia,' said Henri Vauquelin, cutting across her with the calm self-confidence of a man whose calling places him, when he so chooses, above the whims of mere monarchs. 'Prince Roland is asking for you.'

'I beg you will excuse me, Your Majesty,' said Lucia. She did not wait to observe Queen Edwina's reaction to this new development; whatever it might be, she should not let it dictate her conduct.

Henri Vauquelin ushered Lucia back to Roland's bedside, where his apprentice eagerly surrendered to her his seat on a hard chair, together with a jug of beef tea, a porcelain cup, and a spoon.

'He must take some nourishment, ma'am,' said the healer, murmuring in Lucia's ear. 'It may be more welcome from your hand.'

Lucia folded herself into the chair and accepted the jug and spoon almost absently, her attention all on Roland.

Truly he looked shockingly ill, even for a man suffering from magick shock; with the alarming exception of some of Cormac MacAlpine's victims – kidnapped, beaten, and held under interdiction – Lucia had rarely seen such ashen skin on a living person. The sight of him, waxen-faced amidst the white pillows and midnight-blue coverlet, wedged open a door in her mind which for the most part she succeeded in keeping locked up tight, and for a moment she was ten years old again, attending upon her mother's deathbed, at once desperately sad and secretly, guiltily eager for some respite from the melancholic miasma which had enveloped the whole of Castle Hill for nearly a year, spurring her to escapades such as that illicit ascent of Arthur's Seat only to escape it.

But it was a moment only, for she had many years' experience in setting her shoulder to that door and shutting away what lay behind it.

'Roland,' she said, keeping her voice low and (with some effort) even. His wheat-gold lashes fluttered; she set down the jug on the floor by her feet, dropped the cup and spoon upon the coverlet, and bent towards Roland to take his hand in hers. His fingers felt chilly against her palm, but not so much like a row of icicles as previously. *That is one good sign, at any rate.*

She squeezed his hand gently and repeated his name – once – twice – until his eyes fluttered open once more and, after an agonising moment of wandering, found her face.

'Lucia,' he said, a croaking mutter somehow flavoured with deep relief – why? Where had he feared she might go?

'Yes,' she said, smiling down at him – letting her own relief show plainly on her face. 'Here I am. How do you, my dear?'

'I . . .' Roland closed his eyes, wet his lips, opened his eyes again. 'We were in the maze,' he said. 'The . . . the trees were . . . singing?'

Lucia swallowed her astonishment. 'Were they indeed?' she said mildly. 'You must tell me all about it at some other time, when you are better.'

Roland frowned at this, as she had suspected he might. 'Better, how? Were we set upon by . . . Has the maze its own angry Minotaur, now?'

'You are badly magick-shocked,' Lucia explained. With her free hand she smoothed the fall of fair hair back from his forehead. 'We were foolish not to bring along a picnic supper, as it turns out, for

104

I could do nothing for you until your brother came in search of us with a band of guardsmen.'

Roland blinked up at her, his eyes wide and very blue in his too-pale face. 'Lucia, I—'

'You have yet had nothing to eat,' said Lucia, forestalling him. Freeing her hand, she bent to retrieve her jug and took up the abandoned cup. 'I ought not to have kept you talking all this time, when you might have been eating.' She poured a little of the broth into the cup – not too much, lest Roland's hands (or her own) tremble enough to spill it; he would, she was quite certain, resent the indignity of being fed with a spoon. 'Will you drink a little of this beef tea, to begin with? Or, if there is something else you had rather, I am sure—'

Wordlessly, Roland reached for the cup. Lucia handed off the jug to Henri Vauquelin, standing quietly at her elbow, and – for she was herself very hungry, and so tired that her limbs seemed cast in lead – did not try to intervene when his apprentice stepped forward at her other side to help Roland sit up and rearrange the pillows at his back.

'What you did was very well done, Lady Lucia,' said Henri Vauquelin. His voice, she thought, was rather louder than necessary; to whom was he speaking, really? 'Prince Roland was fortunate in his choice of companions.'

'It was fortunate that the night was so mild,' Lucia replied, 'and that Prince Edward came seeking us so soon.'

No one had yet asked either of them, she observed with a strangely detached curiosity, what in the world Roland had been doing to bring this affliction on himself. *That, I suppose, is a conversation for some less eventful hour.*

Henri Vauquelin bent closer and, under the pretext of taking Roland's pulse, said quietly, 'Your bride understates her value,

Highness. You, I trust, will not be tempted to do the same.'

Roland swallowed the remainder of his cupful of beef tea, and, resting the cup amongst the bedclothes by his hip, said solemnly, 'You may be sure that I shall not, sir.'

His voice still much resembled the creaking of a rusted gate-hinge; yet somehow the tone and the words had the character of a vow.

There was a commotion from the direction of Roland's sitting-room; Lucia looked up sharply, irrationally fearing that Queen Edwina might have sent for some even larger and more threatening guardsmen to take her away.

But Roland's mother and brother hovered in the doorway as before, and the only addition to their vigil was—

'Father,' said Roland, in an odd tone compounded of astonishment and trepidation. His hand caught at Lucia's fingers and held fast.

Henry of Britain swept past his wife and eldest son and strode across the room to stand at the foot of Roland's bed.

Henri Vauquelin and his apprentice bowed respectfully; Lucia made to rise from her chair to do the same, but Roland tightened his grip on her hand, and she fell back into her seat with a small huff. 'Your pardon, Your Majesty,' she said instead.

He nodded at her, vaguely, and reached down to grip Roland's right foot through the coverlet – an intimate and oddly endearing gesture, at which Lucia caught herself smiling fondly. *Henry Tudor is not so very grand, after all, when his wee boy is ill in bed*, she thought.

His Majesty did not speak to Roland, however, but to the healer, in the clipped tones of a serjeant-major: 'Tell me. Leave nothing out.'

'Prince Roland is suffering from magick shock, Your Majesty,' said Henri Vauquelin, 'compounded by a prolonged period of exposure, without food or drink, prior to his rescue. Thanks to the

106

Lady Lucia's quick-thinking, however, the consequences are not so dire as they might have been, and His Royal Highness will live to fight another day.'

The King now turned his full attention to Lucia, who was moved by the weight of his intent, measuring gaze to say, 'I assure you, sir, that I did only what anyone would have.'

'Nonetheless, Lucia MacNeill,' said King Henry, so nakedly sincere that his face was difficult to look at, 'we are in your debt.'

'I beg you will not think of it, Your Majesty,' said Lucia.

At Henri Vauquelin's insistence, Lucia was included in the small conclave assembled in Roland's sitting-room, whilst Queen Edwina took her place at his bedside. This seemed to Lucia not altogether as it should be; the Queen appeared well enough contented with her lot, however, and as Lucia had certainly no desire to be shut out of the discussion, she pressed Roland's hand, bent quickly to drop a kiss on the top of his head, and followed Henri Vauquelin out of the room.

The door having been shut behind them, the conference was brief and pointed: Roland was to keep his bed; to be fed on plain, nourishing foods; to be kept warm; to be prevented from any premature experiments in the use of magick, no matter how apparently benign.

'And above all, in cases of this kind,' Henri Vauquelin concluded sternly, 'it is vital that the patient not be upset, or subjected to the least nervous strain. Such as, for example' – and here his eyes settled pointedly on Prince Edward – 'may result from disputes as to which members of the household are to be permitted to bear him company during his convalescence.'

'As you say, sir,' said Edward, looking at his boots.

'As Lady Lucia's company appears to be of material benefit,' the healer continued, 'she is to be given the freedom of his rooms until such time as he is fit to leave them as well as whatever accommodation and assistance she may require. Do I make myself clear, Highness?'

'Entirely clear, sir,' said Edward.

'Very good,' said Henri Vauquelin. 'Now, as to yourself, Lady Lucia: when had you last anything to eat?'

Lucia blinked, considering this question. 'I . . . I cannot now recall,' she admitted at last. 'Certainly I made a very good breakfast—'

'Something will be sent up for you from the kitchens,' said the King, before anyone else could say anything at all. 'At once. Whatever you care to name.'

'To be perfectly frank, sir,' said Lucia, 'I should be heartily glad of breadcrusts and apple-cores at present, so they were plentiful and not actually mouldering. Whatever the kitchen may see fit to send up, I assure you, shall be eaten in its entirety and without complaint.'

King Henry appeared to be considering this carefully.

'In that case,' said Edward after a moment, with a cautious glance at his father, 'I shall order everything that Roland likes best to eat, in case something may tempt him also.'

'An admirably parsimonious solution,' said Lucia. In truth it was an effort of will by now merely to stay on her feet. She turned to Henri Vauquelin. 'May I return to Roland, now?' she asked. 'If you have no further need of me at present?'

'Certainly, certainly.' The healer ran a shrewd eye from Lucia's toes to the top of her head and back. 'In fact, I should advise you to go and sit down as soon as ever you may, my dear, before you fall down.'

'I thank you, sir, very much,' said Lucia. She bowed to the King, and to Edward – no more than a brief inclining of her head, so real was the danger of losing her balance and sending them all sprawling to the floor – then turned away.

As she approached the threshold she heard Henri Vauquelin say, in a low, considering tone, 'That, sir, is a very competent young woman.'

Brighde's tears! I should certainly hope so, said Donald MacNeill's voice, indignant, in her mind's ear. Lucia smiled to herself as she set her hand to the door-handle, and leant her shoulder harder against that other door from which, now more than ever, her memories of her mother's last illness threatened to cast their poisoned caltrops under her feet.

CHAPTER VIII

In Which Lucia Faces the Consequences

As Lucia had good cause to know, an ordinary case of magick shock, promptly and properly treated, need occasion no more serious alarm than an ordinary cold in the head. But a cold in the head can, in particular circumstances, hold the seeds of a more dangerous illness of the lungs; what worse consequences might follow from the exacerbation of magick shock by like circumstances, such as hours spent out of doors, lying on the ground, with no protection from the evening chill, from the river mist?

It was not this question only, however, which disturbed Lucia's sleep.

Two hours since, her guard captain, Ceana MacGregor, had arrived at the door of Roland's rooms, demanding entrance. Lucia had eaten (rather haphazardly) a little of nearly every dish sent up from the kitchens at Edward's instructions; thus fortified, and with Henri Vauquelin's support, she had faced down Queen Edwina's attempt to insist upon her going away to sleep in her own rooms, and at last prevailed; and now, therefore, having left strict instructions with Ceana MacGregor and with Marcus Cattermole, the apprentice healer whose name she had at last succeeded in discovering, that she was to be told *at once* if Roland should wake and ask for her – no matter the hour or the circumstances – had allowed herself to be tucked up for the night, under several layers of blankets, upon the chaise longue in Roland's vast dressing-room.

She had seldom felt so deeply tired, and ought by rights to be dead asleep. In fact, however, she had arrived at that in-between place where exhaustion dragged irresistibly at her eyelids whilst nervous tension kept her thoughts running in circles at breakneck speed. And the thought which most often, and most sharply, surfaced from the maelstrom was this: *If I had not encouraged him, had not given him the notion of listening to the trees in the maze, then he should never have been in such danger.*

When from time to time she achieved a fitful doze, such thoughts followed her into her dreams, so that she stood again with Roland in the centre of the maze, urging him on to new and deeper explorations of the magick of the place, overriding his caution, his doubts, his murmurs of protest – all of them entirely uncharacteristic of the real Roland, and thus, as some half-waking part of Lucia's mind knew perfectly well, not Roland's at all but her own – until the trees drew him in entire, and yew-bark began to grow over his terrified face.

It was rather a relief to her than otherwise, therefore, when in the dark before dawn Ceana padded into Roland's dressing-room, laid a gentle hand upon her shoulder, and murmured in Gaelic, 'Wake up now, and come with me.'

Lucia sat up, heavy-eyed and blinking, her heart hammering in her throat, and found she could summon no words in which to reply. Instead she wrapped herself in the dressing-gown which Ceana held out for her – Roland's, perhaps, but certainly not Lucia's own – and followed her out into Roland's bedroom.

The room was full of light – candlelight, warm and flickering – and in the midst of it Roland was sitting up in bed, staring at something which only he could see, and muttering rapidly under his breath words which Lucia, from this distance, could not distinguish.

Marcus Cattermole, standing on the far side of the bed, caught

Lucia's eye and beckoned her nearer. She stepped forward, her hands clasping her elbows.

'Roland,' she said softly as she approached – once, then again. Did he wake or sleep? Impossible to say: his eyes were open, lips and tongue forming words of some sort; but, on the other hand, he seemed altogether oblivious to his surroundings – seemed not to see any of the several persons haunting his bedchamber, nor to hear Lucia speaking his name . . .

She was near enough now to hear him speaking – muttering, rather – and the more she listened, the more she began to incline towards the view that he was dreaming: though she did not speak such a number of languages as, for example, Sophie or her husband, Lucia was quite capable of recognising many tongues in which she could not express herself to much purpose – and this was none of those.

Or, rather, it was all of them, and more besides: odd unrelated words in more than half a dozen languages – Latin and Greek, English and Français, Brezhoneg and Gaelic and Cymric, and others Lucia could not be sure of – thrown together like crazy-paving and yielding no sense whatsoever. Was Roland attempting some sort of magickal working? It was a troubling thought, in the circumstances, yet it seemed to Lucia that a man who could not string together enough words in one language to form a sentence – coherent or otherwise – was apt to be equally incapable of the concentration necessary for magework.

What, perhaps more importantly, did Roland *believe* himself to be doing, at this moment?

'Roland,' said Lucia, more loudly.

When once more he failed to react in any way, she glanced at Marcus Cattermole, then drew a fortifying breath, let go of her own left elbow, and laid her right hand across Roland's shoulder-blade.

At her touch, Roland came instantly full awake, turning on

112

her and grasping her wrist with a speed and strength of which she should not, a moment ago, have believed him capable. His eyes, wide and wild in the candlelight, caught her gaze and held it.

She winced as the bones of her wrist ground together. Roland observed it – she saw his eyes widen further, his face go still – and his grip relaxed as quickly as it had closed a moment since.

'Lucia,' he said. He sounded as breathless as though he had been running. 'Lucia, what do you here?'

Have we not had this conversation once already? Lucia marshalled her swirling thoughts and spoke as calmly as she was able: 'You are suffering from magick shock,' she said, 'and must stay abed for the present. Henri Vauquelin wishes me to bear you company whilst you are recovering, and your mama has kindly given me leave to stay.'

Roland's face had gone wary. *I have said the wrong thing once again*, thought Lucia, *but what?*

'Monsieur Vauquelin wishes,' Roland repeated. He turned his head a little. Just enough.

Now, too late, Lucia saw her error very clearly. 'I cannot speak for Henri Vauquelin, of course,' she said, and with her free hand reached for Roland's; though his fingers did not return the pressure of her own, nor did he make any attempt to extricate them. 'But if I may venture a guess, his advice was based on his observations of both your behaviour and of my own.'

Roland's gaze swung slowly back to Lucia's face, his brows furrowed in puzzlement. *Again, with smaller words. And may what I am about to say never come to Queen Edwina's ears.* She bent nearer, lowered her voice, and said, 'Henri Vauquelin gave orders that I should stay because you and I both wished it, but Edward and your mama thought it improper.'

What reaction she had expected to this revelation, Lucia could not have said precisely; in light of recent events, however, she had certainly *not* expected Roland's wide, sunny smile – the smile of a child, or of a man who has drunk more than he ought – or that he should regard her with sweet, trustful eyes and say, 'I am glad of it.'

Keeping hold of Roland's hand, Lucia settled herself gingerly upon the edge of the bed. 'Will you lie down again now, and go back to sleep?' she suggested.

Roland looked away again, apparently to study the fall of the coverlet over his knees. 'I had rather not,' he said, very low.

'Bad dreams?' said Lucia, in the same tone. When he did not reply, she added, 'I should not wonder at it. Mine have been very bad indeed.'

'Is there any more of the gooseberry tart?' said Roland, too brightly. He turned his face so as to avoid meeting her eyes. 'Or the duck? I am very hungry.'

This was so transparently an attempt to evade her question that Lucia rather wondered at Roland's trying it on. Nonetheless, if he were offering to eat, she should not be the one to stand in his way.

'I shall go and see,' she said, therefore, and made to rise from her perch on the edge of the bed. But Roland's grip on her hand tightened, vice-like, and raw panic flared in his eyes for just a moment before he pressed his lips together and reasserted his will over his feelings.

'Perhaps Marcus Cattermole may go instead,' said Lucia. She directed at that gentleman a hopeful smile and a small apologetic shrug of her shoulders.

'Of course,' he said, and went away to investigate the remaining contents of the covered trays on the sitting-room sideboard.

Snatching at this moment of almost-privacy, Lucia turned her attention back to Roland. He had loosened his grip on her, but without altogether letting go; his outward composure plainly concealed deep disquiet. This was Roland's first serious encounter with magick shock, she reminded herself, and if he were feeling

114

rather fragile, therefore, it was not to be wondered at. But why should his anxiety take this particular form?

'You are afraid of my abandoning you to your fate,' she said, leaning closer than Queen Edwina would at all condone. 'Though what fate, I have no notion. You need not be, Roland, truly.'

Roland ducked his head. 'Not . . . not of your going,' he said. 'Not that.'

'What, then?' said Lucia, mystified. She waited a long moment for some reply – verbal or otherwise – and when none was forthcoming, at last said, 'Roland, will you not tell me—'

Booted footsteps heralded the return of Marcus Cattermole, carrying a dinner-plate on an invalid's tray. 'I regret that the gooseberry tart was all ate up, Your Highness,' he said, depositing the tray across Roland's knees, 'but there are some of these marchpane-cakes and nearly all the Cheshire cheese, and I have brought you the last of the scones and clotted cream and raspberries.'

'I thank you,' said Roland, reaching for the cheese with his free hand.

Over his bent head, Marcus Cattermole gave Lucia a look which clearly said, *There is more to this matter than we yet comprehend, my lady, and you and I both know it.* Then he withdrew himself to an armchair in the far corner of the room, took up a thick octavo codex which had been resting splayed open upon the arm, and settled down to read, as nonchalantly as though he had been in his own sitting-room.

Lucia cast him a grateful nod which, being bent over his book, he did not see, and resolved to thank him later for his discretion and tact – though she did not doubt that if he felt it needful, he should not hesitate to report all her doings and Roland's to Henri Vauquelin. Then she settled herself more securely on the edge of Roland's bed, at an angle convenient to the tea-tray, and with her free hand secured a scone.

'Roland,' she said, 'may I have the use of my other hand? I should like some clotted cream and raspberries with this scone.'

Roland looked up at her, his face all open, guileless surprise. Lucia waggled her fingers as best she could; he looked down again, this time at their clasped hands, and said softly, 'I – I am sorry – I did not mean—'

He opened his hand, and Lucia – moving slowly and carefully – retrieved hers, deposited her scone on the edge of the tray, and reached for the pot of clotted cream.

'There is something amiss,' she said, keeping her voice calm and even and her eyes on the movements of her hands: splitting the scone, spooning up the cream. 'Something beyond mere magick shock, as though that were not enough to be going on with. I should not for the world attempt to force a confidence – and least of all from you – but . . . if you should feel yourself in want of a confidante, Roland, you need look no farther.'

She chanced a look up – briefly, under her lashes – and saw that Roland was chewing thoughtfully on a marchpane-cake, the other half of which he held poised before his lips. He caught her gaze, swallowed, and, lowering his hand, said, 'You had bad dreams, you said. Tonight.'

Lucia nodded.

'You . . . you are not prone to them, in general?' said Roland diffidently. 'Some people are, I know, though I am not.'

Your sister Sophie, for example, thought Lucia.

'In general, not at all,' she said, truthfully enough. 'But my dreams were very bad tonight, when I contrived to sleep at all. Roland—'

'I hope you have not been too uncomfortable in the dressing-room,' said Roland, a little of his erstwhile solicitude creeping into his tone.

'Not at all,' said Lucia, rather less truthfully; then, pressing on, 'I slept the better for knowing myself within call if you should wake.'

116

Better being a relative term: she had not slept so poorly in many years, but in her own rooms in the Queen's wing of the Palace, she was quite certain, she could not have slept at all.

'I . . . I thank you,' said Roland. He sounded almost shy. 'Was Mama very angry?'

'Your mama, and Edward too, must care for our reputations,' said Lucia, 'as we neither of us take much notice of them ourselves. It is a trying duty, I have no doubt.'

Was that the shade of a smile curving his lips? *Good.*

But the smile, if such it was, was there and gone in a breath, and Roland was saying earnestly, 'I wish you will not antagonise her, Lucia.'

'I have no wish to do so,' said Lucia. Despite herself, her tone was rather chilly. It was not that she begrudged her husband his mother's affection – and the Queen had been very kind to her, Sophie notwithstanding, until their confrontation over Lucia's right to watch at Roland's bedside. *Perhaps someday I may be equally defensive, though I hope I shall not have cause.* 'But—'

'No, no,' said Roland, gesturing with a half-eaten scone like a boy half his age. 'That is not – no. I love my mother,' he said, ducking his head as though half regretting this admission, 'you must never think otherwise, but . . . but I see how she treats Sophie, and . . . and I had rather that you and she were friends.'

Lucia nodded, mollified. 'Her Majesty has made me very welcome,' she said.

For some time, unspeaking, they picked desultorily at the remnants of their impromptu picnic, the quiet punctuated at regular intervals by the *shiff* of turning pages from Marcus Cattermole's corner – a salutary reminder that they were not, in fact, alone.

'Roland,' said Lucia at last, a little hesitant but also desperately curious. 'Roland, what do you remember of last evening? Of the time we spent in the centre of the maze?'

Roland tilted his head thoughtfully, then straightened it again with a wince, rubbing at the side of his neck. 'Almost nothing,' he said. 'Though . . . more now than when first I woke and found myself here. But' – and here his brow furrowed and his voice took on an edge of frustration – 'I cannot make *sense* of the things I remember.'

Marcus Cattermole coughed quietly; Roland turned briefly to look at him before continuing in a much lower tone: 'I am not mad – am I? – to think that you told me to listen to the trees?'

'I did tell you so,' said Lucia, 'and I rather wish that I had not, as events transpired. But it seemed to me that they wished very much to speak to you, and I thought such vehemence must have some reason behind it. Do you . . .' She hesitated. 'Do you remember anything at all of what they told you?'

Roland screwed up his face in thought. After a moment he said, 'When you say *told* . . .'

Lucia inclined her head expectantly; she had not the least idea what he might be about to say, which only made her the more impatient for him to say it. For some time, however, Roland toyed absently with the spoon from the clotted-cream pot, covertly watched the apparently oblivious Marcus Cattermole, tilted his head back to look at the ceiling, and in general did everything but answer her question.

At last, when she had nearly given up hope of obtaining any sort of reply, he looked her full in the face and said, 'When the trees in Alba speak to you, as you have told me they do, *how* do they speak?'

Lucia looked back, nonplussed. '*Speak* is a metaphor,' she said. *Brighde's tears! Is he so much discomfited because he expected* words?

Roland's expression – indeed, his whole bearing – slumped in what looked very like relief. 'Thank all the gods!' he said, loudly enough that Marcus Cattermole glanced up from his book, though only for a moment; then, lowering his voice again and gripping Lucia's hands, 'I suspected myself of going mad.'

'I am no healer,' said Lucia, cautiously, 'to judge *mens sana,* but you do not seem to me particularly inclined to madness.'

She was rewarded with a small, wry smile, and by Roland's letting go of her hands to help himself to the last marchpane-cake.

'My Latin is at fault, perhaps,' she continued, whilst he was still chewing. 'I am fluent enough for most purposes, but this is a magick I learnt in Gaelic, and have never spoken of in any other tongue; perhaps I might—'

'Lucia,' said Roland, touching her hand once more – a gentle, almost hesitant touch, worlds away from his earlier frantic clutching. 'Lucia, *tapadh leat.* Truly, if you had not been with me, had not been so quick-witted, I—'

His use of Gaelic to thank her made her smile, but that he should be thanking her at all—

'No,' she said. She was shaking her head, she found, without having intended it. 'No, I cannot – Roland, had I not encouraged you, not' – she held up a hand to forestall the protests presaged by Roland's gathering frown – 'not *pushed* you to explore a magick with which you had no experience whatsoever, you should not have needed anyone's quick wits.'

'I am not a *child,*' said Roland. He folded his arms across the placket of his nightshirt and frowned more deeply, unfortunately reinforcing the very picture he was attempting to disclaim. 'I am entirely capable of resisting the temptation to experiment, when I choose to do so. You are not to blame for my having chosen otherwise in this case.'

But I am older than you, and have been better taught, Lucia thought, *and plainly I know many things which you do not.* She had also had considerable training in diplomacy, however, and for this reason among others spoke none of these thoughts aloud.

'You are generous to say so,' she said instead.

Roland rolled his eyes, which – more even than the colour returning to his face, and the lively glint to his eyes – reassured her of his eventual recovery. 'Shall we strike a bargain?' he said, smiling cheerfully enough, and offering her his right hand in the Alban manner. 'If I undertake not to thank you for saving my life, will you undertake in return not to blame yourself for its having been necessary?'

Lucia could not help returning the smile. 'Agreed,' she said, and clasped his hand. 'But,' she added, when Roland had gone back to chasing an errant raspberry about the rim of his plate with the clotted-cream spoon, 'you have not answered my question: what can you remember?'

He looked up sharply, spoon poised above the plate. 'You were there,' he said, 'and were not . . . incapacitated, as I was, by my stupidity.' His Royal Highness entirely now, he waved off her protest. 'Your recollection of events, I am sure, must be perfectly clear. What use to you can my vague, confused impressions be?'

'You heard the trees,' said Lucia, simply, 'and I did not.'

Roland studied her, unspeaking, for a long moment.

'And it means so much to you,' he said at last, 'to know the thoughts of the trees?'

Put in such a way, it did seem an eccentric taste. 'It is as I told you,' said Lucia; 'the trees seemed afire to speak to you, and why should that be, unless they had something to say?'

She had meant to stop there – to speak the rational portion of the truth, that is, and not the untidy, sentimental whole of it – but the rest tumbled out of her mouth before she could stop it. 'And – you will think me very foolish, I suspect' – looking down at her hands tensely pleating the fabric of the unfamiliar dressing-gown – 'but I am a stranger in your kingdom, and I suppose I hoped your trees might speak to me of home. I – I hoped, too,' she added, hurrying over the words lest she lose her nerve to speak them at all, 'that you might feel more at home in Alba, if you knew something of the ways of trees.'

Roland was silent so long that Lucia grew apprehensive and chanced a sidelong look up at him – then, seeing his expression, raised her head to look him full in the face.

'I am sorry,' she began. 'I did not mean—'

But Roland caught her hands and shook his head at her, as if too overcome to speak, and her words trailed away into abashed silence.

'A day or two ago, Lucia MacNeill of Alba,' said Roland after a moment, 'I should have said you had not a poetickal breath in your body; you cannot wonder that I should be . . . a little surprised by your saying such things. I have written a deal of poetry myself, I fear, and you may believe me when I tell you that I should have retired from the field in triumph on the strength of such words as yours.'

Lucia, who had not at all intended poetry, and indeed rather regretted the degree of sentimental nostalgia to which she had given way, could not at all think how to reply to this.

'I,' she said, and stopped.

But Roland, for a wonder, seemed to comprehend what she had not said. 'You need not be the heiress of Alba every moment of every day,' he said softly, tracing the tip of one forefinger in a slow circle on the back of her hand. 'There is no shame in leaving a little space to be Lucia MacNeill, from time to time.'

From time to time, Roland of Britain, you are a very wise young man.

She smiled at him, and whatever he perceived in her expression seemed almost to light him from within, so luminous was his answering smile.

After some moments (or possibly hours) spent in the exchange of smiles, with Marcus Cattermole's softly turning pages for accompaniment, Roland said – very low, and in halting Gaelic – 'I do not know at all that I understand the trees; but I believe they tell me, *told* me, that they see an enemy – of mine? Of my father's? Of their own? I cannot tell – and warn . . . *warned* me to beware.'

Lucia sat very still for a long moment, considering this.

'Has your father many enemies?' she enquired after a moment, still in Gaelic. 'Have you?'

'I . . . My father . . .' Roland's voice faltered, then fell still. After a moment, however, he lifted his chin and began again, this time in Latin: 'I do not like to speak of it before you, but I trust you will excuse it, in the circumstances—'

With some effort, Lucia refrained from rolling her eyes. 'You surely cannot suppose me ignorant of the factions in my own kingdom which continue to oppose this alliance?' she said levelly, in the same tongue. 'The objectors are fewer now, and less belligerent – it is not popular to denounce Britain and all its works, as it was before your sister showed herself a hero on Alba's behalf – but some remain. I do not think, however, that any of them could have followed me here without being discovered.

'Though,' she added, 'I shall consult with Ceana MacGregor and Oscar MacConnachie in the morning, and see what may be done to investigate the possibility.'

Roland nodded. 'I thank you,' he said, 'for covering that angle of the matter, and I trust we shall find that there is nothing in it. Closer to home, however – you know, I expect, that some years ago Sophie was among those responsible for foiling a conspiracy upon my father's life?'

Lucia, who had not, rocked back in astonishment; then considered of whom they were speaking, and with a rueful chuckle said, 'I ought not to be surprised at it, upon reflection. This I suppose is part of the tale of the Lost Princess, which everyone in Alba is wild to hear, and which Sophie will never consent to tell any of us?'

'I do not know what tales may be told in Alba,' said Roland, a little stiffly, 'but should you wish to hear a true account of the matter from one who was there, I am quite ready to oblige you.'

There was a rustling from the corner; glancing up, Lucia saw that Marcus Cattermole had abandoned his book, at least for the moment, and was observing them with some interest. When his gaze crossed Lucia's flat stare, however, he blinked self-consciously and said, 'If you have no objection, m'lord, my lady, I should be the better for stretching my legs.'

'No objection whatsoever,' said Lucia.

He rose from his chair, laying aside his codex, and made for the door; Roland watched him out of the room with narrowed eyes.

Lucia settled back in her chair – her own legs were rather in need of stretching – and said, 'Well?'

'Er,' said Roland. 'What *has* Sophie told you?'

'Very little,' said Lucia. 'I know that her mother ran away with her when she was only a baby, because she objected to the terms of the marriage your father had contracted for her; and that she reappeared very suddenly some years ago, but was rarely seen at Court. All of which I knew before ever I met Sophie, and certainly before I discovered who she is.'

'Hmm. Yes.' Roland cleared his throat – ducked his head – smoothed his fingers fussily along the coverlet. 'It was Samhain-night six – five? – years ago, at the Royal Ball. There is always an enormous masqued ball for Samhain, you see. Sophie was there with Lord Kergabet's party – he was not a member of the Privy Council then, indeed I am sure my father had never laid eyes on him since he was first presented at Court – because she and Gray and Joanna had discovered a plot to poison my father.'

Lucia nodded, wide-eyed; news of such a plot had reached her own father's court in Din Edin, though shorn of details –

including, it appeared, Sophie's involvement in the affair – within a month of its failure.

'I can be certain only of what I saw and heard myself, you understand,' said Roland; 'the rest is hearsay, more or less. In any case, the poison was in the libation to the gods, from which the King must drink before pouring the rest out onto the altar. It was Joanna's father who poisoned the wine, and my uncle Edric – Mama's twin brother – helped him do it, though it was not either of them who first had the idea.' Roland's face screwed up in disgust. '*That* honour went to Viscount Carteret, who was then my father's chief advisor; it seems he fancied himself a kingmaker, and meant to promote himself from advisor to King Henry to regent to King Edward before the opportunity passed him by. And he might well have succeeded, too,' he added, 'if he had kept his conspiracy at Court – there was one of the Royal Healers in the plot, as well as Uncle Edric – and not brought Appius Callender and his students into it, in order to get at a better class of poison. And at Sophie, of course.'

'Whatever did he want with Sophie?' said Lucia. 'That is – I should have suspected him of wishing to put *her* on the throne, but . . .'

'An alliance with Iberia,' said Roland. 'Again. He did not think Sophie was truly the Lost Princess, but he meant to marry her off to some Iberian princeling all the same, for if he could not tell one half-Breizhek girl from another, nor could they.'

'Ah,' said Lucia. It had not occurred to her, for some reason, that this danger might have resurfaced; it was no wonder that the subject of royal marriages made Sophie twitch.

'If they *had* believed Callender to be telling the truth,' Roland went on, thoughtfully, 'perhaps Carteret and his co-conspirators might have taken better precautions. Or perhaps not – who can tell? In any event, they did not, and Sophie and her friends used her mother's magick to move about the Palace unnoticed, and my grandmother's magick – you have heard Sophie sing, I suppose? – to stop my father from drinking the poisoned wine.'

'Brìghde's tears!' Lucia breathed.

'Only, none of it was quite enough to stop him from doing what he thought was his duty to the kingdom, by completing the Samhain-night offerings; so she made herself look like her mama, and *that* so shocked him that he dropped the wine-cup, and no one was poisoned after all. There was a deal of fighting after that, and my father ordered all of them arrested, for he was in no state to understand which of them were traitors and which heroes, and there was a trial the next day. Ned and Harry and I saw nearly the whole of it, because Mama would go bursting in to plead for Uncle Edric's life, and spit at Sophie, and we could not stop her.

'They ought all to have been executed for treason, but only Carteret was, in the end; the rest are shut up in the Tower of London still.'

Roland's voice was growing hoarse, and his eyelids beginning to droop; Lucia was therefore not altogether sorry to hear the door open wider, and see Marcus Cattermole slinking back in.

'Well,' she said briskly, 'you ought to sleep again now, if you can. Shall I just—'

She reached for the topmost pillow – meaning to rearrange them so that Roland might recline in more comfort – but halted mid gesture, startled, at his abrupt, involuntary '*No!*'

'Your Highness—' Marcus Cattermole started forward.

Roland ignored him utterly; Lucia flung up a hand – a gesture unconsciously copied from Ceana MacGregor – and their minder subsided, though Lucia could feel the wary tension radiating from him like some overambitious warming-spell.

'I shall stay here beside you,' she said – quietly, as though she had been speaking to a frightened child. 'As long as you like.'

To her own ears the words, the tone, sounded unbearably

condescending; at any other time, she should have expected Roland to scoff at them, and blamed him not at all. But it seemed the lingering effects of magick shock, or of the nightmares of which he refused to speak – or, perhaps, of some other hidden hurt which Lucia could not imagine – still held sway, for instead his stricken expression smoothed out into relief, and he loosed his renewed grip on the sleeve of her borrowed dressing-gown and settled back into his nest of pillows.

'Do you,' he said, so low that Lucia was forced to lean close in order to hear him. 'Do you—Sophie knows a spell, for sleep without dreams; I do not suppose you . . .'

Lucia shook her head in genuine regret. 'I am sorry,' she said, folding Roland's left hand into her own. 'I do know one or two other sleeping-spells, however, and perhaps that may answer?'

'Perhaps,' Roland agreed.

'Close your eyes, then,' said Lucia, and when he had done so, she laid her right hand across his brow, gathered her magick, and began to weave her spell.

'Lady Lucia,' said Marcus Cattermole in a warning tone, as he recognised what she was about.

Lucia looked up just long enough to stare him down, not pausing in her working; then returned her full attention to Roland, whose pulse and breathing were slowing at last into true sleep.

The spell concluded, she gently disentangled their hands and, greatly daring, bent to kiss his brow, then settled herself in her chair by the bedside and composed herself to snatch what rest she might.

CHAPTER IX

In Which Sophie Seeks Reinforcements

'I have a thing to tell you,' said Sophie, erupting into Lucia's sitting-room with her arms full of codices and a quite unaccountable grin spread across her face, 'which I hope may cheer you a little, now that Roland is going on so well. May I?'

Lucia had spent nearly every waking moment with Roland since their adventure in the maze, and was now too exhausted even to speak; she waved a hand at her friend – *Proceed, then* – without much enthusiasm. How could Sophie, who had made the journey from Grosvenor Square to sit with her brother for some hours nearly every day, and had to all appearances worried for him as zealously as his own mother, be so full of sparkling energy now?

Sophie closed the door behind her, surveyed the available seats, and settled herself at one end of the canary-striped sofa. She deposited her stack of codices upon an occasional table, and laid across her knees a leather portfolio tied up with red tapes, which she at once occupied herself in opening.

At last she extracted something from within – a sheet of parchment, it appeared, not large, which had until recently been rolled, for upon being released from the flattening portfolio it at once began to curl inwards from both sides.

Lucia sat up a very little, cautiously interested despite herself.

Sophie leant forward and spread the . . . parchment, yes, it was certainly parchment, across the low table that separated the sofa from Lucia's armchair, and weighted its corners with objects extracted from her reticule: a lump of blue sealing-wax, two copper coins, a heavy silver ring set with some sort of black stone.

Grudgingly, Lucia sat up straight, the better to see the thing on the table-top. It was . . . Was it a map? No: a bird's-eye view of – of a castle?

'Not a castle,' said Sophie. She grinned, and Lucia could not help smiling back at her. 'A college.'

Lucia blinked.

'Lady Morgan College,' Sophie elaborated, touching delicately with one finger the title scroll spread out across the top of the page. 'Established in the reign of King Henry the Fifth, and abandoned at the time of the Princesses Regent, two centuries ago or thereabouts. I disinterred this from a mislabelled pigeonhole in the Palace Archives; I know almost nothing about its provenance, however, as it does not seem to have been included in the archivist's catalogue.'

She looked up at Lucia, bafflingly expectant.

'Abandoned, why?' said Lucia, seizing upon one of the several puzzles presented to her, more or less at random.

'No one knows,' said Sophie. She had begun to exude an air of suppressed excitement, which Lucia could not at all understand, but to which she could not help responding. 'So far as I have been able to discover. Of course, there are a great many books I have not yet read – I have not been long about this business as yet – which may perhaps contain some clue.'

Lucia glanced instinctively at the small tower of books on the table. 'And you have brought me some of them?' she hazarded.

'Oh! No, not at all,' said Sophie. 'That is, yes; I have already read all of those, but you must read them, also, if you are to help me with my project.' She reached for the topmost codex, and handed them one by one to Lucia, who had just time to read their titles as they went by: *An Historie of Lady Morgane College, Oxford. Lady Morganne: A Life, Written by Her Nephew. The Oxford Colleges and Their Patrons. The Lives of the Princesses Regent. A Woman of Substance: The Extraordinary Life of Lady Morgan of Clwyd. A Man of Oxford: Being the Memoirs and Recollections of Arthur Claudius Antony de Coucy, Mag. D.—*

'Your project?' Lucia just succeeded in catching the books now attempting to slide off her lap in both directions, and attempted to herd them into a stack once more. 'What project is that? I do wish you might learn to begin at the beginning, Sophie.'

Sophie paused, still with a book in either hand. 'Oh,' she said, and her mouth twisted, a small self-deprecating smile. 'The beginning. Well—'

There followed a long, thoughtful silence, during which Lucia (familiar by now with Sophie's tendency to drift, and content for the moment to let her do so) examined the codex on the top of the pile, which proved to have been published in the reign of Sophie's grandfather. Arthur Claudius Antony de Coucy, Mag. D., she had concluded by the second folio, had been a dull and self-important fellow almost on the order of Xanthus Marinus, and she rather wondered that Sophie should have persevered through four hundred and forty-eight pages of his recollections.

At last Sophie said, 'The beginning is not at all to the purpose. The *end* is, that I think it is time someone brought Lady Morgan College back to life.'

This extraordinary statement was delivered with the same sunny smile and matter-of-fact confidence with which the Sophie of Quarry Close, tucking a stray curl behind her ear with inky fingers, might have said, *I have decided to walk up to Arthur's Seat tomorrow; should you like to join me?*

This was, Lucia reminded herself, the woman who had set off across a foreign kingdom, alone but for two other young women who did not even speak the local language, to rescue her kidnapped husband from a would-be mage-king – and, against all expectation, succeeded in rescuing not only said husband but half a dozen other prisoners and, indeed, the kingdom itself. A woman, in fact, who made a habit of rescuing entire kingdoms. Resurrecting an abandoned college might well seem a mere rainy-day amusement by comparison.

'And that someone is you, I suppose?' she said, nevertheless. 'You mean to wave your hand, and say, "Let it be so," and there is an end to the matter?'

'Of course not,' said Sophie scornfully. 'I am not such a ninny. Nearly every don in every Oxford college will detest the very notion. My stepmother will tell my father that I am only jealous of Roland, or perhaps of Ned, and attempting to draw attention to myself, and will insist on his ordering me to desist. Joanna will fault my atrocious timing – you were quite right, Lucia, by the by, about Joanna—'

Lucia blinked, confused by this non sequitur; after a moment the mystery resolved itself, and she said quietly, 'Ah,' but Sophie's monologue had run on without her, like a boulder rolling downhill: '—and Jenny and Kergabet will ask me whether the matter might not better wait for a less tumultuous season, and Ned will attempt to reason with me, and say that I need not suppose that all young ladies are as mad for scholarship as myself. And,' she added, folding her hands around one knee, 'my mother-in-law will shake her head and tell Gray very sweetly and sorrowfully that this is what comes of marrying in haste, and without due regard to the views of one's family.'

'Indeed,' said Lucia. She was relieved by Sophie's apparent return to sober reason – though pondering, too, the significance of Gray's absence, and Roland's, from the list of objectors to her scheme.

Her relief and her pondering were alike short-lived, however, for at once Sophie smiled widely and said, 'And that is exactly why I need your help.'

'There is one thing I cannot understand,' said Lucia to Sophie, when next they met, looking up from *An Historie of Lady Morgane College, Oxford.* 'That is, there are many such things in this affair, but one chiefly: why, if – someone – were so determined to see the College closed once and for all, should they have left its buildings standing empty?'

Sophie grinned at her, very much in the manner of a tutor expressing pride in a student's perspicacity. 'Exactly,' she said. 'I have been wondering why the buildings were abandoned, when they might have been used by some other college – there has been at least one new-built since Lady Morgan College was closed – or even knocked down so that the land and the materials might be put to some other use.'

'Indeed,' said Lucia, thoughtful.

'I thought,' said Sophie, absently summoning her teacup and balancing it on her knee, 'that someone must know why things fell out as they did. I had great hopes of a book called *The Rise and Fall of Lady Morgan College*, which was written within a generation of the College's closing – most of the others, as you see' – a careless gesture, here, that nearly sent the teacup flying – 'are concerned with its founding, or with its foundress, and go no further than its period of flourishing – but I could find only one copy, and that had been badly damaged in some sort of flood.'

'An odd coincidence,' Lucia remarked. It did not sound to her like anything of the kind.

'You are no believer in coincidence, I know,' said Sophie, 'but I have no evidence, at present, that any mechanism was at work beyond ordinary negligence and ill fortune. At any rate, I have written to a few friends in Oxford, to beg their assistance in locating more books – beginning with any further copies of the damaged one – but have not had any reply. Besides, it is the Long Vacation, of course, and only the Fellows among them are at all likely to be in college at present.'

'But is it not an odd thing,' Lucia persisted, 'that you should be the first in – two centuries, is it? – to ask these questions? If I were a student in Oxford, I should be quite unable to let such a mystery rest, I think; and do not thousands of people see the College before their eyes every day? The dome of the Temple of Minerva, at least, is visible from quite far off, I believe you said. Did you never attempt to explore the place, in your time at Merlin?'

'Shrine, not temple,' said Sophie absently. Her expression folded up into a thoughtful frown. 'I believe I did mean to do so,' she said, slow and considering, 'but always I had other demands upon my time – or it was the wrong season, or the wrong time of day, or—' She broke off, staring at Lucia in some strange compound of excitement and chagrin. 'I am a fool,' she said. 'I am twelve kinds of fool, Lucia!'

She began a frantic search through the scattered volumes and manuscripts, muttering to herself the while in a hodgepodge of languages, as the fancy took her. Lucia toed off her ridiculous kid slippers, tucked up her feet, and prepared to wait out the fit of investigatory madness.

She had not long to wait, as it proved. No more than a quarter-hour had passed, by Lucia's judgement, when Sophie laid down the last codex she had picked up, flung up her hands, and threw herself into an armchair with a frustrated huffing sigh, for all the world like a five-and-a-half-foot child balked of its desire for sweetmeats.

'You did not find what you were seeking, then?' said Lucia, cautiously.

Sophie blinked at her for a moment, blank-faced, as though she were not altogether certain who had spoken or why; then her gaze sharpened, her face twitched back into life, and she said, 'On the contrary; I have found exactly what I expected to find. Which is to say, nothing at all.' She pitched forward suddenly, dropping her face into her hands, and between her fingers said miserably, 'Oh, Lucia, how could I have been so *stupid*!'

It was not a question, exactly, and Lucia could think of no very useful reply. 'I suppose,' she said after a moment, still feeling her way with great caution, 'that you have had a change of mind on the subject of coincidence?'

'You suppose rightly,' said Sophie, and raised her head. 'I spent two years at Merlin, Lucia, and of course I was not *idle* – I saw my tutor every other day, because I was afraid of falling behind the other students, you know, and I attended as many lectures as I could, and read everything I could lay my hands on – but that I should not even have time to *think*, to *speculate*, after—'

Again she broke off abruptly, this time to stare vaguely off into the middle distance. When she spoke again, her tone was softer, reminiscing. 'When I first saw Oxford – my very first glimpses of it, through the rain, on the day we arrived from Breizh – there was the dome of the shrine, in the midst of those derelict buildings, across the Cherwell, and I felt I had seen it before. And I had, of course; there was a drawing of Lady Morgan College in a book of my mother's. I had read of it more than once, and had pondered what it might mean, that such a College had existed once, and that it existed no longer – what it might have meant for *me*, for such a place to exist in the world, even if I could never come near it.'

133

Lucia felt that a window had been opened to her, briefly, on the blank untalked-of years of Sophie's childhood, and was half afraid to speak lest she break the spell. What must it have been like for that younger Sophie, to know herself cut off from the dearest ambition of her heart? For all the other young women like her – like Lucia, like Mór MacRury, like poor duped Catriona MacCrimmon – who had not had the good fortune to discover themselves to be princesses, with royal fathers willing to reshape the world (or some small corner of it) on their behalf?

'I should imagine you must have done,' she said.

'But between times, somehow,' said Sophie, ignoring Lucia's interjection, 'it slipped my mind. And till that day when I saw the dome, I had forgot all about it.'

Lucia frowned.

'And when first I saw what remains of Lady Morgan College, I felt . . .' Sophie clasped her hands tight together, squeezed her eyes shut, tilted her face up towards the ceiling. 'I felt such sorrow as I had never felt before, nor have felt since – and I have had some cause for sorrow, now and again.'

Lucia nodded.

'But – you will understand, I hope, what I mean – it was not *my* sorrow. Or not mine only. It so overwhelmed me then, I think, because . . . because it was so much larger than myself. I did not understand it at the time, of course. I did not understand anything to speak of, then; everything was strange and wrong and, and simply impossible, and that seemed no different from any of the rest, I suppose. And there was no time, of course. But later—'

She paused, and looked earnestly at Lucia.

'Later, when I did have time, when I was there within reach, *I did nothing.* And not only did nothing, but scarcely thought of it at all.'

'Sophie, you had other—'

'You are not *listening*,' said Sophie, abruptly vehement; Lucia blinked. 'As I did not listen when I ought to have done. It called out to me for help – I heard that call, when no one else did – and then I ceased to hear it; it simply . . . slipped my mind, as though it were no great matter. Do you not *see*, Lucia, what this must mean?'

Lucia did not, and said so. 'And I hope you will not take offence,' she added, 'when I say that I fear you may be reasoning in advance of the evidence.'

Sophie scowled at her; then, unexpectedly, chuckled. 'That is entirely possible,' she conceded. 'But it is also possible – is it not? – for a spell to exist which could produce such an effect.'

'Do you know of any such spell?' enquired Lucia, who did not. 'Spells of concealment, certainly; but what manner of spell could prevent you from *thinking* of a thing which you are perfectly able to *see*?'

'I have not the least idea,' said Sophie. 'But, indeed, if my magick can protect me from the notice of other people – can persuade them that I am not worthy of remark, that the person they see is of no interest to them – then why should not a similar effect be possible on a larger scale?'

Lucia considered this. As a theory, it was not implausible; all manner of things might exist in the world, without one particular person's knowing of them. 'But the books,' she said, waving a hand at them.

Sophie frowned. 'What of them?' she said – not dismissive, but enquiring.

'What I mean is – well, that they exist at all, surely, is evidence that the College is worthy of remark?'

'No,' said Sophie positively. 'Not at all; only evidence that its *history* is worthy of remark. *That* is what I could not find, you see:

135

none of these authors has anything whatsoever to say about why the College was closed, or what became of it thereafter – though some of them at least must have been there to see it – and until just lately, Lucia, *I had never wondered why that should be so.* Does that not suggest to you some manner of magick at work?'

Lucia nodded slowly; it was difficult, indeed, to imagine any other explanation. Except—

'But why now, in that case?' she said.

Once more Sophie rummaged about amongst the codices, and extracted a battered volume upon whose front board was stamped the title *A Dove amongst the Peacocks.*

'This,' she said. 'My mother's book – that is, another copy – which I found by chance in my father's library, not long before you and Sìleas Barra MacNeill arrived in London. If it *was* chance,' she added darkly. 'Finding it made me remember; and I have kept it by me since, so I have gone on remembering. It has taken me all the time since to lay hands on these others, for apart from that plan, they are not in the catalogues, and none of the archivists knew of their being here.'

Lucia examined the book's flyleaf, upon which was written, very small, the single name *Julia*, then turned to the title page. This repeated the title, and below elaborated, *Being the Tale of the Founding of Lady Morgan College, Oxon.* The author, it appeared, was one Charlotte Octavia Boucicault, D. Phil.; the date, more than two hundred years past.

'Well,' she said at last. 'You may leave the other books, and I shall undertake to read them.'

Sophie beamed at her.

'But,' said Lucia, 'I hope very much that you have got a better plan this time than haring off alone, without telling anyone where you are going, and hoping for the best.'

'Well! As to the *where*,' said Sophie, taking this rebuke in good part, 'of course we must go to Oxford; but not yet. I am sorry to say it, but we shall have no chance at all of doing anything – even so much as making the journey, though it is not more than sixty miles – unless I can persuade my father that nothing dreadful will come of it.'

Lucia looked from Sophie to the codex in her hands, and back again.

'Sophie,' she said slowly, reluctantly (for, as Sophie had correctly deduced, she was no less eager than her friend to escape the Royal Palace), 'how can you be sure that it will not?'

'I suppose,' said Sophie, 'it depends upon what you mean by *something dreadful*.'

CHAPTER X

In Which Lord Kergabet
Receives a Letter

Amelia, with Lady Maëlle for chaperon, was gone to a ball given by Madame de l'Aigle in honour of her daughter, with whom Amelia had been at school; Mrs Marshall (who had not been invited) had complained of a sick headache, and, declining all offers of assistance, shut herself up in her room.

The rare dinner *en famille* – more or less – which resulted from this conjunction of circumstances was a relief to Joanna, who had felt for some time as though she walked on eggshells and would be penalised by the Fates for breaking any. The relief, she fancied, was more general also; the family in Grosvenor Square, and Gray and Sophie, had been let into the secret of Roland's alarming brush with magick shock, and of the cryptic warning he claimed to have received from the trees in the King's maze, and to their vivid anxiety for Roland's welfare had been added the strain of keeping these secrets, and the details of Sophie's recent visits to her brother, from their guests.

The conversation over the soup and the fish course, unsurprisingly, had been continually circling back to these subjects: was it, *could* it be, true that Roland – that anyone – was capable of communicating with trees? And, if so, how much store ought to be set by a warning received in such a way?

'This business of talking to trees,' said Mr Fowler, in a *now let us be sensible* tone which at once put Joanna's back up, 'seems altogether too fanciful to me.'

'Roland may be rather fanciful, I grant you,' said Sophie (something of an understatement, in Joanna's view), 'but Lucia MacNeill tells the same tale, and Lucia is no more fanciful than you are, Mr Fowler. It is not impossible, I suppose, that they should both be victims of the same illusion-spell, or some such thing, but—'

'But if both Roland and Lucia can be preyed upon by a mage powerful enough to craft such an illusion, on the very doorstep of the Royal Palace, then the enemy is at the gates indeed,' said Joanna, and Kergabet and Mr Fowler nodded in rueful agreement.

Treveur and Daisy came in with the joint of beef and its companions, and discussion of unexpectedly communicative topiary was suspended until their departure.

'I fear Lucia has put the cat among the pigeons rather,' said Sophie, when the door had closed behind Treveur. Rather than expanding upon this cryptic remark, however, she fell silent, and began tracing one finger round and round the rim of her wine glass to make it sing.

Joanna's mouth was full, but Gwendolen prompted, 'How so?'

'Your pardon?' Sophie blinked at her for a moment, then seemed to catch up the dropped thread of her thoughts. 'Oh! Why, because she would insist on sitting up with Roland all night, not only at first – which might have been excused, in light of the circumstances – but for several nights afterwards. Her Majesty said nothing to me about it, of course – or about anything else, for that matter – but Edward begged me to intercede, for the sake of propriety; as though I should do anything of the kind!'

'Her Majesty would do better to thank her for saving Roland's life, in my opinion, than to fret over the proprieties,' said Jenny, with unusual asperity; and, observing the raised eyebrows around the table at this departure from her usual staunch support of Queen Edwina in all matters not related to her fragile detente with Sophie, she continued, 'Well, and where should you be now, all of you, if *I* were inclined to set propriety above—'

'Above rearranging all of our lives for our own good?' said Gray, lifting his glass to his sister with a small smile. 'Where indeed.'

He looked at Sophie, seated across the table between Joanna and Mr Fowler, and the smile grew tender, crinkling up his hazel eyes. Joanna hastily looked away; but this did not at all answer, for now her gaze crossed Gwendolen's, and she found her own face rearranging itself likewise.

'I have had a letter from Roland,' said Sophie unexpectedly. 'He is feeling quite himself again, he says, and I think – reading between the lines, you know – is growing very impatient with being treated as an invalid. And Lucia has told him of our scheme for Lady Morgan College, and my notion of beginning by exploring what remains of it, and he is eager to assist in the enterprise – or so he says – and volunteers his help in whatever capacity I may deem most useful.'

'Does he, indeed,' said Sieur Germain, thoughtful.

'He is only trying to impress Lucia MacNeill,' Joanna scoffed. The notion of Roland as a champion of scholarship was too ludicrous for words, and as a champion of scholarship for *women*—

Sophie smiled. 'Gift horses, Jo,' she said mildly. 'What of it, if so? At any rate,' she continued, 'I have engaged to go with Lucia tomorrow to call upon Madame de Courcy in Half-moon-street, to tell her of our plans; Jo, Miss Pryce, I wondered whether you might wish to come with us, as Mademoiselle de Courcy is such a particular friend of yours?'

'Why Madame de Courcy, love?' said Gray, looking up from the plate of roast beef and greens which he had been systematically demolishing. 'I did not know that you were at all acquainted with her.'

'Because,' said Joanna, before Sophie could reply, 'Madame de Courcy is clever and well read, and has travelled to Eire and Alba, and to Flanders; and because she has three clever and well-read daughters, who would like nothing better than to be afforded the same opportunity as their brothers.'

'I wonder that Courcy does not arrange for them to study in Din Edin, then,' said Gray. 'As he has a home for them there already.'

Joanna had often wondered the same; Agathe was very young, of course, to be sent to live with her papa in a foreign city, but surely Mathilde and Héloïse, nineteen and seventeen respectively, might perfectly well have gone – with one of their brothers for escort, perhaps.

'If you were a mother of young daughters,' said Jenny, resting one hand (perhaps unconsciously) upon her middle, 'should you rather send them sixty miles to Oxford for their education, or four hundred miles and over the border to Alba?'

'Ah,' said Gray. 'Yes, that is a point, indeed.'

He went back to his dinner, staring vaguely at a spot of sauce upon the tablecloth.

'I should be delighted to come with you,' said Joanna to Sophie – who smiled at her, but rather absently – 'if Lord Kergabet has no objection. Gwen, shall you—'

There was a commotion below – rapid hoofbeats on the cobbles, and a hammering at the front door – and Joanna was out of her seat, in the act of darting to the window to peer down into the square, when the door of the dining-room opened to admit Treveur and a breathless courier in the royal livery, bearing a letter for Kergabet. Joanna quietly resumed her seat, and anxious glances passed up and down the table; such arrivals were not uncommon in the household of His Majesty's chief counsellor, and could not be assumed always to signal a crisis, but given present circumstances in the royal household . . .

Kergabet broke the seal at once and began to read; as he read, the

141

colour drained from his face, and Joanna felt chill tendrils of fear creeping over her skin.

'My love,' said Jenny (by which Joanna knew her to be badly rattled), 'what news? It is not – there is not some worse news of Prince Roland?'

Kergabet laid the letter carefully down beside his plate; when he looked up, his gaze fixed upon Joanna. 'Your father and his cronies, Miss Callender,' he said, 'have escaped from the Tower, and are now at large.'

'*Oh*,' said Sophie faintly. From Gwendolen's place at the table came a sound like a stifled yelp; from Mr Fowler's and Gray's, almost simultaneously, low exclamations assuredly not suited to a lady's dinner-table. Joanna slowly unclenched her fingers from her fork and knife, slowly laid these instruments down upon her plate.

'I do not see how they could have done,' she said, distantly surprised that her voice did not tremble, much. 'They were held under lock and key, and within strong wards – were they not?'

'They were,' said Kergabet grimly. He pushed back his chair and rose to his feet, the letter still in his hand. 'Your pardon, my dear,' he said, addressing Jenny, 'but I must go and see His Majesty at once' – then, turning, 'Fowler, with me.'

Mr Fowler scrambled out of his own seat, leaving his dinner half eaten.

'The rest of you—' Sieur Germain broke off sharply, perhaps recognising that he was, after all, standing in a Grosvenor Square dining-room and not in the barracks-yard of the palace Guard, and resumed in a more moderate tone, 'Jenny, my dear, I trust it goes without saying that your mama need not as yet be burdened with this news.'

'Sir,' said Joanna, making to rise also.

Kergabet turned in the doorway and looked at her; she seemed to feel the weight of his regard, pressing her back into her seat, though that was surely fancy – perhaps, she thought, the shocking news had turned her brain.

'I am sorry, Joanna,' he said. Sincerity rang in his words – and regret and apprehension with them – and Joanna sat up straight in surprise at his form of address. 'Your involvement in their capture is likely to make you a target of revenge, if it is revenge they seek, and I should be criminally careless to expose you more than necessary.'

Joanna drew breath to protest that she did not at all regard any such danger, and had survived worse dangers in the past, but Kergabet forestalled her: 'Were circumstances otherwise,' he said, 'I should of course wish your assistance; but as things stand, you cannot be seen to be involved in this affair. You are too canny a judge of politics to suppose otherwise.'

A dozen arguments sprang to Joanna's mind – the foremost of which, unhelpfully, was, *I shall go mad if you leave me in the dark!* – but sober reason told her that Kergabet was right; any hint of her knowing more than she ought about her father's affairs must be damaging to more than herself. Deflated, she sank back into her chair, leaning her elbows heedlessly upon the table, and watched Kergabet and Mr Fowler out of the dining-room.

A long speechless moment ensued, in which Joanna could feel everyone else at the table watching her and pondering what to say.

What are you afraid of? she asked herself, furious to discover that her hands were trembling and tears stinging her nose. The answer came to her in a heart-stuttering flash: *Whoever or whatever is more powerful than the guards, the locks, and the wards on the Tower of London.*

'I beg you will excuse me, Jenny,' she managed to say, carefully aligning her knife and fork. 'I have rather lost my appetite.'

She rose from the table in her turn, and stalked out of the

room, her gaze fixed in the middle distance so as not to risk seeing anxiety, concern, mistrust – worst of all, *pity* – in their faces.

By the time Gwendolen's hesitant knock (their private signal, six knocks divided into groups of two) sounded at what was presently their shared bedroom door, nearly an hour later, Joanna had had her brief, furious cry, composed herself, stonily ignored the anxious enquiries of Lady Maëlle and Sophie, written out a passionate defence of her right to participate in the manhunt for her father, read it over, torn it into tiny pieces, burnt it to ash in the basin on the washstand, and sat down at Gwendolen's desk to devise a new stratagem – an enterprise in which, thus far, she was signally failing.

'Come in,' she said, squaring her shoulders and turning to face the door.

The door opened slowly, and Gwendolen's narrow face peered round the edge of it, brow furrowed, as though she were uncertain of her welcome in her own bedroom.

'Come *in*,' Joanna repeated. 'And shut the door behind you.' After a moment she added, belatedly, 'Please.'

Gwendolen did so, but having closed the door, leant her back against it rather than crossing to the desk. Joanna had drawn the curtains, shutting out what daylight remained, and that side of the room was dark, out of range of the small lamp which cast its pool of candlelight upon the desk; Gwendolen held out one hand, her lips moved briefly, and a pale globe of magelight drifted upwards from her palm to hover near the ceiling. She stood still a moment more, muttering something under her breath, audible now but incomprehensible: a warding-spell, presumably, against eavesdroppers. Useful skills, both, which Joanna rather envied, though Gwendolen was apt to deprecate her own talent as small and insignificant.

'Are you . . . Are you well, Jo?' she said at last.

Joanna scowled. 'I am perfectly well,' she snapped, hating Gwendolen's diffident tone, hating her father and his misguided ambitions, hating her own weakness in the face of this crisis. *As though* my feelings *were of greater importance than the danger to the kingdom!*

'You don't look it,' said Gwendolen, stepping away from the door.

The unaccustomed diffidence had entirely vanished from her voice, and Joanna exhaled relief. She turned back to the desk, folded her arms upon its polished surface, and buried her face in the crook of her left elbow.

Footsteps approached; Gwendolen's hands settled on her shoulders. 'I know how little you like to be left out of things, Jo,' she said. 'I should not much like it, either, but . . . but I cannot quarrel with Lord Kergabet's reasoning.'

Joanna groaned. 'Nor can I quarrel with it,' she said miserably. 'If I could, I should have done so at once. I do not doubt he has arrived at the logical and rational conclusion, but that does not make me like it any better.'

'Well.' Gwen's thumbs skimmed across Joanna's shoulder-blades. 'You shall soon have thought of a scheme, I expect; you always do. And then we shall—'

We?

Joanna raised her head and half turned to look up at her friend. 'This is not a matter for larking about, Gwen,' she said earnestly, 'like Sophie's Oxford project. I should not care for the risk, if it were only to myself, but these men have killed before – not in battle, nor in their own defence, but by poisoning in cold blood – and if it were not for Sophie and the rest, they should have been regicides as well as murderers. I cannot allow you—'

She stopped, abashed by the scowl gathering on Gwendolen's face.

145

'And what was Cormac MacAlpine, then, if not a murderer and would-be regicide?' Gwendolen demanded, taking a step backwards and folding her arms. 'If *that* was not too much risk, why is this? For you ran towards that danger willingly enough, and made no objection to my running with you.'

'That was different,' Joanna began, indignant, but she could take her protest no further, unable to articulate in what, exactly, the difference consisted.

Cormac MacAlpine had kidnapped Gray – last in a string of captives whose ill fortune it was to be foreigners in Alba, and possessed of powerful magick – with the twin aims of using Gray's power and of ensnaring Sophie for the same purpose; which was, as Gwendolen rightly noted, to sweep Clan MacNeill from the throne of Alba and install himself in Donald MacNeill's stead. He had also, it later transpired, been wooing Sophie's friend Catriona MacCrimmon, whose family harboured some ancient connexion to Clan MacAlpine on the distaff side, with a view to establishing a new MacAlpine dynasty; though, to Catriona MacCrimmon's credit, she had not known the half of the means to MacAlpine's ends, and had behaved with great courage in defying him, once she began to learn the truth. MacAlpine's ultimate threat had been to the throne of Alba – indeed, as it proved, to the kingdom itself – but Joanna, in determining upon her course of action, had been motivated purely by the threat he represented to Gray and, through Gray, to Sophie.

What, then, was different here? Deprived of their head, the traitor Lord Carteret – beheaded upon Tower Hill in the wake of the conspiracy's revelation, as they should all have been, had not King Henry indulged his fit of clemency (*And look what that coin has bought us now, Your Majesty!*) – what threat did her father and his co-conspirators presently represent, and to whom? Of Appius Callender himself she knew enough – or thought she did – to draw some conclusions: he had long been prone to petty score-settling, seldom averse to cheating as necessary to win his small contests of power, always ready to take offence and to put the worst possible complexion upon any word or action of anybody else. Imprisonment had undoubtedly changed him, for how could it not? But still Joanna had no doubt that if left to itself, his mind would turn at once to revenge – and Joanna's own part in bringing about his downfall paled into insignificance beside those of Sophie and Gray, and of Lady Maëlle, and of Kergabet and even Jenny (who had twice had him thrown out of her house).

But as for Gwendolen Pryce . . .

'You are safe enough from my father's attempts at retribution, I believe,' she said at last, 'so long as he does not know what you are to me.'

Gwendolen's arms remained folded, however, and her fine dark brows drew closer together. 'And what am I, then?' she enquired, in what Joanna recognised as a dangerously level tone. 'Am I your pretty, innocent little bride, to be protected from the great perilous world at all costs? A swooning damsel for you to rescue and carry off on your prancing steed?'

The idea was so preposterous – aside from the obvious, Gwen was two years older than herself, and nearly a head taller – that Joanna nearly laughed aloud; but it was clear to her even in her present disconcerted state that this would be an enormous tactical error.

'No,' she said instead. 'No, of course not. Gwen, I—'

'We have made one another no vows, Jo,' Gwendolen continued, cutting across her, 'but surely you understand that were it in my power, I should pledge myself to you before the whole of Britain, by any vow you chose.'

'Yes,' said Joanna, weakly. 'Of course I know that.' She swallowed past the lump in her throat, and went on: 'And *you* understand, I hope, that I feel just the same.'

Gwendolen's expression softened a little. 'I have sometimes suspected it,' she said gravely.

'Then you understand why—'

'Jo.' Gwen dropped to her knees at Joanna's feet, clasped Joanna's hands in hers, and looked earnestly up into her face. 'Suppose that I were the one in danger – should you wish me to spare you the knowledge of it? To refrain from doing all I could to combat that danger, from a desire to shield you alone?'

Put in those terms, the notion seemed not only foolish but repugnant.

Gwendolen had not done, however: 'And you have not forgotten, I hope, that if any one of us had set off alone on that mad sortie to the Ross of Mull, all of those poor fellows locked up in Castle MacAlpine should now be dead, or worse, and very likely all of us with them.

'In any case,' she concluded, 'did you not hear what Sieur Germain said to you?'

Joanna cast her mind back – ran over his words – and after a long moment said, '*Gwen!* Oh, Gwen, how clever you are!'

Gwendolen grinned, and Joanna tugged at her hands until she knelt up far enough to be soundly kissed.

For Kergabet had not said *you must not be involved in this affair*, but *you cannot be seen to be involved.*

It was not until the small hours of the morning that Joanna's busy brain cast up to her, like fortuitous flotsam upon the shingle of her conscious mind, the question of Amelia.

Amelia, whose behaviour Sophie had called peculiar – who had received at least two mysterious letters – whose motives for coming to London (as related by Katell) had seemed so suspect.

These questions had been superseded entirely, in Joanna's mind and no doubt in Sophie's, by the escapades of Roland and Lucia, and now by the potential disaster of the prisoners' escape. Now, however – if it were not merely the effect of a wakeful night, the sort of notion which daylight reveals to be utterly crackbrained – it occurred to Joanna to ask herself whether the three mysteries might not be connected. And if that were so . . .

Beside her, just visible in the faint glow of the banked fire, Gwendolen slept quietly, curled on her side with one hand tucked beneath her pillow and the other just grazing the corner of Joanna's; the bed they presently shared was not a large one. Joanna gripped Gwendolen's shoulder and gently shook it, murmuring her name.

Gwendolen stirred – frowned – opened her eyes at last, her eyelids heavy, and in a voice blurred with sleep said, 'Jo? Is all well?'

'No,' said Joanna. 'I need—'

Gwendolen's eyes opened wide; she sat up straight, as though stung into motion, and reached for Joanna, taking her by both shoulders and peering earnestly into her face. 'What is it?' she demanded. 'Are you ill? Is someone—'

'No one is ill,' said Joanna firmly. 'But I have had an idea – about my father, and Roland's trees, and Amelia.'

Gwendolen favoured her with a sort of exasperated half laugh, flopped back down onto her pillow, and briefly pressed the heels of her hands to her eyes.

'An idea,' she said, through an enormous yawn.

'Yes,' said Joanna. She propped herself on one elbow. 'Does it not seem an odd coincidence that Amelia should be so very eager to come to London, and should be receiving mysterious letters and behaving so much unlike herself, at just the same time when her father has inexplicably contrived to escape what ought to have been the securest captivity?'

Gwendolen, somewhat to Joanna's disappointment, did not

seem particularly astonished by this notion. 'It does,' she said, 'seem a very odd coincidence indeed.'

Then she stretched her long arms above her head, produced another enormous yawn, and said, 'For the gods' sake go back to sleep, Jo. This will all keep for the morning.'

She lay down again, curled up with her back to Joanna, and closed her eyes.

Joanna glared down at her, at the pale shape of her shoulder in the firelight, the dark stripe of her plaited hair. But no better soporific existed than the sound of Gwen's deep, even breathing so near at hand, and at last, in spite of herself, Joanna tucked herself against the curve of her friend's back, and drifted once more into sleep.

Sophie and Gray woke very early the next morning, and arrived in the breakfast-room almost before the breakfast itself – though not before Joanna and Miss Pryce, whom they found respectively demolishing a plate of brioches and yawning over a cup of tea.

'Amelia knows something,' said Joanna at once, and a propos of nothing whatsoever, the moment they crossed the threshold.

'Amelia presumably knows all manner of things,' said Sophie, bemused. Whatever choleric or melancholic humour had led Joanna to flee the dining-room and shut herself up in Miss Pryce's room all yesterday evening, in the wake of Sieur Germain's revelation, had now, it seemed, passed off. 'What—'

'About *Father*,' said Joanna, lowering her voice and leaning across the table. 'Those letters – her insistence upon coming to London *now*, for no good reason – the very odd way she has been going on, since arriving here—'

'Jo,' said Gray, regarding her gravely over the rim of his teacup, 'you understand, do you not, that you are accusing your sister of high treason?'

Miss Pryce blanched.

'No, no,' Joanna said impatiently, 'it is no such thing. I am only accusing her of doing whatever Father tells her; I do not suppose she had the least notion what any of it meant.'

'And what is it you suppose her to have done?' said Sophie. She had spent a miserably wakeful night, and dreamt of horrors when at last she slept; she did not feel capable at present of any degree of reason – but, after all, it was she who had first supposed that Amelia might be hiding something. *Only, I did not imagine anything so dangerous. Or so very, very foolish.*

Joanna made an impatient gesture. 'I have not the least idea,' she said. 'That is, not yet. Nothing particularly dreadful, I should imagine; passing along messages she did not understand to persons of whom she knows nothing, very likely, or arranging for the purchase of items whose purpose she could not divine. Truly, Sophie, you must not suppose that I am seeking revenge upon Amelia, or anything of the kind; I am only thinking of whether she may be able to tell us anything to the purpose.'

Gray nudged Sophie's cup of tea towards her hand; she looked at it, shuddered at the thought of drinking it, and looked away again. 'Has she heard the news, do you suppose?' she said.

'Surely not,' said Miss Pryce. 'Unless Madame de l'Aigle is curiously well informed. We can scarcely be said to have heard it ourselves, and Lord Kergabet was surely the first of His Majesty's court to be told.'

'Amongst the first, at any rate,' said Joanna. 'I agree with Gwen, however: Amelia cannot possibly have heard of it yet.'

She glanced towards the door and went as still as a cornered mouse; Sophie followed her gaze, and saw at once what was amiss.

'Heard of what?' said Amelia.

CHAPTER XI

In Which Joanna Takes Steps

'Miss Callender!' said Gwendolen, too cheerfully. 'I did not think to see you so early today. You must tell us all about Mademoiselle de l'Aigle's ball.'

Amelia frowned very slightly at Gwendolen and – to no one's surprise – ignored her question entirely. 'What is it I have not heard of?' she said, looking steadily at Joanna.

For a long moment Joanna studied her in turn. Framed in the doorway with one delicate hand on the door-handle, Amelia looked beautiful and fragile, her cheeks a little paler than usual, her blue eyes wide.

We are to say nothing to Mrs Marshall; Kergabet was very clear upon that point. But surely he did not mean us to keep Amelia in the dark also? And, besides, if what I suspect of her is so . . .

'I should sit down, if I were you, Amelia,' said Sophie. She patted the back of the chair beside her own; Amelia's frown deepened, and instead she took the seat by Gwendolen's, nearest the door which she had quietly closed behind her. Sophie, apparently taking no offence at this snub, poured out a cup of tea for Amelia and handed it across the table, where it was roundly ignored.

'Joanna,' said Amelia expectantly.

Joanna swallowed; this was more difficult, when it came to the point, than she had had any reason to expect. 'A messenger brought word from the Palace,' she said at last, 'whilst you were out, that the Professor and the others have escaped from the Tower of London.'

'The professor? Which prof—oh, Mother Goddess!' It was as well that Amelia had taken Sophie's advice, however ungraciously, for her pale face grew nearly green and she groped for her teacup with a shaking hand. 'Father? You mean that Father has—? Joanna, how – when—'

Sophie was up out of her seat and going round the table. Amelia saw her approach and turned from it; Gwendolen met her with a gentle hand on her wrist and a soothing murmur of words, whilst contriving also to meet Joanna's eye and nod minutely: *Go on, then.*

Sophie retreated, biting her lip.

'I know nothing more than I have just told you,' said Joanna. Beneath the table, she clenched her fingers in the folds of her gown. 'Had you no warning of this, Amelia, truly?'

Amelia's head snapped up. 'Of course not,' she said, in a passably persuasive tone of outraged astonishment. 'How should I have done?'

'No one blames you.' Sophie's voice was gentle and kind, as though she were soothing a spooked horse. 'If you will only tell us – or tell Lord Kergabet, or Jenny – what you know, what the Professor wrote to you, or bid you do, then I am sure no blame can attach to you for fulfilling the demands of filial obedience.'

'I'm sure I have not the least idea what you mean, Sophia.' Amelia's chin lifted in the old familiar way, the better to look down her elegant straight nose; she shook off Gwendolen's hand on her arm and folded her hands on the tablecloth.

'We know about the letters, Amelia,' said Sophie, still speaking in that gently coaxing tone.

'Which letters, pray?'

Joanna opened her mouth, impatient to have the thing over, but closed it again without speaking when Gwendolen caught her eye and, with another minute shake of her head, warned her off.

'I think you know very well which letters,' said Gray. Like Sophie's, his voice was calm and gentle, his expression kind; but beneath the placid surface something darker lurked, which made Joanna very glad that her brother-in-law's level gaze was not presently directed towards herself. Gwendolen blinked at him in surprise; Sophie made a small abortive gesture, as though she considered attempting to restrain him, but held herself back. She was muttering something to herself, too low for Joanna to hear.

Amelia, however, had either more nerve or less perception than her sisters (or, perhaps, both), for she appeared able to confront him without quailing. 'You may think what you please,' she said. 'It is no business of mine.'

'I think,' said Gray pleasantly, taking a sip of tea, 'that whatever your father and his cronies are about may pose a significant danger to the kingdom – to His Majesty personally – to Sophie and Joanna, and to my sister and her family – and I should not like to believe you, Amelia, so lost to compassion as to protect a quintet of convicted traitors at the cost of your own sisters' safety – to say nothing of your duty to your king.'

He paused for another, more leisurely sip, his gaze steady on Amelia's increasingly tension-taut face. The expectant pause stretched out; Joanna dug her close-trimmed fingernails into the palms of her hands, consumed with the effort of restraining her questions, her impatience, her peremptory demands.

'I have done no wrong to anyone,' said Amelia at last. She was composed, her voice steady, but her hands, too, were clasped so tightly that her knuckles showed bone-white through the skin.

'No one has said so,' said Gray – still calm, still perfectly reasonable. 'But your father and his co-conspirators have done a considerable number of wrongs to a considerable number of persons, and we have all of us a duty to do whatever we may to prevent their continuing to tread the same path.'

'My father—'

'Your father,' said Joanna, furious and unable any longer to bite her tongue, 'has poisoned a man in cold blood, for his own gain, and conspired in an attempt to repeat that achievement on a larger scale. Your father ought by rights to have been beheaded as a traitor. Your father—'

'He is *your* father as well as mine, Joanna Callender!' Amelia cried. She was out of her seat in a trice and leaning towards Joanna, both hands flat upon the table.

Joanna sprang to her feet, almost without intending it, and mirrored her posture, distantly annoyed at being still half a head shorter. 'To my everlasting regret, he is,' she replied; and, surprising herself by the honest laughter that bubbled up from her chest, she continued, 'That is, he was; I find I am disinclined to acknowledge him. Do you know, Amelia, I begin to believe that it was my gift from the gods to be wanted by neither of my parents, loved by neither, so that I might be free to steer my ship to a better harbour, amongst people whose good opinion does not depend upon my parentage, or my sex, or the circumstances of' – she faltered momentarily, then amended – 'of my birth.'

A shocked and ringing silence followed this outburst – Joanna was as deeply shocked at having spoken such thoughts aloud, as any of the others could possibly be to hear them – whilst the two sisters stared at one another across Lady Kergabet's breakfast-table.

This time it was Amelia who broke the stalemate; drawing herself up tall, arms folded, she said, 'It was not Papa's fault, any of it; it was *hers*.' She turned to Sophie. 'Your precious mama's.

155

We should have gone on quite happily, the two of us, if—'

'You cannot possibly know what might have been,' said Sophie, with a surprising lack of heat. 'You were not above three years old when they were married; you knew no more than I did that we were not sisters born.'

Joanna, distracted from her own concerns, looked from one of them to the other with narrowed eyes; this exchange had all the earmarks of a debate continuing after some earlier interruption.

'In any case, Amelia,' said Gray, 'no one supposes that the original notion was your father's; the priests of Apollo Coelispex established at the time that he was recruited into an established conspiracy by Lord Merton, at the instigation of the late Viscount Carteret, because he was a mage of Merlin College and could help them to an appropriately subtle poison for their purposes.'

'But—' Amelia's befuddled expression reminded Joanna that she had not been present whilst the rest of them (together with the conspirators) were examined by the truth-seeing priests; impossible to say what she might know, or believe, about the events leading up to her father's arrest and imprisonment. 'But it was *her* they wanted, as bait for the King.'

'Is that what the Professor told you?' said Joanna. 'It was not the whole truth, if so. And I do not suppose he happened to mention that he had promised you in marriage to one of his students – he had not yet made up his mind which of them to favour – in return for their assistance with his part of the scheme?'

Amelia blinked at her, the very picture of maidenly outrage. 'Mr Taylor had nothing to do with any of it!' she exclaimed. 'Nor dear Mr Woodville, either. And I shall never believe such a thing of Papa; the very notion is ludicrous.'

Gray and Sophie and Joanna exchanged a look of grim surmise. Gwendolen looked on in patient bafflement, trusting presumably that Joanna would enlighten her at some less frantic moment.

'That was not the verdict of the priests of Apollo Coelispex,' said Gray, reasonably, after a moment.

'Then, evidently,' Amelia retorted, speaking with great precision as though she feared what might spill out if she relaxed her vigilance for a moment, 'the priests were mistaken.'

'Amelia, the priests of Apollo Coelispex are truth-seers,' said Joanna. 'His Majesty called upon them precisely for the purpose of ensuring that there should be no mistake in the verdict.'

'But Mr Taylor was not present to be examined!' Amelia protested.

'All of his confederates were questioned, however,' said Gray, 'as were your sisters and I. Of course I cannot say precisely what testimony was given by any other person, but I *can* state categorically that one of Apollo's chosen heard me tell of Woodville's part, and Taylor's, in procuring . . .' He paused, glanced uncertainly at Sophie, then continued: 'in procuring, through highly suspect means, a key ingredient of the poison, at Professor Callender's direction; and that Apollo Coelispex judged my account a true one.'

Amelia's mouth was set in a hard line, and she gazed steadily at a point somewhere between Gray's arm and Joanna's shoulder.

'I am sorry to further tarnish your image of your father,' said Gray at last, more gently. 'But is it not better that we should see the world as it is?'

'I beg you will excuse me,' said Amelia, stiff and formal, to no one in particular. Still meeting no one's eye, she rose from her seat (Gray rose also, as though by reflex), turned away from the table, and set her hand to the door-handle.

It rattled, but would not turn. Gray sank back into his chair. Was it he who had tampered with the door? Or Sophie?

Amelia turned back, strung tight with fury – Joanna flinched away from her venomous expression – and apparently quite free of any such doubt. 'How dare you!' She pointed a shaking forefinger at Sophie. 'Let me out.'

Sophie flinched also, but when she spoke, her voice was steady. 'This is not some petty quarrel over a doll or the seat nearest the fire on a chilly evening, Amelia,' she said. 'I *dare*, as you put it, because you have information which may be material to the welfare of the kingdom—'

'As though you cared two pins for the kingdom!' Amelia's cheeks were flushed, two bright spots in her pale furious face, and her blue eyes burnt. 'As though you cared two pins for anyone but your precious self! How could I have thought you truly wished for peace between us? It was this you wanted all the time, of course it was. It is not enough that you should have taken my father from me – my home – every prospect of a good marriage – now you mean to take even this—'

Even this? Even what? What in Hades is she talking of? Joanna tried to catch Gwendolen's eye, but Gwendolen had no attention to spare for her at present; like the rest of them, she was riveted by Amelia. *Amelia could not hold us more in thrall if she were working some dire magick upon us.*

'—and I tell you plainly, *Your Highness*, I shall not let you do it.'

They regarded one another for a long moment – Amelia stiff and bristling and furious, glaring for all she was worth; Sophie visibly labouring to maintain her calm facade, and only just managing it – and Joanna began genuinely to fear that words had now been spoken which could never be called back. If she did not love Amelia as she loved Sophie – indeed, Amelia had more often been a burr under her saddle than not – once upon a time Amelia had stitched clothes and bonnets for Joanna's dolls, had acceded to her pleas for yet another game of hunt-the-slipper, had held her close and said nothing when, on that first long and difficult night at school, Joanna had slipped out of her own bed, crept about in the dark, and clambered up into her sister's.

'Sophie,' said Joanna quietly, 'let her go.'

Sophie turned to her, mouth opening on some protest or denial. Joanna raised a hand to forestall it and, carefully rising from her chair, edged round the table to Sophie. She felt Amelia's eyes on her, burning; and Gwen's, full of anxious care.

'Truly,' she said, standing a-tiptoe to murmur in Sophie's ear, 'there is no victory to be had here. Whatever she knows – if indeed she knows anything at all, and is not again an ignorant victim of others' machinations – you are only making her the more determined never to tell you.'

Sophie sighed, a soft and almost silent exhalation, and her eyes closed briefly. 'I know it,' she said, very low. 'I—'

Whatever she had been meaning to say, however, she evidently thought better of it.

Joanna clasped Sophie's shoulder – whether to comfort or to restrain, even she herself was not altogether sure. Sophie, at any rate, made no attempt at escape. At length she drew in a breath, let it out, and raised her head to look squarely at Amelia.

'I have never had any wish to hurt you,' she said, 'though I do not suppose you will believe me when I say so. But, Amelia—' She paused; Amelia stood straighter, if that were possible, and glared harder. 'If you insist on protecting your father – on protecting men whom the gods themselves have declared guilty of treason and deliberate murder – that is for you to decide; but we shall none of us help you do it.'

Then she snapped her fingers.

Amelia did not deign to reply, but turned so quickly back to the breakfast-room door that her skirts swirled out behind her. The door-handle turned smoothly under her hand, and half a moment later the door closed behind her with a decisive *snick*.

Sophie sank into the nearest chair, staring after Amelia; the others, warily, stared at Sophie.

At last, with a soft rustle of skirts, Gwendolen straightened in her chair and leant her elbows upon the table. 'Ought I to go after her, do you think?' she said.

'To what purpose?' said Sophie dully.

Gwendolen deflated.

Joanna frowned down at the top of Sophie's head. 'Later, perhaps,' she said, smoothing out the frown with some effort, so as to direct an encouraging half smile at Gwen. 'It is a good notion, but not just now, I think.'

Unless she was much mistaken, Amelia had been mere moments from giving way to angry tears, and woe betide anyone who might happen to witness them.

Sophie flung herself up out of her seat and paced two rapid circuits of the breakfast-room.

'*Cariad*, we cannot even be certain that Amelia knows anything to the purpose,' said Gray, catching her hands as she rounded a corner of the table.

'And we cannot be sure that she does not,' Sophie retorted.

'But in any case,' said Joanna, restraining her impatience with some difficulty, 'there is nothing to be done about the matter now.'

Sieur Germain de Kergabet was not seen again in Grosvenor Square for several days, or at any rate not in daylight. On the third evening he at last reappeared – grim-faced and pale with fatigue, with Mr Fowler, arms full of dossiers, drooping in his wake – well after dinner, and though Sophie and Joanna darted downstairs as soon as they heard the front door opening, Jenny was there before them, bundling her husband off to, in her words, *sleep until the sun is up again.* Sophie, Gray, Joanna, and Miss Pryce had thus to contain their impatient questioning – and, worse, to entertain Jenny's mama – for the remainder of the evening.

This they managed well enough for the first half-hour, as Amelia had a great deal to say of the milliners' shops she and her friend Mademoiselle de l'Aigle had visited in the course of the day, and of Mademoiselle de l'Aigle's brother who had escorted them. Amelia, it appeared, was keeping the ill news to herself, and the recent acrimony was not to be acknowledged outside the closed circle of its participants – for which small kindnesses, after several days' stony silence, Sophie was grateful. But Gray's mother (whatever Sophie might privately think of her from time to time) was neither stupid nor inattentive, and it was not long before, despite the others' best efforts, Mrs Marshall turned to her elder son and said, 'Whatever has Genevieve been doing upstairs all this time? I hope Lord Kergabet is not unwell? Perhaps I may be of some help?'

Gray shot Sophie a look of pure panic, and Joanna began to talk, very brightly and rather too fast, about a fine pair of grey carriage-horses she and Miss Pryce had lately had sight of, almost the equal of Jenny's; to which conversational breeze Miss Pryce trimmed her sails willingly enough, but which failed signally to engage its target.

Whilst this stratagem of Joanna's was going forward, Sophie was wrestling with her conscience, which spoke to her in the gruff baritone of Dougal MacAngus, lecturer in magickal ethics at the University in Din Edin: was it, or was it not, a permissible breach of principle to use her magick to distract her mother-in-law's attention from a matter which they had been expressly instructed not to discuss with her?

A pleading glance from Miss Pryce decided her. 'Miss Pryce,' she said, rising from her chair and drifting over to the pianoforte, 'Amelia, may I impose upon either of you to turn my pages, or perhaps to indulge me in a duet?'

Miss Pryce sprang up from the sofa as quickly as though she had sat upon a hatpin. 'I should be most happy, Mrs Marshall,' she said, and, bending close to Sophie's ear with one hand on her shoulder, 'A lullaby, perhaps? Or something like it?'

'You are very quick, Miss Pryce,' said Sophie, low, and began riffling through her collection of songs in search of the Cymric song which she had so often heard Miss Pryce sing to Agatha and Yvon in the course of this sojourn in Grosvenor Square, and had entertained herself one rainy afternoon by setting down and harmonising.

'Oh, but you must wait for Genevieve!' said Mrs Marshall. 'Whatever can be taking such a time? Graham, do you not think I ought—'

'Let me?' said Miss Pryce quietly, when after some searching the necessary page had yet to come to Sophie's hand, and Sophie yielded up her seat at the pianoforte.

Whilst Mrs Marshall went on talking of Jenny, in fretful counterpoint with Gray's unpractised attempts to soothe or divert her, Miss Pryce settled herself on the piano-stool, flexed her long fingers, and setting them upon the keys, produced an experimental series of chords. Then she looked up at Sophie over her shoulder, and at Sophie's tiny nod, turned back to the instrument and began to play and sing:

Huna blentyn, ar fy mynwes,
Clyd a chynnes ydyw hon . . .

Miss Pryce had a very pretty voice, though not a strong one; it shook a very little with the force of her anxiety. Having seen

162

her, as Sophie had done, with her dark hair shorn to boyish curls, dressed in clothes borrowed from one of Kergabet's grooms, matter-of-factly plotting the theft of an Alban publican's draught horses in the service of a sub rosa rescue mission on the Ross of Mull, such anxiety seemed out of character; but, after all, there came a point in that sort of undertaking after which nothing seemed altogether real, and one could only fight one's way forward, for there was no way back – none of which was necessarily useful preparation for Mrs Edmond Marshall.

For Miss Pryce as for Sophie herself, however, singing appeared calming to the nerves, for as she settled into the burden (*Ni chaiff dim amharu'th gyntun/ Ni wna undyn â thi gam . . .*) the clear mezzo-soprano was steady and sure – and, better still, Gray, Amelia, and Joanna (did Joanna know how clear the longing showed upon her face?) had all turned attentively to listen, depriving Mrs Marshall of her audience.

Sophie laid a steadying hand upon Miss Pryce's shoulder and felt her way into a descant upon the melody. She did not have the words by heart as Miss Pryce did – it was for this reason as much as any other that she had been attempting to find her notated copy – and so resorted to improvised and vaguely Cymric-sounding nonsense; Miss Pryce's shoulders twitched briefly under her hand, in censure or amusement.

Once, long ago, the magick Sophie had inherited from her grandmother by way of her father had flowed out along with her voice without conscious thought, without effort – in fact, altogether without her knowledge, inflicting her cheerful or melancholic or pensive humours upon everyone within earshot. For some years now, however, she had been labouring at the task of bringing it under her conscious control, and acutely mindful of her capacity to do harm by this means; the result was that she had now to find her way into the magick, as well as the music that would carry it forth.

She ought to have chosen some other song, of course – one whose words and melody she knew as she knew the lineaments of her sister's face, or of Gray's – so that she might sing by instinct alone, and devote all her conscious thought to the magick. *But, however, le mal est fait*, she told herself, and, satisfied that she should at least not disgrace herself, sank down into the awareness of her *magia musicae*, surveyed the metaphorical gates with which she had learnt to keep it in check, and began unlocking them one by one.

By the time Sophie and Miss Pryce had sung once through the latter's lullaby and once through 'Llywn On' (the more effective as a spell-song, because Sophie knew it so much better, though it was by no means a lullaby), Gray was yawning enormously, and everyone else appeared to be fast asleep. Miss Pryce turned on the piano-stool, stifling a yawn of her own, and said, quietly astonished, 'Well!'

Sophie crossed the room to perch on the arm of Gray's chair, winding her arms unselfconsciously about his neck (there was no one to see but Miss Pryce, and she, Sophie knew, had seen much worse).

'I ought to feel guilty,' she muttered into the hair above his ear, 'but I confess I cannot quite manage it.'

'Nonsense,' said Gray bracingly. 'Desperate times, desperate measures . . .'

He yawned so widely that his jaw produced a tiny, ominous creaking sound, then scrubbed his free hand through his hair. Sophie leant more fully into his embrace, closed her eyes, and sighed.

It might have been some hours later, or perhaps only a few moments, that she was startled awake by Jenny's voice, exhaustion mingled with sardonic amusement, enquiring, 'And what have we here?'

Sophie sprang up – she had somehow slid down from the chair-arm into Gray's lap, as though her former position had not been humiliating enough – so quickly and carelessly that her shoulder caught Gray under the chin and her elbow jabbed him in the ribs.

'Oof,' he said sleepily, rubbing at his jaw. He blinked up at Sophie, then at Jenny, who stood just inside the drawing-room door, wearing an unseasonably woolly shawl and a bemused expression, and at last said, 'Well?'

'Oh, no,' said Jenny. 'None of that, if you please. You may ask your questions in the morning.'

'Jenny?'

They all three turned at the sound of Joanna's sleep-roughened voice. Joanna and Amelia had dozed off on the blue sofa, one heeling over to port and the other to starboard; Joanna, rousing herself, looked for a moment more like a badger dressed for dinner than like a well-brought-up young lady.

Miss Pryce, at the piano, rubbed one eye and suppressed a yawn. 'What's the hour?' she said.

'I have not the least idea,' said Jenny, 'except that it is past time for all of you to be abed, my wayward goslings. Sophie, what on the gods' green earth have you done to my mother?'

'I—'

'What we shall have to do again before long,' said Gray, 'if we are not to speak to her of what is in all of our minds. I am out of practice in withstanding maternal interrogation, Jenny, and your disappearing upstairs for the whole of an evening was bound to raise Mama's suspicions—'

'There was no help for it,' said Jenny. She cast an anxious look in the direction of her mother; Sophie followed her gaze but found Mrs Marshall still asleep in Jenny's chair, very gently snoring. 'He was half dead with fatigue – and Mr Fowler no better – and he would never rest if I did not *make* him.' Another glance at Mrs Marshall – a furrowing of brows – and then she said, 'Have you thought what you shall say to them, when they wake?'

'There was no help for this, either,' said Gray firmly.

'I do not think I meant your mama to fall asleep, exactly,' said Sophie. Her conscience was prodding her with renewed force now, and she was regretting having yielded to the impulse to end the conversation by any means necessary. 'Only to stop asking questions which none of us dared answer, and threatening with every other breath to charge up the stairs to your assistance.'

'Mother Goddess!' Jenny breathed, her face going rather pale. 'I thank you, in that case, from the bottom of my heart; though I should rather like to ask Lady Maëlle—' An anxious, questing glance about the room. 'Where is Lady Maëlle?'

Joanna and Sophie exchanged a look: Jenny was distraught indeed, if her ordinarily perfect recall of all her guests' comings and goings had been disrupted to this extent. 'She is gone to stay with Lady Karaez,' Sophie reminded her, 'to assist with her lying-in.'

'Yes,' said Jenny, nodding. 'Yes, of course. How stupid of me to forget!' She put up a hand to her head – the movement a near-twin to Gray's habitual gesture, but stymied by the arrangement of her hair – then pressed the other to her eyes.

'Jenny,' said Sophie, approaching her with some caution to lay a hand on her arm. 'Jenny, when had you last a proper night's sleep?'

Jenny's hands came down from her face; she clasped them together, then visibly loosened her grip. 'I have been rather anxious,' she conceded.

'Of course you have,' said Joanna, 'playing hostess to half the kingdom whilst your husband is off doing the gods know what in pursuit of a band of—' She shut her mouth with a snap; swallowed;

166

and after a moment continued, 'Go along to bed, Jenny, I beg. Gwen and I shall be hospitable in your stead; and perhaps things may look better in the morning.'

Or better yet, the afternoon.

Jenny protested, but plainly her heart was not in it, and before long they had succeeded in sending her away to bed, with Gray's arm to help her up the stairs. Sophie, Joanna, and Miss Pryce looked at one another, then studied the two sleepers; at last Sophie said, 'Miss Pryce, come back with me to the pianoforte; Jo, sit down again . . . Where were you? Ah!' Joanna had found her place at one end of the blue sofa and was arranging herself, somewhat implausibly, as though reading the book of philosophical treatises which Gray had left behind on a nearby occasional table. 'Yes, that will do splendidly.'

Sophie sat down at the pianoforte, struck up a rollicking melody in triple time, and poured a judicious measure of magick into a wholly illusory feeling of cheerful energy as she began to sing: '*O, whistle and I'll come to ye, my lad!*'

It was a deliberately provocative choice – a song of the Borders, such as Mrs Edmond Marshall most disparaged, and of unabashed female flirtation, which (by her lights) was worse – and Sophie's magick, or the song itself, or both, soon had the desired effect: first Amelia, then Mrs Marshall, started and snuffled awake, and neither seemed at all reluctant to believe that they had only nodded off briefly, when Joanna told them so.

CHAPTER XII

In Which Sieur Germain Calls a Council of War

Early the following morning Sieur Germain quietly gathered his forces – in the persons of Joanna, Miss Pryce, Sophie, Gray, and Mr Fowler – in the library. To Sophie's secret relief, both her brother-in-law and his secretary looked much the better for their night's sleep: grimly resolute, rather than merely grim.

They seated themselves along the sides of the long reading-table, upon which the morning sun cast blocks of light through the eastward windowpanes. At the head of the table, Sieur Germain cleared his throat.

'This is highly irregular,' he began, 'and I must tell you that I am acting against the wishes of several senior members of His Majesty's Privy Council; but in my view all of you have, for your own reasons, a vital interest in the question at hand, and a right to fuller information than His Majesty may as yet see fit to make public.'

How exactly this assessment applied to Miss Pryce – and not to Amelia – Sophie was not certain; but perhaps, in Kergabet's estimation, Miss Pryce had earned her right to be in all the family secrets by her extraordinary bravery and resourcefulness on the Ross of Mull, and if that were the case, Sophie could not disagree.

'The prisoners have now been at large most of a se'nnight,'

Kergabet continued, 'and as yet we know very little more of their methods or whereabouts than we did on the day of their escape. A general search of vessels departing England, Cymru, and Kernow has been ordered, as well as a search of all conveyances departing London, and descriptions of all the prisoners have been circulated to the Watch Captains of every city and town large enough to possess such a thing.'

Sophie nodded.

'And, of course, as well as such practical measures Lord de Vaucourt and his colleagues have undertaken various scryings and finding-spells – also, I regret to say, to no avail.'

'Perhaps Sophie and I may be of some assistance in that endeavour,' said Gray. Ignoring the wary frown which instantly creased his brother-in-law's face, he continued, 'A colleague of ours in Din Edin was kind enough to teach us some very useful variants on the standard finding-spell, which may be used to extend the spell's range or to continue it over a period of several days.'

Joanna muttered something under her breath to Miss Pryce, presumably in reaction to this statement, which Sophie chose to ignore.

'I thank you,' said Sieur Germain. 'I shall convey your offer to Vaucourt this morning.' He had ceased frowning – in fact, he looked rather pleased – and no wonder: here was a means by which they could be useful, but quite without drawing danger upon themselves or the rest of the household. 'In the meantime, however, I must ask that you bear in mind the danger which these men may pose to the three of you particularly' – he looked gravely at Sophie, Joanna, and Gray in turn – 'and continue to refrain, so far as is possible, from advertising your presence in London.'

'That horse has long left the stable, I fear,' said Joanna.

'I must confess,' said Sophie, attempting to convey the same sentiment with more dignity, 'that I do not see how our presence can possibly be concealed. Joanna is known to the whole of London society, it seems to me, and this past se'nnight excepted, I have been seen with Lucia MacNeill at every gathering of note since I arrived.'

Her brother-in-law gave her a grim little smile. 'Nevertheless,' he said.

Sophie could see his point – she was not a fool – but after such freedom of movement as she had enjoyed in Din Edin, under the eyes of watchers so discreet that she need not remark their presence unless she wished it, the prospect of continuing in what amounted to house arrest held even less appeal than formerly.

'Sophie,' said Joanna, with a small incredulous laugh, 'surely *you* are not objecting to be told not to draw attention to yourself?'

Sophie frowned at her but was forced to concede that this was, in fact, an absurd position for her to take.

'I will undertake to conduct myself with all possible discretion,' she said primly, therefore, and Sieur Germain nodded, apparently satisfied.

'And it need not even be said, I hope,' he continued, now addressing Joanna and Miss Pryce, 'that there can be no question of anyone's riding in the park unescorted, at dawn or at any other time, until this business has been . . . satisfactorily concluded.'

Joanna and her friend, who ought surely to have predicted this, looked briefly outraged; before either could protest, however, Kergabet quelled them with a look.

'There is another complication, however,' said Sophie to her brother-in-law. Briefly she recounted the substance of their tumultuous conversation with Amelia, emphasising her own conviction and Joanna's that Amelia was concealing something connected to her father's escape.

'A complication, indeed,' Sieur Germain sighed. He rested

his forehead briefly on one fist – for just a moment revealing the weight of the cares that pressed upon his broad shoulders – then met Sophie's gaze with a return of his earlier calm resolve.

'I should not expect that Amelia will talk of this to anyone,' said Sophie, 'but – begging your pardon, sir – Mrs Marshall is not a fool; this is not a secret that can be kept for very long, not within this house.'

What she wished very much to say, but – being a guest in Kergabet's house – did not quite dare, was that Mrs Marshall had as much right as any of the rest of them to know what was afoot, if only so that she might take herself off home and out of the way of events.

Sieur Germain acknowledged her words with a curt nod. 'We had hoped, of course,' he said, 'for the expeditious recovery of the prisoners, so that the public need not be alarmed unnecessarily.'

Sophie did not need Joanna's sotto voce gloss to interpret this as *So that this disaster might the more easily be hushed up.*

'Regrettably, however . . .'

'Yes,' said Gray. 'We shall of course be guided by you, sir, but I must agree with Sophie: this news is not likely to improve with age.'

'I shall speak with your mother this evening,' said Kergabet. Had they, in fact, persuaded him of something? Or had he been intending such a conversation in any case?

'I am glad to hear it,' said Gray.

'Lucia MacNeill has already been told what is afoot, however, I hope?' said Sophie. 'I have kept my promise, sir, and said nothing in any of my letters; but Lucia must think it odd that my visits should cease so abruptly.'

'Lucia MacNeill is in the secret, yes,' said Kergabet, and – astonishingly – smiled. 'Oscar MacConnachie had also to be informed, of course, and Lady MacConnachie was all for retreating post-haste to Din Edin, but Lucia MacNeill would not hear of it. "If Sophie Marshall did not flee Din Edin after seeing her father and brother stoned to death in effigy," she said, "why in Brìghde's name should you suppose me willing to flee London now?" She is her father's daughter, certainly,' he concluded in an approving tone.

'I suppose Roland will be feeling very smug,' said Joanna; and, in response to Sophie's questioning look (for this remark seemed to her an utter non sequitur, and in rather poor taste besides), 'His conversation with the yew-trees, you know – the trees warned him of an enemy, he said, and an enemy we surely have.'

'You consider Roland and Lucia's account reliable, then,' said Gray. 'That there was such a message, and that it did indeed come – somehow – from the yew-trees in the maze.'

His tone was not sceptical, exactly – a man who had spent what amounted to whole months of his life in the body of an owl, after all, had not much luxury to scoff at other people's odd tales – but on the other hand, he had not seen all that Sophie had on that mad midnight escapade in Cormac MacAlpine's sacred grove.

Fowler looked up, alert to the possibility of an ally.

'It is all alike to me,' said Joanna frankly. 'It does not seem very plausible, I grant you, but, as Sophie says, Lucia MacNeill is not given to flights of fancy. And,' she added, 'I have seen a great many even less plausible things, Gray, since first you came to stay with us in Breizh.'

'As have I,' said Kergabet, with a small and rueful smile.

And that, thought Sophie, was certainly true, whatever else might or might not be so.

'I do not doubt Roland and Lucia's account,' she said, 'not at all; but what I cannot understand is how those yew-trees should come to have knowledge – let alone foreknowledge – of the prisoners' escape.'

'One does ask oneself that question,' said Gray dryly. 'Among others.'

'We ought to hope with all our might that this is indeed the danger the trees warned Roland of,' said Miss Pryce. The rest of the table turned to look at her. 'Because,' she continued, her quiet voice steady in the face of their collective scrutiny, 'if it is not, then there is some other enemy in the offing, of whom we know nothing at all.'

On this sobering thought their council broke up, Sieur Germain and Mr Fowler to yet another conference with Vaucourt and his staff, and the others to occupy themselves as best they could, without either stirring out of doors or drawing attention to themselves by any sort of unaccustomed conduct.

The letter was postmarked from Oxford, sealed with the owl-and-oak-tree device of Merlin College, and was directed in a crabbed and tiny hand. This hand was not that of Master Alcuin, who had last written to report that, alas, no copy of *The Rise and Fall of Lady Morgan College* was to be found in the libraries of Merlin, Marlowe, Plato, or King's; nor that of Gareth Evans-Hughes, Fellow of Merlin and friend of the Marshalls, with a further report on the contents of the map-room in the Merlin College library. Had one of them, perhaps, recruited some colleague to the cause? Unlikely, but not altogether impossible.

'What is that?' said Joanna, as Sophie studied it.

'I have not the least idea.'

She broke the seal and unfolded the letter.

To Her Royal Highness, the Princess Edith Augusta Sophia, greetings, the salutation ran – not, in Sophie's experience, a promising beginning. She sighed, and read on:

173

It has come to our attention that a movement is presently afoot to re-establish at Oxford, on an equal footing with Colleges hitherto established and presently operating by Royal Charter, a College for female students, on the site of that institution lately known as Lady Morgan College.

Now, how had the letter-writers, whoever they were, discovered this fact? What they spoke of as a *movement* was in fact Sophie herself and whatever friends and relations she was capable of collecting to assist her; should she succeed in obtaining her father's sanction for the project, of course, the case would at once be altogether different, but at present she could not expect His Majesty even to attend to such a request, let alone throw his patronage behind it.

You *are the patron*, she reminded herself – it was a difficult thing to remember, always. *If you can only sway Father to the cause, you shall have the royal coffers – or some fraction of them, at any rate! – at your disposal, and the wherewithal to engage whatever tradesmen, artisans, and workmen may be required.*

But not whilst the King's attention – and very soon, no doubt, the kingdom's – was riveted upon the matter of the escaped traitors.

You may perhaps be unaware, Your Royal Highness, the letter continued, *of the many learned treatises which demonstrate the female mind to be ill-suited for higher learning. A list is therefore appended of several such treatises which may be suitable, and of which copies are known to be held in His Majesty's library.*

'Some very kind Oxford dons,' said Sophie to Joanna, looking up from the letter, 'have undertaken to explain to me why I ought not to worry my pretty head over the question of Lady Morgan College.'

Joanna snorted into her cup of tea: in view of her present state of tight-strung anxiety, a pleasing phenomenon for which Sophie silently thanked her Oxonian correspondents. She read out to Joanna the beginning of the letter, and continued:

Far be it from us to disparage the innate aptitudes and talents of the female sex, which, from the earliest times, has excelled in its proper sphere, that is, in the management of a household and family; of a shop or other concern, of children, as a governess or schoolmistress; or of any number of similarly practical transactions; all, in their way, as essential to the common good as the labours of any farmer, soldier, merchant, or scholar.

Nor do we deny that there may exist the occasional woman capable of those precise, well-regulated, and thorough habits of thought which alone permit the productive study of the complex, inaccessible, or arcane; that is to say, our stock in trade at Merlin or any other Oxford College. Generally speaking, however, young ladies can derive no benefit from being shut away in College libraries and reading-rooms for years upon years; nor does any net benefit to society accrue from their having been thus incarcerated.

'Incarcerated!' Joanna snorted.

'You know how fond scholars are of metaphor, Jo,' said Sophie mildly, and read on:

We urge you, ma'am, not to judge the inclinations and capabilities of young ladies generally by your own exceptional experience, and, instead, to consider as a model your sister-in-law Lady Kergabet, who is admired throughout the kingdom for her hospitality and her capable management of her illustrious husband's household and estate, and not for any attempt, successful or otherwise, to ape the accomplishments of her father, her brothers, or her husband.

'*Ape!*' Joanna exclaimed. 'Of all the unspeakable—'

'Do be quiet, Jo,' said Miss Pryce, unexpectedly, from her corner. Joanna turned sharply to glare at her over the back of the sofa, but to no avail: 'The more often you interject with righteous protests, love, the longer we shall be in getting to the end.'

Joanna's spine stiffened; Miss Pryce's face drained of colour, and her knitting-needles fell still. Then Joanna turned, her mouth already opening on some excuse, some explanation – even, perhaps, denial.

Sophie held up both hands to forestall her and, before she could speak, said, 'You need not hide from me.'

For a long moment they stared at her, wary and still as rabbits surprised by a flash of magelight. Then Miss Pryce nodded slowly, her eyes darting from Sophie's face to the back of Joanna's head. 'I thank you,' she said, low; and then, more firmly, 'Come here, Jo.'

The words themselves scarcely mattered, for Sophie easily recognised her tone: whatever she might say would always have meant, *I thank you for your kindness, but I have not the least intention of discussing this matter with you, either now or at any other time.* She nodded, acknowledging the tone rather than the words.

Joanna rose to her feet – obedient to her friend's wishes, Sophie observed with a wry smile, as she had never noticeably been to anyone else's – and retreated to perch on the arm of Miss Pryce's chair.

'There,' said Miss Pryce, smiling at Sophie and laying down her knitting to take Joanna's left hand in her right. 'I shall pinch her if she threatens to interrupt again.'

Joanna, predictably, emitted a squeak of outrage; Miss Pryce gave her hand a gentle squeeze, however, and she subsided.

176

Sophie ducked her head and cleared her throat to cover the grin she could not quite suppress. Fortunately for her composure – though less fortunately for her good humour – this returned her attention to the letter in her hands, and she sighed, cleared her throat once more and resumed:

> *While not wishing to disparage your own scholarly accomplishments, ma'am, we urge you to heed the wisdom of experience, which confirms that man's sphere is not woman's, and that Dame Fortune does not smile on those who flout this truth; and to take counsel of your elders, and seek some other means of exercising what appears to us to be commendable philanthropic fervour: the endowment of an infirmary or lying-in hospital suggests itself, for example, or the foundation of an infant school . . .*

The names of the signatories occupied nearly a full closely written page: a dozen Fellows of Merlin College, five from Marlowe College, eight from Plato, half a dozen from Shakespeare, four from King's, two from Bairstow. No College Master was among them, but this might mean only that the Masters – who served at the King's pleasure, though chosen by the Fellows – did not wish to antagonise her father. At least five among the Merlin Fellows she had personally annoyed by attending their lectures, first openly and then, having been asked to leave when they deemed the subject matter unsuitable for female eyes and ears, in a suit of clothes borrowed from one of Gray's friends; if only she had been more skilled at disguise, in those early days . . . !

'I wonder,' Sophie mused, 'what the learned Fellows of Oxford think of Lucia MacNeill.'

'*I* wonder what they think of *you*,' said Joanna, with a little snort of derisive laughter. 'It is perfectly evident that not one of them knows the least thing about you; you are the most determinedly contrary person I have ever met, and if I wished to persuade you to do something which you were not perfectly certain of, that is precisely the sort of letter I should write.'

'You are discounting yourself, I suppose,' said Sophie, amused.

'I beg your pardon?'

'From the category of the determinedly contrary persons, I mean. I shall not attempt to deny that I dislike being lectured and condescended to; but that *you* of all people should call *me* contrary . . . !'

Joanna, wisely, did not attempt to argue the point; over her head, Miss Pryce gave Sophie a small, sardonic smile.

'In any case,' said Sophie, 'I fear that the very kind intervention of the learned Fellows is unlikely to produce the outcome they expect.'

CHAPTER XIII

In Which Sophie and
Gray Endeavour to Be Helpful

Somewhat to Sophie's surprise, Sieur Germain's promise to offer her aid and Gray's to Lord de Vaucourt bore fruit within two days, in the form of a brief and exceedingly correct note – delivered to Grosvenor Square by a confidential courier – which formally requested the participation of Doctor Marshall in the search for the escaped traitors. *His Majesty's carriage*, Lord de Vaucourt wrote, *shall call for you and Her Royal Highness in Grosvenor Square at the second hour after noon.*

It was not the most promising of beginnings; still, the relief which Sophie felt at this news of swift reprieve from her present quasi captivity, and from her mother-in-law and Amelia, made her feel almost ashamed of herself. In preparation for this excursion, and to relieve these very mixed feelings, she busied herself in making a mental list of potentially useful spells and in packing up a selection of relevant sources.

'They must be desperate indeed,' observed Joanna, when apprised of this development; 'ordinarily, Vaucourt develops a twitch and a case of hives at the mere mention of your name.'

Sophie frowned, both at her flippant words and at the sardonic tone in which they had been uttered – though it was true, too, that Lord Vaucourt's letter did not mention her name even once. 'I know that you do not underestimate the gravity of the circumstances, Jo,' she said. 'How can you make light of such a thing?'

'Because,' said Joanna, folding her arms defensively across her chest, 'if one does not sometimes make light of grave circumstances, one is apt to fall into despair, and may never succeed in climbing out again.'

Had that been a reference to Sophie's own behaviour, in the dark days after Gray's disappearance from Din Edin? *No, surely Joanna would not be so cruel.*

But the thought lingered, nevertheless.

Joanna tossed her dark head, handed back to Sophie her summons from the Royal Palace, and retreated to the sofa, where she astonished her sister still further by taking up a work-basket, extracting from it what looked very like a half-constructed baby's bonnet, and settling down virtuously to her work. There being nothing more to be done in response to Lord de Vaucourt's note until the promised conveyance should arrive, Sophie sighed, fetched out her own work-basket from behind Jenny's armchair, and joined her.

They sat in uneasy silence for some time, punctuated occasionally by Joanna's bitten-off exclamations of annoyance with her needle (from which the thread had escaped), her thimble (which had let the point of the needle through), and the (apparently insufficient) pins securing the bonnet's brim to its gathered crown. At last Sophie – after many sidelong glances at her sister's deepening scowl – cast up her eyes, laid down her own embroidery in her lap, and said, 'Give me that, Jo.'

Joanna looked up. 'What? Why?'

'Because,' said Sophie patiently, 'I can see that you have got into some sort of difficulty, and I should like to help you out of it. May I?'

She held out her hands, and Joanna, with visible reluctance, surrendered the bonnet. Sophie examined it, assessing the damage:

the gathers had gone askew, crowded together on one side and pulled almost straight on the other. Painstakingly, she picked out two dozen small, slightly uneven stitches, wound up the thread, and set it aside.

'Pincushion,' she said.

No pincushion appeared in her outstretched hand; looking up, she found Joanna regarding her with arms folded and jaw mulishly set.

'Please,' said Sophie, repressing the urge to ask, *Do you know how very much you resemble a sulky child?*

Joanna clearly did know it; without another word, she looked out the pincushion and handed it over, and watched attentively as Sophie unpinned the two halves of the bonnet, redistributed the gathers, and set about pinning them together again.

'There, do you see?' Sophie said. 'If you first pin the middle and both ends, and then quarter each half, like this, you will not have so much trouble.'

'Yes, I see,' said Joanna.

Sophie looked up abruptly at her tone. 'You need not take it so much to heart, Jo,' she said. 'There is more to life than sewing baby's bonnets.'

'It is not *that*,' said Joanna, scathingly.

'What, then?' Sophie handed over the bonnet, now properly pinned.

Joanna took it, retrieved and rethreaded her needle, and began her work all over. Concealing a sigh, Sophie took up her own work again, and silence reigned once more until all at once Joanna's bent head came up sharply and she exclaimed, 'How can you bear to sit here, *sewing*, when out there somewhere—'

'Because,' said Sophie, precariously calm, 'if one does not sometimes sit quietly at home, in the company of people one loves, one is in danger of losing the courage to go forth and do unpleasant things in defence of those people. As I think you know very well.'

181

It was Joanna, after all, and not she, who had begun today's impromptu sewing-circle.

The soft *click-swish* of the door-handle turning made them both look up. The door opened, and framed in the doorway stood Gwendolen Pryce. She was slightly out of breath and had very much the air of one hastening to deliver a message; whatever the message might be, however, it was lost for the moment, for no sooner had her gaze alighted on Joanna's face than her own went wide-eyed with anxiety, and she came quickly into the drawing-room, exclaiming, 'Jo, whatever is the matter?'

'Nothing,' said Joanna, so unconvincingly that Sophie was not at all surprised when Miss Pryce frowned at her and replied, 'If you cannot tell a better lie than that, Joanna Callender, you had much better tell the truth and have done.'

Joanna looked down at her work and set another slow, careful stitch.

'Joanna and I,' said Sophie, 'have been discussing the nature of patience under trying circumstances.'

Miss Pryce turned to her with an expression compounded of surprise and an unexpected comprehension, but said only, 'Have you, indeed.'

Joanna had by now, it appeared, composed herself sufficiently to meet her friend's eyes. 'We have,' she said, 'and I shall tell you all about it in a moment, but you have not run pell-mell up two flights of stairs only to—'

'Oh!' said Miss Pryce, visibly chagrined. She turned to Sophie. 'Mrs Marshall, there is a very grand carriage outside, with the royal arms and two footmen up behind. Do you know where I might find Mr Marshall? You both are wanted, it appears.'

Sophie, startled, dropped her work on the sofa, crossed the room, and peered out of the window in an attempt to gauge the angle of the sun, then down into the street. Sure enough, a carriage bearing the arms of Britain – the lions of England, Normandie, and Maine; the Cymric dragon; the ermines of Breizh and the choughs of Kernow – waited before Lord Kergabet's front door. 'Maître de Vaucourt is before his time, surely,' she muttered to herself – but no matter. It was not as though she were reluctant to begin.

Vaucourt seemed not to share his colleague's opinion that Sophie and Gray ought to be keeping a low profile; surely there could be no more conspicuous means of travel than that carriage, with its plainly visible royal arms, its coach- and footmen in the royal livery, and its four glossy chestnut horses.

'Gray is in the library, I expect,' she said, returning to the sofa and tucking her work away, 'hiding from his mother. I shall go and fetch him. I thank you, Miss Pryce. I shall see you both . . .' When? She had not the least notion. '. . . later.'

Her thoughts already on the task ahead, she went away to look for her husband.

They were alone in the carriage for the duration of the journey, for, the coachman and footmen aside, Maître de Vaucourt had sent no one to escort them – which meant either that he trusted them to need no minder, or that none of his associates could be spared for the purpose. For some time neither spoke; Gray had brought with him a thick dossier from which protruded untidily a variety of pages closely covered in various hands, including his own, and was engaged in perusing it, occasionally muttering to himself under his breath, whilst Sophie looked out of the window, enjoying the brief and necessarily finite absence of other company.

Then the carriage, travelling at speed, took a particularly sharp corner and threw her and Gray against the fortunately well-padded off-side wall, scattering Gray's papers over both *bancs* and the floor.

'Horns of Herne!' said Gray, exasperated. He righted himself and began to gather them up again.

'Do you know,' said Sophie, laughing as she collected the pages which had flown in her direction, 'I believe this may be the first time we have been alone together by daylight since leaving Din Edin.'

Gray blinked at her in apparent bewilderment.

'What have you been thinking of, then?' She glanced through the papers in her hands. 'Cameron's mapped finding, first of all, of course; but I do not suppose Maître de Vaucourt has a spelled map like Rory MacCrimmon's . . .'

'Very likely not,' said Gray, 'if the spell is truly an Alban one, but Alasdair Cameron's having invented it there does not preclude some other mage's doing the same somewhere in Britain. Besides,' he added, producing something which, though not quite the cheerful grin he seemed to have intended, was nonetheless a very welcome change from the grim tension of the past several days, 'other applications exist for a spelled map of that nature, besides Cameron's mapped finding, and I dare say that His Majesty's generals have thought of most of them.'

Sophie handed over her stack of papers; Gray shuffled them back into some sequence known only to himself and lost himself in them once more for the remainder of the journey. For some time Sophie watched him fondly, till at length her gaze drifted to the city passing by without – the people going about their business, happy in their ignorance of whatever person or power had intervened to set free her stepfather and his co-conspirators, and of the purposes (whatever they might be) behind that act.

Circumventing the walls and the locks, the guards and the wards, cannot have been easy, she reflected, *and therefore it must have been worth a good deal of trouble to someone.* Thus much was perfectly evident; but to whom, and why, it was frustratingly difficult to imagine.

* * *

'Your Royal Highness,' said Master Lord de Vaucourt stiffly, bowing, when His Majesty's major-domo had ushered them into his workroom. Having thus disposed of Sophie, he turned to Gray: 'Doctor Marshall. I thank you for accepting my invitation.'

An invitation, was it? thought Gray, with some amusement. *A peremptory summons, I should have said.*

'We could scarcely do otherwise, my lord,' he said pleasantly, 'having volunteered our assistance to begin with. You have work for us to do, I conclude?'

Vaucourt cleared his throat, and looking away, gestured them towards the long worktable in the centre of the room. Gray and Sophie exchanged glances but took two of the offered chairs at the near end of the table. Sophie deposited on the table before her what looked very like a particularly capacious netted work-bag, at which Vaucourt silently curled his lip, and began tugging off her dove-grey kid gloves.

'We thought,' said Sophie, before he could continue, 'that we might discuss the possibility of using Cameron's mapped finding, or something like it, worked in a relay to extend the range of the spell.'

Gray maintained what he hoped was an expression of detached scholarly interest, but inwardly he felt fiercely proud of her, calmly setting out a sensible course of action before a man at least twice her age, whom they both knew to disapprove of her on principle.

Vaucourt, it transpired, had never heard of Alasdair Cameron's mapped finding, but, the nature of this working having been explained, opined that what was wanted was in fact Larbalastier's Spell of Location, and that the requisite set of maps were to be found in the Palace Archives.

'But, however,' he said, 'of course it has already been tried, without success; either the traitors are protected by wards or shielding-spells, or they are beyond the reach of any finding-spell.'

Or both, added Gray to himself, thinking of his own incarceration, in an interdicted cell in a remote part of Alba. 'Hence,' he said aloud, 'Magistra Marshall's suggestion that we employ a relay.'

He caught Vaucourt's twitch of irritation at the use of *Magistra*, but fortunately Sophie did not.

'A relay,' Vaucourt repeated, surprised and sceptical. 'You refer, I suppose, to the collective working of spells of concealment, or of shielding-spells, as practised by military mages?'

Gray could scarcely fault Vaucourt's ignorance of other uses of relays, having himself been entirely unaware that any such working existed until after his Alban friends had employed one in rescuing him from Cormac MacAlpine. 'I have never seen a finding worked using a relay myself,' he said. 'Magistra, perhaps you might describe your experience?'

Sophie reached into her work-bag – which in fact Gray knew to be filled largely with books – and extracted a codex, bound in once-fine but now rather battered bottle-green leather. Setting aside the bag, she opened the book and riffled through its pages until she found the one she wanted, then turned it about and slid it across the table to Lord Vaucourt.

'This is the fullest and clearest explanation I know of the use of relays in finding-spells,' she said. 'I have taken part in several experiments on a small scale, but on the occasion of which my husband speaks – which was, I believe, an experiment on a larger scale, rather than a practised manoeuvre – I was a witness only.'

'Even in Alba, I suppose,' said Vaucourt, not looking up from *On Findings and Summonings: Revised and Expanded, with Illustrations of Specialist Uses Thereof*, 'such a major working must be considered outside the female sphere.'

Presumably he had not remarked the words stamped on the book's front board, below the title:

by Morag Ruadh MacQuarie, Mag. D.
revised and expanded by Rory MacCrimmon, Mag. D.,
and Sophia Marshall, Mag. B.

Sophie caught Gray's eye and, out of Vaucourt's sight, rolled her eyes at him.

'In fact,' she said evenly, 'if memory serves, at least half the mages present were women. I was not among them only because, as it happened, I was too ill to do more than look on.'

Now Vaucourt did look up, frowning. 'You understand, of course, ma'am, that there can be no question of—'

The workroom door opened once more, this time to admit Lord Kergabet and Mr Fowler, and Vaucourt desisted from his argument – wisely, in Gray's view – to greet the new arrivals.

'I suppose,' said Sieur Germain, 'there is no use as yet in enquiring after your progress?'

'An interesting suggestion has been made,' Vaucourt conceded, 'as to the possibility of working a finding-spell collectively, in the same manner as, for example, a regimental shielding-spell.' His eyes narrowed thoughtfully, and when he spoke again there was a suggestion of satisfaction in his voice, quite at odds with the words themselves: 'The notion is not without promise, in theory; but in practice, of course, it is quite impossible.'

'And why should it be impossible?' Sophie demanded.

'Indeed,' said Kergabet, 'why should it? Ordinarily, of course, I should defer to you on any question of magick, Vaucourt, but as my brother- and sister-in-law have considerable practical experience in these matters, I have made it a rule never to dismiss their suggestions untried.'

An expression of raw dislike flashed over Vaucourt's face – there and gone in an instant – as Kergabet and Fowler, uninvited, seated themselves at the table, Kergabet to Sophie's left and Fowler to Gray's right.

'Firstly,' he said, 'the necessary range is too great, even for a collective working; these men may have travelled many hundreds of miles by this time, in any direction.'

'In that case, we must expand the relay, so as to further extend the range,' said Gray. He was struggling to keep his temper, for they should get nowhere at all by shouting. 'More to the point—'

'And, secondly,' Vaucourt continued, cutting across him until Gray gave up in disgust, 'even were it possible to locate them by means of a collective working – which is by no means certain, for in addition to the matter of distance, there is, as Doctor Marshall may remember, every likelihood of their being protected by wards or shields – the nature of a finding is such that—'

'As Master Vaucourt may remember,' Gray broke in, seeing that Sophie's equanimity had begun to fray about the edges, 'the suggestion made was that we employ Cameron's mapped finding – or, as it may be, Larbalastier's Spell of Location – which, of course, does not require that the finding-spell be maintained until spell-worker and target are brought together. You have said, I believe, sir, that an attempt has already been made using the Larbalastier spell?'

'Several attempts, in fact,' said Vaucourt, in an icy tone. 'None of them at all successful.'

'But those attempts did not make use of a re—I beg your pardon, of a collective working,' said Sophie, 'and therefore—'

'Ma'am,' said Vaucourt tightly. 'Far be it from me to disparage your . . . particular talents, but a collective working is a delicate and difficult undertaking, in which each participant must implicitly trust and rely upon all the rest, and a chain which can never be stronger than its weakest link. I cannot reasonably require any of my colleagues or assistants to embark upon so delicate and difficult a project, knowing that its success and their own safety depend on the skill and competence of a woman.'

It was not surprising, exactly; but—

'I confess, Master Vaucourt,' said Sophie (Gray saw, but hoped that Vaucourt might not, how near she was to losing her composure), 'that I do not altogether understand why you should have accepted our offer of assistance, if, as it now appears, you believe we can be of no help to you.'

Vaucourt smiled at her – a tight little smile with no mirth and no friendliness in it. 'Having spent so little time at court, Your Highness,' he said, 'you may perhaps not recognise the importance of diplomacy.'

Gray, who had not the least idea what might be meant by this remark, looked across the table at his brother-in-law, and upon his face beheld an expression of outrage which made him blink in surprise.

'Do I understand, sir,' said Kergabet, 'that two of the most powerful mages in Britain have freely offered their help in resolving the present crisis, and you are intending to *refuse* it?'

'Certainly not,' Vaucourt replied, bristling. 'I should welcome Doctor Marshall's assistance.'

On Gray's other side, Mr Fowler exhaled a sharp *huh!* and muttered under his breath, 'You will wish you had not said that, m'lord.'

Gray himself, his mind frozen in outrage, looked across the table at his brother-in-law, at Sophie.

Kergabet wore a predictably indignant expression, but Sophie – Sophie, who ought to have been incensed at this open, unequivocal insult – met Gray's eyes with a small, resigned grimace.

I had rather swim the Thames in the dead of winter than make common cause with this man, thought Gray, furious. *And yet . . . if any opportunity offers for me to hasten the recapture of Callender and the rest, how can I possibly justify refusing it?*

'Of the pair of us, Maître Vaucourt,' he said, 'I am neither the more powerful, nor the more versatile.'

Vaucourt's expression was utterly baffling: why in Hades should Vaucourt *pity* him?

'Be that as it may, Doctor Marshall,' he said, 'you are the more . . . suitable.'

'The more congruent with your own prejudices, in other words,' said Gray.

'Gray.' Sophie's arm stretched across the table, and her fingers folded over his; magick shivered through their joined hands. 'This is more important than either of us, and certainly more important than my wounded self-regard.'

She spoke deprecatingly — as though this last were a frivolous jest — and her face was perfectly expressionless. Vaucourt actually chuckled, causing Mr Fowler (who knew Sophie rather better) to shake his head despairingly.

Gray turned his hand palm upwards and clasped Sophie's, briefly but firmly. 'As you say, Magistra,' he said, and, turning to Vaucourt, 'I am at your disposal, sir.'

Vaucourt nodded — acknowledgement without thanks — and at once made Gray regret his decision by saying to Sophie, 'If you will excuse us, ma'am . . . ?'

'Certainly.' Sophie let go Gray's hand, rose gracefully from her seat, gathered her books (all but Morag Ruadh MacQuarie's treatise on findings and summonings, which still lay splayed under Vaucourt's hand; Gray made a mental note to retrieve it later), and made for the door, swinging wide around Vaucourt's chair.

Vaucourt summoned two of his assistants, whom Gray vaguely recognised as Merlin men some two or three years younger than himself, and dispatched one to retrieve the maps from the Archives, and the other to gather the rest of the Court mages for another attempt at a finding-spell.

CHAPTER XIV

In Which Joanna and Gwendolen Disobey Orders

Kergabet had not, in so many words, made any promise to keep Joanna abreast of the progress of his investigation. In the course of that first fortnight, however – whether because he considered himself to have made such a promise or because he genuinely wished to hear her views – he contrived to convey some piece of news to her almost every evening, and listened with every appearance of keen interest to her reciprocal news, when from time to time she had any to convey.

Yet though he told her what he could, it was little enough: that the prisoners had contrived to escape without alerting their guards, without visible damage to the premises, and entirely without trace of any sort; that they had left no possessions behind them which might be used in scrying to discover their intentions or their present whereabouts; that the guards did not appear to have been drugged, but a scry-mage in His Majesty's service opined that they might well have been bespelled. The investigation into their disappearance – headed jointly, though not very harmoniously, by Kergabet and by His Majesty's chief mage, Lord de Vaucourt – had as yet discovered nothing of more substance than this, and Joanna felt Kergabet's frustration almost as a physical force whenever they spoke of it. No doubt he was equally aware of the singing tension that gripped her almost always now, compounded of impatience with the slow pace of progress, frustration at her own powerlessness to help, and simple anger at her father. Though of course she was not so arrogant as to suppose that his actions had anything to do with her, or with Amelia – Sophie, or at any rate Sophie's central role in delivering him up to Maître de Vaucourt and the priests of Apollo Coelispex, being a different matter altogether.

Of Sophie and Gray's attempt to assist in the search for the escaped prisoners, Kergabet would say only that things had not fallen out as he himself had hoped, and neither Sophie nor Gray would say anything at all – though their air of suppressed fury, since returning from that initial conference with Vaucourt, and the habit they had developed of fleeing to the library every morning after breakfast and employing Sophie's concealing magick to discourage anyone but Kergabet from remarking their presence there, disinclined Joanna to question them on the subject in any case. They had quarrelled with Vaucourt, Joanna concluded – or Sophie had – and were now pursuing some investigatory avenue of their own, without his knowledge or consent. She wished them joy of it, despite her bitter irritation at being excluded from their counsels.

In her heart of hearts, too, relief flashed guiltily whenever the library door closed behind Sophie, for it meant at least that she was safe at home, and not running off into the gods knew what peril.

Sophie and Gray are not helpless, she reminded herself sternly, beginning to unpick a whole row of stitches which she had set wrongly whilst brooding over the problem of Professor Callender and his friends.

But they were just as capable three years ago, when they first went north into Alba, and much good it did them then!

'They are both still alive and well, are they not?' said Gwendolen. Joanna started violently, knocking the knuckles of her right hand against the arm of the sofa. Had she been thinking aloud, then? It seemed so. *Thank all the gods that Mrs Marshall and Jenny are out paying calls!*

Gwendolen tucked her crewel-work away in her work-basket, then left her chair to kneel at Joanna's feet.

'Jo,' she said quietly, 'you must not fret yourself to death over this business. You have not been sleeping well – have you? Is it the nightmares again? There are shadows under your eyes, and your hands are shaking.'

Joanna, appalled, looked down at her hands – lying idle in her lap now, for she had dropped her latest attempt at fancy-work in her astonishment at being addressed – and saw that it was quite true.

'I am half sick with being penned up in this house,' she admitted.

By Kergabet's decree, the morning rides which had been their settled habit remained suspended; and thus this morning, once again, they sat quietly stitching in the morning-room rather than galloping through the park. Though Joanna thought this precaution ridiculous, for Jenny's sake she had not argued the point, but she was beginning to feel that she should soon go mad if she were not released from this prison – even so large and comfortable as it was.

'And not you only,' said Gwendolen, pulling a face. She sat back on her heels, and after a moment said – as though changing the subject – 'What news from Prince Roland and Lucia MacNeill?'

Joanna sighed. 'None to speak of,' she said. 'I suspect Her Majesty of keeping them under house arrest, for safety's sake – and I confess I cannot blame her.'

'If I were in their shoes,' said Gwendolen, 'I should take ship for Din Edin as soon as I might, and stay there until the . . . the prisoners are back in the Tower, or better yet at the end of a rope.'

Joanna blinked at her, and she scowled, defiant: 'You think me bloodthirsty, I suppose?'

'Not at all,' said Joanna frankly. 'I could not understand at the time what His Majesty was about in commuting the traitors' sentence to imprisonment, and the present circumstances certainly have not changed my opinion on that point.'

Gwendolen's scowl had shifted into an expression of puzzled speculation. She retrieved Joanna's abandoned fancy-work from its scatter across the carpet, stacked the coiled skeins of silk in a tidy heap atop the folded muslin, and placed it squarely across Joanna's lap, then rose to her feet (too neatly by half, for a person with such long legs, thought Joanna in irrational annoyance), turned, and settled herself beside Joanna on the sofa, pressed close against her side.

'But your father,' she began. 'Do you not think—'

'Gwen, you cannot suppose that after all this time – after *everything* – I should still be sentimental about my father?'

Dropping her gaze to her own hands clasped in her lap, Gwendolen said softly, 'I hope you do not think the less of me, because I cannot help feeling sentimental about mine?'

Joanna, shocked out of her indignation, reached for Gwendolen's hands and covered them with her own. 'When your father has been convicted of treason, murder, and attempted regicide,' she said, 'when he has laid a fatal trap for some friend of yours, and without regard to the possibility of its killing you instead, then I shall wonder at your regretting him.'

Raising her eyes, Gwendolen turned her hands palm upwards, the better to wrap her fingers about Joanna's, and produced a grim smile.

Joanna swallowed hard, increasingly aware that this conversation was too fraught, skirted too close to violent emotion, to be conducted in broad day, in Jenny's morning-room, where anyone might interrupt it. She searched for words – some sardonic remark, inflected with gentle humour, which would turn Gwen's grim smile true – but found none; and, not for the first time, she cursed whatever god's whim made her so tongue-tied in the presence of the person with whom she most longed to be eloquent.

The fateful day began in a perfectly ordinary manner: with Joanna and Gwendolen saddling their horses in the stable mews just after waving off Gaël's attempt to do it for them. Trailed by Gaël and Loïc, they rode to the park at a sedate walk – conspicuous only in being two young women riding astride in a Mayfair street – and once through the gates, paused side by side to survey the bridle-path.

In fact, it was no ordinary morning, being the first since the escape of the prisoners from the Tower upon which Joanna and Gwendolen had once more been permitted their daily ride – and then only under escort.

The prospects seemed good: the path was dry and almost deserted, and the sky as clear as it ever was in London. Joanna – feeling half out of her mind with joy simply at being out of doors again – turned her head to look at Gwendolen; Gwendolen met her gaze with a sly grin and, with a minute pressure of her calves and an almost imperceptible twitch of her hands on the reins, urged her chestnut mare, Elain, into motion.

Joanna and Kelvez were only a breath behind her. They walked, then trotted, then cantered past several startled gentlemen ambling along the bridle-path, and at last – when they had outstripped the last of these, as well as their own indignant escort – leant forward and urged their mounts into a gallop.

Kelvez and Elain had been stablemates two years and more and had each other's measure; their own hearts were in the race as surely as their riders', and they flew down the straight leg of the bridle-path neck and neck. At the last moment Joanna urged, 'Just

195

a little farther, lovely!' and they drew ahead by the length of Kelvez's glossy head, just in time to pass under the pair of bay-trees, arching together over the path, that marked their usual finishing line.

They slowed, laughing breathlessly, and rounded the curve at a jogging trot – just as if all were quite as usual, with no vague and ill-formed threat hanging over London like the sword of Damocles.

'I told you I should break your streak, Gwen,' Joanna crowed. As she was turning in her saddle to grin at Gwendolen, a strange young man – wild-eyed, his hair and clothing all anyhow, as though he had slept the night in the wood – came crashing through a weeping beech and onto the path just ahead of them.

He clutched at Elain's bridle, causing her to snort and back and attempt to rear; had Gwendolen been a less skilful horsewoman, Joanna thought, she should certainly have been thrown, and this reckless, idiotic stranger kicked half to death. Kelvez, almost equally agitated, sidled her hooves and tossed her head, and Joanna had both hands full in calming her.

'Which of you is Miss Callender's sister?' the stranger demanded. 'Where is she? I must speak with her.'

Joanna looked up, startled, and very nearly said, *I am*, before prudence and common sense prevailed. 'Unhand my friend's bridle, sir,' she said instead, infusing her voice with the spirit of Mrs Edmond Marshall – chosen as the least obliging person of her acquaintance. 'What do you mean by assaulting us in this manner?'

He let go of the bridle, allowing Gwendolen to back Elain away from him, and lurched towards Joanna. He must truly have been sleeping rough, she thought, as he drew nearer, and not only last night: his clothing had been good once, and being now extremely dirty and growing ragged, looked all the worse for the contrast; his hair was lank and long untrimmed, his face long unshaven and its bones too prominent beneath the skin. He smelt not only of unwashed male body (which was bad enough) but of rank fear – to the horses' more sensitive noses, the smell must be like the fumes of Tartarus – and his eyes—

Joanna could not bear to look at his eyes.

He lunged for her bridle, but Kelvez was having none of it. She snorted and whinnied and made to rear, her ears flattened in warning; whilst Joanna fought to keep her seat, bending forward along the mare's neck to avoid pulling at her mouth, the stranger staggered backwards out of the range of her hooves, with abject terror stamped upon his face.

'Jo!' Gwendolen's voice was firm and insistent. 'Jo, are you or are you not in charge of that horse?'

It was not, perhaps, the approach any reputable trainer of horses would have taken, but it put Joanna very strongly in mind of Morvan, her father's large, patient coachman and stableman-in-chief, who had taught her nearly everything she knew about horses. She had always suspected Morvan of concealing some vast, horse-related magickal talent, for when he spoke, horses stilled and gentled. If so, Gwendolen, she thought, had some of that talent too.

Whether or not there was any magick in Gwen's words, however, her voice cut through Joanna's incipient panic, reminding her that much worse things were possible than falling off a horse.

Ignoring the madman on the bridle-path, therefore, Joanna settled her weight deep in her saddle and stirrups and turned Kelvez's head just enough that, off balance, the mare came down onto all four feet again. Then, seizing the moment whilst she could, she straightened her spine, dug in her heels, and said firmly, '*Walk on.*'

Kelvez sidled uncertainly; but when Joanna once more urged her forward, she seemed to decide to take what was fast becoming the path of least resistance: around the mad stranger and towards Gwendolen and Elain.

Close to, Gwendolen looked a great deal more frightened than she had sounded; Joanna reached for her arm and squeezed it, murmuring, 'Will you trust me?'

'Of course,' said Gwendolen reflexively. Joanna turned away before the doubt already glimmering in her eyes could become a full-fledged objection.

She swung her right leg over to the mare's near side and slid smoothly down to stand on the path. 'Stay here,' she said, handing her reins to Gwendolen and surreptitiously squeezing her gloved hand, 'in case a diversion is called for.'

Then she squared her shoulders, lifted her chin, and turned back to face the madman who was seeking Amelia.

He stood still as she slowly approached him – tensed for flight, like a hare or a deer – and, when she halted just out of arm's reach, visibly restrained himself from clutching at her to prevent her from escaping.

'Who are you?' Joanna said. 'Where are you come from, and what in Hades do you want with Amelia?' *And what*, she added to herself, *do you imagine that Amelia might want with you?* She attempted to imagine an encounter between this man – terror-struck and filthy – and her fastidious sister, and could conjure no version of it which did not end with Amelia's recoiling in disgust and fleeing the scene.

'You do know her, then,' said the man. 'She told me that you often ride here in the mornings, so I have been waiting—she is in London? You must bring her – I must speak with her—'

Joanna folded her arms and glared. 'I shall do nothing of the kind,' she said. 'Do you imagine me to be in the habit of delivering up my friends to the clutches of wild men who assault inoffensive young women in public parks?'

Joanna's glare – she had modelled it on Lady Maëlle's – was well known to make grown men quail, and this one was no exception; but, quailing, he nonetheless stood his ground.

'You must,' he insisted. 'I beg of you—'

'If your business is so very urgent, then, you will not object to give me your name.'

The stranger stared at her for what seemed an age, biting his lip and worrying his hands.

'My name is Henry Taylor,' he conceded at last, and Joanna's unease congealed into horrified disbelief.

'Then where are all the rest of you?' she demanded. 'Six men escaped the Tower and vanished; where are the other five?'

'I shall tell all I know,' said Taylor (if so he was indeed), 'in return for His Majesty's protection. But I must see Am—Miss Callender.'

'If you are playing tricks,' said Joanna, lowering her voice to a furious half whisper, 'if any harm comes to anyone of my acquaintance by your doing, I shall make sure that you live long enough to bitterly regret it.'

Taylor held up his hands in surrender. 'I have no wish to harm anyone,' he said. 'Quite the opposite. That is why I must see Miss Callender, and at once. You need not be afraid; if you are Miss Joanna Callender, then your brother-in-law is Marshall of Merlin College, and I am an old friend of his.'

'You are nothing of the kind!' Joanna exclaimed, outraged. 'You were a tool for my father and the rest of that ill-met company, and hoodwinked Gray into becoming another such. If that is your notion of friendship, Mr Taylor, I think I may safely say that we are none of us eager to call you friend.'

'I do not see that Marshall has done so badly out of it,' said Taylor. He no longer sounded at all mad, to Joanna's relief, but did sound rather like a sulky child.

Joanna did not attempt to argue the point, for it was true that had not Gray been so stupid as to lend himself to Taylor's midnight errand on behalf of his tutor, he should not now have been Sophie's husband, nor the owner of the estate in Breizh which had belonged to several generations of Callenders. *But that is down to our making the best of things*, she reminded herself, *and not to any generous impulse of Mr Taylor's.*

'Tell me what it is you want with Amelia,' she said, though she had a sinking feeling that she knew it already, 'and I shall convey the message. I make no promises as to what she may choose to do with the information.'

It could do no harm to convey a message, she reasoned – whereas the longer she stood here arguing, the greater the risk of irreparable harm to her reputation, and to her protectors', from someone's happening upon this conversation and spreading the tale all over London. If agreeing to carry his message would induce him to go away . . .

And it was not impossible that whatever information he possessed, supposing that he could be induced to part with it, might be genuinely valuable.

'You must bring your sister here,' said Taylor. 'Or see that she comes here. Tomorrow, at the same hour – or, if not tomorrow, the day after. She will not be permitted to come alone, I must suppose; let her bring Marshall with her, if needs be, but no one else.'

'You are very demanding for a man in your position,' said Joanna. Was this some manner of trap? If so, to what purpose? 'Why should either my sister or Mr Marshall agree to such a demand? For that matter, why should I not summon the Watch this moment, and have you taken in charge?'

Under the layers of grime, Taylor's face blanched, but again he stood his ground: 'Because I have information of value, which I shall be disinclined to share if I am arrested and thrown back into prison.'

'Very well; you wish to surrender on your own terms,' said Joanna. That was logical enough. 'Then why not take advantage of your present audience to convey your information directly to His Majesty's ear?'

Taylor first looked baffled, and then – to her astonishment, considering their relative situations – his lip curled, and he said, in a condescending tone with which Joanna was tediously familiar, 'What – you – and your friend?' He waved a dismissive hand at Gwendolen; out of his line of sight, she returned a very rude gesture borrowed from Gaël. 'I hardly think that would answer.'

Joanna repressed a strong impulse to pull off one of her boots and clout him with it. 'As you like,' she said, with her most unladylike shrug. 'I have promised to convey your message; I have made no promises as to the result. If indeed your intent is to turn King's evidence, I expect we shall meet again before very long. Good morning, Mr Taylor.'

And so saying, she turned on her heel and strode away towards Gwendolen and the horses – and the approaching rumble of hooves which presumably heralded Lord Kergabet's grooms.

If her heart was pounding in her throat, there was no need for anyone – and Henry Taylor most particularly – to know it.

Smarting from the tongue-lashing they had received from Gaël and Loïc, Joanna and Gwendolen stopped only long enough to see to their horses before banging through the area door, through the kitchen, and up the servants' staircase. At last they burst pink-faced and out of breath into the breakfast-parlour, where the rest of the Grosvenor Square family, together with Lady Maëlle, were sitting over their meal.

Six faces turned towards the sound of the door, their expressions variously astonished, indignant, and bewildered; six pairs of eyes, beholding the two young ladies in their dishevelled riding-clothes, widened in alarm. Joanna spared a prayer of thanks to Morpheus, god of dreams, that the rest of Jenny's guests were not yet come down to breakfast; she was in no state to put up a front of unruffled calm for Mrs Edmond Marshall.

'Joanna! Gwendolen!' Jenny exclaimed, starting up from her chair with an awkward lurch. 'Whatever is the matter?'

'Henry Taylor,' said Joanna, breathless. 'In the park. Hiding.' She turned to her brother-in-law: 'Gray, he said—'

'You rode straight away to summon the City Watch, I hope and trust,' said Sieur Germain. His tone suggested considerably more hope than trust. 'Rather than engaging in conversation with a convicted traitor and dangerous fugitive from His Majesty's justice.'

Gwendolen's right hand found Joanna's left, concealed behind their skirts, and Joanna pressed her fingers gently in reassurance. Even after all this time, it seemed, Gwen did not entirely trust that some transgression of hers would not inspire Kergabet or Jenny to pack her off back to Papa and the objectionable Stepmama in Clwyd.

'I did consider fetching out the Watch,' said Joanna, truthfully enough, 'but he did not seem to intend us any harm; he is only very stupid about horses.'

Sophie frowned; before she could speak, however, Joanna ploughed onward: 'We are both perfectly well, and the horses likewise, and there has been no harm done to anyone, so there is no need to discuss it. The *point* is that this Mr Taylor says that he must speak privately with Amelia – he would not say why, though I fear it is not difficult to guess – and that he has information of some kind, connected with the conspirators' escape, which he will consent to reveal in exchange for His Majesty's protection and, of course, this meeting with Amelia. I tried to gain some hint as to the nature of this information, but he insists upon speaking of it to you, Gray, and no one else – and only if he is permitted to see Amelia.'

Gray looked deeply baffled. 'Why on the gods' green earth should Henry Taylor wish to confide in me?' he said.

'He called himself your friend,' said Joanna. Gray snorted. 'Which does not accord very well with what we know of him, but perhaps imprisonment has worked some magick upon his heart and mind – or perhaps he has quarrelled with the rest of them, and now finds himself in want of allies. By the look of him, he has not had very good luck since he left his prison.'

'Or perhaps it is a trap of some sort,' said Jenny. 'Whatever is afoot, Jo, I do not like it at all.'

'It may be a trap, of course,' Joanna conceded. 'I have considered the possibility, Jenny, I assure you. I do not know what he hopes to catch in it, however, besides poor Amelia.'

'A mage, one presumes,' said Kergabet. 'Or mages. It would not be the first time.'

Sophie went very pale, and reached for Gray's hand across the tablecloth.

'If it is a trap,' said Joanna, aiming for a calmly reassuring tone, 'it is a very clumsy one.'

'In any case, half of them are mages themselves,' said Gray. 'Unless our information on the subject is very much out of date. And if Henry Taylor expects me to come to his aid, or considers me likely to believe anything he says—'

'And this information which he claims to have?' said Joanna. 'What of that? He must know *something* – perhaps not where the others are now, but at any rate where they have been, and how they contrived to escape.'

'Not to mention who helped them,' Gwendolen put in. When Mr Fowler gave her an astonished look, she said, 'Well, it is perfectly evident that someone must have done!'

So it was indeed, in Joanna's view, though Sieur Germain and his investigators had been at considerable pains to keep their conclusions on this point from reaching the public ear, lest they inflame the rumours of conspiracy already circulating.

'I am perfectly ready to speak with him,' said Gray, 'if Sieur Germain has no objection. But as to Amelia's being exposed to such a risk—'

'*I* have an objection!' Sophie exclaimed, leaping to her feet. Gray twisted round in his seat to look up at her. 'I have *numerous* objections – quite apart from Amelia's going, which of course is perfectly impossible. To begin with—'

'But if I might speed the others' recapture,' Gray said, almost too softly for Joanna's ears to catch. He had caught Sophie's hands – curled into fists at her sides – and engulfed them both in his larger ones, clasped close to his lips. 'You would not have me shirk that task, love, surely?'

Looking away in some discomfiture, Joanna met Gwendolen's eye across the table, and knew at once that she, too, had been unable to continue watching Sophie and Gray.

'No,' said Sophie, with a small, defeated sigh. Joanna heard the rustle of her gown as she resumed her seat, and looked back along the table to see her prop her elbows upon the tablecloth and bury her face in her hands. Her voice, when next she spoke, was muffled: 'No, of course I would not.'

Gray's hand was on Sophie's shoulder, but his gaze was steady on his brother-in-law's face. He did not see, therefore, the moment when Sophie raised her head from her hands, nor the terrifying light in her dark eyes.

Oh, gods and priestesses. She has had an idea, and I fear we shall all of us regret it.

'What say you, my lord?' said Gray.

Sieur Germain, grim-faced, replied, 'Such a summons seems to me highly likely to indicate a trap. I cannot forbid you, of course; but I should strongly counsel you not to go alone.'

'He need not be alone,' said Sophie. Straightening away from Gray's hand on her shoulder, she unfolded herself from her chair, turned to face her husband and brother-in-law, and closed her eyes.

'Sophie—'

The transformation took only a moment – so skilled was Sophie now, so thoroughly in control of her magick, that the intervening stages were scarcely visible to Joanna's eye – and by the time her eyes opened once more, one sister had vanished and the other appeared.

'He need not be alone,' Sophie repeated, in perfect mimicry of Amelia's voice, and smiling Amelia's slightly superior smile, 'for Miss Callender can go with him.'

The silence which greeted this pronouncement was so thick that Joanna's ears fairly rang with it.

'That is a perfectly idiotic notion.' It was Gwendolen who spoke at last; all of them turned to look at her, and she coloured a little but did not look away. 'Begging your pardon, Mrs Marshall. If, as you suppose, these men have set a trap to catch mages, why in Hades should you wish to deliver up two mages instead of one?'

Sophie looked down Amelia's nose at Gwendolen, so entirely Amelia that Joanna shivered. 'You seem, Miss Pryce,' she said, in Amelia's most icily condescending tone, 'to be labouring under a misapprehension. I have no notion of delivering up anything to anyone, and myself and Mr Marshall to Henry Taylor, I assure you, least of all.'

'Nevertheless, Sophie' – Jenny had now found her voice, it appeared – 'I must agree with Gwendolen. I do not see what advantage—'

The faux Amelia shook her head briskly, in the manner of a

hound with water in its ears, and abruptly was Sophie again. 'Have you *met* my sister Amelia, Jenny?' she demanded, laughter warring with exasperation in her voice. 'The advantage is that whatever they may expect of Amelia, they shall not be expecting *me*.'

'Has it occurred to anyone,' said Joanna, 'to ask Amelia's opinion?'

To judge by the looks that were turned in her direction, this suggestion was quite as shocking as Sophie's had been.

'After all,' she continued, pressing her advantage, 'she is not a child; she is six and twenty, or nearly, and surely knows her own mind. Perhaps she may know what this Mr Taylor is about; perhaps he may be willing to tell her things which—'

'Six and twenty or not,' said Lady Maëlle, 'and child or not, Amelia remains a ward of the Crown so long as she is unmarried – as do you, Joanna, you may recall. And, as the duly appointed representative thereof, in respect of your sister, I have every right to decide what is, and is not, in her best interests to be told.'

Joanna and Sophie exchanged a look.

'And do you not think, *Mrs Wallis*,' said the latter pointedly, 'that enough harm has been done already in this family by the keeping of secrets?'

Lady Maëlle winced – just visibly – at the use of her quondam alias and, when Jenny said firmly, 'I quite agree,' acquiesced gracefully enough to Amelia's being consulted.

'Gwendolen,' said Jenny, when this largely silent skirmish had been won, 'will you run up to Miss Callender's room, please, and ask her to come down and speak to us in the morning-room?'

'Yes, ma'am,' said Gwendolen at once, and, with a single enigmatic glance over her shoulder at Joanna, hastened out into the corridor.

* * *

206

'Miss Pryce has been a very long time in fetching Amelia,' said Sophie, worrying at the edge of the fichu which she had taken out of her work-basket for the purpose of hemming it. 'Ought one of us to—'

'*No*,' said Joanna firmly. 'Of all of us, Gwen is the least likely to irritate her simply by existing; we can do no good by—'

She broke off, following Jenny's startled gaze.

Gwendolen stood in the doorway, one hand gripping the jamb; she was out of breath, as though she had been running, yet her face was pale.

'Miss Callender is not in her room,' she said. 'Nor anywhere else in the house, so far as I can discover. Her bed looks as though it had not been slept in, and Mr Treveur says that her boots were not put out to be cleaned, though I am quite sure I saw them last night when I put out Joanna's and mine, and she has left the small drawer of the dressing-table ajar – the drawer where I used to keep my coin-purse, when that dressing-table was in my bedroom in Carrington-street – and I opened it and found a stray copper coin that had rolled to the back' – here Gwendolen held up her other hand and opened it palm up to show the coin's dull coppery gleam – 'but otherwise it was quite empty. And—'

'Enough,' said Lady Maëlle, so sharply that Joanna started in her seat. 'Have any of you seen Amelia this morning? Joanna?'

Joanna shook her head numbly, and one by one the others did the same.

'She went up to bed very early yesterday evening,' said Jenny, her voice slow and heavy. 'Do you not recall?' Joanna, her heart sinking, did. 'She had a sick headache, she said, and I did not doubt her, for she did look ill – I had begun to remark it at dinner. I remember I asked her whether I had not better send you up to her, Lady Maëlle; but she said no, she was going to sleep straight away, and should be quite well in the morning—'

'You ought to have told me,' said Lady Maëlle. Joanna flinched from the furious anger in her voice.

The expressions breaking across their faces, as severally they arrived at the conclusion that, in fact, no one had seen Amelia since the previous afternoon, exactly echoed the sick panic which clutched at Joanna's heart and roiled nauseatingly through her belly.

'I can see now that I ought,' said Jenny – her voice perfectly calm, though her face was waxen and her hands clenched tightly on the arms of her chair. 'But at the time—'

Lady Maëlle drew breath to speak again; Joanna, hoping to forestall her, said, 'Has she had any more mysterious letters? Had she any yesterday?'

Treveur and Madame Joliveau were summoned. No, said Treveur, there had been no letters for Miss Callender by the morning post yesterday, nor the evening post either. However, yesterday being the first of the month, he had been occupied all the afternoon, together with Madame Joliveau and Lady Kergabet, in the settling of the household bills; he was not prepared to swear, therefore, that no letter or message could have entered the house by any other means. Indeed, they agreed, there had been a quantity of messengers, couriers, and so on coming to the door at all hours, since this dreadful business of Dim'zell Joanna's father (here he nodded at Joanna, an apology for having drawn this connexion), and though all the staff of course had strict instructions to let none of these persons past the front door . . .

'I thank you both,' said Jenny at last, and sent them away to question the housemaids, the parlourmaids, the footmen, and (on the subject of Miss Callender's boots) the boot-boy, George – if possible, without exciting their curiosity.

Joanna thought again of horses and stable doors, and rather

fancied that Jenny and Kergabet were thinking the same, but there must be some effort made, at least to delay – for surely they could not prevent it altogether – the moment when Amelia's sudden departure should become fodder for the sort of talk which all were desirous to avoid.

Meanwhile Sophie and Gray had been muttering together in a corner of the morning-room – in their case, an almost infallible sign of magickal doings. Upon the departure of Madame Joliveau and Mr Treveur, they emerged from this conference to resume their seats upon Jenny's new green-and-gold-striped sofa; their faces were grave, and they held hands quite openly (Gray's huge left hand altogether eclipsing Sophie's right), as though they could not quite bear to let go.

'That was a finding-spell, I presume,' said Kergabet. He glanced out of the window, repressed a sigh, and looked at Mr Fowler, who said, 'I shall go and see about the carriage, sir.'

Of course, thought Joanna, very belatedly; they ought to have been about their business long since, and should have been, if not for Henry Taylor, if not for Amelia.

'It was,' said Gray, as the door was closing behind Mr Fowler. 'Either Miss Callender is not within eighty miles of this house, or she is in the company of someone capable of working an extremely strong warding-spell, and of recognising the wisdom of doing so.'

'This Henry Taylor,' said Jenny at once; 'could he do so, do you think?'

Gray's russet-gold-brown eyebrows drew together in a doubtful frown. 'I should not have said so,' he said, 'particularly in light of the description of him which we had this morning – exhaustion and starvation do not tend to strengthen one's reserves of magick. On the other hand . . .'

His voice trailed off, and for a long moment he said nothing but stared vaguely in the general direction of the window, from which were visible the tops of the trees in the square.

'On the other hand?' Sophie prompted patiently.

Gray turned away from the window, blinked several times, and said, 'On the other hand, I have not set eyes on Henry Taylor for the best part of seven years, and even then, we were not friends; I have no reason to suppose my impression of his capabilities at all accurate, and of course no means of knowing what else he may have contrived to learn since last we met.'

'Nonetheless,' said Sophie, 'if, as we believe, Amelia left the house yesterday evening after the rest of us went up to bed – the evidence of the boots, you know – I think the most likely explanation is that she has already got more than eighty miles from London, rather than—'

'Why eighty miles, Sophie?' said Joanna.

'I am drawing a logical inference,' said Sophie primly. 'After the . . . the business in Alba, we recruited all of our colleagues to experiment with finding-spells, so that if anything of the sort should ever occur again . . .' She swallowed, cleared her throat, and continued: 'My range is fifty miles, and Gray's, thirty; ergo, working together, we ought to be able to manage eighty at the least.'

'Mrs Marshall,' said Gwendolen, sitting up very straight, like a pointer which has caught a scent, 'what if – I wonder – the spell you sang, in Din Edin – might that—'

Joanna stared at her, bemused; this inarticulate jumble of words was quite unlike Gwendolen's usual mode of expressing herself. But she knew very well what sort of spell was meant, and it seemed that Sophie did also, for she said at once, 'I am quite prepared to try it; but you know, I think, that on the occasion you speak of, I had had . . . considerable assistance from Lucia MacNeill—'

'Well, as to that,' said Joanna, 'surely Lucia MacNeill would have no objection—'

'*You* may be sure of it, but *I* am not,' Sophie retorted. 'But in any case, Jo, the effect would not be at all the same, because now we are not in Alba.'

Joanna and Gwendolen sat back in disappointment; Lady Maëlle, whose outrage appeared to have subsided to an impotent simmer, said bleakly, 'I apologise for my intemperate words, Lady Kergabet. The blame is mine; I have known that child since the age of three, and ought to have seen that she was scheming.'

The door opened. 'The carriage, sir,' said Mr Fowler.

CHAPTER XV

In Which Sophie and Joanna Conduct an Uncomfortable Interview

'No, ma'am,' said Katell positively. 'And if I did,' she added, with a defiant glance at Lady Maëlle, 'I shouldn't tell anyone.'

She does know something about it, at any rate, thought Sophie. She exchanged with Joanna a look of grim surmise.

'Katell, no one wishes Amelia any ill,' she said. 'She and I have . . . we have not always seen things just alike, as you know, but you surely cannot think that I should take this occasion to crow over her mistakes?'

Katell looked away uncomfortably but said nothing.

'But if she is gone off alone, Katell,' Sophie persisted, 'anything at all might befall her – she does not know London as Miss Joanna does, or Miss Pryce – she has no magick to protect her, nor any other sort of protection either – and with the Professor abroad in the world somewhere, plotting the gods alone know what—'

They ought not to have brought Lady Maëlle with them, she decided. It had seemed a wise precaution, a reassurance to Katell; but it appeared that Katell's habit of shielding Joanna from the Professor's temper had transmuted itself into a determination to keep Amelia's secrets from her guardian.

'Cousin Maëlle,' said Sophie – dubious of success but determined to make the attempt – 'I have just remembered that J—that Lady

Kergabet wished very much to consult you upon, er, upon a matter of midwifery. I do apologise – I cannot think how I came to forget—'

Lady Maëlle, of course, was not taken in for a moment, but Lady Maëlle had not in any case been the target of Sophie's gambit. Her dark eyes narrowed – *I see what you are about, Sophie Marshall* – but she nodded briskly and, saying only, 'We must hope there is no great harm done,' took herself off, very likely to listen outside the library door.

Within the library there followed several further attempts at reasoning Katell into cooperation, which she resisted as steadfastly as before – until at last Joanna's unwonted patience came to a jarring end, and she interrupted Sophie's latest *Please, Katell*, by saying sharply, 'Katell, I wish you will tell us whatever it is you know about Amelia; but if you will not, it does not much signify, for Lady Kergabet has only to scry something of hers, and then we shall know all of it.'

In several respects, as Joanna must know, this last was not precisely true; Katell, however, could only just call light, and to Sophie's knowledge had never seen a scry-mage working close to. Sophie was not much surprised, therefore, to see her defiance begin to waver before Joanna's decidedly unsubtle threat.

The sisters exchanged a meaning look, and by unspoken consent sat back in their chairs and regarded Katell (standing before them with her hands twisted into her apron, her honest face growing pink) in silence. Like both of them before her – for this patient, expectant silence was a weapon which Jenny had deployed against Sophie more than once, and Joanna, in all probability, dozens of times – Katell could bear it only so long.

'It is not fair!' she burst out at last, all furious indignation.

Sophie's ears pricked; she leant forward, clasping her hands between her knees. 'What is not fair?'

Katell paused a long moment – the pause, and Katell's expression, spoke to Sophie of calculation, though that might be only the effect of her own guilty conscience – but at length said, 'That you should be so very cross with Miss Amelia, only for doing what you did yourself.' Misreading Sophie's expression of dismay, she hastily added, 'Begging your pardon, Miss Sophie.'

'Mr Henry Taylor, I presume?' said Joanna with a sigh.

Abandoning her wary study of Sophie, Katell rounded on Joanna. 'And what of it?' she demanded. 'Why should not Miss Amelia run away to be married to a handsome Oxford man, the same as her sister?'

'I did no such thing!' Sophie protested.

Joanna and Katell looked at her, briefly united in disbelief.

'It is quite true,' said Sophie, with some spirit, 'and Miss Joanna knows it as well as I do, Katell, whatever anyone else may say. Mr Marshall and I did *not* run away to be married; we ran away for a different reason entirely, and it so fell out that we were married along the way.'

Joanna hid a most unladylike snort of derisive laughter behind her hand; Sophie glared at her, and she left her seat and began to pace about the room.

'In any case,' said Sophie, returning her attention to Katell, 'Mr Taylor is not an Oxford man, handsome or otherwise; he is a convicted traitor. A man who took part in a plot to poison the King.'

This, it seemed, Amelia had not confided to her accomplice; Katell's brown eyes widened in alarm, and she swallowed hard before saying, 'I am sure that can't be right, Miss Sophie. Or' – her voice grew more confident as she evolved an alternative theory – 'if it *is*, I'm sure Miss Amelia can't have known of it.'

'She did know of it, Katell,' said Sophie gently; 'I know she did, for we spoke of the matter very lately. But I believe she thinks better of Mr Taylor and his friends – and of the Professor, too – than they deserve.'

Behind Katell, Joanna rolled her eyes; this time Sophie could not glare at her without Katell's seeing it, and so she confined herself to a brief crimping of her lips. 'But whatever Miss Amelia may believe of them, Katell, they are *not* good men, and I do not believe she is safe in their company.'

Katell bit her lip and twisted her apron in her hands as though it had been a floor-cloth which wanted wringing out.

'I am sure Miss Amelia would never go away with a young man unless she intended marriage,' said Sophie, pressing her advantage, 'but what Miss Amelia intended and what Mr Taylor means to do may not be the same, you see.' Despite herself, she heard her voice go pleading, felt Joanna's gaze sharp on her face – wondering at her tone, or suspecting her of prevarication? 'Amelia and I have not always been very kind to one another, but if she should come to harm, harm that I might have prevented—'

'She had letters from him,' Katell burst out. She sounded near to weeping – and no wonder, if she was betraying a promise of secrecy. Truly, thought Sophie, it was cruel of Amelia to have put her in such a position. 'He promised to marry her, and to take her where her father is, and that he and the Professor have powerful friends, and will be great men there.'

'Where?' Joanna demanded.

Katell burst into tears, and flung herself at Sophie. 'I don't know,' she sobbed into Sophie's shoulder. 'She never told me that. I don't know.'

Did she know herself? Had she any idea what she was about? Oh, Amelia . . .

And whilst all of us were brangling over whether she ought to be permitted to speak with him, in a public park and in Gray's company, for a quarter-hour, she must already have been planning to elope with him!

But if that were so, then why—

Katell interrupted this promising train of thought by clutching at Sophie's shoulder-blades and sobbing, 'I gave her my word, and now look!'

'All right, Katell,' said Sophie, holding her tight. 'All right. I am sorry that we should have made you break your word. You did right to tell us, I promise you.'

Over Katell's heaving shoulders, Sophie caught Joanna's gaze and held it. *We shall have to ask Jenny to scry Amelia's things in any case.*

To Joanna's surprise, Lady Maëlle was not lurking in the corridor listening at the door, and, indeed, was nowhere to be found. Having given Katell over to the care of Mrs Treveur, the acerbic but kind-hearted Breizhek matron who ruled over Jenny's kitchen, Joanna and Sophie went in search of Jenny. In the morning-room they found Mrs Marshall at work on a vast and complex piece of petit-point, and in the library, Gray, surrounded by stacks of books and poring over an enormous codex – but no Jenny.

They ran her to earth at last in the nursery, nearly at the top of the house, where she was ensconced in a rocking-chair with Yvon curled in her lap and Agatha hanging perilously over the chair-back. All three were listening raptly to Gwendolen, who sat cross-legged on the nursery carpet with a book open in her lap. '*Au bout d'une quinzaine d'ans,*' she read, '*le Roi et la Reine étant alles à une de leurs maisons de plaisance, il arriva que la jeune Princesse courait un jour partout dans le Château, et montant de chambre en chambre . . .*'

Sophie coughed.

Gwendolen looked up sharply. 'What is the matter?' she said.

'Aunty Jo!' said Yvon, pointing with a chubby finger. 'Story!'

Agatha dropped to her feet, ran forward, and caught Joanna and Sophie by the hands. 'Come! Sit down!' she said. 'Aunty Gwen, tell us what happens next to the beautiful Princess!'

Gwendolen glanced up at Joanna as if seeking permission to continue; Joanna nodded minutely, and silently shaped the word *Later.* Gwendolen returned the nod, bent her head to the book, and took up her interrupted tale.

Sophie meanwhile had allowed herself to be towed half across the nursery and deposited on the cushioned window-seat. Rather than joining her, however, Joanna paused by Jenny's chair and, bending close to her ear, murmured, 'It is as we suspected, and possibly worse.'

Jenny's wide hazel eyes fell closed, and her arms about Yvon tightened briefly. 'What had Katell to say?' she said, low.

'A farrago of lies, I strongly suspect,' said Joanna; 'but not her own lies, and, unless I miss my guess, not even my sister's.' In a rapid undertone, wary of Yvon's listening ears, she sketched the purport of Katell's confession. 'But what she did not know – or, at any rate, would not admit to knowing, and by then I believe she had abandoned concealment – is *where.* I hope, therefore—'

'Yes,' said Jenny. 'Bring me something of hers – come to my room, when you have dressed for dinner – and I shall do what I can.'

Joanna blinked, nonplussed. She and Sophie had marshalled their arguments, arming themselves to overcome Jenny's scruples on the subject of scrying Amelia's abandoned possessions without her consent – but here was the skirmish won for them, without a sword drawn.

'I thank you,' she said at last, and, after gently ruffling Yvon's

217

tow-coloured curls, turned away to settle beside Gwendolen on the carpet.

Under cover of their muddled skirts, Gwendolen's free hand found Joanna's and held tight.

'Dougal MacAngus would have my head,' muttered Sophie, sifting through the contents of Amelia's dressing-table drawers, very little of which recognisably belonged to Amelia. Of course even Dougal MacAngus would make an exception in the case of a missing person – but *was* Amelia missing, in that sense, or had she merely made a choice with which her family and friends vehemently disagreed?

Joanna's face appeared around the door of the wardrobe, into which her head and upper body had vanished some time before. 'I beg your pardon?' she said.

'Never mind.' Sophie waved a hand vaguely about the scene of their various transgressions – of the laws of hospitality, of their sister's privacy, of (though as yet only in prospect) the tenets of magickal ethics – and returned to her rummaging.

The results thus far were not encouraging; as well as making a nearly clean sweep of her fungible assets, Amelia appeared to have taken away with her – or otherwise disposed of – all of her jewellery, her brushes and hairpins, her dancing-slippers—

'Aha!' Joanna emerged fully from the wardrobe, and thrust towards Sophie a battered reticule, embroidered with pink and red carnations and closed by a wide ribbon of dull green. Loose threads spilt from the edges of a rent in one side.

Sophie regarded it doubtfully. It was difficult to imagine Amelia as the owner of such a bedraggled object, but had it belonged to Miss Pryce, whose bedroom this ordinarily was, Joanna could not have mistaken it.

'The carnations,' said Joanna, impatient, waggling the limp satin. '*I shall never forget you.* Amelia's friend Claudine Harcourt made this for her when she left school, and Amelia made her one very like it.'

'I shall take your word for it,' said Sophie. 'Have you that copper coin from the back of the drawer . . . ?'

Joanna extracted the coin (or, at any rate, *a* coin) from the folds of her sash and held it up.

They knocked diffidently upon the door of Jenny's room; as Joanna pushed open the door, Jenny turned from her dressing-table, smoothing her skirts over her knees with anxious hands.

'What have you found?' she said.

Joanna produced the carnation reticule and handed it over.

Jenny's eyebrows rose in doubt – exactly as Sophie's had done, not a quarter-hour since – and Joanna, anxious and impatient, bit back a sharp reply. 'It is Amelia's own, I promise you,' she said instead; as a further thought occurred, she added, 'Indeed, I rather wonder that she should have left it behind.'

'She must have packed up her things in a great hurry,' said Sophie.

Jenny flattened the worn and shredded silk across her lap and studied it thoughtfully. 'A gift from a dear friend, perhaps?' she said.

'Yes, exactly,' said Joanna.

'Perhaps,' said Sophie, 'we may find Amelia by seeking out Mademoiselle Harcourt?'

Joanna sighed. 'Perhaps we might,' she said, 'but that Claudine Harcourt – Madame Deschamps she was by then – died four years ago.' Sophie flinched. 'Thrown from a horse, by Cousin Maëlle's account – it was not Amelia who told me of it, of course.'

'Be quiet, please, both of you,' said Jenny, not unkindly.

Sophie reached for Joanna's hand – to still the anxious fidgeting of her own, Joanna suspected – and they sat side by side, unspeaking, whilst Jenny prepared her scrying-spell.

There was not much to see, and they had in any case seen all of it before. Jenny cupped Amelia's abandoned reticule in both hands, closed her eyes and steadied her breathing, and murmured the words of her spell – as obscure to Joanna now as they had been when first she heard them, all those years ago, applied to a ring of keys which Sophie had stolen from the pocket of the Professor's coat.

On this occasion the process seemed to go on for a very long time. Joanna leant up close to Sophie and breathed in her ear, 'What is happening? Is all well, do you suppose?'

As she drew back, Sophie turned to her with a small, unhappy frown creasing her brow. 'Scrying is a closed book to me, Jo,' she said quietly. 'I have not the least idea. I *do* know that a scry-mage must never be interrupted midspell.'

Meaning, in fact, *Hush, Jo.*

Joanna pressed her lips together and called on Lady Juno to grant her patience.

When at last Jenny raised her head and opened her eyes, her expression was surprisingly calm.

'Well?' said Sophie.

Jenny sighed. 'I cannot decide whether this object was well or poorly chosen for the purpose,' she said. 'It was in your sister's possession for more than a decade and strongly associated with her, but it is so thickly wrapped about with aetheric echoes that to find those we are seeking would, I think, be no easy feat for any scry-mage – even one far more skilled than I.'

'Jenny—'

Jenny held up a hand, and Sophie subsided, quivering.

'Fortunately, I am better acquainted with Miss Callender than a more skilled stranger could possibly be, and fortunately, too, the echoes we need are amongst the most recent, though not the strongest, which made my task easier than it might otherwise have been.' She looked down again at the lovingly worked carnations. Where, Joanna wondered, was this interminable lecture leading? 'Less fortunately, your sister's feelings of guilt at leaving behind this last relic of her girlhood friend have created such a strong echo as nearly to obscure those associated with her plans.'

'*Jenny*,' said Sophie, a pleading note creeping into her voice, 'you know I should have no objection, in the ordinary way, to a lecture on the art of scrying, but in this case—'

'I am coming to the point, Sophie, I assure you,' said Jenny. 'From what I have been able to see – and it is little enough, as I have tried to explain – Miss Callender's thoughts, at the time when last she handled this reticule, were on the subject of Mr Henry Taylor—'

'That, at least, is no surprise,' said Sophie, with a grim little nod. 'There is no use in my going to the park as Amelia to meet him, then, I suppose.'

'It would surprise you very much, if you had *seen* him,' said Joanna. Try as she might, she could not make the pieces fit. 'Truly, Sophie, I cannot imagine a man less likely to appeal to Amelia!'

'No doubt he will have found some way of making himself presentable,' said Sophie, waving an impatient hand. 'He is an educated mage, after all – and, by Gray's account, a dab hand at persuading people to do things they ought not. Jenny, what else has Amelia been thinking of?'

'Of Mr Taylor, as I have said,' said Jenny patiently, 'and of her father, and she seems to have been anticipating a journey across the Manche, to Trouville-sur-Mer or perhaps Honfleur. I must stress,' she added, reading their eagerness to start after this scent at once, 'that I cannot say what she *has* done, or where she has gone – only what she thought of doing, or meant to do. And of course it is not unlikely that Trouville-sur-Mer and Honfleur are only two of a long list of possible destinations on the Normand coast, which she happened to remember.'

'But,' said Sophie, 'but, Jenny, when you scried my stepfather's key-ring – over and over, you remember! – you learnt things from it which – what I mean is, *why* cannot you see anything of what Amelia is doing, or thinking, or feeling now?'

'I shall try again, naturally,' said Jenny. 'I shall try every day, if there seems any possibility of its being a useful undertaking. But, as we are speaking of that former example, do you not recall my saying that it was difficult to discover anything of use, because your step-father was so angry with you that I could see almost nothing else?'

Sophie nodded slowly. 'Yes,' she said after a moment. 'I see.'

Joanna let go Sophie's hand, felt about in the folds of her own sash, and after a moment succeeded in retrieving the forgotten copper coin. 'There is this,' she said, holding it out to Jenny. 'We thought the other must be the better source, because it had been hers so long, but . . .'

Jenny folded her long fingers – slender even now, though that would change in the months to come – around the not-quite-circle of dull copper; first one hand, then the other. 'Hmm,' she said, apparently to herself. Then once again she closed her eyes and sank into her scrying, lips moving silently through the words of her spell.

Her face grew pale, first by slow degrees, then all at once.

Joanna and Sophie exchanged anxious glances. Belatedly Joanna asked herself whether Jenny ought to have undertaken this task twice in such close succession (could not this second attempt, at least, have waited till after dinner?) – whether the first attempt had not been too draining in itself, without a second's being added to it – whether they were asking too much of her, and whether the consequence might be magick shock, or . . . something worse.

'But we must not interrupt,' said Sophie. Her face crimped unhappily; she shifted in her seat, and Joanna saw that she was actually sitting on her hands.

Jenny opened her eyes with a small, startled gasp; the copper coin fell from her hand, slid down the slope of her skirts, and rolled across the carpet until it ran against the toe of Sophie's shoe.

'Well,' said Jenny faintly, as Sophie bent to retrieve it. 'Well, certainly I did not expect *that*.'

Sophie laid the coin gingerly atop a nearby occasional table. 'Jo,' she said, 'will you go to the kitchen, please, and fetch back, er, some of Mrs Treveur's beef tea?'

As this irritatingly transparent attempt to get her out of the way – for what purpose, she could only speculate – was also more efficient than ringing for one of the servants to convey a message to Mrs Treveur, Joanna picked up her skirts and dashed down the servants' staircase to the kitchen, though not before glaring briefly at Sophie.

Persuading Mrs Treveur that there was no need to send for a healer (or for Lady Maëlle) took as much time as fetching out and warming the beef tea; when at last Joanna regained Jenny's room, she found a fire dancing in the grate and Jenny and Sophie perched side by side on the chaise longue, heads bent together as though studying something. A fluffy woollen shawl was incongruously wrapped about Jenny's elegant gown of mulberry-coloured silk. Moving closer with her heavy tray, Joanna discovered the object of their study: Amelia's forgotten copper coin, dull and beginning to go green, lay in Sophie's open palm, and beside it another, bright-new, of more or less the same size and shape.

'What has that coin to tell us, that the other had not?' she inquired.

She set down the covered tray upon the hearth, then handed

the cup and spoon up to Jenny, who grimaced at the smell but, at Joanna's severe look, meekly set to.

'There is something very odd about this coin, Jenny says,' said Sophie, holding up the two for Joanna's inspection, 'so we thought to compare it to an ordinary one, and look!'

Joanna looked.

The new coin was indeed perfectly ordinary: on the obverse, a head in profile, recognisable as that of His Majesty the King, and the legend *HENRICUS XII REX*; on the reverse, a stylised sandal of Mercury within a laurel-wreath, and the previous year's date.

The other had been frequently clipped and was half grown over with verdigris, but closer examination revealed that it was not, as first Gwendolen and then Joanna and Sophie had supposed, otherwise an ordinary product of His Majesty's mint. The profile on the obverse was not King Henry's, nor his father's or grandfather's; the lettering round the rim was half clipped away, but Joanna could just make out *ANS* along the right-hand edge, and *FRA* along the left. On the reverse, what at first appeared to be a bundle of sticks resolved itself, when held at a particular angle to the light, into a fleur-de-lys.

'That is not so very strange, is it?' she said, after a thoughtful moment. 'This coin is a long way from home, certainly; but if it was Amelia's, then it came here by way of Breizh, and coin from the Duchies crosses into Breizh and Maine and Normandie often enough in the course of trade, when relations are good.'

She studied Jenny's troubled expression, relieved to see that at any rate her face was no longer the colour of a tallow-candle.

'There is something else, I collect,' she said. 'What is it?'

Jenny swallowed another spoonful of beef tea, then set the half-empty vessel aside and folded her hands upon her knee. 'The coin was Amelia's, in fact,' she said, 'but only very lately;

she did not acquire it in the course of some ordinary transaction, but received it – received an entire purse of coin from the same source, not only copper but silver and gold – by the hand of a stranger, with instructions for its conveyance to some third person.'

'But *who*?' Joanna demanded.

'Had I been able to identify either of these mysterious persons,' said Jenny mildly, 'I should already have told you so. I was not.'

'And who made the coin?' said Joanna, in a more moderate tone – there was certainly nothing to be gained from antagonising Jenny. 'Or ordered it made? And where?'

Jenny shook her head. 'It was not made in Britain,' she said, 'but that much we knew already. The reverse is a fleur-de-lys; one or other of the Duchies seems indicated, as you have remarked yourself. More than that, at present, I cannot say.'

From below came the bright peal of the dinner-bell.

'Do you feel well enough to come down with us, Jenny?' said Sophie, laying a hand over Jenny's, still clasped upon her knee. 'You are still a little pale, I think – Jo, do you not think so?'

'I am perfectly well,' said Jenny firmly, before Joanna could make any reply; rising from her seat, she put off her shawl and went to the mirror to scrutinise her hair. This done, she turned back to them, hands on hips, and added, 'Come along!'

Joanna and Sophie followed her obediently out of the room. If Joanna chanced to remark that Jenny's gait was a trifle more measured than ordinarily, or that she kept a firmer hold of the bannister when descending the stairs, she was not so foolish as to mention it aloud.

CHAPTER XVI

In Which Gray Receives a Commission

There were guests for dinner, whom it had been too late to put off: Sir Herbert and Lady Beaumont, their eldest son, and their daughter, upon whom Mrs Marshall had matrimonial designs on behalf of her son Alan; for after the first, shocked reaction to Kergabet's news of the escaped prisoners, Mrs Marshall had quickly returned her attention to her chief aim in coming to London. Miss Beaumont was a perfectly inoffensive young lady – indeed, thought Sophie, she was very pretty, with her tawny-gold hair, finely sculpted features, and warm smile – and perfectly friendly to Mrs Marshall; the enthusiasm which the latter (and possibly also Lady Beaumont) supposed that young lady to possess for the absent Alan, however, appeared entirely her own invention.

Nevertheless Jenny had, at her mother's request, invited Miss Beaumont and her parents not only to eat dinner but also to spend the evening in Grosvenor Square. The evening party was to include more than a dozen further guests, among them – and here Sophie anticipated considerable chagrin on her mother-in-law's part – three unmarried young men, all of them personable, reasonably intelligent, and of larger fortune than Alan Marshall, as well as Madame de Courcy and her two eldest daughters.

Jenny had also intervened – or, rather, had outmanoeuvred her mother's intervention – in the seating arrangements, so that Miss Beaumont was seated to Sieur Germain's left, with Gray on her other side, and as far as possible from Mrs Marshall.

No one mentioned Amelia. Lady Maëlle, Sophie discovered, had invented an invitation from a cousin to an extended house-party at the fictional cousin's husband's estate in Kent, received by Amelia in the course of the previous se'nnight and taken up yesterday afternoon. Being who and what she was, she had succeeded in persuading Mrs Marshall to swallow this unlikely tale as though it were entirely plausible, first, that Amelia should have been in possession of a cousin with an estate in Kent and said nothing of it to anyone, and, second, that she should have abandoned London for the country when the London season was yet in full swing. And now, though Sophie knew her to be furious with Amelia, furious with herself, and half sick with fear that something far worse than an ill-considered elopement might have befallen her, she was calmly eating quail *en croûte* and discussing the relative merits of two different breeds of sheep with Sir Herbert Beaumont.

Where Lady Maëlle had been since leaving Sophie and Joanna alone with Katell, Sophie had not the least idea. There had been no opportunity before dinner to convey to her what Katell had confessed, or what Jenny's scrying had discovered, and Sophie itched with the desire to do so – to, if she were honest with herself, lay the whole of it before her erstwhile guardian like a child bringing her small woes to her mama.

Instead, however, she gathered her wandering wits, turned to the young man at her side, and in as ordinary a tone as she could manage said, 'Have you been long in London, Mr Trenoweth?'

Mr Trenoweth smiled winningly. 'A twelvemonth only,' he said.

'And how do you find it?'

'I find it very well supplied with beauty,' said Mr Trenoweth.

'And with dancing, and spritely conversation. I am very fond of dancing,' he added.

As Sophie was also very fond of dancing, this topic served them well for some time.

'I hope Miss Callender may be enjoying herself in Kent,' said Mr Trenoweth at length.

This remark rather startled Sophie, both by its unexpected consonance with her own thoughts and because she had not known Amelia and Mr Trenoweth to be at all acquainted with one another. When she did not at once reply, Mr Trenoweth frowned at her and said in quite a different tone, 'Mrs Marshall, are you quite well? You are very pale.'

Sophie drew her mother's magick about her, imagining it as a veil – so finely woven as to be nearly invisible, yet obscuring the truth of her feelings from her face – and said, 'Perfectly well, I thank you. I hope the same. I am not acquainted with these cousins, but my sister seems to have been pleased by the invitation.'

She had learnt from Joanna, though not without many a painful moment of revelation, the trick of telling plausible lies: only the word *cousins* was genuinely untrue.

'You are acquainted with the Mesdemoiselles de Courcy, however, are you not?' said Mr Trenoweth. His tone was light, almost offhand, but his expression betrayed his interest.

'A little, yes,' she said. 'The eldest is a great friend of my sister Joanna and of Miss Pryce.'

'They are known in London society to be *clever* and *bookish*,' said Mr Trenoweth. 'One does not altogether know what to make of such remarks.'

'Indeed?' Sophie raised her eyebrows. 'Speaking for myself, I think I should begin by considering their source.'

A sudden, startling grin flashed over his face, there and gone in a moment. 'That is the interesting thing, you see,' he said, sinking his voice to a confidential murmur. 'I have heard my sister call them so, and Miss Callender – Miss Joanna, that is – do so also; yet they do not appear to mean at all the same thing by the words.'

'I see,' said Sophie, who thought she did. 'If I may contribute my pinch of salt to the soup-pot' – this was an expression adopted from Donella MacHutcheon – 'I am not so well acquainted with the ladies in question as either Jenny or Joanna, but what I do know of them, I like very much. Mademoiselle de Courcy, I believe, is a great student of politics and of history, and I have heard my sister say that Mademoiselle Héloïse – she is talented, you know, which her sisters are not – takes a considerable interest in alchymy.'

'Does she, indeed,' said Mr Trenoweth, thoughtfully. 'And, if I may ask – I fear it is a great impertinence! – what think you of Miss Beaumont?'

Startled, Sophie glanced down the table at her, and found her smiling up at Sieur Germain. Too far away to distinguish their words, Sophie nonetheless thought she recognised her brother-in-law's expression as akin to the look of kindly but slightly weary patience he so often wore when conversing with Mrs Edmond Marshall.

'I think,' she said after a moment, choosing her words carefully, 'that Miss Beaumont is a kind, sweet, biddable young lady, who has not had much encouragement to think for herself.'

Mr Trenoweth followed her gaze, his thoughtful frown deepening. 'Hmm,' he said.

Then the table turned with the next course, and Sophie left Mr Trenoweth to the care of Jenny and talked determinedly of nature-poetry, Latin and Gaelic and English, to Mr Fowler, until the end of the meal.

'A word, if you please, Marshall,' said Sieur Germain quietly, drawing Gray aside with a hand on his shoulder.

'Sir?' Gray followed obediently, and not so quickly as to draw attention; when they had reached the secluded corner behind Miss Pryce's harp, he asked, 'Have you had news of the prisoners?'

'Yes,' said Sieur Germain, 'and no. There have been reports, of course, almost since the moment their escape became public knowledge – sightings of them in every hole and corner of the kingdom, and it is a task for Hercules himself to discover which of them may be true ones, if any. But our business together is something else entirely.'

Gray turned so as to continue looking at him whilst also keeping the rest of the party in his line of sight.

'As you know,' Sieur Germain continued, 'I have – or, rather, His Majesty has – agents in cities and towns across the Duchies, all of whom send in ciphered dispatches as best they may; their reports do not always arrive regularly, or in the intended sequence, and at times rumour is reported as fact, and only later corrected. When first one of our men in Touraine reported that local men were being recruited to serve a man calling himself Imperator Gallia, as you may perhaps remember, we all thought it as likely to be a practical joke as not—'

Gray nodded; he did remember, and could not deny that the notion still struck him as unlikely to the point of absurdity.

'Yet this same man – or, rather, the same title, whether or not the same man is meant – has been mentioned in no fewer than half a dozen other agents' dispatches since, which of course is not proof but does suggest that there exists something worth investigating.

'Moreover, dispatches from our border garrisons in Breizh, in Maine, and in Normandie have lately reported that some large force is massing beyond the Loire, and another in the Comté de Blois and northward, on the borders of Maine and Normandie. The arms of Blois have been sighted, and of Anjou, Poitou, Touraine, and Acquitaine, among others—'

'Together?' said Gray, astonished.

Though no great follower of politics, and still less of military campaigns, he was at any rate aware that the Comté de Blois and the Comté de Poitou had been making attempts these seventy years and more to wrest the territory of Anjou – which, with the Comté de Touraine and the British province of Maine, lay between their own – from the Duc d'Acquitaine, each claiming a right, on behalf of their respective liege-lords, to defend it from the depredations of the other, and from the no longer particularly credible threat of British reconquest. Even had one of them prevailed at last, what could have induced the others suddenly to make common cause?

'Indeed,' his brother-in-law said dryly. 'You will thus perhaps understand the Privy Council's . . . curiosity.'

'Certainly,' said Gray, 'but—'

'Now, all of this is very curious, of course; but more lately my colleagues and I have ceased to be intrigued, and begun to be alarmed, for the reports we have been accustomed to receive have grown more infrequent, and for the last fortnight have ceased altogether. And that, Marshall, is where you come in.'

'I beg your pardon, sir,' said Gray, equally baffled and alarmed, 'but I do not see . . .'

'Do you not?' Sieur Germain chuckled, but quite without humour. 'Miss Joanna warned me to expect as much, I admit.' Whilst Gray was digesting this rather extraordinary remark, he continued, 'I wish to send you as my eyes and ears to Ivry, on the River Eure, where we have a cavalry regiment garrisoned and, as it seems, a large mixed force from several of the Duchies encamped opposite, lest we be tempted to cross the river, one supposes. And, from Ivry, where the trail leads you – without stirring up further hostilities, that is, for we have enough to be going on with at present without making, or provoking, an outright declaration of war.

'What has become of our agents in the Duchies? Can all of them have been captured? Killed? Suborned? How, and by whom? Who is it that calls himself Emperor of Gaul – if such a person exists indeed – and what is he about? And,' he added, 'it will not have escaped your notice that according to your sister's scrying, the absent Miss Callender was bound in the same general direction when she departed this house – or, at any rate, believed herself to be so.'

Gray discovered that he was gaping, and shut his mouth with a snap. 'I,' he began, and stopped. 'Do not misunderstand me; I am eager to be of service, as I have said – and also to ensure Miss Callender's safety; but I confess I do not altogether see why I should be more suited for *this* service than another. There must be . . . officers – agents – men trained to such work, and familiar with the territory—'

'Indeed,' said Sieur Germain once more, 'but none whom I, and the redoubtable Lady Maëlle, can trust as we both trust you.'

Gray swallowed against an incipient stammer. 'I thank you,' he managed, 'very much indeed. Both of you. May I ask, however—'

'Certainly you may.'

'Do I reason correctly, from your talk of trust and the lack thereof, that you also have reason to suspect the existence of . . . sympathisers . . . within Britain's own ranks?'

'It is not impossible,' said Kergabet gravely, 'though at present I have no specific suspicions of the kind. You hesitate,' he added – Gray's ears burnt in embarrassment – 'yet I know you do not lack for courage. You have reservations as to some aspect of the business; explain them to me.'

'I hesitate,' said Gray, 'because I cannot imagine what qualifications – beyond my loyalty to my kingdom, and your trust in me – I might possibly possess for a reconnaissance mission on the borders of the Duchies, with daring rescue to follow.'

Kergabet's eyebrows rose. 'Can you not?' he enquired. 'You have been trained in defensive magicks; you have seen battle, of a sort; you are an educated man, and a student of languages as well as a powerful mage; you have survived several months' imprisonment and' – a delicate pause; then – '*mistreatment* at the hands of a most unscrupulous enemy, and even when rescue seemed most remote, did not agree to his demands. Can you truly imagine no reason for my choice?'

Gray blinked.

'By that account,' he said slowly, 'I should seem the best man for the post.' He did not add that the said account did not sound to him at all like a description of himself.

'Indeed,' said Sieur Germain, with a small chuckle behind his hand.

A more urgent thought occurred to Gray, 'You are aware, I am sure, of what befell Sophie, whilst I was imprisoned in Alba?'

Kergabet sobered abruptly. 'Certainly I am,' he said.

'Then you will understand . . .' Gray hesitated. But Kergabet *would* understand, if any man could. 'You will understand that I should prefer to have Sophie with me, as a partner in this undertaking.'

'Graham,' said Kergabet. Having made this startling beginning, he paused, folded his arms, and regarded Gray long and thoughtfully before speaking again. 'I am well enough acquainted with your character, I believe, to feel certain that you should never have made this suggestion, even to me, unless in your considered opinion the danger to her were less – or at least no greater – in accompanying you than in remaining here.'

'That is so, sir,' said Gray gratefully.

'That being said, however,' his brother-in-law continued, 'it is not I who must be convinced, you understand, but the Princess's father; and I tell you frankly that the odds of your succeeding in that endeavour are infinitesimally small.'

Gray nodded, disappointed but unsurprised. His Majesty – who knew Gray so little, and Sophie scarcely more – would not see, as Kergabet had done, the extent to which Gray's request grew from a concern for Sophie's . . . not *safety*, for to attempt to keep Sophie safe was akin to clipping the wings of an osprey and keeping it in a cage, but her happiness and well-being. He would understand it, rather, as reflecting selfishness on Gray's part, or headstrong foolishness on Sophie's.

Yet the thought of once more subjecting Sophie to the distresses of a separation – of doing so willingly and deliberately – and, almost worse, the prospect of breaking the news to her of his departure on an adventure in which she could take no part, and of which he could tell her almost nothing . . .

On the other hand, was it likely that he should be knocked on the head, taken captive, and held under interdiction, as he had been in Alba? The former, he conceded, was not out of the realm of possibility, though he hoped he should not be so caught off his guard a second time; but that an army on the move should have any means to hold a mage under interdiction – no, surely not.

So far, so reassuring; unfortunately, Gray could not help following out this line of reasoning to its logical conclusion: *Far safer and easier to execute him on the spot.*

He swallowed. 'I doubt not you are right, sir.'

'Are you *mad*?'

'*Cariad*—'

Gray shut his mouth abruptly as Sophie whirled to face him across the expanse of their bedroom, more nearly afraid of her than he had ever been before. The gods knew that he had witnessed more

than one display of fury, of outrage, of self-destructive anguish –
had been caught up in the destructive wash of her magick, had
suffered for it, though never so painfully as Sophie herself – but
never till this moment had that fury, that outrage, that anguish,
with all the force of their shared magick behind it, been directed
squarely and consciously at *him*.

He had not expected her to be *pleased* by Kergabet's proposal to
send him alone to the Normand border, or with his own inclination
to accept it – naturally not. After all, however, she had encouraged
him to work with Lord de Vaucourt, despite the latter's making it
insultingly clear that her own assistance was not wanted; she had
conceded, if reluctantly, to his meeting with Henry Taylor, before
Amelia's flight rendered the subject moot. Had he not had some
justification for supposing that she might be similarly understanding
in this case?

Sophie's face was starkly pale, save the twin scarlet patches of
her cheeks; her eyes, darkened from warm brown to the black
of water under river-ice, sparked dangerously, and her hands
clenched ivory-knuckled in the folds of her sea-green gown.

'I had rather go with you than alone, love,' Gray said. She glared
at him, dashed furious tears from her eyes with one trembling hand,
but appeared to be letting him speak. 'Can you doubt it? I had a
thousand times rather have you with me, for my own sake; and for
yours, I had rather – I had *always* rather – you had useful work to do
than be mewed up in idleness, waiting. But can you not see – it is as
you told me, when Vaucourt would not accept your help, though he
so badly needed it – this is a matter of more import than either of us.'

To his vast (if secret) relief, Sophie appeared to be listening.

'Kergabet has not much liking for the notion of sending you into
what may soon become a field of battle,' Gray continued, 'but if the
choice were his alone, I believe he should agree to it, for he knows

both of us well enough to . . . to *believe* what we may be capable of, if he cannot altogether understand it. But, Sophie, it is not Kergabet who must be persuaded, and certainly not I; and I cannot blame him for wishing to set things in motion at once, rather than spending' – he had nearly, disastrously, said *wasting* – 'the gods know how much time in attempting to persuade your father.'

'*I* could persuade him,' said Sophie darkly. 'As I persuaded your mama to leave off her badgering, not so long ago—'

'But you would not,' said Gray, attempting to keep his tone both gentle and implacable. 'Not in such a case. And, besides, love, that is a method for the moment only; you should not be out of his sight for a quarter of an hour before he had all of London in an uproar, searching for you to bring you back to him, when instead—'

'When instead we ought all to be seeking the Professor et al., yes,' said Sophie.

The righteous fury had all gone out of her now, and left her resigned and sadly diminished. Gray – near tears himself, to his shame, for he liked leaving her no more than she liked his going – held out his arms, and Sophie crept into them.

'You will come back to me,' she said, her voice muffled by the fabric of his coat. 'You will come back safe, and not . . . not . . .' What words was she repressing, behind that swallowed sob? 'Promise me.'

'Of course, love.' Gray bent to kiss the top of Sophie's ear. *And if by some mischance I am too long about it for your liking, I expect you shall turn up again to rescue me.*

CHAPTER XVII

In Which Sophie Loses an Argument

Sophie saw Gray off just after sunrise – with solemn, quiet dignity, their true farewells having been made in the privacy of their bedroom, in the course of the night just past – and, having watched the anonymous hired carriage round the turning of Grosvenor Square and out of sight, turned back towards the house and climbed the steps with leaden feet. At the top of the steps she paused for a long moment, breathing slowly and carefully, and drew the veil of her concealing magick over herself from head to toes. *I am carved from marble, like the statues of Ceres and Proserpina in the square. I am clothed in armour as wise Minerva, and no barbed word can pierce it.*

Then she pushed open the door.

Breakfast was a painful ordeal, and Sophie escaped Mrs Marshall's volubility, Sieur Germain's silent remorse, and the cautious, quiet compassion of everyone else, as soon as she decently could, wishing all the while that she had thought to ask for her breakfast on a tray in her room.

Having retreated thither, however, she found it still worse, strewn with Gray's possessions – those not needed for his journey rooted out of their proper places and not yet tidied away – but firmly and indefinitely bereft of Gray himself; having indulged in a brief, useless, and infuriating fit of weeping, she smoothed away the evidence of her distress, tidied her hair, put on her best hat, and went downstairs to request conveyance to the Royal Palace.

Sophie had never before sought an audience with the King of her own volition, without prior invitation, and the process proved frustratingly lengthy – a just punishment, Sophie reflected, for her frequent reluctance to visit her father. *After all, he is the King of Britain; he has more pressing matters to attend to than a visit without portfolio from a wayward child.*

Or had he, on the contrary, deduced the purpose of her visit, and did he seek to avoid discussing it?

In any event, after being twice told that His Majesty was occupied with urgent business, and on a third visit kicking her heels in the rose-garden for well over an hour, she was at last summoned by a steward and conducted to His Majesty's study.

'Sophia!' King Henry rose from behind his desk and came forward to kiss her. 'You are well my dear, I hope?'

'Father,' she said, attempting a smile. 'I am well enough; and yourself?'

'As you say,' he replied, drawing her with him to sit on a lion-footed sofa at the far end of the room from the desk. 'Well enough.'

They spoke for some time – a little awkwardly, perhaps, but no more so than was usual for the two of them – of matters of mutual interest; the health and well-being of the Grosvenor Square family and of Queen Edwina and her sons having been duly canvassed, His Majesty revealed that the King's Own Cavalry Regiment, in which Prince Edward held a captain's commission, was preparing for active duty in Normandie, and wished to know how, in Sophie's opinion, matters stood between Prince Roland and Lucia MacNeill – which forced Sophie to admit to herself, if not to him, that she had no longer the least idea.

At last she could bear the weight of her unspoken purpose no longer, and without further preamble said, 'Do not you think, Father, that I have a duty to assist in the search for my sister?'

King Henry raised his fine-drawn white brows. 'Your sister?' he said.

'Stepsister, then,' said Sophie impatiently. 'We were brought up together, in the same house, the same family, such as it was; my mother was the only one Amelia ever knew, for her own died when Amelia was no more than a baby. We believed ourselves sisters for seventeen years; and I am capable of many things, Father, but not of overcoming an attachment seventeen years in the making.'

A year ago, three years ago, indeed, she should not have believed herself capable of such a speech; for some time before the sudden and irreversible disruption of their lives, Amelia and she had antagonised one another as, perhaps, only sisters can, when the comradeship of childhood has been curdled by jealousy and resentments only too clearly understood. But now Amelia was missing, very likely in dire trouble, and whatever Sophie's feelings towards her might be in the ordinary way, it was impossible to imagine abandoning her to her fate.

'And Lord Kergabet has sent Gray to Normandie to look for her,' she continued, rising from the sofa and turning to face her father. 'Not that only, of course, but partly that.' She had been wrong, she saw by his expression of surprise, to suppose that he had guessed her reason for wishing to see him; had he thought that Gray should for a moment consider not telling her where he was going, and why? 'I am only asking to be permitted to follow him there, and help in whatever way I am able.'

'It is quite impossible for you to go to Normandie, my dear,' said His Majesty. To his credit, he spoke regretfully, but a reluctant denial was a denial nevertheless, and brooked no protest.

Sophie drew breath, nevertheless, and made one. 'On the contrary, Father,' she said, 'it is quite impossible for me to remain here without my husband. You have not forgotten, I hope, what

239

befell the last time Gray and I were separated by hundreds of miles?'

Gray, had he been present, might have pointed out (as he had pointed out to her during one of the quietly stormy conversations that preceded his departure) that unless the separation were a long one, and as he was not likely to be imprisoned under interdiction in the course of this journey, the likelihood of those consequences' being repeated was small. He might very well have been swayed, too, by the King's perfectly sensible assertions as to the dangers to which she would be exposed, so near the contested borders.

He was not present, however, being at that moment somewhere between London and the military garrison at Ivry, on the River Eure, and Sophie therefore felt entirely free to make use of whatever weapons might best serve her purpose.

'Sophia, a cavalry regiment is no place for a woman—'

'Have none of the officers wives, or daughters?' Sophie persisted. She turned on her heel and began to pace, lest the nervous energy engendered by this conversation spill out in some less acceptable manner.

She knew, and her father must also be well aware, that armies attracted camp-followers – the wives and sisters and daughters of the common soldiers, who in return for a half share of the daily ration did the cooking and washing for their own men and many others besides – and that therefore it was entirely likely that the Ivry garrison had already plenty of female inhabitants. *It is no place for a* gentlewoman, *I suppose he means.*

Rather than giving voice to any of these unhelpful thoughts, she said, 'Women serve in Donald MacNeill's household guard. Ceana MacGregor – Lucia's guard captain – was the finest archer of her clan when she was my age.'

Her father raised his eyebrows.

'I may not be capable of drawing a bow or swinging a sword,' said Sophie, in answer to his unspoken question, halting and folding her arms, 'but a mage-officer trained me in defensive and offensive magicks. I am not helpless, Father, I assure you!'

The King sighed. 'It is not that I think you helpless, my dear,' he said. 'Only that I do not wish to fling you headlong into danger, to no good purpose.'

'But you are sending Ned,' said Sophie quietly.

Ned will be King of Britain one day, he might have replied, *and her defence is part of his duty*; or, *Ned has been trained in arms, and in defensive magicks, since he was a child.* He might even have circled back to his original argument, by pointing out that Ned was a man, and she a woman, and the battlefield was not her place.

Sophie was prepared to rebut any or all of these answers: she was the Princess Royal and owed a duty to her kingdom as much as Ned did; she had seen real combat (if on a small scale), as he had not. Instead, however, her father looked at her with every one of his years writ clearly on his face, with the weariness of ages in his blue eyes (so like her brothers'; so different from her own), and said, 'I have lost you once, Sophia. I could not bear to lose you a second time, knowing so well what I had lost.'

Oh, Ned, thought Sophie, adding this to her mental list of things which she knew but must never reveal to any of her brothers.

'Papa,' she said – she had never called him so before, but the word was out before she could think better of it – 'you cannot protect me by packing me in goose-down and locking me up in a strongbox until the trouble is over! When you opened the box again, Gray and I should both be withered away, as we nearly were when he was Cormac MacAlpine's prisoner in Alba, and all your precautions wasted.'

She drew nearer to him, and dared to lay a hand upon his arm; he was looking down at her with such intensity, and wearing such a stricken expression, that she scarcely knew how to meet his gaze.

'You do not love me any the less, I think,' she continued, nevertheless, 'because I am not so biddable as I might be, or so eager to please.'

As she had hoped, this drew a wry smile and a fond, if rueful, chuckle. 'No, indeed,' the King conceded.

'And I swear by the Lady Diana,' said Sophie, taking her courage in both hands, 'by fleet-footed Mercury and Ceres of the hearth, that I can be of far more use to you – to the kingdom – in the field than I could possibly be at home. Only send me where my husband is, Father, and you shall see what we may accomplish together.'

It was not an idle promise; though each of them might be powerful alone, the rite of marriage *confarreatio* had linked their magicks so that together, working in concert, they were capable of quite remarkable things. Reminding His Majesty of the grave dangers of their connexion had perhaps begun to sap his determination to keep her here – out of one sort of danger, but bearing steadily towards the other; slowly, if distance were the only thing separating them, but with terrifying rapidity if things were to go ill with Gray, as they had in Alba – and Sophie hoped that this recollection of its power might complete that work.

Truly, however, she had always felt at sea in her dealings with her father – this near-stranger who knew at once so much of her and so very, very little – and the present conversation was no different.

King Henry, as Sophie had remarked before, knew the value of patient silence in unsettling his opponent. He deployed this weapon now, watching her calmly as she struggled to keep silence also; and before long she broke.

'I shall run away after him if I must,' she said, recklessly honest. 'I had rather not – I had very much rather not – I do know the duty I owe to you, Father, though you may not think it – but I shall not let any harm come to Gray on my account.'

'I do not doubt it,' said her father, disconcertingly calm. *Does he suppose I do not mean what I say?*

'A-and if I am forced to run away,' Sophie went on, 'I shall be all alone, or as good as; I cannot ask anyone else to follow me against your wishes—'

'Sophia!' The King held up a hand, and Sophie's impassioned argument fell away into silence. Again he let the silence stretch, until at last he said 'It was foolish of me, of course, to suppose that you might have grown less reckless with age, or less single-minded. May I propose a compromise?'

His raised brows, the slight tilt of his chin, made clear that the question was not pro forma; if Sophie wished to know in what this compromise consisted, she must say so.

And do I so wish? She could not decide.

But if a path existed which did not require her either to submit to an indefinite separation or to defy her father outright and embark on a solitary flight across the kingdom, did she not owe it to Gray, and to herself, to seek it out?

'You may,' she said, folding her hands together to still their anxious fidgeting.

'Should you begin to experience any . . . symptoms which you recognise as connected with Mr Marshall's absence,' said His Majesty, 'or should you have reasonable grounds to suppose him likewise affected, you will inform me at once, so that I may arrange for his swift return; and in the meantime you will abide by my decisions on this question, and will give me your word not to attempt to follow him.'

Sophie pressed her hands together more tightly, and said nothing.

'However,' the King went on, 'I shall not insist on your kicking your heels at Court; so long as you are adequately guarded, I shall

243

make no objection to your travelling a little way – to Oxford, for example – should you have some project in view, which I believe you have. You should have less leisure to fret and borrow trouble, I think, if your mind were better occupied.'

'You mean, I collect,' said Sophie, 'that in exchange for my agreeing to stay quietly in England whilst Gray is risking his life in Normandie, I shall be indulged in my – what was it those learned Fellows called it? – my *philanthropic fervour*, with respect to Lady Morgan College? Are you certain, sir, that you wish to extend your hand into that particular hornets' nest at present?'

Her father winced, just perceptibly, at her tone. And truly, thought Sophie, was his approval of this venture of hers not precisely what she had been hoping for, when she read the profoundly irritating letter from which she had just been quoting? To do the thing openly and properly, with His Majesty's backing, and the resources to match her ambitions for the place, and a royal writ to fling in the teeth of those Fellows who thought it their right (nay, their calling) to thwart her?

But the price he asks . . .

She forced herself to consider the matter rationally. If only she could ask someone's advice – Gray's, of course, for preference, but then, if Gray were here, she should not have been in this equivocal position to begin with. Jenny or Lucia or Mór MacRury, Sophie was certain, would give her intelligent and sensible counsel; even Joanna could at least have offered another perspective on the matter, though Joanna's own decisions were as apt to be impetuous as soberly considered.

Well, then: if Gray were here, or Jenny or Lucia or any of them, how might they advise me in this case?

'May I,' she said, looking up at her father, 'may I have a little time to consider?'

'Certainly, my dear,' he said. He patted her shoulder – an awkward and diffident but oddly comforting gesture – and returned to his writing-desk, where he took up the topmost of a stack of dispatches and bent his gaze to it, effectively leaving her alone with her thoughts.

Sophie resumed her pacing, to and fro before the broad window, and began attempting to trammel the said thoughts into some sort of order.

First, then, the truth: her insistence on following Gray to Ivry was half anxiety (for Gray and, yes, for herself) as to the consequences of a separation, and half resentment at being mewed up in London, at loose ends and quite useless, whilst Gray and Ned and Sieur Germain and even, in her own small way, Joanna were doing their part against the twin threats of the Duchies and the escaped conspirators, and for the rescue of Amelia. No very noble motive, that – and undoubtedly His Majesty knew it.

A further truth: her motives for seeking the rebirth of Lady Morgan College were no less complicated, and perhaps no more likely to withstand scrutiny. Of course she wished – quite unselfishly, if she did not mistake her own feelings – that young women of scholarly bent should have the same opportunity as their brothers for useful and challenging study, without having to beg for a place at the University in Din Edin, an expedient to which very few of their fathers were likely to agree in any case. But, too, she smelt a mystery clinging round the walls of Lady Morgan College, and burnt to puzzle it out. Why had it, after centuries of modest but respected scholarship, having educated thousands of students – including several daughters of dukes and even kings – and easily holding its own with the newer men's colleges, having attracted the personal patronage of the Princesses Regent in the reign of Edward VI, suddenly been closed? And not simply closed, but very nearly erased from history?

Lady Morgan had not been the first Oxford college to close its doors; Bairstow, for instance, stood on the erstwhile site of another college, nearly as old as Merlin, and (according to the Museum of the History of Magick) set up explicitly as a rival to it. Beaufort College had opened with great fanfare under the patronage of the Duke of Somerset, and for nearly three hundred years had been a great success, even luring some notable Fellows away from Merlin; but before it reached its fourth century, it had begun to lose its Fellows, its students, and its reputation to its elder rival, and at last faded into obscurity, until its land had been purchased and its buildings improved and expanded, under the patronage of the Duke and Duchess of Grafton, into the present Bairstow College.

The whole of this history, with many additional minutiae which Sophie had not troubled to commit to memory, was documented in dozens of histories of Oxford, of magick in Britain, and of Beaufort and Bairstow Colleges, readily available in the library of this last as well as in those of Merlin College and of the Museum of the History of Magick. To judge by the extant recorded history of Lady Morgan College, on the other hand – as Lucia MacNeill had astutely remarked – the whole of it might as well have been plucked up from the bank of the Cherwell by a curious god or goddess and never seen again.

Except that the residents of Oxford, town and gown alike, saw it every day, half buried in rust and rubble and ivy, but unmistakably present – a corpse at the feast, so to speak.

Who owned the College buildings, and the land on which they stood, now that the College itself was no more? Why did no one seem to know, or even to wonder, and why had no one ever attempted (so far as Sophie had been able to discover) to make any other use of it? What, in the name of Clio, of Minerva, made all the histories stop short of the end of the tale?

Confess, Magistra Marshall: you fancy yourself a solver of mysteries, and worse than that, you fancy yourself cleverer than all those historians, than all the tens of thousands of Oxonians who have failed to solve the mystery since the Princess Edith Augusta's day.

If that is not hubris, my name is not Sophie Marshall.

Whatever her reasons – selfish or great-hearted, noble or altogether the reverse – certain it was that restoring Lady Morgan College to its former state was an aim dear to Sophie's heart. With the overt approval, if not the true patronage, of the King himself, that aim would become an attainable one; or, at the least, more attainable than formerly. A college, after all, is not only bricks and mortar, window-glass and furniture, pens and paper and books, but the people to use them – the Fellows, the tutors and lecturers, the students. Though sober reason told her that there had been clever, curious young women like herself in Lady Morgan's time and thereafter, and would be again, who would leap at the chance to study as eagerly as she had, what of all the fathers, the brothers, the husbands like Appius Callender, like Edmond and George Marshall, whom they should have to persuade to allow them that chance? And where should Sophie find the tutors and lecturers to teach them, when so many of the Fellows of other colleges had gone out of their way to express their disapprobation of the very notion?

There was, in other words, an uphill battle before her, in which even royal backing was no guarantee of victory.

Nevertheless, it was also true that were her father not making her this offer as a distraction, as a bribe to keep her feet safely (as he believed) on English soil and away from the armies of the Duchies – had there, in other words, not been far more urgent and important work for her to do, if only she were permitted to do it – she should not have hesitated even a moment before accepting it.

Am I truly considering cutting off my nose to spite my face?

She was wearing a path in the carpet of her father's study, Sophie found; she forced herself to stillness – swallowed hard – looked down at her clasped hands.

No.

'If I am to accept your terms,' she said at last, 'I must have your sworn word – your oath on . . . on the bones of my mother – that should Gray find himself in need of rescue – which the gods forbid! – there will be no delays, no arguments—'

'I am prepared to give my sworn word in the matter of a rescue mission,' her father said, holding up a hand to stem the mounting tirade, 'provided that it is understood that any such mission shall be undertaken by persons of suitable training and experience.'

Not, in other words, Sophie translated, *by yourself and your sister.* In fact, however – had he only been willing to acknowledge it – no person living could be better suited to this task than herself.

'Yes,' she said. 'That is understood, of course.'

In any case, we must pray that it does not come to that. Gray should not be wandering about Normandie alone, after all, but in the company of a regiment of soldiers; he was perfectly well able to look after himself, and, after the near-catastrophe in Alba, would be on his guard against . . . what? *There is the rub, indeed; he cannot know what awaits him there, and nor can any of us.*

'Then . . .' She hesitated, swallowing back what she feared might become bitter regrets; on no account would her father agree to her following Gray to Ivry, and it was futile to wish it, but remaining in England nevertheless felt like an abandonment. 'Then, yes, Father, I agree.'

Lucia was playing at chess with Roland – they were more or less evenly matched, being both apt to open with great caution and to grow increasingly reckless as the game progressed – when a discreet knock upon the half-open door of her sitting-room, where Ceana

MacGregor and Conall Barra MacNeill stood guard, heralded the arrival of Sophie Marshall.

She looked altogether wretched, and Lucia was half out of her seat, crying, 'Sophie! Whatever is the matter?' when Sophie's eye fell on Roland, turning towards her in alarm. Before Lucia's astonished eyes, Sophie's ashen cheeks warmed to a healthier colour, the reddening of recent tears faded from her eyes, and something almost like a smile curved her lips.

'You will never guess,' she said, in a voice, again, almost entirely like her own. 'My father has given me leave to mount an expedition to Oxford, and I am come to ask you – both of you, though I did not know that I should find Roland here – to be of the party.'

Roland, not surprisingly, was looking from Lucia to Sophie and back again, wearing a frankly baffled expression. During his convalescence – or at any rate until her stepfather's escape from imprisonment had prompted her brother-in-law to confine her to the house – Sophie had been a regular visitor, and Lucia had believed the pair of them to be developing something approaching mutual confidence. It seemed, however, that Sophie was not prepared to allow her brother to witness her present distress, or to know its cause.

'Of course we should be delighted!' said Lucia.

'Yes, of course,' Roland agreed, ready enough despite his evident puzzlement; getting into the spirit of the thing, he said, 'When does this expedition of yours set forth?'

'I . . . I hardly know,' said Sophie. She reached for the high back of Roland's chair, which was nearest, misjudged the distance, and swayed on her feet.

Lucia's heart plummeted into her boots; Roland leapt up, knocking the chessboard askew and half the chessmen onto the floor, and each of them caught one of Sophie's elbows to guide her into the seat he had vacated.

'Roland,' said Lucia sharply, 'fetch your sister a cup of tea – put a great deal of honey in it, if you please – and whatever cakes may be left from the tea-tray—'

She desisted – he was already up and moving, pouring honey into her own empty teacup with one hand and sweeping a dozen uneaten cakes and petits fours onto a clean plate with the other – and dropped to her knees beside Sophie.

'What is it?' she demanded, low. She spoke in Gaelic; it would not prevent Roland from understanding, but it would at any rate slow him down. 'Something is very much amiss; if I did not know better, I should say—'

'Kergabet has sent Gray to Normandie,' said Sophie miserably, in the same tongue. 'To spy for him – he believes there may be traitors in the ranks of my father's army – and to look for my sister Amelia, who has run away with one of my stepfather's henchmen, or so we have concluded. And,' she added in quite a different tone, sitting up straighter and scrubbing one forearm roughly across her eyes, 'I ought not to have told you any of that, so you will forget all of it straight away, if you please.'

Roland appeared at Lucia's shoulder with the cup of heavily sweetened tea and the plate of cakes; Lucia took them from him with a smile of thanks, set the plate upon the abandoned chessboard, and thrust the teacup into Sophie's hands.

'Drink this,' she said firmly, reverting to Latin, 'and when you are feeling more yourself, you shall tell us all about it.'

PART THREE

Oxford and Ivry

CHAPTER XVIII

In Which Gray Occasions Some Surprise

It was a little past noon on a blazing-blue Marday when a Normand farmer's cart – driven by the farmer's stocky, tow-headed fifteen-year-old son, whose conversation through the whole of their slow, bone-rattling journey had, despite Gray's efforts, consisted entirely in variations on the two themes of *When I am old enough to go as a soldier* . . . and *If my father knew what my sister Ginette has been at with that Breizhek corporal* . . . – deposited Gray before a beflagged and imposing tent in the military encampment east of the city of Ivry. Having assisted in disentangling his passenger's belongings from the cured hams and rounds of cheese which constituted the remainder of his cargo, and tucking away with a broad grin the coins Gray dropped into his hand, the boy vaulted back up onto the driving-seat, took up the reins, and clucked his father's patient draught horses into motion.

'*Au revoir, monsieur!*' he called cheerfully over his shoulder as the cart trundled away.

The large young men standing sentry outside the tent eyed Gray with disfavour. Gray, however, had stared down, if not *many* a greater man, at any rate more than one; and, though not so broad in the beam as these fellows, he was half a head taller than either. 'I am to report to Colonel Dubois,' he said, drawing himself up very straight. 'My name is Marshall; I have letters for him from London.'

The sentries' expressions of distrust were altered not at all by this explanation, but the left-hand one did unbend so far as to say, 'Wait here, sir, and I'll enquire.'

He turned on one heel and vanished into the tent. His fellow contrived somehow to stare straight ahead whilst nevertheless visibly keeping Gray under his eye. The effect was rather unnerving; were they trained up to it, Gray wondered, or were men chosen for this duty because they possessed a natural gift for silent, stolid intimidation?

Surprisingly quickly, the vanished sentry reappeared, holding open the tent-flap and gesturing Gray within.

Colonel Dubois, at first blush, answered Gray's every expectation of the archetypal regimental commander; standing tall and straight behind his desk to receive his visitor, he possessed a cragged and weathered face bisected on the vertical by a nose as crooked as Gray's own – perhaps for the same reason – and on the horizontal by pale sharp eyes which swept over Gray's person in a single assessing glance. Only in one particular did he deviate from the Platonic ideal: he had evidently been working in his shirt-sleeves, for his regimental coat hung by its shoulders from the back of his chair.

'You have letters for me?' he said, holding out one hand.

'Yes, sir,' said Gray. Outside the Colonel's tent, he had stood to attention in a conscious attempt to intimidate the suspicious sentry; here, before the man himself, he found himself doing so quite involuntarily. He handed over Kergabet's letter of introduction, and with it the file of documents, tied up in red tapes, which until this morning had lain concealed beneath the lining of his trunk.

Colonel Dubois set aside the dossier and, following a minute examination of Kergabet's seal, broke open the letter. Gray watched him reading it, noting that he wore his chestnut-coloured hair longer than was the fashion in England, drawn back tightly and clubbed at the nape of his neck, and that it was liberally, but unevenly, streaked with grey; that three fingers of his left hand bore unmistakable evidence of having been broken and then poorly set, without benefit of a healer (talented or otherwise); and that there depended from his waistcoat pocket, on a sturdy leather thong, a soldier's talisman in silver, stamped with the emblem of Mars on one face and of Mithras on the other.

At length Colonel Dubois looked up. 'Have you never thought, yourself, Mr Marshall,' he said, 'of accepting a commission?'

Gray blinked. 'There was some thought at one time, indeed, of my going into His Majesty's service,' he said, carefully eliding the ownership of these thoughts, 'but in the end I proved better fitted for a scholar than an officer.'

'A pity, that,' said Colonel Dubois. 'There is a great demand for men of your particular talents.'

'My talents, sir?' Gray enquired, puzzled. What in Hades was in that letter of Kergabet's? 'Er – you mean a facility with languages, I suppose?'

'Languages?' The Colonel's eyebrows inched up his forehead like chestnut-furred caterpillars. 'No, of course not. Mr Marshall, Lord Kergabet gives me to understand that you are a shape-shifter – is it not so?'

Oh. 'Yes, sir; it is certainly true. I did not – that is, I was not aware of Lord Kergabet's having mentioned the matter to you.'

'And, if I may enquire, your other form is . . . ?'

Gray blinked again. 'An owl, sir,' he said. 'A Great Grey. It is native to—'

'A night-scout, by Mithras!' Colonel Dubois exclaimed. 'Yes, a great pity that you should be wasted in a library carrel.'

Rather than pursue this line of conversation, however, he reached for the file Gray had brought him, untied the tapes, and began reading through the topmost of the papers within, whilst Gray stood silently pondering what the next move in the game might be, and studying with interest the interior of the first military command-post he had ever seen. It was, in its way, not unlike the rooms of many a Fellow, lecturer, or student of his acquaintance – spartan in appearance, filled with the tools and detritus of an all-consuming profession – but meticulously well ordered. The interior was lit by a magelight lantern suspended from the tent's central peak; that it was magelight was apparent from its steady, silent glow and the lack of heat or smoke, but its colour was strange, a warm yellow rather than the usual cool blue-white.

'The quartermaster uses coloured glass in the lanterns,' said Colonel Dubois. Gray started slightly – had his host been reading his thoughts? – but, of course, he must still have been gazing at the ceiling, puzzling over the lantern, when the Colonel looked up from his reading. 'To guard against night-blindness. Now: to business.'

He took up a brass bell from one corner of his folding desk and rang a brisk peal upon it; this summoned a slight young man, wearing a lieutenant's coat and a patch over his left eye, who gave his commanding officer a smart salute and Gray a respectful bow.

'Mr Morvand,' he said, 'Mr Marshall is seconded to Captain Tremblay's company for the present, and may wish to go out with the scouting-party at dusk. He is to be billeted with the night-scouts. Kindly escort him there, and then to the Captain, wherever he may be at present. And see that he has a bed, and so on.'

'Sir,' said Mr Morvand. He turned to Gray and enquired, 'Have you much kit with you, Mr Marshall? Er, much baggage, that is?'

'That may depend on your definition, I suppose,' said Gray doubtfully. 'My things are outside, I believe – we unloaded them before the fellow with the cart went on to see the quartermaster—'

Colonel Dubois cleared his throat in very audible impatience, and Gray exerted himself to overcome his dithering: 'There is not more than I can carry, at any rate,' he said, and, to the Colonel, 'I thank you, sir.'

The Colonel grunted a vague dismissal, already absorbed once more in Lord Kergabet's dispatches and entirely oblivious to Lieutenant Morvand's parting salute.

They collected Gray's possessions – a small brass-bound trunk and a pair of valises – from the hard-packed ground before the Colonel's tent. The trunk, containing books and other magickal impedimenta, Gray had carefully packed himself; the valises containing clothing, brushes, shaving kit, and other necessities of travel had been packed for him in great haste by Sophie with help from Daisy, as Gray had been almost on the point of climbing into his brother-in-law's carriage for the journey to Brighton without them. Morvand, having attempted to lift the trunk, was glad to cede it to Gray and carry the valises; the attempt left him red-faced not, Gray judged, from physical exertion but from a sense of his own inadequacy.

'You have lately seen battle?' said Gray, to distract him.

'Not battle, exactly,' said Morvand, ducking his head. 'A skirmish, involving weapons and magework, which both sides afterwards regretted. Near Klison, on the Sèvre.'

Now that they were out in the open, crossing the central square of the encampment (and drawing not a few curious stares), Gray saw that in addition to whatever injury might be concealed beneath the eye-patch, his companion walked with a pronounced limp, and he slowed his own long stride to compensate.

'You were wounded there?'

'I was.' Mr Morvand shrugged, as best he could manage with a valise under either arm. 'Lord Mithras smiled upon me; some others were not so fortunate. The healers did their best with what remained; I am of less use in the field now, but the Colonel knew

257

my father, and has been kind enough to give me useful employment as his aide-de-camp.'

Gray caught back, just in time, the words *I am sure you are very useful to him*, which (though true) must have been unbearably condescending.

'These night-scouts,' he said instead, 'what sort of men are they?'

'They are men of Breizh, as I am,' said Mr Morvand, rather stiffly – as though his name and his manner of speech had not declared as much already. He turned his head minutely to glance up at Gray, then turned his one eye back to the way ahead. The camp – like Colonel Dubois' tent – was excruciatingly tidy, the tents arrayed in precise rows, the cookfires distributed with mathematical exactitude. Over all of it drifted the smells of smoke and, faintly, of horses.

'My wife is Breizhek-born,' said Gray, slipping easily from Français into Brezhoneg. He watched his companion sidelong, in his turn, as he added, 'That country breeds brave spirits, in my experience.'

Mr Morvand's shoulders straightened minutely, and his chin lifted a little. *Did he truly think I should think the less of him, only because he is a man of Breizh?*

'Mr Ollivier and Mr Lécuyer,' said Mr Morvand, 'are perhaps rather reckless than brave. Though not so reckless as the day-scouts, for at least they make their sorties under cover of darkness. Ollivier is a barn-owl, and Lécuyer – some other sort of owl, a brown one, but I cannot say which.'

So that is what the Colonel meant by his cryptic remarks about owls.

'They are shape-shifters, then?' Gray enquired. 'Are all the scouts . . . ?'

Mr Morvand waited some moments for an end to this question before supplying his own: 'Are all of them shape-shifters, do you mean, sir? Or owls?'

Gray himself was not perfectly sure which he had meant. 'Shape-shifters,' he decided. 'How many are there here in your camp?'

'Four scouts to each company, sir,' said Mr Morvand promptly, 'and we have only four companies of the regiment here at present.'

'*Sixteen* shape-shifters!' Gray could not imagine such a thing; he had not met more than three others in the whole course of his life.

'Oh, no, sir,' said Morvand, and produced the first genuine smile Gray had seen from him. 'Sixteen scouts all told; only those in Captain Tremblay's company are all shape-shifters, however, and very few of the rest. Most of the mage-officers are in Captain Tremblay's company, you see, because—oh, I beg your pardon, sir.'

He halted abruptly, turned on his heel – valises and all – and led Gray back twenty paces or so, to a tent which was exactly like all the others, but for a pair of scarred and pitted fence-posts driven into the ground before the door.

Morvand deposited the valises at his feet and rapped sharply with his knuckles against the nearer of the two posts, calling in Latin, 'Hallo the scouts!'

There was a long pause; Gray shifted the heavy trunk in his arms, pondered putting it down, and decided that he had rather not be required to pick it up again. Then the tent-flaps parted, and a stocky young man with a head of auburn curls and a most unmilitary two-days' beard stumbled halfway out into the sunshine, rubbing one eye with the heel of his free hand. He was very evidently off-duty, clad only in linen drawers and a shirt with neck and cuffs unlaced and gaping.

'Mr Marshall, may I present Mage-Lieutenant Arzhur Lécuyer of this regiment; Mr Lécuyer, Mr Graham Marshall of, er, London.'

Mr Lécuyer sketched a gesture vaguely reminiscent of a salute; Gray, who had not the least notion of the proper protocol for a civilian greeting an officer so thoroughly out of uniform, made him rather a stiff bow in return.

'The Colonel's compliments, Mr Lécuyer,' said Morvand, saluting somewhat less smartly than before, 'and Mr Marshall is to be billeted with you and Mr Ollivier for the present, and to join you on duty tonight if he so desires. I am to see his kit stowed away and then take him to see Captain Tremblay. The quartermaster's boys will be round with a bed and so on presently.'

What, Gray wondered, was comprised in the phrase *and so on*?

Lieutenant Lécuyer blinked up at him, then turned back to Morvand, his eyes narrowing. 'Billeted with us, why?' he said, switching into Brezhoneg. 'What does he mean, "join us on duty"?'

'I believe,' said Gray in the same tongue, concealing a smile, 'the Colonel feels that we may prove birds of a feather.'

Mr Lécuyer gaped at him a moment.

'You speak Brezhoneg,' he said.

'As I have just been telling Mr Morvand,' said Gray, allowing the smile now, 'my wife was born in Breizh. I am from Kernow myself; the tongues are not dissimilar. For example—'

The tent-flap opened again, and another stubbled, bleary-eyed face appeared, twisted into an expression of irritation beneath an uneven fringe of dark hair.

'Ah, Mr Ollivier,' said Morvand, who appeared to be enjoying himself.

The introductions were repeated – this time in Brezhoneg; Mr Ollivier emerged from behind the tent-flap, revealing himself to be half a foot taller than his fellow officer and clad only in his uniform breeches, but did not cease to look annoyed.

'What is it to do with us?' he asked Morvand.

Morvand shrugged – this conversation, thought Gray, was growing less martial by the moment – and said, '*You* may have a burning wish to go aboard your commanding officer, but I have not. The Colonel wishes him billeted with you. I expect he has good reason.'

Lécuyer, who had begun to look more alert, narrowed his eyes at Gray. 'What did you mean, "birds of a feather"?' he said.

With Morvand's help Gray bestowed his gear in a corner of Ollivier and Lécuyer's tent – less slatternly in appearance than its occupants' own persons might have suggested, it reminded Gray very strongly of a certain species of undergraduates' rooms at Merlin – and shifted the two camp beds to make room for a third. Gray eyed the dimensions of these and repressed a sigh; like the cots aboard the *Asp* and many a bed in the posting-inns where he had lately been sleeping, they were at least a foot shorter than himself. Then, with a brisk *Kenavo deoc'h! – Until we meet again* – Morvand left the two lieutenants to their own devices, and conducted Gray to the presence of their Captain.

Mage-Captain Tremblay was a lean, dark man of perhaps five-and-thirty, upon whose face life and military service had scored deep lines as well as a single long, thin scar from temple to cheek. Impeccably and immaculately clad, not a hair out of alignment, he was difficult to imagine as the immediate superior of Lécuyer and Ollivier.

Seated behind his camp desk, he frowned at Morvand through the entirety of the Colonel's compliments and the forms of introduction, then frowned at Gray, and at last said dismissively, 'I cannot spare any of my men to nursemaid a civilian attaché.'

Gray counted ten, in Greek, before replying, 'I have not the least intention of disrupting your operations, Captain; my charge is to observe the movements of forces in the Duchies on behalf of Lord Kergabet in London, not to interfere in any way with yours. Colonel Dubois has suggested that I might join your night-scouts on this evening's patrol – that is, if you have no objection?'

The frown deepened. 'Has he, indeed,' said Captain Tremblay. His voice was a deep, irritable rumble. 'And why in Hades should he do that, hmm?'

Gray glanced aside at Mr Morvand, whose rigid, wooden-faced stillness suggested either suppressed terror or suppressed mirth. *The mages are nearly all in Captain Tremblay's company*, he had said, and then had begun some sort of explanation which had never been concluded. The most logical conclusion, however, was simply that His Majesty's army considered it wisest to place mage-officers under the command of one who understood their ways – not to speak of their tricks.

'I should never presume to speak for Colonel Dubois,' he said, 'but I expect, sir, that I have been seconded to your company, and to your night-scouts in particular, because my particular talents are well matched with theirs.'

Captain Tremblay, he observed detachedly during the silence that followed, had a face very like an osprey's.

Then the Captain produced a short, sharp bark of laughter, brought his palm down flat upon his thigh, and said, 'An owl-mage, by Jove! I should never have guessed it.'

'Nevertheless, sir,' said Gray mildly.

'Sit,' said Captain Tremblay, waving one hand at a battered camp-stool in the corner. Gray fetched it out, set it before the desk, and, rather doubtfully, folded himself on to it.

'Off with you, Mr Morvand,' the captain continued. 'My duty to the Colonel, that is, and I shall see Mr Marshall safely returned to his quarters.'

'Sir,' said Morvand, who had been lurking near the door. He produced another of his sharply executed salutes for his superior officer, bowed politely to Gray, and took himself off.

The moment the tent-flap fell behind him, Captain Tremblay

tugged at his immaculate neck-cloth, exhaled a gusty sigh, shrugged out of his coat, and relaxed into his chair as though his strings had been cut.

'Le Floc'h!' he called, and in Brezhoneg continued, 'Have we any of that claret left?'

A dark-haired young man – very young indeed, and also in his shirt-sleeves – emerged from what Gray now saw must be an interior room of the captain's tent. 'Sir?' he said, in the same language. 'Yes, we have, Unc—er, Captain. Will I fetch it?'

Out of the newcomer's line of sight, Captain Tremblay rolled his eyes. 'Yes, Mr Le Floc'h. The bottle, and two glasses, if you please.' He turned to Gray, and, reverting to Français, said quietly, 'My sister's boy. All manner of talent, alas, and very little in the way of either wits or common sense. I have undertaken for her sake to give him a profession and keep him out of trouble.'

'Are we,' said Gray carefully, 'speaking in Français so that your nephew should not comprehend us, or because you suppose me not to understand you when you speak to him in Brezhoneg?'

Captain Tremblay's languid gaze abruptly sharpened. '*Brezhoneg a ouzit?*' he demanded – the third man today to ask Gray this question – rocking forward across his desk. 'How comes this?'

Shifting into Brezhoneg and leaning his elbows on Captain Tremblay's desk, Gray explained, also for the third time today.

'There is some . . . ill feeling, I believe,' he concluded cautiously, 'between the Breizhek officers and the rest – or perhaps one side or the other is imagining it – but certainly Mr Morvand seemed very concerned that I should not think him or his countrymen disloyal, and I do not see why that should be unless some such accusation has been lately made . . .'

Tremblay cleared his throat, looked over Gray's shoulder, and met his eyes with visible reluctance.

263

'Tales have been spread,' he conceded at last. 'No one will own to beginning them – or to repeating them, for the matter of that – yet still, of course, they spread. Somehow the armies of the Duchies have lately developed an ability to take our forces by surprise, and we appear to have lost our talent for doing likewise. To the military mind, this combination of circumstances inevitably suggests that the enemy has been receiving information on our movements.'

'Yes,' said Gray, frowning thoughtfully. 'Even to *my* mind, Captain, that seems a likely explanation, and it is certainly one that has occurred to more than one mind at Court.'

Captain Tremblay gave a quiet snort of laughter. 'Indeed,' he said. 'And so, of course, the Breizhek troops are suspect—'

He broke off abruptly as Mr Le Floc'h returned with a half-empty bottle of claret and two glasses. The young man made to pour out the wine, but his uncle waved him off – kindly enough – with an order to *see to the horses and the tack*, and when he had retreated, poured it out himself.

'Your very good health, Mr Marshall,' he said, raising his glass.

'And yours, sir,' Gray replied.

After a moment, picking up the dropped thread of their earlier exchange, he said, 'I do not entirely see, however – forgive me – why the premise *The enemy appears to have some means of knowing what we are about* should lead inevitably to the conclusion *The Breizhek troops are guilty of treating with the enemy.* The threat to all three provinces is equally great, surely; why should any of them be more amenable to treason than the others?'

Captain Tremblay drained his glass in one long draught and chuckled ruefully as he refilled it. 'You are not a student of politics, I conclude,' he said; and without waiting for Gray to reply, continued, 'The Duke of Breizh was granted the right to levy his own troops only five years since; hundreds of Breizhek officers resigned their commissions in other regiments in order to take up commissions in those newly levied by the Duke, and their loyalties have been suspect ever since.'

Gray considered this, already mentally composing the beginnings of a report to Lord Kergabet. 'But you did not,' he said slowly, 'nor any of the Breizhek officers whose acquaintance I have made thus far today. That is—' He paused, wondering whether he had misunderstood – 'that is, Colonel Dubois' regiment is not a Breizhek one?'

'It is not,' said Captain Tremblay. 'But the Colonel is Breizhek-born himself – though of a Mainois father, like myself – and an honourable man, if tediously attached to military pomp and ceremony.' He took another large swallow of wine. 'Those who departed their Normand or Mainois or English regiments are suspected of serving Breizh above Britain,' he said, 'whilst those of us who remain are suspected of harbouring divided loyalties, and of informing against our fellows – the ordinary sort of regimental rivalries, boiled up with political in-fighting into a most unpleasant ragout. It is the most natural thing in the world, therefore, that when any disloyalty is suspected, we should be at the head of the queue.'

Gray sighed.

Today, for the first time since embarking on this absurd journey, circumstances – Morvand's wary sideways look, and finding himself one flying shape-shifter among many, and the half-clothed Ollivier and Lécuyer in their dishevelled sleeping quarters, and now *this*, which he ought to have anticipated – made him grateful that Sophie was hundreds of miles away.

'Now!' Tremblay exclaimed after a moment, cheerful once more, 'You wish to fly out with the night-scouts, do you? What is it you are hoping to observe?'

* * *

Ollivier and Lécuyer stripped to their skins quickly and without ceremony – like undergraduates at the public baths – baring with no trace of self-consciousness whipcord-muscled limbs and torsos marked with a bewildering variety of small scars. Their talk and laughter never flagged, and Gray, encouraged, followed their example – only to falter in the sudden, shocked silence that engulfed the magelight-lit campaign-tent when, for a moment, he turned his back to his companions to fold away the shirt he had just pulled off over his head.

'What made those marks, my lord?' Ollivier enquired, after a long moment. 'Er . . . if I may ask?'

'A man with a horsewhip,' said Gray shortly, 'in a dungeon in Alba.' *Not that it is any affair of yours.* 'Shall we get on with this business?'

He turned back to face them, concealing for the moment the almost mathematically parallel rows of scar tissue that striped his back and shoulders, which repeated applications of healing magick had blurred and softened but could not erase. They were gaping at him, just as he had feared they might; yet it was not pity or disgust he saw in their faces, but . . . something else altogether.

'You are soldiers, both of you,' he said, not troubling to hide his impatience. 'You must have seen such marks before – or worse things.'

Lécuyer swallowed hard and gave a sharp nod; his right arm twitched, as though he were restraining himself from offering a salute.

'Colonel Dubois will send a runner with the signal,' he said, 'very soon now.'

Gray nodded. 'I should like, if it does not inconvenience you,' he said, 'to observe the process – I am a scholar, you know, and I have not many opportunities to—'

'Oh, look all you like, my lord,' said Ollivier, cheerfully enough. He glanced at Lécuyer, who shrugged.

They crouched on the dusty floor of the tent, balancing on the balls of their feet and the tips of their fingers. Ollivier closed his eyes and spoke his shifting-spell almost inaudibly, his lips pressed close together and moving as little as possible; Lécuyer drew his arms forward to encircle his shins, then bowed his forehead to his bent-up knees, hiding his face entirely. Whereas Gray's own transformation tended to happen slowly – those desperate, panicked shifts in the dead of an Oxford night and in the woods on the Ross of Mull excepted – His Majesty's scouts took no more time to put on their talons, wings, and feathers than to strip off their clothes; before Gray had even begun to guess at their choice of spells, there stood before him, blinking their round dark eyes in the lamplight and stepping delicately away from foot to foot, a pale-faced barn owl and a large brown-and-tawny eagle owl.

'Well,' said Gray.

He stepped out of his own drawers – much easier to do it now than later – and crouched down in his turn, feeling each small lump and pebble against the soles of his feet, then tilted forward until most of his weight rested on his toes.

This working no longer required much conscious thought; once summoned, his magick flowed easily into the channels of his owl-shape, and muscles and sinews followed in its wake. His bones were lighter already, primaries springing through the skin of his arms, his bare toes splaying into talons.

Owl-shaped, Gray remained taller than his companions – though less so than before – which Lécuyer, the eagle owl, clearly found irksome. Gray spread his wings cautiously, conscious of the number of things he might possibly dislodge or damage; Lécuyer spread his own, slightly longer, in answer. Ollivier, the barn owl, bobbed his head and hooted in avian laughter.

Perhaps fortunately, the dark head and broad shoulders of the Colonel's runner leant in through the tent-flap before the conversation could proceed any further. 'Ready to be off, are we, gentlemen? The sun is well down.'

He threw open the tent-flap, revealing himself to be wearing a lance-corporal's uniform and a falconer's heavy leather gauntlets, and crouched down to lift first Lécuyer, then Ollivier, onto his wrists. Then, for a long moment, he frowned at Gray, who tilted his head and stared back. At last an idea seemed to occur to him; he shifted the eagle owl from his left wrist to his right – the barn owl ruffled his feathers indignantly, but finally shuffled a little way up his arm to make room – then extended his left arm towards Gray.

'I am Lance-Corporal Kerambrun, my lord,' he said. 'If you will permit me . . . ?'

It was not a graceful process, and Gray's temper was not improved by the knowledge that Ollivier and Lécuyer, as well as having seen the evidence of his experiences in the bowels of Castle MacAlpine, were watching him hop and flap about to keep his balance. Gray's weight was evidently less than Kerambrun had expected, which occasioned some shifting of the passengers. At length, however, Lance-Corporal Kerambrun straightened up and emerged from the scouts' tent, with an owl on either wrist and a third clinging to his shoulder, and strode eastward through the twilit camp.

CHAPTER XIX

In Which the Princess Royal Mounts an Expedition

'*And what on* earth has he told his mother?' said Lucia, incredulous, when Sophie had finished her tale. She had risen from the floor and resumed her seat on the far side of the small table which held the abandoned chessboard, and was leaning forward, her elbows resting on her knees, in rapt attention.

Sophie peered at her over the rim of her teacup, clasped tightly in both hands; the tea was almost too sweet to drink, but the heat seeping through the porcelain warmed her chilled fingers. 'That, I expect,' she said, 'he has left to Lord Kergabet.'

'I certainly should do, in his place,' said Roland unexpectedly, and with some feeling.

Sophie and Lucia looked up at him in surprise.

'Well,' he said, his cheeks going rather pink. 'Mothers can be rather . . . excitable—' Then, recollecting perhaps that both of his companions had lost their mothers before the age of ten, he muttered, 'Never mind,' and turned away to make a noisy pretence of tidying the tea-things on the sideboard.

'In any case,' said Sophie, 'it is entirely possible that Gray's mama will be pleased as much as alarmed; his father planned a military career for him, you see, and went so far as to purchase him a mage-lieutenant's commission, when he was nineteen. It was because Gray refused to leave Merlin College and take it up that Edmond Marshall disinherited him.'

Roland had not ceased to rattle the teacups, but Sophie fancied she could see his attentive listening in the set of his shoulders.

'I mean no disparagement of your husband, Sophie,' said Lucia, whose russet-gold eyebrows had flown up at the words *mage-lieutenant's commission*, 'but truly it is difficult to imagine a worse notion.'

Sophie laughed – a shaky, ragged-edged thing, but laughter nevertheless. 'Quite so,' she said; 'still, I must suppose that Kergabet knows what he is about. This must go no further,' she admonished. 'I ought not even to have told the two of you, but it beggars belief that either of you should—' She swallowed, and against her better judgement took a large swallow of too-sweet tea.

'Of course we shall neither of us say anything to anyone, Sophie,' said Lucia. Her tone suggested that she was suppressing further comment on the general theme of *What do you take me for?*

'Certainly not,' said Roland indignantly; after another moment, in a more diffident tone, he added, 'May we help you plan your expedition to Oxford, then?'

If Sophie's heart was no longer entirely in her Oxford scheme – if, in fact, a considerable proportion of it was in Normandie with Gray – it seemed her friends were prepared to embrace it wholeheartedly. Watching as they set aside their misgivings, and the many other demands upon their time, to assist her in planning and undertaking the initial exploratory visit to Oxford, Sophie strongly suspected that the interest and assistance of Kergabet, Jenny, and Mr Fowler, at any rate, was owing not to any personal enthusiasm for the scheme but to a wish that Joanna should be got out of the way of the search for her father, and that Sophie should be diverted from pining over Gray's absence.

In light of the last such occasion, she reflected, it was not an idle worry.

Lucia's reasons for participating in the scheme she judged to be two parts genuine enthusiasm and one part longing to escape the Royal Palace; Roland's, almost entirely a wish to please Lucia. As for Joanna and Miss Pryce . . .

But there again, when have I ever been able to discover what either of them is thinking?

Whatever might be the motivations of the participants, their eager energy made quick work of the planning, and she was duly grateful.

That Mr Goff and Mr Tredinnick, her faithful shadows since first she and Gray set up housekeeping in Oxford years ago, should be of the party, was taken as read; His Majesty, however, had insisted upon the addition of a further half-dozen guardsmen under their joint command – despite Sophie's protests that this could only serve to make them conspicuous – and Lucia MacNeill's guard captain, not to be outdone, had volunteered herself and her troop as escort.

Lucia had rolled her eyes at this – Ceana MacGregor, Sophie had learnt early on, had known Lucia from birth and had been captain of her personal guard for the past decade, and the two were accustomed to take quite astonishing liberties with one another. Ceana MacGregor, however, had folded her arms and said, 'Either we all of us go to Oxford, Lucia MacNeill, or none of us goes, least of all yourself,' which pronouncement caused Lucia to throw up her hands in exasperation and give in.

The party which eventually departed Grosvenor Square for Oxford, therefore, comprised one prince, four ladies, and sufficient men- and women-at-arms to have cowed any but the most enterprising assailant.

* * *

Having taken possession of the entire first floor of the Dragon and Lion for the accommodation of her retinue, being the only respectable hostelry in Oxford presently able to offer hospitality to such a large party, Sophie left the other ladies to their unpacking and, in the sole company of Mr Tredinnick, set off on foot up the High-street towards the Broad, and Merlin College.

The Porter manning Merlin's gate was unfamiliar to her and showed no sign of knowing who she was. Quite prepared for this eventuality, Sophie nodded to Mr Tredinnick, who stepped forward and said affably, 'We are come to see Doctor Evans-Hughes; is he in college at present?'

The Porter narrowed his pale-blue eyes at them but conceded grudgingly that Doctor Evans-Hughes was indeed in his rooms. 'Is 'e expecting you?' he enquired.

'No,' said Tredinnick; 'that is, not today in particular. Mrs Marshall' – nodding at Sophie – 'has been in correspondence with him, however, and forewarned him of our coming.'

This was true, assuming that Sophie's latest letter, posted two days since, had been opened and read. In any case, if Gareth had not been here, Master Alcuin certainly should be, and could be counted upon to welcome them in.

The Porter looked askance at this, but, having informed Mr Tredinnick that *female visitors* were not permitted to wander the College grounds unescorted, sent one of his minions to enquire whether Doctor Evans-Hughes were willing to come down to the Porter's Lodge to speak with them. Sophie and her companion loitered comfortably upon the pavement, observing the sparse late-summer foot traffic along the Broad and looking up at the walls of Merlin. Not so long ago, she had been – and Mr Tredinnick had pretended to be – a student there, and it surprised her to find that she did not much regret giving it up.

Gareth Evans-Hughes arrived on the heels of the Porter's boy – as rumpled as ever and rather rounder, pink-faced and out of breath – and upon beholding Sophie, shocked all present by nearly bowling her over in the enthusiasm of his greeting.

'Sophie Marshall, as I live and breathe!' he exclaimed, standing back with his hands on her shoulders. He continued, rather less accurately, 'How well you look! I did not look for you until tomorrow at the earliest. But let us not stand talking in the street; come in, come in!'

Ignoring the Porter's scandalised glare, he ushered them through the gate, signed the Porter's book on their behalf, and led them across the Quad to his staircase.

It being the Long Vac, Merlin was very sparsely populated, and they passed no more than half a dozen persons, Senior Fellows mostly, along their way. Sophie nonetheless took the precaution of making herself inconspicuous; there was no benefit to be gained from attracting attention to herself, or to Gareth either.

Having ushered them into his sitting-room – less altered even than himself, with the same creaking armchairs, the same shelves of odd and miscellaneous artefacts, the same haphazard stacks of books as when Sophie had last seen it – Evans-Hughes turned to Sophie and said, 'Wards, I think?'

'Indeed,' she said, and at once reached for her magick to work the strongest warding-spell she knew.

'Now,' said Gareth briskly, when she had finished, reaching behind a bronze knotwork buckle and a badger's skull to retrieve his welcome-cup, 'who is your friend, Sophie, and where in Hades has your husband gone off to?'

Sophie introduced Mr Tredinnick and Gareth to one another, put off the latter's second query with the promise of a fuller explanation *later*, and gratefully accepted his welcome, though the wine he poured into the small, battered copper goblet was so sweet that she had to restrain a grimace. Gareth himself was not so nice – upon tasting it, he had screwed up his face, swallowed hard, and said, 'The wine steward will have his little joke' – but what a host might permit himself to say about his own hospitality, a guest ought not.

They all sat down, Sophie and Mr Tredinnick arrayed before Gareth as though they had been his students come to read him their essays; Gareth leant forward with elbows on knees, clasping his hands before him, and said, 'I have found something in the Merlin Library, Sophie, that I think you shall like; but before I fetch it, will you – *can* you – tell me what you are about? And – if the, er, circumstances permit – why Marshall is not come with you? That is,' he added, hastily and quite needlessly, 'there is no reason on earth why you should not both do just as you please, of course! It is only that I am accustomed to your being inseparable.'

Sophie sighed. She was as sure of Gareth Evans-Hughes as she could be of anyone – else she should not have involved him in her scheme to begin with – but too many people were already in the secret of Gray's whereabouts.

'Gray is on an errand for his brother-in-law,' she said instead, 'which is as much as anyone may be told about it; and I am here to break into Lady Morgan College' – she could not help smiling at her two companions' identical expressions of shock at this turn of phrase – 'and poke about in its library – hence my request.' She leant forward in turn. 'You did find something, you said? May I see it?'

Gareth's face, which had creased unhappily at her refusal to elaborate on Gray's circumstances or whereabouts, broke into a smile, and he sprang up from his seat to rummage about in a desk drawer.

'Here we are,' he said at last, turning back to her, and handed over a long roll of parchment, yellow with age and beginning to crumble at the edges, tied up near each end with incongruously bright-new blue tapes. He looked about him, frowning a little. 'Let me just . . .'

'Er, perhaps this table, sir?' said Mr Tredinnick.

'Yes! Yes, that will do very nicely.'

Gareth hurried the scattered notes and documents into an untidy stack and removed it to the top of his desk; Sophie, having untied the tapes, slowly and carefully unrolled the parchment onto the table-top thus exposed, anchoring each side with the tips of her gloved fingers. Although rerolled smoothly, it showed irregular creases, as though having been rolled once, it had then been sat upon for some time.

Above and below her fingertips, the corners curled persistently inwards, but Sophie scarcely remarked it; she was staring, transfixed, at the centre of the parchment, on which was drawn, in a firm meticulous hand, a detailed plan labelled *Lady Morgan College, Oxon.*

'Gareth!' she said, looking up. 'Wherever did you find this?'

'It was rolled up and forgotten at the back of a map-drawer,' he said, 'where it had been squashed flat for the gods know how long; I am surprised that it did not fall into bits the moment I touched it.' He was moving about the room, gathering . . . what? 'None of the librarians or archivists knew it was there, or even that it existed – or at any rate none of them would admit to knowing – nor what it was; how in Hades did *you* know that I should find it?'

'It was a bow drawn at a venture entirely, I admit,' said Sophie frankly. 'That is, I know that Lady Morgan College exists – or did exist – and I supposed that plans must have been drawn of it; and several of the books I have found on the subject mention the existence of such a plan.'

Gareth came back to stand beside her at the table, and now she saw what he had been about. Carefully he lined the edges of the spread-out plan with a series of small objects – the skull of some small creature, about the size of Sophie's palm; a miniature brass lamp; an ancient-looking stoppered bottle of smoky-blue glass; a paper-knife with a handle in the shape of a porpoise; and so onward – to prevent its curling up again.

'And having found a view of the place forgotten and uncatalogued in a pigeonhole in the Palace Archives,' she continued, while this proceeding was going forward, 'it seemed to me that Merlin's Archives, being older, might also possess uncatalogued documents of which no one knew anything. Of course,' she added, 'we should have staged our invasion in any event, but now we shall be better able to plan our campaign.'

She bent her head again, tapped one index finger on the blank space labelled *Great Quadrangle* (like Merlin's, a quadrangle in name but not in shape), traced the footpaths that crossed and intersected it. *Library*, she read, arching across the outline of an oblong structure. *Refectory. Undergraduate Rooms. Portress's Lodge.* And – yes, there! In the upper left-hand corner, just where memory suggested it ought to be – a small, perfect circle with a square portico, adorned with a tiny drawing of an owl and, inscribed across a decorative scroll, the words *Shrine of Minerva Sophia.*

'The dome,' she said, more than half to herself. 'The green dome.'

'Ma'am?' said Mr Tredinnick, politely baffled.

Sophie blinked away the memory-vision of the compact copper-green dome, dimmed by mist and rain, rising above weed-grown walls and empty windows. 'This,' she said, pointing, 'is a shrine to Minerva as Sophia, personification of wisdom. My namesake, or one of them – the one my mother chose for me.' She paused, swallowed hard, and continued: 'More importantly for present purposes, it is visible from the near bank of the Cherwell, and appears on the plan exactly where I expected to see it, which means, I hope, that the plan can be trusted to reflect the thing itself. Now, I wonder, has the draughtsman recorded the date . . . ?'

Three dark heads bent over the plan, searching – Gareth with a magnifying glass unearthed from the chaos of his desk; it was Mr Tredinnick, however, who at length exclaimed, 'There!' extending a sturdy forefinger towards a stylised representation of a tree, seen from above, in the lower right-hand corner.

'By Jove! You have sharp eyes, Tredinnick,' said Gareth, in a tone of admiration quite untainted by envy or resentment. He held the glass over the little tree-top, and the three of them leant still closer – their heads nearly touching – to peer through it at the minuscule letters twined into the stylised branches.

'*Edwina Antonia Calixta fecit,*' Sophie read aloud; the feminine name surprised her but, upon consideration, ought not to have done. '*Anno xii Henricus VIII.*' She paused, eyes closed, to wrestle with the mental arithmetic. The Princess Julia had been born in the tenth year of her father's long reign, and Prince Edward in the twenty-eighth . . . King Edward had succeeded to the throne at the age of nine, and the College – so far as she had been able to determine – had been closed in the second or possibly the third decade of his reign . . .

'This was made within fifty years of the College's closing,' she said at last. 'More or less. Of course a great deal may change in fifty years, but – this is a marvellous find, Gareth, truly.'

She grinned at him, and his round plain face lit up with his answering smile.

The smile quickly faltered, however, as his gaze returned to the plan of Lady Morgan College. 'Sophie,' he said, slow and careful, 'are the rumours true? That you mean to . . . to sponsor a college for women, as Lady Morgan did?'

Sophie studied his expression – troubled; hopeful? – for some time before replying, 'If I can manage it, yes.'

'There is a good deal of . . . of feeling against it,' said Gareth. 'At Merlin particularly, but in the other Colleges also.'

'The august Fellows have made their views very clear to me, never fear,' said Sophie dryly. Where was this leading?

'Sophie, why did you not tell me?' The question did not surprise her particularly, but the *tone*—

'Why do you suppose? My father is not indulging me in this scheme from any real interest in its success, but only because— well, never mind exactly why, but to keep me *out* of something else entirely; there is every chance that this will all end in some costly and humiliating mess. Can you suppose that I wish to bring my friends into such a mess with me, who must go on living and working at Merlin when I have run back to Din Edin with my tail between my legs?'

Mr Tredinnick, whose presence Sophie (from long habit) had momentarily forgotten, laughed aloud. Sophie turned to glare at him; subsiding to a chuckle, he said, 'Begging your pardon, ma'am, but if you were at all disposed to run *away* from trouble, I should soon find myself out of work.'

Gareth, infuriatingly, joined in Tredinnick's laughter, and Sophie glared harder at both of them, to little avail. Exasperated, she turned away and stared resolutely out of the window.

'If you have quite finished,' she said coolly, after a moment. They caught her tone and subsided, and Sophie turned away from the window again to address her friend. 'I may take it, I collect, that – in principle, at any rate – you are rather in favour of my scheme than otherwise?'

'Certainly I am,' said Gareth. His soft tenor voice held a trace of indignation, and the Cymric tilt that marked his speech in Latin, ordinarily almost too subtle to hear, had become very pronounced. '. . . but, there, I had forgotten that you are not acquainted with any of my sisters.' The bright grin resurfaced momentarily, though now with a wry edge. 'If you had been – and my sister Angharad particularly – you could not doubt it for even a moment.'

It was always a clever sister, Sophie reflected – half jubilant, half rueful – to make a man think twice about this matter; never, it seemed, any sense that the generality of women might benefit from, or might have any right to enjoy, the privileges which their brothers serenely accepted as their right. *Gift horses*, she reminded herself sternly, not for the first time.

'I am very glad to hear it,' she said, taking care that none of this inward argumentation should show on her face or in her voice. 'And when – if – when matters have progressed a little – if it seems likely that—'

She paused, looking at her hands. The investigation into Merlin's Archives, though it had yielded such unexpectedly useful results, had been only half the reason for this visit – the more or less official, the openly acknowledged half. They were now come to the other, of which Mr Tredinnick was very likely to disapprove – and not without reason. *Can I afford to trust Gareth with this secret? On the other hand, how should I account for myself before the gods, if I did not use all the resources at my disposal?*

'I have another favour to ask of you,' she said at last, making up her mind.

Mr Tredinnick straightened his shoulders and frowned. 'Mrs Marshall—'

It was not often that Sophie made use of her rank to cow her father's guardsmen; she did so now, however, without compunction, for her sisters' sake. 'Mr Tredinnick,' she said, her tone as much the Princess Royal as she could make it, 'you may wait in the corridor outside, or you may stay here and refrain from interfering, and from revealing to anyone else whatever you may hear. The choice is yours; I suggest you make it at once.'

'Ma'am.' Mr Tredinnick set his teeth. 'I am yours to command, of course.'

She waited long enough for him to decamp, should that be his intention; when instead he settled himself in a corner, perched on a tall stool tucked between two bookcases, she turned back to Gareth and extracted from her reticule the only other possession of Amelia's which she had been able to discover: one of the pair of silver-and-garnet ear-drops given to her by the Professor for her sixteenth birthday, which Katell had found trodden into the thick carpet beneath the dressing-table in the Kingfisher room. The others she had had to leave behind in Jenny's care, if she were not to be required to confess to Jenny – and, worse, to Lady Maëlle and Joanna – that she intended revealing their private trouble to a rank outsider.

'This belonged – *belongs* – to my sister Amelia,' she said, unfolding the handkerchief in which she had wrapped it and holding it out on her flattened palm. 'She has . . . That is, we have reason to believe that she has run away with, with Henry Taylor.' Speaking over Gareth's shocked intake of breath, she hurried on: 'As you knew Mr Taylor in his student days, you will understand why we are anxious to locate her. Gray's sister, as you may know, is a scry-mage of some talent, and she has done her best with some other objects of my sister's, but she has not the training you have, Gareth, as she herself is the first to admit, and so . . .'

Gareth had listened to all of this with a troubled frown, and in silence. If she desired his help, she must ask for it outright.

'And so,' she said, measured and deliberate, 'I should be very much in your debt, Gareth, if you were to consent to scry this ear-ring, though I have not its owner's permission to do so, and tell me what you see of my sister, which may shed any light on her present circumstances or whereabouts.'

After another long, considering silence, Evans-Hughes sighed, leant forward, and reached for the ear-drop in Sophie's hand. 'Your sister would not be the first young woman to follow her own inclinations in marriage, in opposition to her family's,' he said pointedly, 'nor the first to take this means of doing so, and sometimes with good reason. If you had not said *with Henry Taylor*, Sophie, I should refuse to have anything to do with the business, and I should advise you—'

'If Henry Taylor were not in the case,' Sophie retorted, 'or someone very like him, I should be wishing my sister joy of her choice, not joining in the hunt for her. What sort of hypocrite do you think me, Gareth Evans-Hughes? But it *is* Henry Taylor, and therefore—'

'And therefore, I shall do as you ask,' said Gareth. 'Now, be quiet a moment, if you please.'

Sophie clasped her hands in her lap, pressed her lips together, and did her best to keep still.

At length Gareth surfaced from what Sophie could only call a trance and laid Amelia's ear-drop carefully upon the table beside the weighted-down parchment.

'Marshall has gone off to Normandie to look for your sister, I suppose?' he said.

Sophie, startled, recalled that just before introducing them to one another, Gray had ducked his head to murmur in her ear, *Evans-Hughes is a good, solid man, and trustworthy; but you must always bear in mind that he is at least twice as clever as he looks.* And it was not, perhaps, very difficult to draw the necessary connexions in this case. 'Yes,' she conceded.

At least he has not guessed what else Gray is about.

'Not a bad guess,' said Gareth, rather cryptically, 'but not far enough.'

'Gareth—'

'I apologise.' He held up a hand, then, absently, began turning the delicate silver filigree round and round between the fingers of the other hand, studying it as though, having just probed into this object's accreted secrets, he now could not imagine what its original purpose might have been. 'Your sister-in-law has told you, I expect, that . . . May I call her Amelia?'

Sophie shrugged; what could it matter?

'That Amelia, at the time when she was making ready to leave London, believed herself to be bound for Normandie, by way of Portsmouth and then Honfleur?'

'Yes,' said Sophie, 'more or less. Is that—'

'That is certainly what she *believed*, yes. But, as you say, Henry Taylor.' Gareth sighed gustily, and his shoulders sank back against the threadbare damask of his chair. 'Or perhaps—well. Not so far from Honfleur,' he said, recapturing the thread of his narrative after this cryptic digression, 'as the crow flies more or less north – and very near indeed to Dover, as the ship sails – is the port of Calais, in the Comté d'Artois, which presently owes allegiance to the Duc de Bourgogne.'

'And . . . Amelia is going to Calais? Or has gone there?'

'Oh! Certainly. From London to Dover, from Dover to Calais. And from there . . . from there,' Gareth repeated, 'things are murkier; but Bourgogne is known to be friendly with Orléans, though of course it does not follow that Artois should necessarily feel likewise—'

'Gareth,' Sophie broke in, 'my sister?'

He had the grace to look a little sheepish; it made his face suddenly altogether familiar, and Sophie bit her lip to tamp down a wholly unexpected pang of regret for those things at Merlin College which she had loved, and those persons who had welcomed her unreservedly, during her brief and difficult sojourn here – Gareth Evans-Hughes included.

Quickly, before she could lose her nerve once more, she said, 'Amelia left London intending to marry Mr Taylor; did she—have they—'

She scarcely knew which of the two possibilities was the more dreadful. On the one hand, an elopement without some reasonably official form of marriage, should it become known, must materially damage any gentlewoman's reputation and prospects; but, on the other, for Amelia to be the wife of Henry Taylor . . . !

This time Gareth took pity on her stammering. 'In fact, so far as I have been able to see,' he said gently, 'not only has there been no marriage, but from Dover your sister appears to have been . . . to be travelling alone.'

'Travelling alone!' Sophie exclaimed, incredulous. '*Amelia?*'

What to think of this development? Sophie could not imagine. On the one hand, the world was full of perils for a woman – particularly a young and beautiful woman – travelling alone; on the other hand . . .

'Go on,' she said.

'Well,' said Gareth. 'The aetheric echoes attaching to this . . . item' – he gave it another vaguely baffled look – 'have by now been very much attenuated, you understand; but your sister, so far as I can tell, has been thinking very little about Henry Taylor – I fancy he disappointed her, not by refusing to marry her, but by attempting to alter their destination; but that may be only my imagination, you understand – and a great deal about their original plan, in which she was to be reunited with her beloved papa, and of how she might accomplish it for herself, without Taylor's assistance. Also, of the much happier life she shall have, when her papa is a great man again, and when—'

He shut his mouth abruptly, with a guilty look.

Sophie sighed. 'Tell me.'

After some hesitation, he said, '. . . when you are not in it.'

With few exceptions, it was only what Katell had told them, or they had known, already; why should it sound so very much worse now? Sophie sat very still, concentrating hard; a friend Gareth might be, but still she had no intention of going all to pieces in front of him.

'Sophie?' he said hesitantly, after what might have been a moment or half an hour.

With some effort, she forced herself to meet his gaze. 'Where?' she said. 'Do you know, can you tell, Gareth, where this reunion is to take place?'

'Alas, I cannot,' he said. 'And what I *can* tell you, I regret to say, makes no sense at all.' He frowned, shrugged his broad shoulders, dropped Amelia's ear-ring back into the folds of Sophie's handkerchief, and handed it across to her. 'According to your sister, who had the tale from Taylor,' he said at last, 'Appius Callender is presently employed as an advisor to the Emperor of Gaul.'

CHAPTER XX

In Which Gray Reconsiders Long-Held Prejudices

The passage through the encampment of Lance-Corporal Kerambrun and his passengers drew a considerable number of stares. This surprised Gray – Lécuyer and Ollivier in their owl-shapes must after all be a familiar sight here – till he recollected that only the night-scouts themselves, Colonel Dubois, Mage-Captain Tremblay, and, it now appeared, Kerambrun knew of this particular manifestation of his talent. The rest must all be wondering at two owls' having become three.

Over the course of a long and frankly indolent afternoon largely given over to sleep and games of chance – for Captain Tremblay's night-scouts, it appeared, enjoyed a somewhat equivocal status in their off hours, which were many, as a consequence of performing a difficult and wearing duty in which none of their fellows could replace them – Ollivier and Lécuyer had given him some notion of their modus operandi. Though in fact they flew patterns, separately and together, designed to give them sight of as much of the land below them as possible – just as a patrol on foot or on horseback might spread out and quarter their ground, in order not to miss any square foot of it in their passing – their survival might at any time depend on their not appearing to do so. All the scouts, it appeared, had of necessity become scholars of the behaviour, hunting techniques, and flight patterns of birds of prey, so that they might pass for natural, ordinary birds and attract no untoward attention.

'Tanguy had an arrow through his left wing, once,' Ollivier had said, and all of them shuddered. 'Though that was in the heat of battle. He has never been sure whether it was excellent aim or appalling luck.'

Tanguy, Gray found upon enquiring, was one of the company's day-scouts, a *milan royal* in his shape-shifted form, and through a fortunate landing and the immediate assistance of a talented healer, he had survived his ordeal with no lasting ill effects but a slight stiffness of his left arm in damp weather.

'He must have kept his head remarkably well,' said Gray, 'to have stayed aloft long enough to make any sort of landing.'

He was thinking, as from time to time he could not prevent himself from doing, of the occasion when he had himself attempted to go aloft on a badly injured wing; remarking that his companions were looking at him curiously, he discovered that he had clasped his right hand protectively over his left shoulder. Hastily he pretended to be scratching an itch.

'Tanguy is made of quicksilver and cast iron,' said Ollivier, allowing him the pretence. 'Whatever does not rebound from his fortunate hide seems to pass straight through him without leaving a mark. Well,' he amended, 'not much, at any rate.'

He and Lécuyer had grinned, then, and Gray had made himself do likewise, grateful to them for letting the awkward moment pass.

The night-scouts, it must be said, had surprised him – and Mage-Captain Tremblay, too; none of them at all suited his notion of an army officer. Even Colonel Dubois, as seen through the lens of his gruff kindness to young Mr Morvand, was altogether more . . . *human* than Gray had expected. For a moment, even, he caught himself pondering whether his father might not in fact have had his best interests in mind, in purchasing for him a mage-lieutenant's commission and urging (no: *ordering*) him to take it up. Here he was, after all, making genuine use at last of what was otherwise an obscure and largely impractical, if impressive, skill which had cost him a great deal of time and painful effort to attain, in the company of other men who had undertaken the same single-minded – some might say mule-headed – journey; they were, some of their manners aside, not brutish louts but brave and clever men who treated him as a respected comrade.

If they accorded him that respect for all the wrong reasons, well . . .

The plan they had ultimately made, such as it was, would allow Gray to conduct his own reconnaissance, closer to the ground, without much interference from the others, and would assure him of hearing their full reports whilst not committing himself to reveal every detail of his own observations (or his own purposes) in return.

And what, indeed, do you hope to observe that they shall not? he asked himself now, derisively. Both Lécuyer and Olliver had been flying these twilight sorties for years; both had been stationed at Ivry for some months and knew the territory as he could not possibly do. And of course it was not to be supposed that he should happen upon Professor Callender and his cronies, or upon Henry Taylor and Amelia, in the fields and woods round Ivry at night.

To Ivry, Sieur Germain de Kergabet had said, *and from Ivry, to where the trail may lead you.*

In Captain Tremblay's tent, the three owls perched on the scarred and battered poles of a wooden contraption clearly built for this purpose, peering at the map unrolled upon the Captain's desk.

'Here, here and here, you see,' said Colonel Dubois, pointing, 'are the positions of the encampments reported by the scouts of

Captain Howells' company this morning, when they returned at the third hour before noon. Tanguy and Fournier reported seeing no movement during the afternoon, apart from the ordinary business – foraging and scouting parties and the like,' he added, aside, in Gray's direction.

Unthinkingly – as though he had been conversing with Sophie – Gray bobbed his head in acknowledgement of this explanation.

Questions were bubbling up in his mind like a pot a-boiling: *What concealing-spells might the armies of the Duchies be employing? Have they airborne scouting parties of their own? How numerous are these nearby encampments, and whose banners do they fly?* – and, less worthily, *If one of us should be injured, or worse, how shall anyone here know of it?* For almost the first time in his life, he would gladly have traded his wings for his human voice in order to ask them. What fool had thought he and the night-scouts ought to be briefed after shifting and not before?

'Steady on, Mr Marshall,' Captain Tremblay murmured, and Gray discovered to his chagrin that he was bobbing anxiously up and down, shifting from foot to foot, in a most undignified manner. He ruffled his feathers apologetically and settled his wings, though inwardly feeling no calmer.

The briefing, such as it was, concluded with an offering to Mithras, the soldiers' especial deity, and to Lady Minerva, whose sacred bird was the owl; and at last by Captain Tremblay's unlocking a battered dispatch-case and extracting from it an equally battered ledger and three small leather bands hung with miniature soldiers' talismans.

'Sixteen,' he said, reading aloud from the inner surface of the first band; Kerambrun made a note in the ledger. 'One-and-twenty. Three.'

Gray cocked his head, eyeing the odd objects in Tremblay's hand

and pondering whether they might be charms of concealment such as he had worn once or twice before; Lécuyer and Ollivier, however, put out their left feet and waited patiently whilst the bands were fastened on by Kerambrun. Gray, when his turn came, followed their example.

'Should anything befall you,' said Kerambrun quietly, as his quick fingers worked the tiny buckle about Gray's leg, 'which the gods forbid, any mage-officer in the company, whether or not he has ever laid eyes on you in either form, could work a finding-spell to seek this talisman, and so find you.'

Well, that is one question answered, at any rate. Again Gray bobbed his head in acknowledgement, and hoped that his relief might not be outwardly visible.

The three owls were then conveyed to the camp's forestward edge and up a ladder to the makeshift watchtower, from which – without further unnecessary ceremony – they were tossed out one by one.

Gray knew perfectly well that his attention ought all to be on the ground below him, the forest all around; but after these earthbound months in London he could not help, for the first few exhilarating moments, simply glorying in being aloft. He coasted to a convenient branch – surveyed the forest floor below, seamed by meandering tree-roots and inches deep in leaf-mould – spotted a *belette* creeping from tree-trunk to tree-trunk, and repressed his owl-body's urge to dive after whatever it might be hunting – dropped from his branch again, spreading his wings, and launched himself once more into the night air.

His position was equivocal, his companions temporary, his present task dangerous and of dubious utility; yet a part of him – and no small part, at that – rejoiced, happy as, in all his life, only flying and Sophie's company had ever made him happy.

That night's patrolling – and all the next several nights' – yielded no startling or even particularly interesting intelligence with respect to the troops massing along Britain's frontiers. Their numbers seemed to be increasing, but slowly; they were, to all appearances, as solidly entrenched as their counterparts of His Majesty's army; the juxtapositions of hitherto warring dukes', counts', and viscounts' banners – though certainly baffling – were only what Kergabet had led Gray to expect.

When not aloft, Gray wandered about the camp, taking note of what the officers and men and camp-followers spoke of; striking up an apparently idle conversation whenever he could; and becoming friendly with the sentries, so as better to observe the camps' many comings and goings. Though apparently exploring idly and at random, he had actually been proceeding in accordance with a plan of the camp, consulted almost daily with Colonel Dubois, on which he was steadily marking off each tent, picket, and cookfire – and there were now very few persons in the camp with whom he had not had some contact; yet thus far all his overhearings, all his faux-casual questioning, had revealed nothing more unsavoury than petty thefts and a tendency to lewd and sometimes cruel jesting. Most had heard the name Imperator Gallia; many had specific, often contradictory details to relate; but all dismissed it as the species of rumour always liable to be spread by troops wishing to unsettle and intimidate their opponents.

Unbeknownst to Kergabet – or, at any rate, without telling him of it – Gray had succeeded in absconding with one of Lord de Vaucourt's spelled maps, and throughout his sojourn at Ivry he had been using it to work Cameron's mapped finding, nearly every day – but thus far no trace of Amelia, Appius Callender, or any of the other conspirators had he found.

The situation had, in fact, all the earmarks of a stalemate, and after nearly a se'nnight Gray was on the point of giving it up – was laying plans to move on from Ivry, over the frontier into the territory of Blois, in search of Amelia, the absconded traitors, or both – when the decision was taken out of his hands.

He had come very near to all three garrisons on various occasions – near enough to note the details of banners and to make approximate counts of men and horses – and always had felt, even in owl-shape, the telltale raising of hairs (or, in this case, feathers) up the back of his neck, which warned him of the working of magick. From this evidence together with that of Ollivier and Lécuyer, as well as of the day-scouts Fournier and Tanguy, and of the several mage-officers who took it in turns to accompany Captain Howells' infantry scouts, Gray concluded that the three most proximate enemy encampments almost certainly had mages of their own, and that very possibly these mages had worked (or were presently working) some manner of protection, illusion, or concealment.

And if that is so, he wrote, concluding today's dispatch to Lord Kergabet, *all of our observations are – or may be – as good as useless, for we cannot know for certain what is truth, and what illusion.*

Having laboriously enciphered his text and burnt the unenciphered original, he sealed the enciphered copy and tucked it into an inner pocket of his very unmilitary coat, locked away his writing-case in the bottom of his trunk, and made for Colonel Dubois' command-post.

Gray had been sleeping badly, alone in his too-short bed amidst the noisy bustle of the camp's daylight hours; he missed Sophie most fiercely not at night, when the twin imperatives of surveillance and survival occupied the lion's share of his attention, but during the long, restless days. They could not correspond except by way of Kergabet – even this dubious privilege was a compromise, which he dared not protest lest it, too, be withdrawn – and to end each day without telling Sophie of its happenings large and small, without hearing in return what had occupied and preoccupied her, unsettled him far more than he judged it ought.

Nevertheless, Sophie and he had learnt many things in the course of their years in Alba, one of which was that their magicks linked them, whether they themselves were together or far apart. Though none of their researches had taught them any means of controlling or influencing this link, by patient experiment they had learnt to see one another's magick, in the same way that every mage sees his own.

His dispatch delivered, Gray ducked back into the night-scouts' tent, shrugged out of his coat and slung it across the lid of the trunk, and carefully folded himself into his borrowed camp bed. Then, closing his eyes, he sank deep into the consciousness of his own magick; having found it – a vast dim autumn rose of blue-green flame – he felt cautiously outwards into the warm dark, seeking the frail bright thread which, at this vast distance, was all he could see of Sophie's. It came, when at last he grasped it, with a faint, aetherial chorus of treble voices – which Gray had half expected – and a bright anticipatory spark of excitement, which he had not.

What are you about, Sophie-of-mine? But whatever it was, at any rate Sophie was not – at this particular moment – sunk in melancholy. *I wish you well of it, love, and may the gods grant us leisure to tell all our adventures very soon.*

Outside, some heavy object fell to the ground with an ominous clatter, and a man's voice shouted, 'Mars and Mithras! Have a care!'

Gray's eyes flew open; Lécuyer stirred in his sleep; Ollivier flung up one arm and let out a single stentorian snore. Gray chuckled wearily, closed his eyes once more, and at last drifted down into sleep.

* * *

After a long, unbroken spell of fine weather, that night brought a lashing rain, the occasional clap of thunder, and a tense twilight conference amongst the night-scouts and their captain as to the advisability of a sortie.

'Ollivier cannot possibly go,' declared Lécuyer, folding his arms across his chest; for a wonder, they had both dressed in full uniform, if not very carefully, and Lécuyer wore in addition a vast great-coat which smelt strongly of lavender-oil. 'You know what his feathers are like; he should be waterlogged and in need of rescuing within a quarter-hour, and what good is that to anyone?'

Ollivier glared, but did not attempt to contradict him. Gray was no expert on the physiology of *Tyto alba*, but it was true that the soft feathers which enabled barn owls to fly so silently in dry weather must absorb water to a dangerous degree when it was wet.

Captain Tremblay pressed the bridge of his nose between thumb and forefinger and sighed. 'I am sorry to say it, Mr Ollivier, but that is certainly true. Mr Marshall' – he turned to Gray – 'what experience have you of flying in wet weather?'

Gray considered this question carefully, listening to the keening of the wind and the drumming spatter of the rain against the canvas roof and walls. A great deal of his flying, in fact, had been done in wet weather, but he had never had reason to go aloft on a night like this one, and it was not the rain but the wind which gave him pause. Too, this lashing rain would impede even his owl's eyes, making reconnaissance difficult if not impossible – even if he and Lécuyer were fortunate enough not to be blown off course or, worse, against a tree.

On the other hand, if I were a general contemplating an invasion, I should make use of any circumstance which seemed likely to shield my movements from the enemy. What might we fail to see tonight, should we choose the prudent course?

293

'I can give you no promises,' he said at last, 'but I am prepared to make the attempt.'

'Good man!' Tremblay clapped him on the shoulder – the left one, which had ached all day as it always did when the air was damp and chill.

'Captain, is this wise?' said Ollivier.

Gray turned to look at him, startled; he had observed before now that Captain Tremblay's men, and the mage-officers in particular, observed the forms of military discipline only as the humour took them, but never before had he seen any of them issue so direct a challenge.

'Tell me, Mr Ollivier,' said the Captain dryly, 'which of us commands this company?'

'Your pardon, sir,' said Ollivier. He did not look remorseful, however – or even abashed – and Gray was irresistibly reminded of Joanna at thirteen, fearlessly berating persons older and more powerful than herself when she believed them to be in the wrong; she was grown more politic now, and to his surprise he rather regretted the change.

Ollivier, indeed, was not deterred: 'Can the Colonel not wait till morning for the next report?' he said. 'It is a difference of only a few hours, and at what price?'

'Kannig,' said Lécuyer, who looked acutely uncomfortable. 'Hold your tongue, idiot.'

'I shall not, then,' said Ollivier, turning on him. 'And which of us is the idiot, to insist on flying in this unholy mess? Not I.'

They looked ready to come to blows, and Gray was as much relieved as startled when the furious tension between them was broken by Captain Tremblay's saying, in a tone of well-controlled ire, 'Enough. Mr Lécuyer, Mr Marshall, you will make ready to go aloft in half an hour's time. *Mr* Ollivier, you will go back to your quarters at once, and I should advise you very strongly not to be seen outside them before tomorrow morning. Is that clear?'

'As a midsummer sky, sir,' said Ollivier, through gritted teeth. He saluted smartly, turned on his heel, turned up the collar of his coat, and vanished into the driving rain.

There is a story there, thought Gray, gazing after him. Ollivier, in his observation, had no less courage than any of the other scouts, though he was rather less reckless; it was not cowardice or an excess of caution, presumably, which had pushed him to such behaviour.

Gray and Lécuyer, avoiding one another's eyes, turned up their collars likewise and followed Ollivier out into the rain and wind. They were very damp indeed – Gray particularly – by the time they reached their own quarters, and Lécuyer flung off his dripping great-coat and collapsed upon his bed with a theatrical groan, one arm across his face.

Ollivier had shed his regimental coat and wrapped himself in a thick travelling-rug, and was pacing to and fro, already wearing a path in the packed-earth floor. He looked daggers at the oblivious Lécuyer and, when Gray shrugged out of his coat and sat down gingerly on his own bed, at once sat down beside him.

'If you *must* go, do keep an eye on him,' he said, low, before the startled Gray could protest this liberty. 'He is as brave as a lion, and he has no more sense than a rabbit.' He leant closer and added, almost inaudibly, 'And there is something uncanny about this storm.'

'Shut *up*, Kannig,' said Lécuyer. His words were muffled by his coat-sleeve, but his exasperated tone was entirely audible. 'I have not needed a nursemaid these twenty years. You had better take your dry night's leisure and thank Jove for it, than to be making such an almighty row.'

Ollivier, on his feet once more and glaring down at his

brother-officer, scoffed. 'You were quick enough to stop *me* from flying,' he said; when Lécuyer made no reply to this, he continued, 'If I hear tomorrow that you have been taking stupid risks, Arzhur, I shall kill you myself. And not quickly.'

Then he curled up on his bed – muddy boots, travelling-rug and all – and closed his eyes. He was still feigning sleep when Kerambrun arrived to collect Lécuyer and Gray.

A sound like a hound's barking caught Gray's ear through the tumult of the storm, away off to the north-east. He pondered it, curving his wings to catch an updraft and gliding perilously above the tops of the trees. It came again – from the general direction of the largest enemy camp, but . . . higher? Yes: not a hound's bark but the call of an eagle owl sounding the alarm. *Lécuyer has found something he wishes me to see.*

There was another possibility, of course, but for the moment Gray resolutely refrained from considering it.

He answered the call with a series of low hoots, and – somewhat to his surprise, for the wind had risen to a sort of keening wail – was answered in turn by another brief volley of barking. Each hearing made the source easier to pinpoint, and before long Gray had sight of his quarry, clinging damp and bedraggled to the bottom-most branch of an enormous oak-tree half overcome with mistletoe. Lécuyer, catching sight of him in turn as he glided in, greeted him with a more usual *oohu-oohu-oohu.* For some time they huddled close for warmth, quite unselfconsciously, Gray's right foot nearly overlapping Lécuyer's left; then Lécuyer tilted his body forward and, with a powerful thrust of his legs, dropped away from the branch. Gray followed him as closely as he dared, skimming close to the forest floor.

They reached the river, swollen by a full day's heavy rain to within a foot of the near bank, and Lécuyer sheered away upwards, climbing high above the rushing water, above the new-felled trees on the far bank, above the camp which for at least a fortnight had flown the banners of lords beholden to Blois, Poitou, Anjou, Artois, and Bourgogne so puzzlingly side by side. New banners had been raised alongside and above them – the number was larger than before – but the lashing rain made them impossible to distinguish.

But this, whatever it might mean, was neither the worst nor the most astonishing discovery to be made that night; for as he followed Lécuyer's circuit of the camp, farther aloft than either of them ordinarily flew, he saw that it appeared to have tripled in size since the previous night – even, in fact, since this morning's report from Fournier and Tanguy – and that yet more troops – foot-soldiers and cavalry, pikemen and archers, teams of horses pulling siege-engines, trebuchets, and huge carriage-mounted saltpetre-cannon of the sort armies use when they have no battle-mages to sow large-scale havoc amongst the opposing force – were pouring towards it along the southern road.

Gray had always found this body less sensitive to the presence of magick than his human one, but down the back of his skull and all along his spine there now crawled a prickling sensation in reaction to someone else's spell-work. Were there mages – trebuchets and cannon notwithstanding – amongst those steadily moving columns of men and horses below? Doing what exactly? Or had Ollivier been correct in supposing that this storm was not of natural origin? If so, were the persons responsible en route to the enemy camp, or were they in residence already?

They circled the camp twice more, attempting to see as much as they could of its drastically altered configurations; the rain grew heavier, harder – solidified into tiny hailstones, striking with painful force – and Gray began more seriously to consider Ollivier's theory.

Navigating the increasingly violent wind was becoming exhausting; a sharp ache in his left wing began to demand his attention and quickly grew impossible to ignore. At last, subordinating curiosity to common sense after a particularly punishing buffet of hailstones, he called to Lécuyer, and when the latter had circled back to him, gave the agreed-upon signal for *injured, returning to camp*. Had Ollivier been with them as usual, Lécuyer might have seen him across the river, into friendly territory, and then turned back, but in the circumstances, Gray was not surprised to be escorted all the way back to the eastern watchtower of Colonel Dubois' encampment.

He was surprised, however, at how closely Lécuyer followed him – their wingtips sometimes almost brushing – and astonished by the commotion that greeted their return. It was customary (or perhaps a rule of military conduct) for the scouts to be divested of their identifying leg-bands and returned to their quarters before resuming their natural form, but they had no sooner alighted in the watch-tower than Lécuyer was exploding from owl to man – mother-naked and entirely heedless of the fact – and bellowing, 'A healer, quickly! He has caught an arrow through the wing.'

Oh, thought Gray vaguely. *Those were not only hailstones, then.*

Someone had slung a great-coat about Lécuyer's shoulders; kneeling on the rough boards of the watchtower, he gathered Gray's owl-body gently into his arms, tucked him between the great-coat's overlapping layers, and began to descend the ladder. Gray shut his eyes, wound his talons into the rough wool, and held on.

CHAPTER XXI

In Which Sophie Dispatches a Message, Joanna Commits an Error in Judgement, and Lucia Makes a Discovery

'*Imperator Gallia?*' *Joanna* repeated, her face folding up into a frown. 'But the Emperor of Gaul is only a rumour, surely – a monster invented to frighten the common soldiers. You do not suppose—'

'Amelia evidently believes in him, at any rate,' said Sophie, rather more crossly than she had intended. 'Unless, of course, one prefers to take the view that my friend Evans-Hughes has invented the tale for his own amusement.'

The two of them were presently in sole possession of the bedroom which Sophie was to share with Lucia, Sophie curled in the room's one armchair and Joanna sprawled across the counterpane. Gareth, who had accompanied Sophie back to the Dragon and Lion and thereafter dined with the party from London, had then volunteered to conduct them on a guided tour of those of Oxford's sights which could be seen in the interval between dinner and dusk. Lucia, Roland, and Gwendolen had received this suggestion with enthusiasm; when Joanna would have joined them, however, Sophie had leant casually towards her and muttered in her ear, 'I have something to tell you about Amelia,' after which Joanna had promptly developed a headache, and elected to remain behind.

'Well,' Joanna sighed, 'of course if anything casts the Professor in a flattering light, poor Amelia will happily swallow it whole. In any case, however, I do not see that that titbit gets us much forwarder. But Dover . . . Dover is very suggestive.'

'It suggests a wish to leave Britain as quickly as possible, certainly.'

'Dover,' said Joanna, pushing herself up on her elbows, 'is the most heavily fortified port along the Manche, precisely because one can very nearly throw a stone across the strait from Calais and strike the ships in the harbour. Its entire garrison is on alert for the fugitives from the Tower, of whom Henry Taylor is one.'

'Seen in that light,' said Sophie, thoughtful, 'it seems a most peculiar choice for him to have made.'

'Exactly,' said Joanna. 'And in fact, according to your friend, from Dover Amelia went on to Calais alone, and neither of them was apprehended – nor even *seen*, so far as we know. Now, of course, the garrison and the local constabulary were on the lookout for the conspirators travelling together, not for one of them with a woman, or a woman alone, but no British ship's captain who valued his livelihood would have given either of them passage to Calais without papers of some sort—'

'Woodville, the forger?' Sophie suggested.

Joanna replied with a noncommittal sort of hum.

'At any rate,' said Sophie, 'this must all go to Kergabet, as soon as may be. If I write my letter at once, shall you have time to help me encipher it this evening, so that one of the guardsmen can deliver it in the morning?'

Joanna yawned hugely and rolled over onto her back. 'I shall help you this time,' she said, 'but after this I shall make you do your own enciphering. Hurry up, then! The light is going.'

Sophie called a globe of magelight, then another, and sent them to hover amongst the rafters. Then she extricated her writing-case from the bottom of a valise and sat down at the small spindle-legged desk, more decorative than practical, to begin her letter.

'I am glad she is not with Taylor,' she said, 'but I do wish she had not gone off all alone.'

Early the following afternoon, in a state of mingled excitement and trepidation and armed with a three-hundred-year-old plan of their quarry, an assortment of tools, and a borrowed ladder, Sophie's party approached the main gate of Lady Morgan College. Constructed from close-set wrought-iron bars, the gate was set in a tall, narrow archway flanked on either side by long wings of dressed Headington stone, whose windowless ground-floor walls were almost less forbidding than the broken-paned casements brooding dark above them. The gate was locked, and a heavy chain, wrapped several times and secured by a large padlock, anchored it to the gatepost. In the interstices of the ivy-leaves, Sophie saw that the whole arrangement had rusted to a near-uniform russet-brown. She ceased to fret that no one knew where to look for the keys to these locks, and began to wish for draught horses and a dredging-hook.

She and Roland and Lucia, however, had unlocking-spells at the ready. Sophie's was one she had learnt from Gray and had never failed her before; perhaps it was made for well-kept locks, however, for its sole effect on the rusted padlock was to strike a few sparks. Roland's brief, emphatic spell made the padlock groan, shedding flakes of rust, but still there came no telltale clicking of tumblers. Frowning, Roland tried it twice more, with the same result.

'The trouble with mages,' said Joanna, coming forward to peer at the lock, 'is that you cannot conceive of a problem to which magick is not the solution. Gwen, come and see whether you cannot pick the lock, as you have such a talent for it!'

'*Joanna!*'

301

Sophie, glancing over her shoulder, saw that Miss Pryce's face was flushed red.

Joanna, who had not been looking at her friend when she made her careless pronouncement, now wore an expression of dawning horror.

'I believe,' said Sophie – both to draw the others' attention away from the unfortunate Miss Pryce, and because she had herself had an idea – 'that picking locks requires equipment which we have not brought with us. We *have* brought a ladder, however, and Mr Goff has got an axe.'

'Only a wood-axe, ma'am,' said Goff apologetically, 'for doors and the like. It would not do much good against an iron gate, even rusted . . .'

Ceana MacGregor tapped Mr Goff smartly on the shoulder and, when he turned to face her, held out her hand for the axe. He frowned, but surrendered it.

Ceana made for the padlocked gate, then hefted the axe and drew it back up over her right shoulder, the wrong way about, with the sharp edge upwards – which puzzled Sophie until it came down again, powerful and precise, and the blunt end of the axe-head rang against a single link in the great rusted chain. Two more precise blows upon that same link – two more again – a last and it exploded into flakes of rust and shards of metal. Sophie scratched absently at the bridge of her nose.

Ceana MacGregor propped the axe, head down, against the wall beside the gate, and with assistance from Goff and Roland began unwrapping the chain. It was a long and noisy business – during which, to Sophie's intense discomfort, a furious whispered argument between Joanna and Miss Pryce continued unabated.

At last the chain was reduced to a heap of rusted links at the foot of the wall, and Sophie and Lucia converged upon the gate's own locking mechanism.

'Hmm,' said Lucia, in an interested tone; shifting (perhaps unconsciously) from Latin into Gaelic, she said, 'there is magick *in* this lock, and I believe it still lives.'

'*Lives?*' said Roland, sceptical. 'Like . . . like the yew-hedge?'

Lucia smiled a little at this cryptic query and said, 'A little like. This iron gate is farther from its roots even than your tamed and trammelled yew-trees, but it has not quite forgotten them; and the lock . . .'

She turned to look at Sophie, a solemn, meaning look. 'Like calls to like,' she said. 'Iron to iron. I shall try my spell, but I think . . . I think the lock's own magick may be—'

'The key?' Roland offered sardonically, stepping up beside Sophie.

Lucia ignored him; she had leant her head against the bars of the gate and was murmuring low and quick. To Sophie's eye, no effect was forthcoming.

'As I thought,' murmured Lucia, stepping back a little.

Gwendolen Pryce had drifted closer without Sophie's noticing, and now said quietly in Latin, 'May I be of any help?'

'Have you a pocket-knife about you?' said Lucia. 'Or a pen-knife? And can you call fire?'

'I have,' said Gwendolen, in a doubtful tone, 'and I can, but why—'

'Well, give it here, then!' Lucia's tone was eager.

Gwendolen hesitated; Lucia thrust out a hand insistently and repeated, 'The *knife*. And call me a small flame to light, to light . . .' She rummaged in a capacious pocket of the riding-habit – split-skirted and tailored above to mimic a man's dress – which she had insisted on wearing for the purposes of this venture, and pulled up a stub of candle. 'This. Here.'

'*Lucia,*' said Roland, urgent. 'Is this wise?' There was no response.

Sophie studied her friend – the quivering tension in her stooped shoulders, the slim fingers wrapped tight round the bars of the gate, the pale sliver of her profile, her one visible eye intent on her work.

Lucia meant to give her own blood to the lock in hopes of inducing it to open; so much was clear, to Sophie if not to anyone else. Was this a brilliant or a disastrous notion? Or was it, perhaps – like many a notion of Sophie's own – brilliant or disastrous only as subsequent events might decide?

Sophie nodded once at Miss Pryce, who, though her dark-curved brows rose in surprise, stepped forward with her pen-knife in one hand and took the candle-stub from Lucia.

'The flame must be hot,' said Lucia, low. 'As hot as you can manage. Pass the blade through.'

Sophie only just heard the whispered *Flammo te!* before the wick burst into flame – a tiny flame, blue-hot and precisely controlled. Gwendolen Pryce knew her business when it came to minor magicks, though seemingly incapable of greater ones.

With a steady hand she held the pen-knife's small blade in the flame – one breath, two, three – then wrapped Lucia's splayed fingers about its handle and, abandoning magickal for more prosaic methods, blew the candle out.

Lucia loosed her hold on the gate and with her right hand raised the knife to the pad of her left forefinger. Now Roland at last saw what she had in mind, and Sophie caught him by both elbows just in time to arrest his panicked lunge towards her.

'*Nuair a thig air duine thig air uile*,' Lucia murmured – *what befalls one, befalls all* – as she nicked the pad of her finger.

Roland growled; Sophie gripped his arm to restrain him and dimly registered that Ceana – despite her very evident disapproval of Lucia's proceedings – was doing the same on his other side.

'Whatever she is about,' said Sophie, low, 'we must not interrupt it.'

Lucia regarded her bleeding finger, dripping steadily onto the blade of the knife – then, as though it had been the most natural thing in the world, crouched down and, holding the knife in her left hand, slid the blade slowly into the keyhole.

For a moment, nothing happened. Then came a sudden smell of hot iron; Sophie's nose began to itch, so fiercely as to be almost painful; at almost the same time, Lucia yelped and staggered back from the gate, dropping the knife and cradling her left hand against her chest.

Ceana MacGregor caught her – just – when she stumbled and nearly fell headlong. The rest converged on her in a rush.

'Stay *back*,' Ceana snarled. She was holding Lucia upright with both arms locked about her ribs, but not without difficulty: Lucia – pale as her own candle-stub but still intently focused on the centuries-old lock – was struggling mightily to get free.

'Lucia,' said Sophie, very firmly and as loudly as she dared. 'Lucia, look at me.'

Lucia blinked, blinked again, and abruptly ceased her struggles to escape. Ceana MacGregor eased her hold, though without releasing it.

'The lock needs blood,' said Lucia, as calmly as though she had not been fighting tooth and claw against her own guard captain just moments ago. 'My spell was an adequate substitute for the key, but the locking-spell cannot be broken in that way; it must have blood. Not *my* blood, however; the spell has made that very clear.'

She held up her left hand, palm up, and Sophie saw that the skin of her hand, the palm and all five fingers, was burnt to blisters.

'And yet, why leave even such a loophole as that, if they truly meant it never to be opened again? Why, indeed – as we have asked ourselves before – not knock down the walls and buildings, and make some other use of the land beneath?'

'More to the point,' said Miss Pryce, who had gone back to the gate to retrieve her knife and was wiping it clean with her handkerchief, 'how are we to know whose blood, if anyone's, will appease the spell, and how are we to undertake the trial without anyone else's being hurt?'

Sophie considered. 'Suppose,' she said after a moment, 'suppose that the lock and the spell expect the key and the blood, respectively – as Lucia believes they do – one might . . . er . . . apply the latter to the former, and so provide both at once. And as we have already dealt with the lock itself – have we not, Lucia?'

Lucia nodded without looking up. She had unwrapped Ceana MacGregor's makeshift cold compress from her hand and was studying her burnt fingers.

'Then one might find another object of the same length and circumference,' said Sophie, beginning to look about her. 'A key with no bit, so to speak, to serve the same purpose—'

'But it must be iron,' said Lucia, urgently. 'You are thinking of a tree-branch, Sophie, or something of the sort, but it must be iron, like the lock itself. Not wood or bone – not even steel.' She held up her burnt hand.

'Very well,' said Sophie. She studied the gate, the height of the windows; considered the lower east wall, the height of the ladder. It was growing late in the afternoon, and everyone must be wanting their dinner. No – this problem, alas, would not be solved today.

'A tactical retreat,' she announced. 'We shall return tomorrow, properly armed. Mr Goff, I should be obliged if you would seek out a trustworthy blacksmith; perhaps the innkeeper may tell you where one is to be found.' Using a piece of string, she made crude measurements of the keyhole and noted them down on a page of her commonplace-book, which she tore out and presented to Mr Goff.

He looked deeply dubious, but nevertheless said, 'Ma'am,' and after glancing at the torn-off paper, folded it and tucked it away in a coat-pocket.

'Back to the inn, then,' said Sophie briskly, concealing her restless frustration as well as she was able, 'for dinner, and a healer, and our beds.'

By a variety of stratagems, Joanna contrived largely to avoid Gwendolen during what remained of the afternoon and evening. At last, however, the company retired for the night, and there was no more evading the continuance of the afternoon's dispute.

By now she had, by slow degrees, talked herself out of her self-righteous insistence that Gwendolen ought not to be angry with her, and returned to that first access of remorse; she hoped that Gwendolen's temper, too, might now be cooled, at least a little.

'I am sorry, Gwen,' she began, without other preamble. 'It is true that I did not know how strongly you should object to my saying what I said, but still I ought not to have said it, and I am sorry.'

Gwendolen, leaning against the edge of the dressing-table, arms folded, in a pose of wholly unconvincing nonchalance, gave her a long, measuring look.

'I believe you,' she said at last, unsmiling.

Joanna winced. To be believed was something, but in this case it was evidently some considerable distance from being pardoned.

'You know, I hope, that I should never hurt you by intent,' she said. 'Perhaps, if I understood why—'

Gwendolen cut her off with an impatient huff. 'Can you truly imagine no reason why I should be reluctant to advertise a talent for breaking and entering?' she demanded. 'None whatsoever?'

'I do not see that it is any different from an unlocking-spell,' said Joanna – not for the first time – 'which Sophie and Roland and Lucia had no objection to being seen to work.'

'It is *different*,' said Gwendolen, through gritted teeth, 'first,

307

because very few common thieves can work an unlocking-spell, and second, because powerful mages of royal birth may do any number of things with impunity, which the cast-off daughters of heavily indebted country squires cannot afford even to be suspected of doing. Particularly' – she raised a hand to fend off Joanna's protest – 'if those daughters should happen to be engaged in equivocal and secretive intimate friendships with the protégées of men prominent at Court.'

Joanna closed her eyes for a long, silent moment: *Lady Venus, wise Minerva, guide my tongue, or I shall say entirely the wrong thing once again.*

'You surely cannot think my father any better prize than yours,' she said carefully. 'And I hope you do not suppose yourself any less solidly under the protection of Lord and Lady Kergabet than I am?'

Gwendolen stared at her in frank astonishment. 'Jo, you are Lady Kergabet's sister-in-law,' she said. 'And it is plain to see that they love you for yourself. Of course I am grateful to Lady Kergabet for taking pity on me that day at the Griffith-Rowlands', and for all the rest of it, but—'

'You are quite wrong,' cried Joanna, equally astonished at this thorough misinterpretation of the facts. Seeing Gwendolen's fine dark brows begin to draw together in a frown, she hurried on: 'I do not say that Jenny did not *begin* by feeling sorry for your plight, but how can you suppose *now* that she does not love you? And – and in any case *I* love you, Gwen, and they should protect you for my sake even if they did not.'

Then – abashed at this uncharacteristic eruption of passionate words, and cut to the heart by Gwendolen's expression of wonder at hearing them – she retreated to the washbasin to splash cool water upon her burning cheeks.

When the shades of Gwen's father and stepmother, and of that tyrant Mrs Griffith-Rowlands, are judged in the realm of Hades, I hope they may all be condemned to the fires of Tartarus, for having made my Gwen believe no one but her dead mama could love her.

When at last she turned away from the washstand, still drying her hands on the inn's crisp linen towel, she found Gwendolen standing before her, near enough to touch. Without her conscious volition, her hands came up to clasp her friend's slim shoulders, and Gwendolen stepped forward into her arms.

'You must never doubt it,' Joanna whispered fiercely. 'Not for a moment.'

'Nor you,' said Gwendolen, muffled into Joanna's hair.

Joanna pulled away just far enough to look up into Gwendolen's deep brown eyes. 'And you must never think you have any cause to be ashamed,' she said. 'I ought not to have spoken as I did, without your leave, but a useful skill is always worth possessing, and I spoke from pride in your skill, not . . . not from any other motive.'

Gwendolen swallowed hard, pressing her lips together briefly; then she smiled – a small swift thing, but warm and full of affection – and said, 'I thought, perhaps, your motive was to open that rusted old gate. But perhaps I may be mistaken?'

Joanna laughed aloud, and kissed her.

All the same, she thought, not for the first time, *I should very much like to know what* your *motive was for learning to pick locks.*

CHAPTER XXII

In Which Gray Receives a Message and Makes a Decision

Gray woke to watery late-afternoon sunshine slanting through an open tent-flap, and prudently took stock before attempting to sit up. This was not his too-small camp bed in the night-scouts' tent, but one of many identical ones set in tidy rows in a much larger tent – really a sort of pavilion, a canvas roof and walls which could be rolled up to admit fresh air and sunlight, supported by sturdy wooden posts. The regimental infirmary, then; and to judge from its lack of occupants, whatever offensive action might be contemplated by the force across the river had not yet begun.

Someone had dressed him, not in his own clothes but in a worn linen nightshirt, too small but scrupulously clean. His left arm, bent at the elbow, was bound flat against his ribs with a square of linen folded into a sling, which also held in place the folded bandages padding his shoulder; the shoulder yet ached a little, but the throbbing agony he remembered was nowhere in evidence. His head, on the other hand, felt as though he had spent an evening attempting to outdrink his brother George, and the whole of the succeeding night regretting it.

An arrow through the wing. Lécuyer's words echoed in Gray's mind. There were healers here – very skilled ones, clearly – and Lécuyer had lost no time in delivering Gray into their care; but even so, such a wound could not be recovered from in a single night. *I shall not be flying for some days, I suspect.*

Pinned to the blankets at the foot of the bed with a clothes-peg was a flat object, more or less white and more or less rectangular: a letter? Gray struggled to sit up, to lean down after it. An indrawn breath snagged in his throat, and he coughed. By all the gods, when had he last had anything to drink?

Help arrived in the form of a young man, clad in an odd hodgepodge of uniform breeches and boots and healer's robes, bearing a *cantine* of water. He then insisted on taking Gray's pulse, changing the dressing on his shoulder wound, and testing the motion of his arm, by the end of which operations, his patient was in a very fever of impatience.

'Is that a letter for me?' Gray inquired, low, when the healer had finished and was preparing to take himself off again. 'May I read it?'

He held out his right hand to the healer, who gave him a dubious frown but unpinned the letter and handed it over. Awkwardly one-handed, Gray broke the seal. His brows rose; not Kergabet's hand but Joanna's had enciphered the contents. What could this portend?

Upon deciphering, the message proved brief – a mere few lines, padded out with nonsense. *In Oxford*, it read. *Have consulted GEH; A is gone to Calais, not to Honfleur, and not with T. Means to join Papa, whereabouts unknown, and person styled Imperator Gallia. Not a rumour? Go carefully. S.*

Gray stared at it for some time, questions boiling up in his mind: why should Sophie go to Oxford – or rather, why should her father consent to her going? Calais, not Honfleur; meaning that Amelia sailed from Dover? *Not* with Taylor? Then with whom? Not all alone, surely? And where was she (were they?) going, in the end?

At any rate – all relevant observations having by now been reported up the chain of command, and there being no evidence whatsoever amongst the garrison of conversation with the enemy – Gray had already concluded that he could do no more good in Normandie.

He folded Sophie's letter away and, for lack of a pocket of his own to stow it in, folded his fingers around it. Then – moving slowly at first, until he was certain that he should not fall over – he extricated himself from the camp-bed, climbed to his feet, and went in search of his boots and a pair of trousers, without which he did not quite dare accost Colonel Dubois.

Gray departed the camp at Ivry with even less ceremony than had attended his arrival a se'nnight since – shortly before dusk, on horseback, with a few necessities distributed into a pair of saddle-bags (together with a small purse of coin from Anjou, Orléanais, Picardie, Poitou, and Champagne, helpfully provided by Colonel Dubois); the rest of his possessions he had left behind in the care of Mage-Captain Tremblay. As soon as he could safely do so, he meant to wander into enemy territory in the dark; if, somewhere in one of the Duchies, someone were indeed calling himself Emperor of Gaul, then Gray had only to keep his ears open and his origins and identity concealed, and soon enough he should discover where to seek his quarry.

Or so I hope.

Around him, the camp hummed with preparations – improvements to the regiment's defensive position, chiefly, though Gray and the rangy grey gelding Colonel Dubois had lent him were also passed by troops of grim-faced grooms shepherding strings of horses in from their picket-lines outside the camp proper. From time to time he received a respectful nod or even, once or twice, a salute; word had spread of the civilian night-scout who had matched the feat of the acclaimed Mage-Lieutenant Tanguy. *My father would be pleased, at any rate*, thought Gray, suppressing an ironical twist of his lips as he gravely returned a passing cavalry-officer's greeting. Not that, should this sortie of his succeed, his father was ever likely to hear anything of it.

Gray had written, enciphered, and dispatched a report to Kergabet – parallel to the official version and, he suspected, rather shorter – giving a detailed account of his observations of the camp on the far bank of the River Eure, in which was enclosed a brief message of thanks to Sophie, together with a précis of his plans. Perhaps more usefully, Tremblay had unlocked his dispatch-case once more and made Gray a temporary gift of one of the talismans stored therein – the one marked *XXI*, which he had worn on his first sortie with the night-scouts; this small piece of insurance presently reposed in an inner pocket of his coat, and Tremblay had proposed a regular rotation of finding-spells by means of which he and Colonel Dubois should be apprised of Gray's approximate location at least once every day, unless and until he reached the limits of the available mages' range.

There, Sophie-of-mine: I am leaving you a trail to follow, as best I may, should . . . anything befall me.

He wished more than ever, now, that she had been here with him; how much more might he hope to accomplish, with two pairs of eyes to observe, two sets of ears to listen, and Sophie's magick to wrap them in unremarkable obscurity? But he had made her a promise to return to her safe and whole, though plainly (he flexed his injured shoulder irritably, and thanked Aesculapius for talented healers) it was too late to return actually unscathed; and Gray hoped he was not a man to break a promise to his wife.

The grey gelding rejoiced in the name of Tonnerre, which in Gray's experience thus far could not have been less a propos to its placid, accommodating temperament. Having passed the outer pickets, they ambled through the gathering dusk in a more or less southerly direction, roughly parallel to but out of sight of the River Eure and, it was to be hoped, any sentries or scouts posted by the force massed on its opposite bank.

The size of that force had more than tripled, the number of siege-engines doubled; the heavy saltpetre-cannon had been added to the array of weaponry visible along the far bank, and new banners to the collection flying from the peaks of tents and pavilions and from the watchtowers facing the British camp. But no sortie had been made, either to attack or to parley. What might they be waiting for?

The lights of Colonel Dubois' camp behind him, Gray dug in his heels, urging Tonnerre into an easy canter.

The night was well advanced, and a gibbous moon lighting Gray's path in black and silver, before it seemed likely that he should be able to cross the Eure without being seen or heard from the enemy camp. Fording the river left him drenched to the hips, chilled, shivering, and at odds with the world at large and Tonnerre in particular – no one had mentioned to him, for reasons best known to themselves, the gelding's particular dislike of running water. But here he was, and a warming-spell repaired the worst of the damage, or at any rate rendered man and horse willing to tolerate one another once more.

By noon they were ambling into a village – middling prosperous, to all appearances, and in most respects indistinguishable from any farming village in Maine or Normandie – and looking about them in search of their breakfasts. The village proved, surprisingly for its size, to possess two inns, at opposite ends of its principal street; their signboards proclaimed them to be, respectively, the Lion d'Or and the Cheval Blanc. Gray, after some thought, chose the former.

Gray's meal was a very long time in coming, and when at last it appeared, was garnished with pre-emptive apologies for its quality – the muster of the Seigneur de Déols had marched through the village three days since, and the inn's cook, indeed half its staff, monsieur, had marched off with them, without so much as giving notice! – which, sadly, proved entirely justified.

The beds at the Lion d'Or, on the other hand, were clean and dry and free of vermin – though Gray, after his night's journey, would gladly have slept on a horse-blanket in the stables.

The following morning, having inadvertently slept all afternoon and most of the night and feeling much the better for it, Gray loaded his saddle-bags, mounted up, and set off again, attempting to look as though he had some notion of going somewhere in particular. He could not, of course, turn back in the direction he claimed to have come from, nor was there any purpose in retracing his actual route – in addition to which, what wandering scholar would ride towards an army when he might so easily ride away from it? But if Amelia, with or without Taylor, had landed at Calais, then his best chance of intercepting her, surely, lay in travelling north-east, to Picardie and Artois. He therefore set his face more or less east once more, towards – eventually – the great River Seine.

The next several villages, with their several inns, offered generally better provisioning but not, in the main, much more useful conversation, and the endlessly repeated finding-spells continued to turn up nothing whatsoever. Gray began to curse himself – very quietly, rolled up in Ollivier's borrowed travelling-rug in shared bedchambers at night – for believing that this wild-goose chase of his might have any other result than his eventually coming to the end of his coin and either starving to death or being hanged as a thief.

On an unseasonably wet and chilly day he arrived at dusk in a village which had no inn as such, but did possess a public-house – denominated Le Bouclier d'Argent – in whose hayloft, for a small price, travellers might spend the night. Here the cook and her minions remained, but the matériel for her art was lacking, having been eaten or simply requisitioned by a passing cavalry troop.

Conversation amongst the half-dozen persons poking dispiritedly at their unappetising dinners, however, showed more promise. Being asked his name and business, Gray declared himself once more to be Guy Marais of Poitiers, in Poitou (which he had judged sufficiently distant that most persons he encountered were unlikely to know it any better than he did himself, from reading histories and travellers' accounts), and to be a scholar travelling the Duchies seeking employment, or, failing that, to visit as many libraries as possible. Having thus persuaded his new acquaintance that he was odd, eccentric, and almost certainly harmless, he assumed an affable and perhaps slightly foolish expression, and for some time let their talk flow over and around him.

Three were merchants from Arras en route to Tours, old acquaintance travelling together for safety and economy. A father and son had been stranded by the recent storm and were now making their way home to their farm near Anet. The sixth man was, so he said, a priest of Ceres, and had been travelling on the business of his temple in Orléans. Like Gray himself, he said little, but unlike Gray he did not try to hide that he was listening attentively to all that the others said. They all spoke in Français, in deference to the farmer, who had no Latin, and his son, who had very little; Gray's Français was as different from the priest's, the Artésien merchants', and the farmers' as they were from one another, but no one, it appeared, remarked it as Normand rather than Angevin.

In the Duchies as in Britain, it seemed, relative strangers taking one another's measure are apt to talk about the weather. In the present case, however, thought Gray, the weather bore talking of — such a storm, the grizzled farmer and his son agreed, had not been seen here for many years, and the cold, wet weather since was out of the ordinary, also.

'Has there been much damage to the crops hereabouts?' Gray enquired, more or less generally, after nearly half an hour's such desultory talk. 'Or is there like to be?'

'With the goddess's goodwill, there will not,' the priest of Ceres replied.

'And without it?' said the farmer's son, with a sardonic half smile. His father frowned at him, and he subsided.

'You are come from Orléans, I believe you said?' one of the merchants said, addressing the priest. 'Have you found things very . . . unsettled along the way?'

Observing the priest covertly, in profile, Gray saw him frown briefly before smoothing his face into blankness. 'Here and there,' he said.

The merchants, severally and together, related at some length their misadventures on the road from Arras with their goods and gear. They had been forced several times to alter their planned route, either to avoid armies on the march or because, the said armies having passed before them and eaten the local populace out of house and home, they could no longer expect themselves, their servants, or their beasts to be lodged or fed; they had heard such rumours of happenings in and around Orléans that they had decided to swing wide around it on their outward journey, and return that way from Tours instead.

'Could you,' Gray ventured, hesitantly – if military strategy was not his strong suit, trade was perhaps still less so – 'might there not be a market for your goods amongst the soldiers themselves? So that you need not travel all the way to Tours after all?'

The eldest of the merchants gave him a pitying look which Gray had seen before. 'When one has woven webs of exchange over many years, monsieur,' he said, in a sentential tone, 'when one's word is trusted by one's associates even at a great distance, because one has never broken it, one does not simply leap at the first opportunity of turning a profit, at the risk of tearing all those webs to shreds.'

'And besides, Médard,' said one of the others, a lean man perhaps in the middle forties, 'there is no great demand for fine tapestries or carpets in a soldiers' camp.'

He grinned. The rest of the table laughed aloud; the butt of all this mirth glared at his friend, but not without a small, rueful chuckle at his own expense.

'I had thought of visiting Orléans,' Gray said, seizing his opening before the conversation could turn again; improvising hastily on a strong ground of truth, he continued, 'on my return journey. I have heard much of the libraries at the temples of Minerva and Apollo Grannus there. Ought I to avoid it, do you think? And what of Paris?'

'From what we have heard along the road,' said the third merchant, 'Paris is no better.' He was the youngest-looking of the three – not, by Gray's estimation, very much older than himself – but did not seem to lack for self-confidence. 'They are building ships to go up the Seine to Rouen, and out to the Manche.'

There had been, in less unsettled times, some considerable degree of trade between Paris and Rouen by way of the River Seine; by the man's tone, however, this was not the sort of ship he spoke of.

'Oh?' said Gray. 'Er . . . what sort of ships? And who is "they"?'

'Ships with saltpetre-cannon mounted aboard,' the young merchant elaborated. He seemed rather to be enjoying himself. 'As for *who*—'

The priest, Gray saw too late, was giving him a rather more interested and penetrating look than before.

'You are a scholar, monsieur, I think you said?' he enquired. 'In search of some employment?'

'I am,' said Gray – immensely glad, not for the first time, that he had not tried his powers of invention further.

'A scholar of what, if I may ask?'

The truth is safest. 'Of magick, monsieur,' he said.

The priest of Ceres smiled. 'How fortuitous,' he said. 'Monsieur . . . Marais, is it? I believe we may be of use to one another.'

That tone of voice, too, Gray had heard before. It was the tone in which, one very strange day years ago, Appius Callender had invited him to spend the summer in Breizh: the tone of a man disguising a command as a friendly invitation.

But I need not obey this man's command unless it serves my own purposes, Gray reminded himself. He was not that boy of barely one-and-twenty, almost equally lacking in friends and funds, and forced to choose, in effect, between incarceration as his tutor's guest and an accusation of murder. Perhaps most importantly, he had – unlike that frightened, baffled younger version of himself – the full use of his talent, and the certain knowledge that he was not alone in the world.

He returned the priest's smile and leant back a little in his seat. 'Do tell, monsieur,' he said.

So it was that by the following morning, Gray found himself travelling south through the Île-des-Francs in the company of one Charles Durand, priest of the Temple of Ceres, who wished to make him known to the man he called the Emperor of Gaul.

CHAPTER XXIII

In Which Roland Makes
Himself Surprisingly Useful

In the morning, armed with several slim iron rods made to Sophie's specifications by an obliging blacksmith, and sundry other useful tools, they renewed their assault upon the College gate. Sophie and Lucia – her good spirits much restored by the attentions of the talented healer whom Roland had insisted upon summoning from the Infirmary – had sat up late the previous night in their room, racking their brains for some better method than crude trial and error, but, in the almost total absence of information, had been forced to concede defeat. Accordingly, therefore, Joanna produced a wax candle in a brass holder, and held it steady whilst Gwendolen called fire to produce another of her focused, blue-hot flames; Sophie carried a basin, soap, and towels borrowed from the inn; and Lucia extracted from her reticule a bodkin and a stack of clean handkerchiefs collected from the rest of the party and passed the former through the flame.

'Let me be first to try,' said Ceana MacGregor, predictably.

She did not so much as flinch when Lucia ran the bodkin deep into her thumb, or when she squeezed it to encourage the blood to drip onto the first of the iron rods. But when tried in the lock, Ceana MacGregor's blood, like Lucia's, had no effect upon the spell at all.

There followed a brief debate between Sophie and her guardsmen as to which of them should make the next attempt, which Mr Goff won — only to discover that, alas, his blood was no more to the spell's taste than Ceana MacGregor's.

Mr Tredinnick, Miss Pryce, and Joanna all tried their luck, to the same effect, before any of the others would agree to either Sophie's or Roland's doing so. The morning was wearing on, however, and the discouraging failures (and bloodied handkerchiefs) mounting up; when Joanna was nursing her bleeding right thumb and Mr Goff beginning to talk of calling in the rest of the guardsmen presently off-duty at the inn, and Ceana MacGregor of summoning some of her subordinates, to try their luck, Sophie and her brother exchanged a meaning glance, and Roland said firmly, 'I shall take the next turn.'

At his own insistence, Lucia turned over to him the iron rod smeared with his blood, to be tried in the keyhole. Sophie tensed involuntarily as he inserted it. So much occupied was her mind in anticipating the outcome that she did not register the stiff *click-clank* of the tumblers turning, or even the low groan of the hinges, until Roland said, in a stupefied tone, 'The . . . the gate is opening.'

Through the ivy-covered gateway Sophie went — magick buzzed in her mind's ear like swarming bees, then rippled as a sheet of water falling — and before she quite understood what she was doing, she found herself the first living person in more than two centuries to set foot inside the walls of Lady Morgan College.

She stopped in her tracks, causing someone to jostle her shoulder and someone else to tread painfully on her heel, and stared about her.

Even in the dungeons of remote Castle MacAlpine on the Ross of Mull, she had never seen such thorough dereliction. So high was the frontage that only the verdigris-green dome had been visible from

321

without – or was there magick at work there, too, concealing the true state of things from the casual observer? – but here within, massive oaks and plane trees (and one lightning-split horse-chestnut) spread their branches overhead in a near-unbroken canopy, and underfoot the carpet of leaf-mould and acorns and rotting conkers was ankle-deep in places, interrupted by springy tree-shoots at various stages of growth. Clusters of primrose-yellow and harebell-blue swirled about the feet of the great old trees, like supplicants on their knees before the great gods.

Oak-trees, thought Sophie vaguely, *are sacred to Jupiter.*

With a scraping and a creaking of hinges, the gate closed (or was closed) behind them; and then silence. Utter silence, but for the breathing of the five women and three men who stood just inside the gate, suspended in Sophie's indecision.

Sophie drew a deep, slow breath, shut her eyes, and reached for her magick. The unspeakable relief of finding it just as usual took her aback – she had not understood until this moment how much she had dreaded the reverse, had feared that they might be crossing the boundary of an interdiction – and she stood for a moment perfectly still, steadying her breathing, willing her pulse down from its panicked hammering in her ears. That done, she reached out cautiously, seeking touchpoints in the not-quite-space about her: near at hand the bright red-gold touch of Lucia's magick, to which her own had once been linked; far away, so far as to be nearly undetectable, the deep blue-green thread of Gray's, linked to hers still though the connexion was faint and attenuated by the distance between them. Gray's magick had had a flavour of feathers about it for some time now, and on one recent night the sizzle of stormy weather and a worrying flash of pain; this morning, however, it tasted only of deep sleep.

Easy to ponder the significance of this, to worry at the possibilities like a terrier with a rat, to be drawn aside from the concerns of the here-and-now—

Sophie gave herself a mental shake, drew in her wandering wits, and put forth the tendrils of her magick to prod (carefully, gently) at the barrier which logic suggested must enclose the College grounds. At first she could detect nothing, and frowned in bafflement; had she and her companions, in passing through the circumference of the spell, somehow released or erased it? Such a thing was not impossible – not, at any rate, more impossible than some of the other things they had seen and done since arriving in Oxford – but it would be an odd sort of mage, or group of mages, who so constructed any sort of barrier-spell as to permit some unknown future invader to undo it.

And, besides that, there is *something. I felt it, and I feel it still.*

No, she corrected herself almost at once, remembering: *There are two things.* Two layers of magick – and of quite different magicks, if she had read the signs aright – one encircling and enclosing the other.

Those generations-ago mages, whoever they had been – even this much, none of the books she had found and read could tell her – what had they been thinking, what seeking to achieve?

Following the logic of that thought, and peripherally aware of her companions' soft footfalls all about her, Sophie shifted and broadened the focus of her explorations; it might be a cleverly modified concealment-spell, the thing she sought, but equally it might be some species of warding-spell, of shielding, of protection – all related, of course, but nonetheless distinct from one another. And there, *there—*

That shimmering inner layer followed the exterior walls, she found – unsurprising – but curved high overhead, too, and – astonishing! – deep beneath her feet. A shielding-spell, or the essence of one, a perfect sphere constrained and contorted by the shape of the walls about its middle, like a ball of wool forced through an arm-ring.

The magick tasted familiar, somehow – not like her own, or Gray's, or Lucia's, not *like* that of anyone she knew, and yet . . . and yet. The scent of it echoed in her mind's ear, as though she should recognise it if only she could find just the right angle of observation. She touched it with a tendril of her magick (a single petal of the blue-white flame-flower by which her mind chose to represent her power, pulled out into a fine thread), steeling herself against some hostile reaction. To her astonishment, however, the only response was a brief shiver, rippling outwards from the point of metaphysickal contact like the concentric waves a still pond makes when a small stone is dropped into it; it was not hostility she felt, shimmering back along that hair's-breadth tendril of her magick, but . . . surely it could not be . . . recognition?

Now, the outward layer, on the other hand—

A hand on her arm wrenched her back to the world of leaf-mould and ancient, overgrown trees; she opened her eyes to find Joanna peering anxiously up into her face.

'Sophie,' she said quietly, 'is all well? Ought we to proceed, or . . . ?'

Sophie felt anxious eyes upon her from all sides. She straightened her spine, squared her shoulders, and said, 'We proceed. Mr Tredinnick, the maps, if you please.'

Mr Tredinnick unshipped from his shoulder the heavy cylindrical case which held the rolled-up maps, and which Sophie herself, to her intense irritation, had not been permitted to carry. The map she wanted (actually the plan of the College located by Evans-Hughes at Merlin) was fortunately the outermost; there being no flat surface to hand, Mr Goff offered his own back for the purpose, and Sophie – acutely uncomfortable, but unwilling to risk unnecessary delay – unrolled the parchment and flattened it across his broad shoulders, holding it in place with one palm to each of its short edges.

The others crowded round them, so close that Sophie experienced a strong desire to scream.

'Here we are,' she said, nodding at the point towards the lower edge of the plan which represented the gate. Nodding at it was quite useless, but she had no free hand to point with. 'Miss Pryce, may I ask—'

Miss Pryce's slim hands pressed flat the two corners nearest her, and Sophie retracted her right hand and tapped her forefinger upon the spot where – more or less – they now stood. 'Here is the Shrine of Minerva; here, the Library, and there the Refectory.'

They had planned to investigate the Library first of all, if they should find the buildings still standing – though it had been a long morning already, and the Shrine of Minerva was temptingly near . . .

Lucia rested one forefinger on the representation of the Library; she glanced up from the map, then down again, orienting herself. 'That way, I believe,' she said, pointing. 'But the way is not very clear.'

Indeed, the way was choked with brambles – almost entirely dead for lack of sunlight – and twilight-dark besides, for the canopies of two plane-trees and a horse-chestnut met overhead in that spot, and between them contrived to block almost all the sunlight that elsewhere filtered through the branches.

'Well, then,' said Roland cheerfully, 'shall we begin?'

Either he was quite unintimidated by the prospect before him – buoyed up, just possibly, by his unexpected (and quite unearned) success with the gate – or he was developing into a far better actor than Sophie had hitherto suspected. For her purposes, however, it did not much matter which.

'Certainly,' she said, and began rolling up the map.

The guardsmen obligingly hacked their way through the worst of the overgrown brambles and half-fallen trees. Here and there they

325

found the remains of a footpath by the crunching of gravel under their feet, but the place was so still and silent around them that Sophie could not help feeling, uneasily, that they were treading through a tomb. The others followed; conversing at first in whispers, they fell silent one by one, and went unspeaking, single-file, their footsteps slow and cautious as her own.

The College Library hove into view after perhaps a quarter-hour – at a distance which ought not to have taken half that time to traverse – half buried in ivy and old-man's-beard but instantly recognisable by its two long wings and square central tower. The main doors were easily enough located by reference to the plan, but it took some time, even with three wood-axes to yesterday's one, to hack away the creeping growth that covered them. So oppressive was the pervading silence that the sound of the axe-blades biting into tough ivy-stems and glancing against stone came, perversely, as something of a relief to Sophie.

She started at a brief touch on her arm, but it was only Roland. Drawing in close beside her, he bent his head to speak in her ear: 'Are you quite sure of this, Sophie?'

Sophie stepped back and turned to look at him. 'What makes you ask?' she said. 'You were eager enough this morning, at the gate.'

Roland pursed his lips, wrinkled up his forehead, and scuffed one boot-toe in the leaf-mould underfoot. 'It is too quiet,' he said at last.

'It is that,' Sophie conceded. 'I do not quite know what to make of it.'

'*La belle au bois dormant*,' said Roland. 'That is what I make of it.'

'I believe that cryptic utterance was intended to convey some very deep meaning,' said Sophie, after a long moment, 'but I must tell you, Roland, that I have not the least notion what it might be.'

She surveyed the scene before her, telling herself that she was the captain of this small expeditionary force and was merely gauging its progress. The truth was that since the moment they had all passed in the gate, a cold vague dread had been creeping through her, winding frigid fingers about her heart; sober reason told her that, if any dire fate was to befall any of her party, it could not be avoided by her watchful eye alone, but nonetheless she did not like to let them out of her sight. Mr Goff and Mr Tredinnick were resting from their assault on the ivy, whilst Ceana MacGregor knelt at the foot of the door, prying up matted grass-roots from between the paving-stones with her belt-knife; Joanna and Miss Pryce had spread out the College plan on the lowest step and were discussing it (or something else) in low voices, and Lucia, inexplicably, was picking flowers.

'*La belle au bois dormant*,' Roland repeated, unhelpfully. 'You must know the tale, surely!'

'Joanna knows it, I am sure,' said Sophie, 'but—'

'Knows what?' Joanna raised her head and turned round to look at Sophie and Roland.

'The tale of the beautiful woman in the sleeping wood,' said Sophie.

'No, no,' said Joanna. She sprang to her feet, dusted her hands on her skirts, and descended the three steps in one casual jump. 'It is the woman who sleeps, in the tale; the wood goes on growing for a hundred years – or was it a thousand?'

'A hundred,' said Miss Pryce, descending the steps more sedately in Joanna's wake. 'Surely you remember! You heard me reading this tale to Agatha and Yvon very lately – it is Agatha's favourite at present. The princess pricks her finger on the spindle, and the curse of Alecto, of which she ought to have died, is softened by the blessing of Melpomene, so that instead she falls into a deep sleep, and the whole of her father's palace likewise. They sleep for a hundred years, whilst the wood grows up all about them, until they are freed by the bold and handsome prince who contrives, with the blessings and aid of the Lady Venus, to break through the barrier of the wood and wake the princess.'

'Was it Melpomene, Gwen?' said Joanna, screwing up her face in thought. 'I thought it was Thalia.'

'Oh, certainly, perhaps it might be,' Gwendolen agreed.

Sophie considered this in silence for some moments, and at last, turning to Roland, said, 'The resemblances are striking, I must concede.'

'But the wood,' said Roland. 'The *trees*. That is what made me think of it – that, and the terrible quiet. The prince needs the help of the Lady Venus, you see, because the trees are not merely standing in his way, but waging war against him.'

At this last Lucia, who had wandered into hearing distance whilst Roland was speaking, looked up sharply from her fistful of wildflowers. 'You hear them?' she said. 'You are quite sure? What do they say?'

'You know it is not like that,' said Roland. He sounded rather cross. 'They do not want us here; that is all I know.'

'Roland, what—' Sophie began, but got no further before Lucia and Roland's conversation went on over and without her.

'Do not want *us* here?' said Lucia. 'Us, particularly? Or—'

'Do not want anyone,' said Roland. 'I think. That is, they wish to be left in peace. That is – truly, Lucia, you ask too much!'

To Sophie's astonishment, Lucia did not dispute this accusation, but only said, 'I am sorry.'

Roland blinked.

'These trees will not speak to me at all,' Lucia went on; Roland's eyes widened, as though this surprised him. 'I do not know why they should, in point of fact; who am I, to the trees of Lady Morgan College?'

'And why should they speak to me?' Roland demanded. 'This was a domain of women – of women *scholars* – and I am neither of those things; why in Hades should the trees speak to me, of all people? Yet they do, more or less. Plainly there is no logic or reason in the case.'

Joanna, edging close to Sophie whilst Roland and Lucia were absorbed in their debate, stretched up on tiptoe and muttered into her ear, 'I confess I do not find this tale of speaking trees more persuasive with repetition.'

'Hush, Jo,' Sophie murmured. Tredinnick and Goff had begun to swing their axes again, and she was struggling to hear anything over the din.

'But it was your blood that opened the gate,' Lucia was saying. 'You cannot deny it – indeed, you were rather preening yourself on it not two hours ago. And if the gate—'

A tremendous cracking sound, and the sharp unsettling shriek of metal striking metal.

'Your Highness,' called Mr Goff, from the top of the steps. 'We are through the door.'

Sophie hesitated – how could she leave that cryptic conversation unexplored? – but the others were surging past her and up the steps to the Library doors, and so she made haste to follow, calling a light to hover over her shoulder as she went, for beyond the splintered oaken doors lay a profound and palpable darkness.

When she would have stepped through the new-hewn doorway, however, the crossed handles of Mr Goff's axe and Mr Tredinnick's halted her in her tracks. 'Begging your pardon, ma'am,' said the latter, 'but you'll not be going first. Anything might be lurking in there.'

'But—'

'Consider our poor nerves, ma'am,' said Goff, politely but firmly, 'and imagine our fate at your honoured father's hands if anything should befall you that we might have prevented through *perfectly reasonable* precautions.'

The heavy stress which he laid upon those two words, Sophie felt, was entirely superfluous to requirements – but it was true that she ought not to force them into such an equivocal position.

'Very well,' she said, graciously enough; 'I concede to you the honour of first setting foot in the pages of history. Give me that lantern,' she added, in a more prosaic tone.

Mr Tredinnick handed it to her, and she chivvied her magelight into it and handed it back.

'I thank you, ma'am,' said Mr Goff, with a little bow which Sophie strongly suspected of irony.

'I beg you will not think of it,' said Sophie.

The two guardsmen turned their faces to the ruined door and, moving confidently but cautiously, in single file, stepped over the threshold. Sophie and the others crowded around the opening – torn into the wall of ivy like a wound – and watched them, or their magelight lantern, away into the deep, dark stillness.

CHAPTER XXIV

In Which Gwendolen Makes a Discovery

After what seemed a very long time – though judging by the movement of the sun, it was no more than a quarter-hour at the most – Goff and Tredinnick emerged once more from the gaping doorway, looking very sober and rather wide of eye, but otherwise none the worse for their experience.

'If it please Your Highness,' said Tredinnick. His jaw tightened briefly. 'There seems no immediate danger within.'

'But?' said Roland, after a moment.

Tredinnick hesitated, and exchanged a worried look with his comrade.

'But there is something within,' said Goff at last, 'that . . . something that may pose a risk to your safety, sir, and to that of the Princess.'

Lucia saw the lift of Sophie's chin and repressed a sigh. Did Sophie's guardsmen, after so many years' close observation, understand her so little?

Then, glancing from Sophie to the two men who stood upon the steps, she saw the expression of betrayal which Tredinnick was directing at Goff – Goff who was, Lucia remembered now, a countryman of Sophie and Joanna's, born and raised in the province of Breizh. For the first time it came home to her that Roland's kingdom might be as rife with shifting and conflicting loyalties as her own, and as difficult to navigate.

'What thing, Mr Goff?' Sophie enquired.

The two guardsmen shifted from foot to foot and looked anywhere but at Sophie or each other. Goff was again the first to yield to Sophie's expectant silence: 'Not . . . not so much a *thing*, ma'am,' he said, speaking miserably to his boots. 'More of a feeling. Er. A feeling of dread.'

Sophie pressed her lips together briefly. 'I see. Mr Tredinnick, do you concur?'

Tredinnick raised his head. 'Yes, ma'am,' he said.

'That does not seem very dangerous,' muttered Gwendolen Pryce.

The next step in the dance was entirely predictable. 'Mr Goff,' Sophie said, 'give me that lantern, if you please.'

Less predictably, Goff descended the steps and did so. He said something to Sophie as the lantern changed hands, which made her smile very slightly and Joanna, overhearing, produce and quickly muffle a snort of astonished laughter.

'Sophie,' said Roland, 'I do not think you ought—'

Sophie spun to face him, eyes blazing, and – as though actuated all by the same impulse – Lucia, Joanna, and Gwendolen hurriedly converged to separate them.

'Sophie, there is no need for that,' Lucia heard Joanna say soothingly, behind her, as she herself caught Roland by the shoulders and said, low and urgent, 'I beg of you, Roland, do not antagonise your sister.'

'I am not *antagonising* her,' he protested, sinking his voice to match hers. 'I am attempting to keep her safe.'

'To hear you,' said Lucia, 'one would think you did not know Sophie at all. Truly, Roland, I can think of nothing more likely to antagonise her than an attempt to shield her from the consequences of her own decisions, in the course of an expedition under her command.'

Roland's brows drew together and his lips pursed up at her military terminology, or perhaps at its use in connexion with his sister. 'Do you have *any notion*, Lucia MacNeill,' he said, vehement through gritted teeth, 'what my fate will be at my father's hands should any harm befall Sophie?'

Lucia had not the patience at present, she decided, to debate with Roland his imagined hierarchy of paternal affection. She dared a look back over her shoulder and found Sophie consulting with Goff and Tredinnick over the draughtsman's plan of the College Library which Sophie's historian friend, Gareth Evans-Hughes, had unearthed from a drawer of uncatalogued plans and charts in the library at Merlin College.

'There is no stopping her,' she said, turning back to Roland, 'short of knocking her flat and sitting on her, which I hope we can all agree to be an overreaction in this case. If you are wishful to keep your sister safe – or at any rate to be on hand to make the attempt—'

'Yes, yes,' said Roland impatiently. He shrugged out of Lucia's grip on his shoulders, caught her hand in his – she drew breath in surprise, and returned his grip with interest – and started up the steps.

'I hope we may not regret this, Jo,' Gwendolen muttered, her shoulder pressed close against Joanna's in the dark. All about them loomed silent shrouded shapes – bookcases and tables and reading-desks. Outside, the sun had been shining; here the air – as unnaturally still as in the quadrangle – was dry as paper-dust and cold as Midwinter Night.

Joanna, greatly daring, found Gwen's hand and squeezed it. 'We have done many a stupider thing,' she said, 'and lived to tell the tale.

333

What horrors are we like to find in an abandoned library, worse than those we saw on the Ross of Mull?'

Gwendolen (who had been so brave on that dreadful night, so calm and so quick-witted) shuddered a little and pressed closer still. 'But all the same,' she said, 'Mr Goff and Mr Tredinnick are not wrong: I do feel something here, Jo, and it is most unpleasant. As though . . . as though we were not wanted.'

'That is only damp, I expect,' said Joanna stoutly.

The magelight lantern, followed closely by Roland's and Lucia MacNeill's lights, was drawing farther ahead. Gwendolen called her own small globe of magelight and sent it aloft to hover above their heads.

A pale shape, very nearly human, leapt into relief in the light of Sophie's lantern. There was a chorus of gasps and yelps – Joanna's among them – which gave way to a startled burst of laughter from the vanguard when Tredinnick, tallest of the party, held the lantern aloft to reveal a perfectly ordinary marble statue of Minerva with an owl upon one shoulder, set in a raised alcove to the left of a massive set of oaken doors.

Lucia MacNeill's light grew brighter, illuminating the doors and the large square signboard upon the rightmost, which read in large letters, *Closed Stacks*. The doors bore heavy wrought-iron handles, gracefully curving left and right.

Sophie turned to face the others, her eyes alight with a dangerous glee. 'Mr Goff!' she said. 'Opened you this door, in the course of your reconnaissance?'

'No, ma'am,' said Goff. 'In any case I should have supposed it locked.'

'We shall see, then,' said Sophie. Turning away again, she set her hand to the right-hand door-handle.

Joanna, watching with her heart hammering in her ears, saw

Sophie's shoulders tense and her elbow draw sharply back an instant before Roland, Sophie, and Lucia MacNeill, in voices taut with dismay, said, 'Oh, *no*.'

It was not surprising, of course, that a college library should contain a very large number of books. Nor was it astonishing, after two centuries' neglect, that the said books should be in a distressing condition. But this was not mere neglect; this was vicious, wanton destruction. The foreboding which had pressed upon her (upon all of them, if Mr Tredinnick and Mr Goff were to be believed) since the moment of entering the building grew abruptly heavier, as though someone had thrown over her shoulders a cloak lined with lead.

For a dizzying, horrified moment, Sophie was transported back to the Master's Lodge of Merlin College as she and Gray had seen it on the night of Lord Halifax's death – a wasteland of torn and half-burnt codices, broken glass and toppled furniture, the hiss and crackle of flames, the thick air choking her – and began instinctively to look amongst the mangled books for a human victim. With an effort she wrenched herself back to the present, gently disentangled herself from Roland's hand gripping her elbow, and advanced into the wreckage of the closed stacks.

She picked her way cautiously amongst the debris, picking up objects more or less at random – here the front half of an edition of Virgil's *Eclogues*, there a single page of Cymric verse – and gently putting them down again. Puffs of dust rose underfoot at every step.

The mutilated books, the overturned chairs and tables and reading-stands, her own hands moving before her, grew blurred and indistinct; Sophie heard someone muttering, louder and louder, *Who could—how could—what monster has done such a thing?*

Only when gentle hands took hold of her shoulders, turning her away from the wreckage, and pressed her face into Lucia's shoulder, did she recognise that the outraged muttering was her own, and that she was weeping.

'I was wrong,' she said, raising her head and surveying her little company. 'I was wrong – Gray was wrong – we were all of us deluded. There is nothing left here, and we shall never be permitted to rebuild it, any of it. I am sorry to have so misled all of you, and wasted so much of your time and – and—'

Sophie turned away from Lucia and sat down hard on the filthy floor, her back against the end of a bookcase, wrapped her arms about her shins, and hid her face against her drawn-up knees. She was distantly aware that she was behaving like a thwarted child, but to have come here with such bright hopes, so have poured so much hard work and will and magick – even, quite literally, the blood from their veins – into the effort to gain access to this place, and then to find it in such a state . . .

'Sophia Marshall!'

Sophie looked up, startled – then farther up, into her sister's furious face looming above her.

'How *dare* you!' said Joanna. 'After – after *everything*, Sophie, how dare you give up, when we have come so far, only because some sheep-witted, ham-handed dolts have made a mess of a few old books!'

Gwendolen stood at Joanna's right elbow, and Roland at her left with Lucia beside him; beyond the circle of their anxious, indignant faces, Mr Goff and Mr Tredinnick hovered, inwardly debating, Sophie supposed, whether this constituted a threat of the sort against which they were meant to be protecting her, or a salutary check upon her temper.

'It is not *a few old books*, Jo!' Sophie protested. She did not trouble to keep her despair from leaking into her voice or from showing on her face. 'It is *thousands* of books – it is *all* the books – there may be some that existed nowhere else. Even to collect up all the fragments would be the work of a month, before we could begin piecing them together, to see what has been lost; and as for repairing them—!'

Lucia MacNeill dropped to her knees in the dust and debris and caught one of Sophie's hands in hers. 'A college is not its books, Sophie,' she said. 'A college is the minds and hearts and voices of its scholars – its Fellows, its students – and the knowledge they make together. This' – she tilted her head at the destruction – 'hurts my heart as it hurts yours; but a library can be rebuilt, Sophie, within as well as without.'

Sophie blinked slowly, considering this. There was a large and obvious flaw in Lucia's reasoning: at present, Lady Morgan College lacked not only books (or, at any rate, books in a condition to be read and used) but Fellows, students, librarians, servants, gardeners, patrons, tutors, and lecturers as well. And what hope had they now of discovering the secrets of the place, if even its ordinary, everyday possessions had been visited by such destruction?

'Sophie,' said Joanna again – her voice not angry now, but sharp with sudden worry. She crouched directly in front of Sophie, hands on her knees for balance, and looked searchingly into her face. 'Sophie, this is not . . . you are not missing Gray again, as you did in Alba?'

This query, at which Roland's brow furrowed in confusion, sharpened Sophie's mind as perhaps nothing else could have done at this moment. 'I,' she said, and bit her lip in concentration. 'No, I think—'

She let her eyes fall shut, reached inwards with practised ease and then, tentatively, outwards – found the thread of Gray's magick once more, and gauged the strength of her own. 'No,' she said positively, opening her eyes. 'He is far away, and, I think, going farther still, but – no.'

The exercise of seeking out her link to Gray, however, had made her senses more awake to the presence of other magicks around her, and it became clear to her now that the foreboding which had dogged all their steps since first they passed the College gate was not a product of anyone's imagination but a real and very nearly tangible thing. That it was, in fact, exactly what some long-dead mage, or mages, had meant subsequent intruders to feel.

Well, then: whoever you are – were – I decline to oblige you. Sophie smiled down at her knees. Then she turned the smile upwards and outwards, let it begin to blaze away the fog of despair in which she had been about to lose herself, and levered herself to her feet.

'My apologies for my outburst,' she said briskly, dusting her hands on her skirts. 'I shall not let it occur again.' *I hope.* 'Mr Goff – Mr Tredinnick – Ceana MacGregor – I believe we have useful work here for your troops to do; you may assign the most careful of them to begin collecting and organising all of this . . . material . . . so that it may be properly catalogued hereafter.'

'Ma'am,' said Mr Goff. Ceana MacGregor nodded.

Sophie looked about her, and found she could imagine the skewed and gaping shelves straightened, repaired and filled with books once more.

Though the mere sight of it very evidently pained her, Sophie insisted – over the protests of the others – upon a full exploration of the ruined library stacks. This proved a fortunate choice, however; the destruction, they discovered, was far less complete than had at first appeared, and they left the closed stacks greatly encouraged, to proceed to the reading rooms.

It was in the Fellows' Reading Room – once a place of ease and comfort, even luxury, to judge by the shapes of the dust-furred sofas and the array of cobwebbed bottles and decanters upon the side-board – that this strange day began to grow even stranger.

'Jo,' said Gwendolen, sending her small magelight up to hover near the ceiling, at the corner formed by the room's south and east walls.

The corner was occupied by a triangular glass-fronted curio-case, well above six feet tall, from behind whose square panes (only one of them broken, for a wonder) could be glimpsed, inter alia, a bronze knot-work buckle, several large shells, a silver welcome-cup entirely black with tarnish, and a small bust of Hypatia of Alexandria. What might be on the top of it, however, Joanna could not possibly determine.

'If you will give me a leg up,' said Gwendolen – as though they had been discussing the logistics of mounting a particularly tall horse – 'I shall be able to get it down, I think.'

'Get *what* down?' said Joanna.

'Once I have laid hands on it,' Gwendolen said patiently, 'perhaps we may discover what it is.'

Joanna, grumbling more for the look of the thing than from any genuine reluctance, took a knee and cupped her hands to boost Gwendolen up the last few inches.

The thing which had caught Gwendolen's eye proved to be a box: a perfectly ordinary oblong box, or chest – such as a lady might use to keep her jewellery in, or her love-letters – of polished wood, with brass hinges to one side and a robust lock to the other. Perfectly ordinary, that is, but that over the course of two centuries it appeared to have gathered no dust.

Joanna and Gwendolen looked at one another, and at Lucia.

'Sophie!' Joanna said. 'Come and look what Gwen has found.'

Gwendolen carried the box to the table by the vast cold hearth on the west wall and set it down very carefully, as though she feared it might burst into flame. Sophie straightened up from investigating the bottom drawer of the sideboard, and they gathered round the table, Roland and Tredinnick having set out to investigate the bindery where once on a time, according to Edwina Antonia Calixta's plan, the College's librarians had maintained and repaired their own books.

The lock resisted first Gwendolen's attempts upon it with a pair of hairpins and Joanna's paper-knife, and then Lucia's unlocking-spell, but opened with a soft *snick* when Sophie laid her hand upon it and murmured, '*Libera quod hic habeant in carcere.*'

The four of them exchanged a look of trepidation; then Sophie carefully lifted the hinged lid of the box – like the lock, the hinges seemed not to have remarked the passage of time, for they swung easily and silently.

Within, the box was lined with crimson velvet, unworn and unfaded by time, and filled with closely written pages; perched atop them, a folded and sealed letter was directed – in a flowing, exuberant hand – *To she who has succeeded in opening the box.*

They stared at it, frozen in a silence pregnant with terror and exhilaration, the length of four long breaths. Joanna could hear the others breathing – fancied, indeed, that she could hear their hearts beating, though it must be only her own pulse hammering in her ears.

Then Lucia MacNeill said, in a sort of strangled whisper, 'That will be you, then, Sophie.'

Sophie made no reply, unless her quickened breathing might be so construed.

'Ought we to read it here?' said Joanna, when the silence had again begun to stretch unbearably. 'Or take it away with us?'

'Ought we even to touch it?' said Gwendolen. 'Is it not likely to be a trap?'

She was staring at the open box, Joanna saw, like a mouse watching a cat: wary and preternaturally still, as though seeking to make herself invisible. *That is Sophie's bailiwick, Gwen; the rest of us had better not attempt it.*

'What sort of trap?' said Joanna, practically.

'It may be poisoned.' Gwendolen looked down at her, brow furrowed with worry. 'Or – or perhaps removing the letter from the box may trigger some other sort of trap, or—'

Her next horrible idea remained unspoken, however, for she broke off abruptly when Sophie reached out, picked up the letter, and broke the seal.

When – contrary to her expectation – no flash of mage-fire or magickal explosion followed, no shriek of pain or sudden swoon, Joanna relaxed minutely; from which she understood, as she had not before, how tightly she was wound. Wincing, she flexed her fingers and shifted surreptitiously from foot to foot.

There was not much else to be done: Sophie was reading the letter – if letter it was – in a tense, breathing silence, whilst everyone else watched her doing so; and though Joanna should not have hesitated, in the normal course of things, to ask importunate questions, peer round her sister's shoulder, or demand that the letter be read aloud, the present atmosphere made all of these possibilities altogether unthinkable.

She could, however, edge closer to the box, the better to peer at the topmost paper in the stack, and this she did – though very slowly, so that Sophie might not remark it.

The swooping hand was the same as that which had directed the letter, and not easily intelligible; Joanna found herself wishing that the document had been only enciphered, rather than written two centuries ago by someone now long dead, and thus impossible to interrogate. Sophie, she supposed, must often have encountered documents of similar or even less recent vintage, in the course of her studies; at any rate, though her perusal of the mysterious letter was by no means rapid, it seemed not to be giving her any particular difficulty. The documents which crossed Joanna's desk in the course of her work, by contrast, were seldom more than a month old. Not for nothing, however, had she spent so much of the past five years in translating the hurried shorthand notes of a variety of persons into legible and consistent fair copies; she had grown adept at spotting patterns, and at leaps of logic premised on nothing more than the vague shape of a word.

And the shapes of the words before her now . . .

No. Surely not.

She blinked – blinked again, hard – but having resolved the swooping whorls and decorative loops and slashes into intelligible words, she could not unsee them.

Being the true tale of the deathe and life of Edward, by the gods favour Rex Britannicus, in the VIth yr of hys reigne

attested this XVth day of May, anno XX Edw. VI R.

by his sisters—

It was a forgery, surely – it could not be what it appeared – could it? *The* death and life *of Edward* – what in Hades could that mean? Joanna's fingers itched to reach for the page, to turn it over so that she might see the next.

She glanced at Sophie, and found her gazing at the last page of the letter as if transfixed.

'Tell me I am not mad,' she said abruptly, thrusting the pages at

Joanna, who was nearest. 'Look at these . . . these signs-manual, and tell me I am not mad.'

Joanna stared at it – Lucia MacNeill and Gwendolen crowded in to do the same – they exchanged incredulous glances, and stared still more.

The names were unmistakable, written in letters nearly as high as the preceding paragraph, and each underscored with a complicated arrangement of interlocking horizontal loops:

Mathilda Julia

Edith Augusta

'Either that is the cleverest forgery I have ever seen,' said Joanna last, 'or this letter was written to you by the Princesses Regent.'

CHAPTER XXV

In Which Sophie Reads a Letter

'*Must we stay* here?' Roland was pacing – both irritable and irritating – an increasingly rapid circle round the Fellows' Reading Room. 'Whatever this mysterious box has to tell us, can it not be told . . . elsewhere?'

'If you cannot be still, Roland,' Joanna snapped, 'I beg you will at least be *quiet*.' She spun on one heel to address Lucia: 'Can you not knock him down and sit on him?'

Lucia had for some time been resisting a strong urge to do exactly this, not least because she was not entirely certain of succeeding. She shook her head at Joanna, who, with a small huff of impatience, turned back to Sophie. Tempers were fraying on all sides, it appeared.

I cannot knock him down and sit on him, but perhaps . . .

'Roland,' said Lucia quietly, laying a hand on his arm, when next his fretful peregrinations brought him near. He paused, turned, met her gaze; his eyes, blue as the sky at Midsummer, burnt fever-bright, and beneath her hand his arm quivered with tension.

'Can you hear it?' he said. 'It has not stopped since we set foot in this room.' In a tone as near to desperate pleading as she had ever heard from him, he repeated, '*Must* we stay here?'

Lucia heard nothing out of the ordinary – nothing but Roland's quiet near-panic and the others murmuring together as they deciphered Sophie's ancestral artefact – but it was true that the atmosphere in this room was charged as even the quadrangle, with its still air and whispering trees, had not been. *Was* there something in this place, something only Roland could hear? Were Roland's pacing, Joanna's snappish temper, Lucia's own restless anxiety, linked by something more than their strange uncertain circumstances?

'What do you hear?' she said. 'Is it . . . It is not the trees again, surely? I should hear them, I think – at least a little – if it were that.'

'No,' he said, twitching. 'Not trees. Voices . . . voices and *bells*. Why *bells*, by all the gods? Can you – are you quite sure you cannot hear them, Lucia?'

His voice had risen by now from a low murmur almost to a shout, and from behind Lucia there came a furious bellow: 'Roland, *be quiet!*'

The next moment found the five of them gaping at one another in speechless shock, and Sophie – whose bellow it had been – most staggered of all.

There is *something here*, thought Lucia grimly, *tangling us up and bending us awry.*

The question was whether that something resided here, in the College Library – and thus could be run away from – or whether it was tied to that box which only Sophie could open, or to its bizarre contents, and thus would follow them wherever they might go.

'I think,' said Sophie in a quite different voice, high and a little shaky, 'we ought perhaps to resume this conversation elsewhere.'

In the still sun-dappled air of the quadrangle, the trees shivered and rustled, and Lucia and Roland – walking arm in arm, pressed close together, though they seemed not to know it – looked anxiously about them, and started at small sounds.

Sophie carried the box. It seemed to grow heavier and heavier – it was only that her arms were not so strong as she had thought, she told herself firmly – and she was reminded of Gray's midnight misadventures in Oxford long ago, of his description of Henry Taylor cradling the teakwood box which, as Sophie and her friends discovered much later, had held a beating human heart to be used in the Professor's arcane poison. Might the contents of this quite different box, she wondered, prove equally deadly?

They collected their much-reduced bodyguard at the College gate, to which – eventually – they had been persuaded to return and wait, in case of inquisitive passers-by. Mr Tredinnick's eyes widened at the sight of them; Mr Goff and Ceana MacGregor seemed disposed to ask questions but were stared into temporary silence by Joanna.

The return journey to the Dragon and Lion was slow and subdued, as though all of them felt – as Sophie certainly did – far more drained by their afternoon's labours than the nature of those labours warranted.

She surveyed her troops, as she fancied a general might, and made a decision.

'The baths first,' she said firmly, 'and then dinner, and then this horrible box.'

'In the sixth year of our brother Edward's reign,' Sophie read, peering down at the manuscript page on the table before her,

> *a sickness came upon him, which, for the first time, all the skill and all the art of the Royal Healers proved powerless to amend. Then as now, the greatest threat to our kingdom was that of retribution from Ferdinand of Aragon and his allies amongst the other Iberian kings, on behalf of his daughter, the first*

Queen Catherine; a strong hand on the reins was, and remains, necessary to Britain's survival.

Our father Henry was – like his patron Jove – impetuous, headstrong, and apt at times to be ruled by the bodily passions, but—

'Jove's blood!' Roland exclaimed, starting up in his chair. 'Do you suppose they dared speak of him so when he was alive?'

'If they did,' said Joanna, sotto voce, 'it was no more than he deserved.'

Too restless to sit still, she had eschewed all of the available seats in favour of loitering before the window, only half seeing the bustle of the inn-yard below. Gwendolen, standing just behind her left shoulder, prodded her reprovingly in the ribs; Joanna ignored her.

'I expect,' said Sophie dryly, 'that had either of the Princesses been in the habit of insulting their father to his face during his lifetime, they should not later have found themselves among their brother's Regents. If I may continue?'

—but he was not a fool; indeed, he possessed both a formidable intellect and an unparalleled grasp of political strategy, though all too often overridden by less noble concerns. In divorcing Catherine of Aragon, he did not act in ignorance of the likely consequences but, rather, in defiance thereof, and in full confidence of Britain's capacity to defend her own interests. For this reason, when the full consciousness of his impending demise came upon him, he took great care in dictating the terms under which his successor – our brother Edward – should be guided during the years of his minority.

In another kingdom, perhaps, or in other circumstances, Henry might simply have named one of his daughters – both intelligent women; both thoroughly educated in history, politics, and the theory and practice of magick; the elder already of an age to rule, and the younger very nearly — as his successor. Both Eire and Alba, for example, have from time to time been ruled by women of exceptional strength of character, and neither, we feel bound to note, has been rendered a less formidable foe thereby.

Lucia MacNeill produced a small, appreciative chuckle.

Our father, however, Sophie continued, *knew such a course to be politically impossible in Britain, and therefore, in the interests of averting consequences which might well have escalated to the point of civil war, chose what seemed to him the next best course, by appointing both of us — together with Edward Seymour, Earl of Hertford (later Duke of Somerset) and brother of our late stepmother Genevieve Seymour, and Hugh Dudley, Earl of Warwick (later Duke of Northumberland) — as Regents to the child Edward.*

If you, unknown and yet-unborn scion of the House of Tudor, have any knowledge of history, you will of course know what next befell: the attempt by Somerset to install himself as Lord Protector, and of Northumberland to blow up the spark of conflict with Aragon into the full flames of war; their trial, conviction, and execution on charges of high treason, and our unexpected victory in remaining Edward's sole regents until his majority; Edward's successive betrothals, and their various failures; his illness at the age of fifteen, and the struggles for dominance which ensued; his marriage in the following year, and — the Lady Juno willing — the tale of his descendants, down to your own day. What you cannot know — what no one presently living knows, excepting our two selves, nor ever will know from our lips whilst we live — is the true tale of that illness. This we

set down here, both as a caution for others who may suffer the
same temptations, and as a protest against that other precaution
which Edward, against our counsel, intends to take, that of
casting into perpetual oblivion that seat of learning which fed
and nurtured us, and many another young woman of intellect
and spirit, and thus gave us both the knowledge of a means to
save him, and the audacity to make the attempt.

We intend no disloyalty to our brother, to our King, or to
our kingdom. Indeed, in every particular we have acted from
a determination to safeguard both the King's person and the
kingdom itself.

'Yes, but what in Hades did they *do*?' Joanna had spent a great
deal of time, these past several years, in cultivating patience; but
this aggravated avoidance of the point – and perhaps, too, she
grudgingly conceded, whatever mysterious current had so affected
all of them whilst they stood about in the College Library – was
making her skin crawl and her gut clench and her fingers twitch,
not only in impatience but in something very like dread.

'If you will listen instead of interrupting,' said Sophie, 'perhaps
we shall all find out.'

Joanna turned from the window and glared at her, but made a
show of pressing her lips tight shut.

If you now hold in your hands this manuscript, and have
read so far as this—

'Then you have the patience of Prometheus,' muttered Roland,
and Joanna, Gwendolen, and Lucia erupted in entirely inappropriate
laughter.

Sophie, frowning, raised her voice and overrode them:

*—and have read so far as this, then you have done what
Edward and his Privy Council (from which we have long been
banished, for the offence of keeping the royal sceptre of Britain
safely in our brother's hand) are bent upon preventing: you
have opened the gates of Lady Morgan College, gained entrance
to the Library, and succeeded in opening the box into which
this manuscript will shortly be sealed. We commend your
perseverance; we tremble at your temerity. May the gods protect
and aid you in confronting whatever dire peril has led you here.*

Sophie turned over the page from which she had been reading;
before she could go on to the next, Roland said, 'Why should they
suppose that we – that is, that the reader of their words – should
be in dire peril? I mean to say – of course there is danger to the
kingdom, but—'

'Why indeed?' echoed Lucia, stepping in (to Roland's visible
consternation) before he could further entangle himself. 'After
all, Sophie, you did not suppose any such peril existed when you
conceived your idea. And – I am sorry to say it, but so it is – we
should none of us be here at all, had your father given you leave to
go where the true peril is, or appears to be.'

'One does ask oneself these questions.' Sophie, looking grim,
lowered her gaze to the paper before her.

*Know, then, that this last illness of Edward's did not come
near to killing him, as it had done more than once before, but
killed him indeed; that we, his sisters, bargained with the gods
for his life, and that the bargain we struck gave back his spirit to
the world of flesh and blood, in exchange for the lives we should
have had, as wives and mothers. Our life's blood flows now in
his veins; our three hearts beat in time; we have taken his ills*

upon ourselves, and our lives are bound up in his. When he takes ship for Elysium at last, we shall go with him — or, as it may be, shall go down to the depths of Tartarus, as punishment for our desperate arrogance, in thwarting the will or whim of the gods.

What we did was done for the best, as we have said, for Edward had no heir — nor even a wife — at the time of his death, and though already he showed promise as a shrewd and even-handed ruler, with much of our father's wit but little of his grosser appetites, we could not predict (or, rather, could predict all too well) what scoundrel, fool, or wastrel amongst the wisted limbs of our family tree might be seized upon to succeed him — or what pretenders might emerge from Bourgogne or Acquitaine, or even from Aragon, to press their suits by claim of law or, worse, by force upon our kingdom's body.

'What a very unappealing metaphor,' said Lucia, wincing.

'Quite,' said Sophie.

Nevertheless, Edward, upon being told of our great feat and sacrifice when he came of age, declared it a crime against his person (for being in such dire straits, we had not sought to know his wishes, nor sought his consent to what we meant to do) and against the gods (whose will it had clearly been, he said, that he should die on that day, at that hour), and exiled us from his Court. We have taken refuge here, at Lady Morgan College, which has extended to us her protection and welcomed us back within her hallowed walls — but, as we know in our heart of hearts, only so long as nothing is known of our crime, our sacrifice. Edward of Britain and the Fellows of Lady Morgan College agree on very few points, but on the subject of the ancient magick of blood and stone, their views are both alike distressingly rigid.

351

'"The ancient magick of blood and stone,"' Lucia repeated thoughtfully. 'What can that mean, do you suppose?'

'I have not the least idea,' said Sophie. 'I must say that this is quite the longest and almost the least useful description of a magickal working I have read in my life; the Princesses Regent appear to have modelled their prose style on that of Xanthus Marinus.'

In case Edward should carry out his scheme to consign Lady Morgan College to oblivion – as at present we think very likely – we feel duty-bound to record, for posterity if for no other purpose, what the transgression was that has led to the dissolution of his College and the revocation of its Royal Charter. Had we understood at the time that we should be sacrificing not only our own future, but those of the thousands of young women who might have passed through the gates into this place of learning, of knowledge, of seeking after wisdom, we should have acted, not differently, but with infinitely more regret for this consequence of our choice, which falls not on ourselves but on others. Notwithstanding these regrets, however, it is our considered opinion that to permit our brother's early death to open the way for disorder and strife in the kingdom we love as fiercely as he does himself were the worse betrayal of the two.

Who can say how we may be remembered, if at all? But Edward VI shall be remembered as a good and wise king, and thus we shall have our posterity.

Sophie looked up once more, blinking owlishly. 'And that,' she said, 'is all there is of it. As well that we have no need to replicate their grand mysterious working, for they have told us nothing whatever about it!'

'Sophie, they were writing a deathbed confession, not reporting the results of an experiment for the *Transactions*,' said Lucia MacNeill, much more gently than Joanna could have managed.

'And, as you say,' said Roland, 'we have no need of such a working.'

The four women exchanged a long, meaning look, but made him no reply.

'At any rate,' said Joanna, when the silence threatened to grow impossibly long, 'we have solved your mystery, Sophie. Only, I do not suppose that we ought to make this tale public.'

'We should certainly put paid to any notion of restoring Lady Morgan College, if we did so,' said Sophie dryly.

'*Did* the Princesses Regent die along with their brother?' said Lucia.

'Oh, indeed,' said Gwendolen. 'It is a well-known tale. King Edward perished in the sinking of the frigate *Titania*, en route from Portsmouth to Honfleur, and his sisters on the same day, of a fever, in the infirmary of the Temple of Minerva at Bath – they were old women by then, for Edward's reign was a long one. And now I suppose we know why.'

A shiver seemed to pass through all of them, then, though the day was warm and the inn's sunny sitting-room, with its south-facing windows warmer still.

There was a long, thoughtful silence, until at last Sophie said, in a small voice, 'Suppose Lady Morgan College *is* cursed? Suppose the Princesses Regent *did* thwart the will of some god or gods, and were punished accordingly? Ought we to . . . ought we to interfere?'

'*Think*, Sophie,' said Joanna, in some exasperation. 'If, as their confession claims, they bargained with the gods for their brother's life, then the worst that can be said of them, in that respect, is that perhaps they sought to play one god or goddess off against another, which I daresay most of us have done more than once; it is not a greater crime in this case, surely, simply because the gods in question happened to take notice.'

'And, besides,' she added, 'have not whichever god or gods sought

Edward's death, if so any of them did, had ample opportunities to kill off his descendants? There have been Tudor kings on the throne of Britain almost without interruption since the time of Henry the Great's father; that does not seem to me a sign of divine disfavour.'

'No-o,' Sophie conceded, her brow crinkling in earnest thought. 'But that this working of theirs was so great a secret that even in confessing to it they should avoid describing how it was done – does that not suggest something very . . . very wrong? Or, at any rate, very dangerous?'

'Or possibly both,' said Joanna, who did not disagree with her sister's analysis – only her conclusions.

'There is another possibility, of course,' said Lucia thoughtfully.

'Oh?'

'Have you never, in making your own notes on a particular working, used some form of shorthand to refer to another working, which you need not explain in detail because you know it well already, or have made fuller note of it elsewhere?'

'Certainly I have,' said Sophie, 'but I should not do so if I were making notes for someone else!'

'Not even if the working referred to were one which that someone else might also be expected to know perfectly well?' Lucia countered. 'That is, if you were to write me out instructions for a sleeping-draught, I daresay you should not begin them with half a page's worth of explaining how to call fire to boil the water?'

'No,' said Sophie again. 'So, then, your theory is that this . . .' She shuffled through the pages in her hands. 'This *ancient magick of blood and stone* is – was – common knowledge amongst . . . whom, exactly?'

'The Fellows of Lady Morgan College, to begin with,' said Joanna, 'as we are told they disapproved of it. They must have known of it in order to disapprove, though of course it does not follow that they *understood* it.'

354

Sophie chuckled darkly. 'As a particular contingent of the Fellows of Merlin have lately demonstrated,' she said. 'Though, in fairness to them, I am no longer altogether persuaded that *I* understand what we are about in this business.'

'That may be,' said Joanna. 'But I cannot think that, because one pair of female mages once overstepped the bounds of magickal ethics, they – we – must therefore all be forced to piece together what education we can from scraps and fragments, for lack of any organised alternative. After all, to hear Gray tell it, Merlin men have created magickal disasters enough, without their College's being closed and forgotten in punishment for their mistakes.'

'*That* is certainly true,' said Sophie. 'Indeed, not even treason on the part of a Senior Fellow—'

She broke off at the sound of brisk knocking on the sitting-room door, started a little, and began gathering the papers into a stack and stuffing them back into the box. When she had closed the lid and stowed the box away under the table, she snapped her fingers to release her wards upon the room, and called, '*Quo vadis?*'

'An express is come from London for Mrs Marshall.' It was the voice of the innkeeper himself – he who but rarely climbed the stairs on his twisted leg – and Joanna sprang up from her chair to cross the room and open the door.

'Our apologies for having kept you waiting,' she said, and thanked him.

Even before she had closed the door and turned back to the others, Sophie was at her shoulder, reaching for the letter in her hand. Its source was perfectly evident – it was directed in Mr Fowler's hand and bore Kergabet's personal seal – but whether it contained good news or ill was impossible to guess.

* * *

Sophie sank down into the nearest available chair, her heart pounding, and broke the seal on Sieur Germain's letter. As she unfolded it, a smaller enclosure fell out, enciphered in a more careful version of Gray's large untidy hand. Which to read first? Sieur Germain's letter was not enciphered, and thus might be read quickly; but a message from Gray . . . !

In the end she could not bear the suspense, and read her brother-in-law's missive straight through before setting her mind to the task of deciphering her husband's. Neither was long. Sieur Germain wished her to know that Gray had been safe and in one piece when last heard from, but was intending to go into the Duchies in search of the conspirators and Amelia; he thanked her and Joanna once again for the information they had forwarded; and he wished to be told at once should they run across any more.

Then, the first alarm over – *safe and in one piece* might conceal a multitude of hurts, but it was enough to be going on with – she smoothed out the even briefer note from Gray and studied it. He had scratched in the numerals of the date at the top, very small: *That was Mercuriday, and therefore . . .*

'Sophie!' said Joanna, peering over her shoulder. 'You have not *memorised* all the cipher keys?'

'Why not?' Sophie did not look up; the deciphered message was taking shape, and she could not spare the time to argue with her sister. 'There are not so very many. It is no different from getting Greek noun declensions by heart. And it was you who said I must learn to encipher my own letters, Jo.'

Am going carefully, the message read; *the regiment will have a means of finding me.* She smiled at his use of her own words, then said, very low, 'But going where?'

PART FOUR

Orléans

CHAPTER XXVI

In Which Gray Makes
a New Acquaintance

Three days into his journey to the soi-disant Emperor's court, in the company of Monsieur Durand of the Temple of Ceres, Gray had yet to settle in his own mind the question of his companion's motives. Had he seen through Gray's Angevin incognito and pegged him as a spy? Had he, on the contrary, been taken in by it, and seen Gray as a useful recruit to his master's cause? Was he, too, reserving judgement, awaiting some revealing word or act which should sway him in one direction or the other?

And was it his business, truly, to quarter the countryside in search of unemployed scholar-mages whom he might tempt into vowing their service to a man who was, at least at present, Emperor of nothing and nowhere?

From the first their conversation had been subtly guarded; Durand was not inclined to loquacity, and what he did say was not notably revealing. But he had said that the Emperor was gathering scholar-mages to his court; Gray, for his part, played the eccentric scholar-mage to the hilt, discoursing at length on the theory and practice of illusion-spells and quoting all the dullest authorities he could think of, whenever an opportunity offered.

Durand, he learnt, possessed only the most rudimentary magickal talent – capable of calling light and fire, and of small summonings, and no more than that – but he claimed other powers granted by his patron goddess, including that of blessing farmers' crops on her behalf.

Being a priest of Ceres in the countryside, moreover, Durand could command food and lodging gratis, or, rather, in return for blessings and divinations rather than coin, which at any rate spared Gray's increasingly thin purse, though he salved his conscience by trotting out his best mending-spells for the benefit of their hosts. They rode briskly, and soon they were threading their way between one lord's encamped troops and another's, approaching a great walled city on the bank of what proved to be the River Loire.

The city was not under siege, whatever the appearances, Durand assured him; these were the Emperor's own liege-men, gathering here to march with him upon the King of Britain. Gray, lost in frantic calculations (how far was he now from Colonel Dubois' regiment and Tremblay's mages with their finding-spells? How soon, as the owl flew, could he reach them with a message?), replied somewhat at random.

The banner flying from the central tower of the castle keep bore a familiar-unfamiliar blazon: on a crimson field, three vaguely triangular flowerlike emblems in white – the arms of Orléans! *Yes, now I see* – surmounted by three fleurs-de-lys and what looked very like a Roman eagle.

'The banner of the New Empire of Gaul,' said Durand grandly.

Once past the sentries and the walls – thanks to the countersign supplied by Durand – Gray was conducted to the castle keep, surrendered Tonnerre to the ministrations of a groom, and was himself handed over to an unsmiling chatelaine accompanied by two pages. She took in his travel-worn clothing, his dishevelled hair, his general air of road-weariness, and burst into a rapid stream of orders; Gray was borne off to the baths, his clothing was taken away to be laundered, and the rest of his possessions vanished up a staircase 'to the mages' quarters'.

Gray saw them go with considerable trepidation.

Two hours later, however, scrubbed, shaved and barbered, dressed in clothes which, if they did not quite fit him, at least were not caked in the mud of every road, track, and farmer's field between Ivry-sur-Eure and Orléans, he was conducted to a small, bare cubicle – almost entirely like a prisoner's cell, but for possessing clean bedding on the narrow bed, a window out onto the keep's central courtyard, and an open doorway – where he found his saddle-bags slung over the foot of the bed and his own clothes, still warm from the laundress's iron, hung up on pegs on the opposite wall. The saddle-bags appeared not to have been tampered with, though of course a man who was collecting mages might have at his disposal more than one means of effecting a search.

If I am to be kept prisoner again, Gray reflected, *at any rate I shall be kept comfortably this time.*

The notion was no more appealing for that, however.

Yet another page appeared shortly thereafter to conduct him into the presence of the great man.

'You are Monsieur Guy Marais of Poitiers?'

At first glance, Henri-François, Duc d'Orléans and self-styled Emperor of Gaul, was not much to look at – a small man, dark of hair and eyes, clad in buckskin breeches, gleaming boots, and a blue velvet coat adorned with a frankly absurd array of gold braid, and lounging in a massive chair of ornate design which made him appear smaller still – and certainly did not look as though he should inspire terror. The tense shimmering feeling of the air all about them, however, told a different tale altogether; this man fairly radiated power – both magickal and otherwise – and was accustomed to use it without scruple or compunction.

'I am, Your Imperial Majesty,' said Gray. He had thought the address absurd, when Durand instructed him in how to address the Emperor *so that you may not disgrace yourself, or me*, and he thought it so still – what was this man Emperor of, after all, but some thousands of men and a few square miles of town? – but not by any betraying twitch of lip or eyebrow did he show it.

'And you are a mage?'

'I am, sir.'

Henri-François d'Orléans sat back in his chair – or, rather, Gray decided, his throne – and studied him, narrow-eyed, in a manner which suggested that he was looking beneath the surfaces of things. 'There is vast potential here, certainly,' he murmured, after a moment; and then, shifting his gaze to Gray's face, 'Show me.'

Gray blinked. 'Is there,' he said, 'any particular working which you should like to see demonstrated? Sir?'

Orléans waved a careless hand, but his gaze on Gray perceptibly sharpened. 'All those of which you are capable,' he said.

Take care what you ask this man for, thought Gray, ruefully. He did not mean, of course, to reveal *everything* of which he was capable; shape-shifting was too distinctive a working to risk, and no scholar-mage such as he was claiming to be would be expected to have a store of offensive spells at the ready, though some might be capable of a shielding-spell or two.

He began by calling an ordinary globe of magelight, then split it into two, then four, and sent them to spin in a circle overhead: a foolish trick, entertainment for children. He asked for a candle and called fire to light it, working as neatly and precisely as he knew how, then drew raindrops from the air (fortunately rather damp) to put it out again. Then summoning-spells: the book from the top of the stack at the Emperor's left hand, then the embroidered handkerchief which one of the Emperor's attendants had just slipped into his pocket. He worked an illusion-spell to create a facsimile of Charles Durand's hat – the *catch*, the necessary clue to distinguish illusion from reality, a sprig of bright orange forget-me-not tucked over one ear. He set strong wards about himself, the Emperor, and his attendants, and invited them all to try whether they could pass through them.

To his secret dismay, Orléans – though none of the others – could, and did, brushing at his shoulders as though sweeping aside strands of cobweb clinging to his coat.

This man is more powerful even than I feared. Had he sprung a trap from which he should not be capable of escape? *We shall see . . .*

'A promising display,' said Orléans at last.

Gray bowed.

'Walk with me a little, Guy Marais of Poitiers.'

Gray, beginning to be sorry he had ever left London, followed him – up to the battlements, as it proved, whence they could see the great River Loire, the great bridge spanning it to give access to the city from the south, the wide flat vista spread out all about them.

'My legions,' said Orléans, his expansive gesture taking in the thousands, tens of thousands, of men encamped outside the walls to the east, north, and west.

'If I may be permitted an observation, sir,' said Gray mildly, 'you appear to be preparing for war.'

Orléans turned slightly, leaning one elbow on the battlement, and gave him a long look. 'Tell me, Monsieur Marais – where have you been travelling of late, that you should only now have arrived at this conclusion?'

Gray attempted a self-deprecating laugh but was conscious of its not succeeding very well. 'My pursuits and those of kings and armies do not often intersect,' he said. 'I confess that when I accepted

Monsieur Durand's invitation to be presented to his patron, I did not expect to find myself in the midst of a military campaign.'

'All Gallia is at war at present, Monsieur Marais,' said Orléans gravely, 'or soon will be. For centuries we have fought amongst ourselves, when we ought to have made common cause against our common foes, to recapture the lands lost to Rome and build a new empire.'

Gray swallowed. 'I see,' he said. 'Given such vast and well-equipped armies as you appear to have mustered, however, I confess I do not see what need you have of scholar-mages in your war of empire.'

'*Our* war,' Orléans corrected. How could so soft-spoken a man project such menace? 'I am only the gods' instrument in this matter.'

'The gods of Rome,' Gray said, testing a hypothesis.

'The great and true gods,' said Orléans, confirming it.

Perhaps this may explain his appeal to Appius Callender, thought Gray; like not a few other persons of his class and education, Callender was, or had been, conspicuously dismissive of the local gods whose worship was so much a part of the lives of, for example, his tenant farmers. Though, for the matter of that, flattery and other sops to his self-consequence might explain it equally well. *The mystery is Callender's appeal to him.*

'Nevertheless—'

'Julius Caesar,' said Orléans, 'by the gift of the gods, was a mage of great talent and exemplary skill, by which means he was able to wrest lands and peoples from lesser, undeserving gods, to bring them the gift of the Pax Romana, and so merited the title he bore in life and the godhood he was granted thereafter.'

Gray tried to look as though the connexion between his query and this unprompted and oddly tilted (not to say wildly inaccurate) lecture on Roman history were perfectly clear to him.

'Julius Caesar, Divus Iulius, died at the hands of a conspiracy of traitors' – *as King Henry nearly did, at the hands of Callender and his*

364

friends, thought Gray – 'and in time the empire he built passed into the hands of those whom the gods had not chosen, and thence into decline and irrelevance. But the Roman people – we citizens of the old empire, made worthy by our allegiance to the great gods of Rome – can build a new empire, can reconquer the lost lands, which now are throwing away the power of their prayers and offerings on small, unworthy gods, and create a new Pax Romana for their peoples.'

By killing those peoples' own gods, or those who serve them? Not even the mad emperor Nero ever conceived such a monstrous idea.

Gray was too much appalled to speak (though not too much to wonder what in Hades this man was about, to be spouting these mad ideas to a perfect stranger of whose loyalties he knew almost nothing); fortunately, his companion swept on unheeding: 'The histories tell us that Caesar's sorcerer-centuries were the key to his success in the field; less well known is the key to the sorcerer-centuries themselves: that to every sorcerer in the field were linked two more behind the line of battle – his reserves – to strengthen him and replenish his magick. The barbarians thought them invincible, and often they had only to be seen to take the field in order to win their battles.'

He smiled in a manner that chilled Gray to his bones. 'You wished to know what use I have for scholar-mages? I have built a new sorcerer-century, and am building another, and my sorcerers need reserves.'

'Linked,' said Gray, now fighting a strong urge to leap off the battlements, shift, and fly away – or, as was far more likely, shift and plummet to his death in a hail of arrows. 'Linked, how?'

He could imagine it, he thought, far more easily than this man suspected – a bond like his link with Sophie, but drawing all one way.

'Oh, you understand well enough what I am speaking of, I think,' said Orléans, as though in reply.

Gray controlled a startled exclamation: a reader of thoughts, or a seer of magick? Either was dismaying, in the circumstances. Upon further thought, Gray decided that the latter was most likely; had Orléans truly been capable of hearing his thoughts, he should long since have been clapped in irons, at the very least.

'We need not go so far at present, however,' said Orléans, in what he perhaps imagined to be a reassuring tone. 'Come – you shall see what we are building here.'

Gray could think of few things he desired less, but he had been given a task, and he meant to carry it out. What he had expected to be the most difficult aspect of this ill-advised operation – to persuade the men whom he had helped to convict of murder and attempted regicide that he had decided to throw in his lot with them – took on a rather different aspect, now that he understood what fate awaited them. How had Orléans persuaded them to consent to it? *No – surely they have been tricked, misled, coerced.*

And Amelia – what in Hades has Amelia to do with this mess?

'Certainly, sir,' he said.

The first surprise was that all of them appeared quite contented – even pleased – with their lot. What Orléans called *the mages' work-room* was vast, bright, and warmly sunlit, and the dozens of men in it (they were all men) were engaged in perfectly ordinary pursuits, from the purely scholarly to the more practical – one fellow was distilling some disturbingly bright green solution in a series of alembics, many were reading, and several were debating good-naturedly the merits of several disparate spells of concealment. One or two appeared to have dozed off in their armchairs. Might any of these be Kergabet's missing agents? Impossible to say.

Not one, so far as Gray could determine, was at present working any sort of magick. The atmosphere was busy and cheerful, like . . . *like the nursery at Grosvenor Square, in fact.* Strangest of all was the fact that not one of them took the slightest notice of their master or his companion.

Gray tucked these thoughts away for later contemplation.

He picked out Callender and the healer Lord Spencer almost at once, and he thought he could guess to what employment Orléans had put Taylor and Woodville, strong young men trained in offensive and defensive magicks. What had become of Lord Wrexham, Queen Edwina's brother – the one member of the conspiracy, absent the late Viscount Carteret, entirely without magickal talent – was less easy to guess, but of course wherever he was he should not be in this room. More puzzling was the absence of Lord Merton, erstwhile Fellow of King's College, Oxford, and certainly a mage of considerable power. Perhaps, despite his age, Orléans meant to put him in the field?

Orléans ushered Gray out of the workroom again. 'A thing of beauty, is it not?' he said happily. 'Nothing can disturb them when they are busy about their work. But you, I think, will wish to see the other side of the coin. You are young and strong, and if I do not mistake, you have hidden depths; should you choose to join us, your place will be in the field, not in the workroom.'

Did Gray imagine the sinister ring to that *should you choose*? He rolled his left shoulder, testing its range of motion, and was unspeakably relieved to feel no unusual twinge of pain. *I can fly if I must, then. That is well.*

They found the Emperor's sorcerer-century – not quite a century, in fact, though more than a half-century – conducting manoeuvres in a large flagstone courtyard. Behind them – in the midst of a group of other young ladies seated on a bench along the courtyard's far wall, all watching the mages whilst hemming, or pretending to hem, some long strip of white linen – was Amelia Callender.

CHAPTER XXVII

In Which Sophie Receives a Deputation

The excavation of the library continued through the next several days. Ceana MacGregor ruthlessly organised her forces into salvage and triage parties, depending on their skill with letters and languages, as a result of which the work progressed more quickly than any of the rest had dared hope.

Lucia and Roland took charge of collating texts in Latin and Français, Sophie and Evans-Hughes of those in English and Cymric, and Master Alcuin, recruited for the cause over dinner at the Dragon and Lion, of those in Greek.

Joanna and Gwendolen, for their part, were charged with cataloguing the results of the work of everybody else. They pitched their camp in the library's tiny map-room, whose contents were in comparatively pristine condition. In the intervals of receiving more-or-less complete codices to catalogue, they took out and examined the maps and charts; there were hundreds of them, of which, by the afternoon of the third day, they had examined perhaps five dozen.

'I do not suppose they are much good for any but an historian,' said Gwendolen. She was gazing thoughtfully at a large, intricately decorated map of the Iberian peninsula – at least four centuries out of date. 'But how beautiful some of them are!'

'Not this one,' said Joanna, drawing out a small map of Britain and the adjacent Duchies, badly foxed, which had somehow adhered to the back of a larger one. 'It cannot ever have been as beautiful as yours, there, but it has certainly nothing at all to recommend it now!'

They spread it out, nevertheless, and studied it, standing side by side at the sturdy table. This room was very nearly private, if, as now, one stood out of sight from the half-open door; Joanna dared to lean her shoulder into Gwendolen's, and to tilt up her face to kiss her friend's cheek. Gwendolen tamped down a smile, and nudged Joanna's shoulder in return.

'What on earth *is* it?' she said, after a moment. 'It looks very old – older even than that Iberian one.'

'Yes, I should think it may be,' Joanna agreed.

No well-supplied court cartographer had drawn this map. The rough and ready lines, the cramped script, suggested a military man working in the field, marking out rivers and roads and waggon-tracks, the ponds that might serve to water cavalry and pack-horses, the villages and farms where supplies might be replenished and officers quartered at need, the obstacles and fortifications that must be taken into account in planning and executing a military campaign. Borders had been drawn and then scratched out, till in some long-contested territories – along the River Loire, for example – the map was a palimpsest.

Joanna searched the map for a date, for the name of a king, for any indication of its age, and found none, but the borders of Britain shown upon it – those uppermost, and most recently drawn – were those of the time of Henry the Great, not vastly different from their own.

'What are those red . . . things?' said Gwendolen, leaning close and pointing with one forefinger. 'Here, and along here, and there?'

'I have not the least idea.' Joanna bent closer, too, and peered at them. 'Fortifications, perhaps – the way they are placed suggests it, there along the border of Breizh with Anjou.'

'Well, perhaps. But look there—'

Joanna did. That spit of land protruding from the Breizhek coastline, south-west of Gwened on the Gulf of Morbihan, was surely Kiberon; which, if she did not greatly err, put that oddly placed grouping of red marks – much the largest, for the rest were single or in pairs – square amongst the Stones of Karnag.

'How peculiar,' she said, almost to herself.

'Jo,' said Gwendolen then, fingertips gentle on Joanna's wrist. 'Jo, look at this.'

In one corner of the map, half obscured by a dark stain which might have been anything from strong tea to human blood, was drawn an aggressively straight-sided rectangle, filled to the edges, in an entirely different hand from that which had labelled the map's cities and provinces, with Greek.

'*Not* Greek,' said Gwendolen. 'At least, I think not.'

Greek but not Greek. That rings a bell . . .

Joanna fetched Master Alcuin away from his stacks of dismembered codices and stood shifting from foot to foot whilst he peered at the blotched letters through a magnifying glass and hummed interestedly.

'Not Greek,' he confirmed at last, looking up. 'We have seen this trick before, Miss Joanna, have we not? Some other tongue set down using Greek rather than Roman characters—'

'But, Master Alcuin, what does it *say?*'

He chuckled. 'Patience, my dear,' he said. 'I shall transcribe it for you, and then we shall see.'

Gwendolen fetched him pen and paper, and Joanna a four-legged stool, and they settled down to watch.

To Joanna's chagrin, the message taking shape under Master Alcuin's pen made no more sense in Roman characters than in Greek ones; till, several words along, she recognised that the unnamed annotator had disguised the message not only through the use of the Greek alphabet but also by writing it backwards. 'Start at the end,' she said, and Master Alcuin said, 'Ha!' and did so, tracking his progress through the final-or-first sentence with his left forefinger.

'Sophie!' Joanna bellowed, some two dozen words later. 'Sophie, come here at once!'

The Brezhoneg words were sometimes oddly spelt, but the message was perfectly clear for all that. *This map*, the new transcription read,

> *shows the anchors of the magick of blood and stone, which Argentaela ar Breizh, wife of Nevenoe, devised and sealed with her blood to protect her husband's kingdom, which Ahez daughter of Alan, King of Breizh, brought as dowry to her English husband, which the queens of Britain have preserved as once it preserved us from the longship raiders of the north, from the mage-warriors of the east, from the great golden ships of Iberia to the south. Look to the stones when danger threatens, and may the old gods preserve us all.*

'"Sealed with her blood,"' Sophie repeated. '"The magick of blood and stone." This place is steeped in blood, it seems to me.'

Lucia, Roland, and Evans-Hughes, drawn presumably by Joanna's calling to Sophie, had by now all crowded in at the map-room door.

'It is also steeped in persons who do not explain themselves,' Lucia remarked. 'We may now be said to know what this magick of blood and stone was meant to accomplish, and where it originated; but we are no nearer understanding either what it does, or how.'

'It does sound very like Ailpín Drostan's spell-net, however,' said Sophie – more thoughtful than revolted, now. 'The blood of the rulers, the bones of the land. And its purpose must have been similar. One wonders how the Princesses Regent shaped it to their very different ends, for which it seems to me very ill-suited, and what on the gods' earth gave them the notion to attempt it.'

As the afternoon sun began to dip below the tops of the library windows, the party returned as usual to the Dragon and Lion, there to wash off the accumulated filth of their excavations, change their clothes, and eat their dinner. Ordinarily, they were left to their own devices until the first two of these proceedings had been completed; on this occasion, however, they had not even reached the staircase to the first floor before they were hailed by the innkeeper, who informed Sophie that there were *some gentlemen from Merlin College waiting for you in the parlour, ma'am.*

They looked at one another in consternation.

'Who can it be?' said Gareth. 'Alcuin and I are here already, and none of your other acquaintance, I am quite sure, are in college at present.'

'What does it matter?' said Sophie, gesturing comprehensively at her filthy boots, the streaks of grime down the front of her gown, the hand-shaped smudges where she had tucked up her skirts to climb a ladder. 'I cannot possibly meet anyone at all, looking as I do at present. I was ashamed to be seen in the street.'

The gentlemen in the parlour, having presumably heard the telltale sounds of a large party trooping in at the front door and starting up the stairs, emerged into the corridor. Gareth had been mistaken; with Professor de Guivrée and Professor Langsdale, alas, she was very well acquainted, to their mutual irritation.

'Evans-Hughes!' exclaimed the latter, taking in the filthy canvas overall which Gareth, with his usual foresight, had put on over his own clothes that morning, and was now taking off and folding inside-out over one arm. 'Whatever can you be doing here?'

'He is just going,' said Sophie firmly, giving Gareth's broad back a purposeful shove in the direction of the front door. He attempted to resist; she stared hard at him, and after a moment he relented and, *Thank all the gods!*, went away.

'Professor Langsdale,' said Sophie, turning to her visitors with an unfelt smile and motioning them back into the public parlour. 'Professor de Guivrée. To what do I owe this unexpected honour?'

They eyed her with more than usual distaste – some of it for herself, she supposed, and the rest for the appalling state of her clothes, her hair and very likely her face. She stared back, unblinking, as she drew out her magick to tame her hair and smooth both dust and dismay from her face, for the brief perverse satisfaction of seeing them goggle at the change. She did not invite them to sit down; perhaps they might take the hint and refrain from lingering.

Professor Langsdale cleared his throat. 'We are come on behalf of the Senior Fellows of Merlin College, er, Mrs Marshall, for the purpose of—'

'Magistra,' Sophie corrected him.

'I beg your pardon?'

'As I hold a master's degree in practical magick from the University in Din Edin,' said Sophie, 'I am correctly addressed as *Magistra Marshall*.' The honorific did not much matter to her in the ordinary way, but it seemed necessary to remind these men of her right to it.

'Er.' *It is sticking in his craw, right enough, the old goat.* 'Magistra Marshall. Am I correct in supposing that you have elected, despite advice to the contrary, to proceed with this business of a college for young ladies?'

Sophie gave him an edged smile. 'You are correct in supposing that you have failed to warn me off, yes.'

'And, er. What is your husband's view of this, er, venture?'

'My husband's view?' Sophie repeated, surprised. 'He supports it entirely. Why should you imagine otherwise?'

'And yet he has, er, has not accompanied you to Oxford.'

'My husband,' said Sophie, her tone as chilly as she could make it, 'has duties of his own.' She paused, and added conversationally, 'Before you continue your representations, professors, it may interest you to know that this venture, as you put it, is under the personal patronage not only of the Princess Royal' – she smiled demurely – 'but also of His Majesty the King.'

As she had surmised, this flummoxed them; to harass and browbeat *her* was one thing, to attempt the same upon their sovereign quite another.

They were not entirely deterred, however, and did not take themselves off until Sophie had pretended to listen to a quarter-hour's worth of variations on the theme *Lady Morgan College was an experiment that failed and need not be repeated* – throughout which she was continually thinking, *If only you knew!* – and allowed them to hand her a petition signed by some number of Fellows of Merlin and other Colleges, which she had no intention of reading. As a result of this visit, or visitation, she arrived at the dinner-table late, wearing mismatched ear-drops, and so cross that Joanna and Lucia began making cautious enquiries as to her well-being.

When, therefore, one of the innkeeper's daughters knocked at her door early the next morning, to inform her that there was *a, er, a gentleman below wanting to see you, ma'am*, her first instinct was to tear off the boots, stockings, gown, and shift she had just put on, resume her nightdress, and go back to sleep.

'Sophie?' said Lucia, her voice blurred and sleepy. 'Is all well?'

'There is another deputation downstairs in the parlour,' said Sophie crossly. They had neither of them slept well. 'With another petition, no doubt. I shall just go and tell them to go away.'

She closed the door behind her, descended the stairs as quietly as their tendency to creak permitted, rounded the turning into the parlour, and stopped dead, her mouth falling open in shock.

The man who stood fidgeting nervously by the fireplace mantel was not another Fellow of Merlin – was not, any longer, an Oxford man at all. A man of her father's age, lean to the point of emaciation, his pallid face surmounted by a sweep of greying hair: Lord Merton, lately of King's College and friend – or, at any rate, co-conspirator – of her stepfather, Appius Callender.

'Mrs Marshall?' said his younger, more solid companion. 'My name is Henry Taylor.'

After a moment's gobsmacked silence, Sophie – without pausing further to consider her approach, or thinking the circumstances through – marched across the parlour, took Taylor by the lapels of his ill-fitting coat, and said, 'What in Hades have you done with my sister Amelia?'

She did not altogether recognise that she was shaking him – and so preventing him from answering her – until a sharply indrawn breath behind her made her pause, turn, and behold Roland and Joanna standing in the doorway.

'I-I-I have not seen your sister,' Taylor managed. He was green in the face and breathing in shallow gasps. 'Not since we parted on the Dover road. I-I tried, I asked her – but she would go.'

Sophie let go of his coat and swung away from him, exasperated.

'Where?' Joanna demanded. '*Where* would she go?'

Henry Taylor could not possibly have been more outraged by this turn of events if he had been truly innocent of all wrongdoing. *He* had never intended to take Amelia to Calais, he said indignantly; *he* had meant to throw himself on the King's mercy, and had only wished to speak to Amelia – to bid her a proper farewell – before doing so.

'How came you to be on the Dover road together, then?' said Joanna, deeply sceptical. 'And what have you been doing with yourself, in all the time since?'

Had she not said all along that Amelia would not have eloped with the unwashed, uncombed, half-lunatic man she and Gwendolen had encountered in the park? But it was not very satisfying, in the event, to be proved right.

'Hiding, chiefly,' said Taylor, his righteous indignation fading into weariness. 'Evading the City Watch. I called at my sister's house, when she was not at home, and helped myself to some of her husband's coin – he will never miss it – and a suit of his clothes. And in the end I came back to Merlin.' He shrugged. 'I had that in common with Marshall, always, though I do not suppose he knew it; we had neither of us any other home.'

Joanna kept her expression impassive in the face of this bid for compassion. *I shall consider feeling sorry for you when we have rescued my sister.* On the heels of this thought came another: that she and Sophie, out in the wide world with their vastly expanded families, had begun to think of Amelia as though she were not the eldest of them but the youngest – and, worse, to treat her accordingly.

Roland, who had quietly left the room whilst Joanna's attention was occupied elsewhere, now returned to stand at her shoulder once more. 'I have asked the innkeeper to send for the Watch,' he said, low; then, a little louder. 'Sophie, come here.'

Predictably, rather than obeying, Sophie turned to glare at him. Roland sighed. There came the sound of footsteps – coming down the stairs, not along the corridor – and then Joanna felt Gwendolen's hand on her shoulder, and Lucia was crowding in behind them, peering around Roland's head.

Roland squared his shoulders and took a step forward. At once Taylor and Merton tensed, wary, and brought up their hands defensively as though to do . . . what? Roland, in any case, seemed quite unintimidated. 'I arrest you in the name of His Majesty the King,' he said firmly.

They goggled at him. Roland had always been a good man in a crisis, Joanna reminded herself; it was in the small ordinary difficulties of everyday life that he tended either to forget, or to make far too much of, the dignity of his years.

'The City Watch has been summoned,' he went on; 'I should advise you to go with them without argument, when they arrive. In the meantime, however, let us sit down like reasonable people and discuss how we may be of use to one another. Sophie, will you set us a ward?'

Sophie blinked at him (*horses, stable doors*, thought Joanna) but after a moment nodded, closed her eyes, and began muttering a spell. Roland waited patiently for its conclusion before turning his earnest gaze squarely on his . . . prisoners, Joanna supposed she must call them. They seated themselves, looking rather like stunned oxen, on two hideous armchairs.

'You have information of value to us,' he said. 'My sister and I have the ear of the King' – the prisoners' eyes widened as, belatedly, they recognised to whom they were speaking – 'and I, at least, will undertake to intercede on your behalf, should you put us in the way of locating Miss Callender.'

'And tell us who it was that abetted your escape,' Joanna added prudently, from the doorway, 'and why.'

'Indeed,' said Roland.

Taylor and Merton conferred in voices too low for Joanna to distinguish. At last Merton said, 'How are we to lead you to Miss Callender when neither of us had any hand in her departure from England?'

'We know,' said Sophie, 'that my sister left London with the goal of rejoining her father at the court of the Emperor of France. Presumably you must know, or at any rate suspect, who is meant by that epithet, and where he has his court?'

'You will speak for us to the King?' said Lord Merton. 'We have your word upon it?'

'You have,' said Roland.

'You sought us out, Lord Merton,' Sophie said quietly. 'You sought *me* out, in fact. Why do so, if not because you have something to say to me? Whatever it is, very soon now you shall have to say it to the Watch Captain, who may be less inclined to compromise.'

'I had hoped,' Merton said, grimacing, 'to retain both my life and my liberty, and to give warning without further risk to myself. I am not a traitor, Your Highness—'

Roland and Sophie exchanged an incredulous look.

'What I did,' Merton insisted, 'I did for the good of the kingdom, as I saw it. I could not have predicted this consequence. I am acting now from the same motive; I cannot speak for any other person.'

'Go on, then,' said Roland. 'And do not be too long about it.'

Merton frowned at him. 'The man who calls himself Imperator Gallia,' he said, 'is the Duke of Orléans, and Orléans is where you shall find him, unless he be now on the march with his armies. He has anointed himself a second Julius Caesar, and aims to unite all of Caesar's Gaulish and Frankish territories, and thereafter to build a new Roman Empire. He is collecting mages, as well as the armies of his followers, because he aspires to control sorcerer-centuries such as those which struck terror into the hearts of Caesar's conquests.'

His auditors digested this for some moments; then Lucia MacNeill ventured, 'Is he mad, think you?'

'Quite mad,' said Taylor positively. 'He – by way of his agent in London, that is – agreed to aid our escape, and promised that we should be granted posts in his court, in return for information – harmless enough information, it seemed at first – until, before we knew where we were, we were all become his liege-men – his creatures, I should rather say.'

'For myself,' said Roland, in a distant tone, 'I do not think I should seek out convicted traitors as my liege-men.'

'That is because you do not understand the circumstances,' Taylor snapped. 'Lord Carteret was Orléans' liege-man before he was King Henry's.'

Does this mean, can it mean, that this self-styled Emperor was somehow behind Carteret's plot? How far down, how far back, does this rabbit-hole extend? And how could the priests of Apollo Coelispex, discerners of truth and falsehood in the minds of men, have failed to discern such a momentous truth as this one?

Into the astonished silence which greeted this revelation, Taylor continued: 'Poor Amelia was the go-between – though she believed she was only sending parcels to her papa, of course, along with her own. By the time the day arrived, I had already made up my mind that I wanted no part of the Emperor's court, and had written to Amelia to beg her to come to London – we should go to Eire, perhaps, I thought, or Alba, or to the Low Countries, and put all of this business behind us. But it was not so easy as I thought to escape from the escape – so to speak – and then . . . well. When the time came to choose, she did not choose me.'

He did not appear to have noticed how widely this version of his intentions departed from his initial protests of innocence. *Wished only to say a proper farewell, indeed*, thought Joanna.

'And you, sir?' said Roland, turning to Lord Merton. 'What is your tale?'

'Whether or not Orléans is mad, I cannot undertake to say,' said Merton. 'But he has certainly an idée fixe on the subject of this restored empire of his, and of the Roman gods. I am a follower of the Roman path myself, like most educated men,' he added, in an explaining tone, 'but to speak of enforcing Pax Romana by stamping out the worship of all other gods is another matter altogether, and an aim to which I cannot lend myself.'

He concluded this speech with a decisive nod and sat back in his chair.

'I confess,' said Roland, 'that I had rather hoped for more concrete intelligence with which to act upon your warning. What are my father's generals to do with the information that their opponent has declared war on the old gods? Does he mean to declare war on Britain? When, if so? Is he likely to be amenable to terms? What numbers has he, and how deployed?'

There was a small, stifled sound to Joanna's left; darting her eyes in that direction, she observed Lucia gazing at Roland in pleased approval. *There's for all your poetical wooing, Roland,* she thought, rolling her eyes. *You had only to talk to her of tactics and strategy, after all.*

Alas, however, neither of their informants had been near enough to Orléans' councils to acquire any of the intelligence Roland sought.

'I have promised to intercede on your behalf,' he said at last, 'and I shall not go back on my word; but when next you decide to throw yourself on the King's mercy in return for information, I should advice you first to build up a greater store thereof.'

It happened at this moment that the Captain of the Watch knocked loudly on the door of the Dragon and Lion, and Roland, glancing that way to gauge the source of the noise, met Lucia's gaze and held it. Joanna saw him register her appreciative expression – saw his cheeks flush and his eyes brighten in response. Then the men of the Watch in their heavy boots were clomping along the passage and crowding through the parlour door, and in the bustle of handing over the prisoners and impressing upon the Watch Captain the importance of their being transported *at once* to London and given into the custody of Lord Kergabet and Lord de Vaucourt, the moment passed.

CHAPTER XXVIII

In Which Lucia Attends a Concert, and Lives to Tell the Tale

Having dispatched both Taylor and Merton, and an explanatory missive on the subject thereof, to Kergabet in London, Sophie's party sat down to eat their breakfast and take stock. They had by now collected and sorted all the damaged codices from the library of Lady Morgan College, and had pieced together and catalogued most of them, but they had still to explore the Shrine of Minerva Sophia. Further discussion decided them, however, that the following morning must suffice for this endeavour, and that thereafter they should return with their prizes to London, where they might study them in more comfort and be in the way of more quickly hearing any news.

The reclaimed books and maps were packed up under Ceana MacGregor's direction into a large number of crates and dispatched in a hired cart, tightly covered in oilcloth in case of rain, to the Royal Palace. The box containing the confession of the Princesses Regent, however, and the mysterious map which seemed to belong to it, Sophie wrapped carefully in layers of clean linens and packed into her own trunk. She was not altogether clear, in her own mind, what she meant to do with either of them, but the letter in the box was directed to her, in a way, and she felt a responsibility for its secrets.

Indeed, its secrets weighed upon her like a cloak of lead.

They arrived in Grosvenor Square to find that Mrs Marshall, disappointed in the matter of Miss Beaumont, had decamped to Glascoombe. Lady Maëlle remained, but to Sophie's eye she seemed reduced, as though the loss of Amelia – in effect, her last child – had altered her in some fundamental way. Sophie and Joanna, feeling guiltily that they, too, had abandoned her in rushing off to Oxford to go exploring, exerted themselves to demonstrate their affection, but though she smiled at them and called them good girls, as though they had been children once again, nothing they could say or do appeared to make the least difference to her melancholy.

Some days after their return to London, the Grosvenor Square family, together with Roland, Lucia, Edward, Delphine, and Harry, attended a concert at the Apollonium. The mood in the city was oddly buoyant, following the very public return of two of the escaped conspirators to the Tower of London, in consequence of which – and of the private knowledge that the others were almost certainly hundreds of miles away – Lord Kergabet had relaxed his strictures on public appearances by Sophie and Joanna. Delphine (who was very fond of music) had lobbied strenuously in favour of this engagement, as had Edward, who was to depart with his regiment but two days hence and therefore was more than usually inclined to indulge his wife.

It was not precisely like being amongst friends; it was not the Royal Palace, however, and the company was in general a younger and more carefree set of persons than were to be met under the careful chaperonage of Queen Edwina. Alas, Sìleas Barra MacNeill had insisted upon Lucia's wearing one of her new gowns, a stiff and thickly embroidered creation in which sitting was uncomfortable (and dancing nearly impossible), but the music, when it began, was very lovely, and it was pleasant – if very odd – to be reunited with the Oxford party, in this altogether less consequential atmosphere.

At the first interval, they rose from their seats and moved out to the terrace. Roland and his brothers trooped off to fetch glasses of wine for the ladies of the party; Sophie, Delphine, and Gwendolen had their heads together, comparing notes on the performances they had just heard, whilst Joanna propped her shoulders against a pillar and studied her programme with an abstracted air. Lucia stepped away from them a little and leant her elbows upon the balustrade, gazing out at the busy River Thames below.

'Lady Lucia?' The speaker, when she turned to look at him, proved to be a dark-haired young man, not much taller than herself, with bright hazel eyes. He wore, if she did not mistake, the uniform of a cavalry lieutenant.

'I am she,' she said, cautiously.

'I beg your pardon,' he said in Latin, with a bashful smile which, despite herself, Lucia found rather charming. 'I know we have not been introduced. My name is Arzhur Kermorgant. I have a most particular reason for wishing to speak with you—'

Lucia did not see the threat until it was very nearly too late: his arms had closed behind her, mimicking a lover's embrace, and what later proved to be the tip of a tiny clasp-knife was nosing gently at the fabric of her stiff, uncomfortable new gown, scraping amongst glass beads and gilt thread and seeking the best opportunity to slide in between her ribs.

It was fortunate – for both of them, as it transpired – that Ceana MacGregor had insisted on teaching her the rudiments of self-defence, and fortunate too that Lucia's instinct, when events moved too quickly for thought, had always favoured magick over force. The heiress of Alba did not panic, did not cry out, did not for a moment lose her composure; she was reaching for her magick, flinging it out around her on the words of a shielding-spell, almost before her conscious mind had acknowledged the danger.

And then her assailant was flat on his back at her feet, the knife (so small, honed so deadly sharp) skittering across the polished floor, and other people (so many people!) exclaiming and running about and shouting for someone to call for the Watch. Lucia stared down at the man who had attacked her, dry-eyed and perfectly steady but for the painful hitching of her breath, and concentrated on slowing her heartbeat.

He lay motionless, his eyes closed. Dead? *He looks very young. Almost a boy.* His chest rose and fell. *Not dead. Hail Brìghde!* Lucia did not shrink from the notion of killing, when killing was required – a chieftain who did so (as she had tried to explain to tender-hearted Sophie) was no chieftain at all – but he was so very young, this would-be assassin, and in any case it had *not* been required. *Besides which, had you killed him, he could not answer your questions.*

Running footsteps approached from several directions – the patter of dancing-slippers, the thump of heavy boots – and Lucia raised her head, slow and careful, and took a wary step backwards, then another, pressing her spine against the pillar that interrupted the balustrade.

'Lucia!' Sophie's voice, breathless and worried – then Roland's – Joanna's, Gwendolen's – and finally a gruff familiar baritone: 'My lady! Are you hurt?' Conall Barra MacNeill, Ceana MacGregor's second-in-command. Whose head Ceana MacGregor would certainly have, and his guts for bowstrings, if any harm came to Lucia through some negligence on his part.

Casting only the merest glance at the stranger who lay insensible upon the floor, Roland strode towards Lucia and reached out to her; she shrank away in spite of herself, and Sophie and Gwendolen caught his elbows and held him back.

'A moment, I pray you,' she said, astonished to find her voice steady. For the ears of the approaching guardsmen, her own and King Henry's both (here because she and Delphine and the Princes were here), she forced into it a note of command: 'I am quite unharmed; there is no danger now. Stand down.'

Conall Barra MacNeill glared the King's guardsmen out of countenance, and knelt by the young man's shoulder to examine him more closely.

A melodic *skrrr* caught Lucia's ear; when she looked that way, there was Joanna Callender straightening up from the floor with some small metallic object in her hand, held between the halves of a folded handkerchief. 'His weapon, I believe,' she said, and Lucia watched her hand it over to the guard captain – Prichard, yes, that was his name.

'I must go and speak to Jenny, and keep her away from . . . this,' Joanna muttered, and strode away, neither asking leave nor taking it.

'Lucia,' said Sophie's voice again, nearer this time; while all this was going forward, it seemed, Sophie had drawn level with Conall and was hovering there, prudently just out of Lucia's reach (though not, of course, Lucia could not help remarking, out of reach of an offensive spell). 'Thank all the gods you were not hurt!'

'Not in the least,' said Lucia. 'Let no one tell you that learning a trustworthy shielding-spell is a waste of effort.'

Now, *now* she heard the betraying tremble in her own voice – *Steadfast in the face of danger*, she thought, in bitter self-mockery, *and undone by a kind word from a friend.*

She put out a hand, thinking to keep Sophie at bay, but Sophie, misunderstanding, caught her hand and held it, and stepped over the stranger's splayed limbs to stand at Lucia's side, curving one arm protectively about her shoulders. In spite of herself Lucia leant towards her a little, feeling chilled and trying very hard not to shiver.

'Lucia, will you not come and sit down?' Roland had escaped from Joanna and Gwendolen and was approaching, with great caution, from Lucia's other side. 'You look—that is, you must have used considerable magick, I think, in defending yourself – Sophie, you will help her to a chair? – I shall fetch you something to eat.'

He turned on his heel and hared off in the direction of the supper-room.

It now occurred to Lucia that her shielding-spell might have used more magick than, had she been thinking at all at the time, she might have intended. Certainly it was comforting, a balm to her pride, to suppose that it was magick shock and not simple cowardice that made her feel chilled and light-headed and weak at the knees.

And clever of Roland to have deduced (or had he only guessed?) what had happened, before she had said anything to him about it.

Lucia and Sophie were still gazing down at the would-be assassin when Roland re-emerged onto the terrace; he was carrying two plates, one piled with strawberry tarts, the other with delicate slices of ham.

'Please, Lucia,' he said again, 'will you not sit down?'

'I will sit down,' she said, turning from Sophie's encircling arm to look him full in the face, 'if you will undertake to ensure that I shall be present when this man is questioned.'

'I—' Roland faltered, then said, 'If it be in my power – yes. You have certainly a right to hear whatever he may have to say for himself.'

He did not altogether like the notion, Lucia could see. She allowed herself to be steered to a chair near the terrace doors, from which she could both observe ongoing events and devour her strawberry tarts and ham.

Having seen her settled, Roland returned to the scene of the attempted crime, where Captain Prichard and Conall Barra

MacNeill were concluding a businesslike search of the unconscious youth, now bound at wrists and ankles, and – by their gestures – contesting possession of their prisoner.

The latter interrupted their debate with a low groan, and by stirring and attempting, with no success whatsoever, to sit up.

'I—stay here, Lucia,' said Sophie abstractedly. She patted Lucia's shoulder and darted off.

Lucia took stock of herself – *yes, much better!* – then stood up (gripping the chair-back for the first moment, to be safe) and followed.

Conall Barra MacNeill looked up at her approach and came forward, frowning, in an attempt to head her off. 'There is no use at all in my ordering you back to the Sasunnach castle and to bed, I suppose,' he said.

'None whatsoever,' Lucia. 'Is there any use in my offering you that chair, to spare your knee?'

Conall glowered down at her, his arms folded across his broad chest. 'You may be heir to the chieftain's seat, Lucia MacNeill, but I have not forgotten the time you put a hedgehog in Ceana MacGregor's parade helmet, or the time—'

Lucia held up one hand to signify her surrender.

Fortunately – for Roland, missing the substance and misreading the tone of their rapid, low-voiced exchange, appeared to be on the verge of wading into it in Lucia's defence – Joanna now came hastening back, with Prince Edward in his scarlet coat close on her heels. Delphine, to Lucia's relief, was nowhere in sight.

'Roland!' cried Edward. '*Quomodo vales?*'

Roland – with interjections from Lucia and the rest of the witnesses – explained.

Edward stood over the prisoner, now seated, more or less, with his back against the balustrade – was the young man's regimental coat his own, Lucia wondered, or part of a disguise? – and fixed him with a no doubt forbidding glare.

'Explain yourself, Lieutenant,' he said. 'What is your name? Your regiment? What reason can you possibly possess to attempt such a vile deed?'

'I-I-I am Derrien Robic, C-captain – Your Royal Highness – I serve in Colonel Maheux's regiment, presently quartered north of the River Huisne, in Maine – I—' He gazed about him in what looked like genuine bewilderment. 'M-may I know of what crime I am accused? And . . . I beg your pardon, my lords . . . where I am?'

The gathering erupted at this point into confused debate, which was ended at last by Edward's saying, loudly and very firmly, 'Captain Prichard, take this man to the Palace and confine him to the interdicted chamber, if you please.'

'Sir,' said Prichard, offering a crisp salute.

He signalled one of his guardsmen, and they began to pull Derrien Robic to his feet.

Lucia, however, was not inclined to sit quietly whilst her assailant's fate was decided by others. 'A word, Your Highness,' she said.

Their faces turned towards her, Roland's wary, Edward's astonished.

'Truly, Lucia,' said the latter, 'there is no need to trouble yourself further over this business; my father employs guardsmen and mages for exactly this purpose, and you may be assured that those responsible for this outrage upon a guest of his house – of our house – shall be suitably punished.'

Struggling to keep her temper, Lucia said, 'Your father may impose whatever punishment—' Lucia could see Prince Edward drawing breath to overrule her, and raised her voice a little: '—whatever punishment he sees fit, with my blessing, but first we must know how, and *whom*, and *why*—'

'Lady Lucia' – and Edward's voice was louder still, though quite without any show of temper – 'as a guest of—'

'Ned!' said Roland, between gritted teeth. 'Lucia has every right to know why she was attacked, and by whom.' His composed expression, to judge by the rhythmic clenching of his left hand at his side, was costing him some effort to maintain. 'Her being our guest is rather an argument in favour of her request than not, I should have thought. If *I* had been so used—'

'You are not a lady!' Prince Edward insisted, his voice lower now, but not the less vehement for that.

Lucia blinked.

'No more is Lucia,' said Roland, and, before anyone could protest, 'not in the way you mean. She is the *heiress of Alba*, Ned – or had you forgotten?' His eyes, like his brother's a vivid blue, glinted with ill-timed mischief as he added, 'I am at fault, of course; I ought to have compared Lucia's case to your own, and not to mine.'

The expression of outrage that bloomed over the Crown Prince's face as he digested this statement forced Lucia to clap one hand over her mouth to stifle a sudden, *entirely* inappropriate upwelling of laughter. She had admired Roland's unexpectedly able handling of Merton and Taylor in Oxford, but to hear him taking her part, and with such conviction, was something else again.

His gaze found hers – swift and furtive, seeking her approval, but with an almost-hidden glint of answering laughter in his eyes – and she grinned at him (though only for a moment) as fiercely as she knew how.

'What we need,' said Lucia, 'is a spell-seer.'

'Is it?' said Sophie doubtfully. 'To see what, precisely? Even if, as we suppose, Mr Robic was acting under some manner of compulsion, surely it will by now have passed off – or been broken – and there will be nothing left to see.'

'One of Lord de Vaucourt's apprentices is a spell-seer,' said Roland, 'and not altogether insufferable – Macsen Griffiths, you know. Will I send a steward to fetch him?'

They had, collectively, persuaded both Captain Prichard and King Henry, who could overrule Lord de Vaucourt, to permit the three of them to attend the formal questioning of Robic, though not to lead it. No one had authorised them to invite further persons into the business; but, as Sophie had heard Joanna say more than once, absolution is often more easily gained than permission.

'Yes,' said Sophie. 'Do so.'

They were a party of four, therefore, when they made rendezvous with Captain Prichard and Lord de Vaucourt outside the door to the Palace's interdicted chamber. Vaucourt raised his eyebrows at Griffiths, and then at the other three, but desisted when all four of them returned him the same level stare.

Captain Prichard unlocked and unbolted the door and pushed it open, then strode into the room to retrieve the prisoner. Having seen (and occasionally experienced for herself) the consequences to a powerful mage of imprisonment under interdiction, Sophie was prepared for his drooping posture, his miserable expression, and the faintly green hue of his pallid face; Roland, however, looked altogether horrified when Prichard, having bound Mr Robic's hands once more, led him out into the corridor.

She edged closer to him and murmured, 'It will pass off soon enough.'

Mr Robic, for his part, regarded her in mute and miserable appeal. Sophie set her teeth. What in Hades did he suppose her willing (or even able) to do on his behalf, after what he had so nearly done?

* * *

Some two hours later, they had begun to conclude that there was nothing useful to be learnt from this exercise. Griffiths had given it as his considered opinion that some faint trace of compulsion indeed lingered about the prisoner, but he could form no impression of the spell's author or of its intent or motivation. Mr Robic himself appeared genuinely to remember nothing of what he had done, or why.

An idea occurred to Sophie, halfway through the third or fourth of these retellings of cavalry manoeuvres, stable duties, disputes among the common soldiers, and supervising the unloading of fodder and other supplies. She could, in theory, by means of a song-spell such as the one she had employed to divert her mother-in-law's attention from Lord Kergabet and Jenny, compel a person to speak the truth; could she also, perhaps, compel him to speak a truth which he did not consciously remember?

Lord de Vaucourt would never permit it, she told herself. But . . .

But what if Lord de Vaucourt did not know? Reaching gently for her magick, she began humming under her breath, weaving melody and magick together into a call for the revelation of hidden truths. Griffiths shot her a sharp sideways glance, but refrained from betraying whatever it was he saw.

The prisoner stumbled once more to the end of his recital. This time, however, the low monotonous voice, beyond even weariness, did not stop at '. . . and reported for patrol duty with my men,' but continued: 'And when we rode out, we were ambushed in our own woods by men of Orléanais.'

Everyone sat up straighter; no one spoke.

As though this one misstep had jarred loose all the rest of the contents of some tight-packed secret cabinet, he went on – and on – in the same hollow monotone.

'There were two officers and six men, none mounted. They

391

strung lines across the trees at chest height, and so scraped us off our horses' backs. Stupid of me not to see it. One was a mage-officer, which in general none of the Duchies' troops employ. Perhaps he was a spell-seer, for he looked at all of us and singled me out, and I was the only one of us able to do more than call light.

'He sent the rest back to camp. Bespelled them somehow, I think, for no alarm was raised. And I . . .' For the first time, he faltered – then swallowed hard – and at last went on. 'I must call myself a deserter, I suppose. The mage-officer . . . spoke to me. I cannot recall even now what he said. But I knew at once what I must do. He gave me . . .'

He paused.

'May I have my hands free?' he said. A humble petition, eyes downcast.

Vaucourt and Prichard exchanged a look.

'Very well,' said Prichard after a moment, and untied them. 'He gave me this,' said Mr Robic. His slim, callused right hand dipped into the pocket of his coat, and brought out what looked like an ordinary copper coin, dull and green with age. 'In case I should be caught, or fail in my task.'

He raised the coin to his lips. Sophie saw what he was about to do in the heartbeat before he swallowed it; she leapt forward out of her seat, shouting, and Lucia and Roland with her – but too late, too late, too late.

CHAPTER XXIX

In Which Joanna Draws Conclusions, and Gray Is Taken by Surprise

Having spent the night of the disrupted concert with Lucia at the Royal Palace, Sophie was returned to Grosvenor Square early the following evening in a state of numb, unspeaking horror which Joanna had seen before.

'What has *happened?*' she demanded, clasping Sophie's chilled hands. Treveur, who had been hovering in expectation of collecting Sophie's hat and gloves, instead vanished momentarily and returned with a woollen shawl, which Gwendolen wrapped about Sophie's shoulders.

Sophie's throat worked; she blinked slowly, once, twice; her lips opened, then closed again.

'You are ill,' Joanna decided. 'Let me take you upstairs and tuck you up in bed, and ask Lady Maëlle to—'

'No,' said Sophie. Her throat worked again. 'Not . . . I am not ill. This morning . . . The young man who attacked Lucia – he had been bespelled—' Her silence being now broken, the words tumbled from her lips faster and faster. 'The interdiction delayed the inevitable, but the effect wore off, I suppose, or—and he remembered. He told us what he knew – what little he knew – but then he – then he—'

This was not a conversation for the front door, but there was no question now of going upstairs, or anywhere else; Sophie was weeping almost too much to draw breath, and clutching at Joanna as though she feared her being snatched away.

The storm at last eased, however, and Joanna and Gwendolen succeeded in spiriting Sophie up to her bedroom via the servants' stairs, so as to avoid for the moment any further necessity to answer questions. Over the course of the next hour, the ugly tale slowly emerged.

'And if I had not made him speak,' said Sophie, 'then perhaps—'

'*No*, Sophie,' Joanna said firmly. 'He was to be punished for his failure, whatever you did or did not do; that much is clear.'

For some little time they all three sat silently contemplating the horror of it.

To fall on one's sword might be an honourable end; but this – this poisoning-by-proxy – had been no more or less than foul murder.

'Orléanais,' said Joanna at last.

'I beg your pardon?' Sophie looked-up, dull-eyed.

'On the one hand we have, by Mr Robic's account, a mage-officer from Orléanais,' said Joanna, 'who bespells a young Breizhek officer to compel him to commit . . . well, both murder and treason, to begin with. And a very *particular* murder, which if successful might have been expected to outrage not only Britain but Alba as well; certainly it must end any hope of alliance between us, and perhaps – very likely – it might constitute an effective casus belli, and thus draw our attention to our northern border and away from the eastern ones.

'On the other hand,' she continued, 'by the evidence of Lord Merton, we have the Duc d'Orléans, who styles himself Imperator Gallia and desires to control all the former territory of Roman Gaul, principally including, we must suppose, Britain's own three provinces on that side of the Manche. Who seeks to bring all the peoples of this empire of his to the worship of the Roman gods alone. Who has somehow persuaded at least half of his neighbours to unite under his banner, and who apparently is searching the Duchies for mages to train up to his sorcerer-centuries – meaning, I suppose, to erase the only two tactical advantages which we have always had over the armies of the Duchies.

'We know now, in fact – do we not? – where Gray is likely to be, and the Professor and Amelia too.'

Sophie nodded; she did not look comforted.

'I quite see why a man who is collecting mages should be eager to get his hands on Mr Marshall,' said Gwendolen, 'but what should this Imperator Gallia want with your sister?'

Joanna had asked herself this question more than once, and thus far had arrived at no satisfactory answer.

'I think,' said Sophie, after a long moment, 'I think that is the wrong question to ask.'

'What is the right one, then?' said Joanna.

'What I mean is – perhaps it is not a matter of his wanting Amelia, but of Amelia's wishing to go to him. That is, to go to the Professor.' At Joanna's sceptical look, she hurried on, her eyes brightening as she warmed to her theory: 'Amelia was always devoted to the Professor, and he to her, insofar as he was capable of devotion. Certainly he valued her above either of us. She was mistress of Callender Hall, and now she has nothing – or at any rate, *believes* she has nothing – and she told us, in so many words, that she does not believe him guilty. She was in correspondence with Henry Taylor – perhaps secretly but certainly without Cousin Maëlle's knowledge, for I cannot imagine her allowing it – and perhaps even thought herself in love with him, who can say? And he, or the Professor, or this agent of Orléans whom Taylor spoke of, or all three of them, will have filled her head with tales of what a great man her papa is, or will be, at the Emperor's court. It is not impossible, is it, that she should consider the alternatives apparently on offer, and choose that one?'

There was another long silence.

'If that is so,' said Gwendolen at last, 'then . . . ought we to be seeking to rescue her from herself?'

'Perhaps not,' said Sophie. 'Perhaps she is perfectly well and happy with the Professor at the court of Orléans. Or perhaps she has been robbed by highwaymen of all she was carrying, or kidnapped, or has fallen into a ditch and broken both her legs, or perhaps—'

She stood up and began pacing about her bedroom.

'You must not entertain such thoughts, Sophie,' said Joanna firmly.

Her thumbs pricked – Sophie's pacing had taken on a manic edge, her slim hands twisting and untwisting Gwen's handkerchief, and her brow was furrowed in furious thought. *I know that look, the gods help me.*

Amelia! Gray's lips had shaped the first syllable of her name by the time his mind caught up and stopped him from calling out to her. She had not seen him, or had seen him but was choosing to pretend otherwise; she appeared absorbed in her companions and her work.

Orléans stood beside him, observing with satisfaction the, it must be said, admirably well-coordinated manoeuvres of the seventy-odd young mages as, in response to some signal from their leader, they wheeled leftward in unison, disposed themselves in a half circle about a massive straw-stuffed target mounted on a wooden cart, and let loose in a rippling wave with bolts of flame and lightning – and then, when the target was well aflame, drew water from the air to quench the fire.

Orléans shifted slightly, turning from the blackened, sodden remains, and tilted his head to look up at Gray; he was a small man, no taller than Joanna, but by some alchymy of the mind made his own height seem the Platonic ideal, and Gray's an unfortunate defect. It had been years, Gray reflected, discomfited, since he had been so tempted to stoop in an attempt to conceal his height.

'A fine sight, are they not, my sorcerer-century?' he said, smiling faintly. 'Though not, as you have justly remarked, quite a century as yet.'

'Indeed,' Gray replied, somewhat at random; he had not said any such thing aloud – or had he?

'I must just speak a moment with my centurion,' said Orléans, and turned away.

Five, six, seven steps; then Orléans spun on his heel, suddenly, and with a minute flick of two fingers, drew a gout of flame out of the air and sent it streaking back towards Gray.

Almost before the threat had registered in his conscious mind, Gray was throwing up a shielding-spell to block it. The flame struck; the shield dimpled slightly with the force of its impact, recovered, and sent it skittering harmlessly away in tiny showers of sparks.

'That was very well done,' said Orléans. 'For an itinerant scholar.'

'The road has its dangers, from time to time,' Gray replied. 'And I have had very good teachers.'

His heart was pounding, not from exertion but from shock at the suddenness of the attack. With an effort, he slowed and deepened his breathing, until at last his pulse slowed.

'So I see.' Orléans stood with feet spread, hands clasped behind his back, and considered his . . . not *guest,* for there had been no rite of welcome; his experiment, perhaps? 'And I see also that I was quite correct in my initial estimation: you, Monsieur Marais, would be altogether wasted in the reserves.'

Gray's thoughts scrambled for purchase on this new cliff's-edge. He had thought the possibility of being yoked to one of Orléans' battle-mages a credible threat; this, now, was a far worse fate which until this moment he had not even thought to dread.

'I . . . do not take your meaning, my lord.'

Another faint smile. 'On the contrary, I am quite certain that you do.'

I cannot aid this man in his misguided war against the old gods, who made these lands, and those who serve them. Not even to speak of the notion of forging a link between his magick and some other person's who was not Sophie, which made his stomach churn. *But if I refuse outright to give him what he wants, I shall have learnt almost nothing of use, and I shall lose all possibility of rescuing Amelia.*

Always supposing, of course, that Amelia was willing to be rescued.

The mages finished their drilling and were dismissed; they dispersed, some sloping away across the courtyard, others lingering to exchange flirtations with the ladies. Several of the younger men paused before Amelia, but she only glanced up at them and smiled briefly – the barest curve of her rosy lips – before returning to her work.

Perhaps it was a matter of rescue, after all. *Time will tell, if I can contrive to gain some.*

Gray turned back to Orléans, plastering a smile over his deep unease, and said, 'I should like to hear more of your sorcerer-century, my lord.'

'Should you, indeed?' said Orléans, with a tolerant smile. 'I regret I have no more leisure to attend you this afternoon, but I shall appoint you a guide. Decurion Rousseau!' he called, fortunately turning away in time to miss Gray's startled expression. *Decurion?*

One of the young mages raised his head, turned; bent again to murmur something to Amelia, then strode towards his . . . master, in fact, if the expression of slavish devotion upon his face were any sign.

'My lord,' he said, bracing before the imperial presence.

'I have brought you a new recruit, Decurion.' Orléans opened his hand in Gray's direction, and Rousseau's gaze followed the gesture – left, then . . . up.

'Monsieur Guy Marais of Poitiers,' said Orléans. 'Monsieur Marais, Decurion Auguste Rousseau, of the second sorcerer-century.'

Gray bowed; Rousseau returned the gesture. Orléans, favouring them both with a benignant smile, said, 'Rousseau will show you about the place, and you shall dine in the officers' mess. *À la prochaine*, Monsieur Marais; *on se reverra ce soir.*'

Shall we, indeed.

Gray and Rousseau stood side by side, unspeaking, until Orléans had vanished through an archway on the far side of the courtyard. Then Rousseau turned to Gray and said, in a not unfriendly tone, 'What brings you to the Emperor's service, Monsieur Marais?'

Go carefully! This man is a true believer in Orléans' idée fixe, or at any rate in Orléans himself.

'I have sworn no oath of service as yet,' said Gray cautiously. 'I am a scholar of magick; I have been travelling in search of some useful employment, and hope to find it here. And yourself?'

'The Emperor is a great man,' Rousseau declared, with a proud smile. 'I am honoured to serve him in advancing his great vision.'

'I should like to hear more of it,' said Gray. 'He is a spell-seer, I think, the Emperor?'

Rousseau perceived some insult in this query, it appeared, for he drew himself up a little and said, 'The Emperor is a master of all kinds of spell-work, and sees many things which ordinary mages cannot. His talents come from the gods themselves.'

'All magick is a gift from the gods,' Gray countered reflexively; and then, seeking to soften what might be heard as a further insult, 'So we are taught. As Gaius Sejanus Domitianus had it, *Magick is the gods' gift to mankind, and their curse.*'

'Ordinary magickal talents are only an accident of birth,' said Rousseau, with the assurance of one reciting a well-learnt lesson. 'The Emperor has been elected by the gods to a great destiny, like Julius Caesar before him, and thus they have granted him extraordinary gifts with which to fulfil it. Naturally one of these gifts is that of discerning those who may best serve him in establishing his great empire and respect for the true gods.'

I have heard that line of argument before. In very similar words, though in a quite different tongue, had the late Cormac MacAlpine justified his forcible kidnapping and enslavement of foreign mages – Gray and Sophie among them – to feed their magick into his distant ancestor's great spell-web. *And talking of spell-seers . . .*

'Then,' said Gray, 'I should imagine he has seen something in me which he believes he can turn to good account.' *As Cormac MacAlpine did before him.*

'I saw the scholar-mages in your master's workroom, earlier,' he went on, hoping to steer the conversation in a more productive (and less hazardous) direction. 'They seemed . . . very much immersed in their pursuits – indeed, I do not think they at all remarked our presence.'

'Well, we have been drilling all this time,' said Rousseau, as though this explained everything. 'The sorcerer-century, that is. So naturally the fellows in the workroom would have no notice to spare for the outside world.'

Gray considered that *naturally*, and found he did not at all like its implications.

Rousseau's tour of the makeshift *palais imperial* – the Château d'Orléans – culminated in a second stroll along the battlements.

'We are just in time,' said Rousseau cryptically, peering over the chest-high battlement wall.

Gray stepped up beside him, rested both palms on the top of the wall, and followed his gaze. Down in one of the camps below, a crowd of men, moving in as graceful a unison as Rousseau and his companions had earlier done, were carrying out some sort of exercise with a dozen saltpetre-cannon, aimed apparently at nothing, in what might once have been a turnip-field.

'What are they—'

His query was cut off by a bludgeoning roar as all twelve cannon erupted into smoke and flying . . . what?

'Horns of Herne!' said Gray reflexively. He rubbed at his ringing ears.

Rousseau glared up at him. 'We do not call upon the lesser gods here,' he said.

Gray blinked, then nodded. 'Your pardon,' he said. 'I was taken by surprise.'

For reasons which Gray could not entirely fathom, this drew a broad grin from his companion. 'Chain-shot,' he said, gesturing down at the cannon-crews now spread across the field like reapers. 'To slice through enemy cavalry.'

By which he means, in fact, my brother-in-law Ned. Gray repressed a shudder. Below, strings of men, their hands oddly overlarge in thick gloves, were gathering up lengths of heavy chain and neatly coiling them.

In the air with Ollivier and Lécuyer, in conversation with Colonel Dubois or Mage-Captain Tremblay, Gray had begun to think that perhaps the military life might have something to recommend it. The mental image of iron round-shot or those heavy chains falling amidst the ranks of men and horses superimposed itself on these memories of camaraderie and mutual assistance like night-soil emptied onto the spread pages of an illuminated codex.

And I am all alone here, he reflected, fixing his gaze determinedly on the activity below so that he should be in no danger of meeting Rousseau's eye. The mages of Captain Tremblay's company might yet be capable of finding him – impossible to say – but there existed no possibility of his communicating with them, except by returning to Ivry.

Orléans might be a spell-seer, but Rousseau certainly was not, and Orléans, at present, was not by. Gray shut his eyes and reached for the thread of Sophie's magick; finding it as bright and strong as ever, he opened his eyes, swallowed hard, and turned to Rousseau with a bright but unfelt smile.

'Impressive, indeed,' he said.

'Impressively noisy,' said Rousseau, 'and useful in its way, but the Emperor's war will be won by the sorcerer-centuries.'

And what is it they do, then, which is worse than this?

'I can well imagine,' said Gray; the lie coming easily now, he added, 'King Henry's army has nothing to match either one, I believe.'

Dinner in the officers' mess was a more formal affair by far than the equivalent in Captain Tremblay's company. Gray made the acquaintance of the Centurion of the second sorcerer-century – an Orléanais man of about Sieur Germain de Kergabet's age, whose dark eyes assessed him with swift calculation – and at least half a dozen more decurions, Rousseau's fellows, as well as a string of officers of the infantry, cavalry, and artillery, also denominated in the Roman style; they dined upon elegantly dressed joints of meat which were, nevertheless, so tough and stringy that Gray shuddered to think what the Emperor of Gaul was feeding his common soldiers, and drank (all but Gray) a very great deal of not very good wine, which led to some disintegration of the aforesaid formality. Gray nursed his first glass until the last bottle ran dry, the better to keep his wits about him.

After dinner Rousseau walked with him back to his tiny cubicle in the mages' barracks and left him there.

Gray sat down rather heavily on the bed (for lack of any other seat) to think things through. *Have I, or have I not, become a soldier in Orléans' army?* He had taken no oaths, made no promises – indeed, had not so much as answered a relevant question in the affirmative – yet here he was, and it was anyone's guess what might be coming on the morrow.

The correct course of action seemed self-evident: to abandon his saddle-bags and the clothes on his back and fly for his life, the moment he could safely do so. He had already collected valuable intelligence on the situation, of which Colonel Dubois (and, through him, Lord Kergabet and the King) ought to be apprised without delay; that done, the next stage of operations would be in capable hands, and Gray might either be of practical use in carrying it out, or, if his assistance was no longer needed, be permitted to return to London, and Sophie.

He rolled his left shoulder once more, experimentally – reached for his magick, to gauge what remained to him following his displays for Orléans – gave sober thought to the matter, and judged it possible. The difficulties lay elsewhere: here, as in the British garrison, one was almost literally never alone. If he were to depart, it must be by night, whilst the greater part of the place was asleep, and the men standing sentry duty presumably focused on threats from without.

Well, at any rate I should do well to catch some sleep whilst I can.

When Gray woke, the barracks were silent around him – or, at any rate, the only sounds to be heard were those of sleeping men. He rose from his bed; disrobed quickly and methodically, folding away his clothes as he went so that he should not appear to have departed in haste; wrapped himself togalike in the darker of the two

403

woollen blankets provided along with the bed-linens; and stepped out through the doorway of his cubicle (it had no door, and only three-quarters of a wall) into the long, narrow corridor.

There was, he had noted earlier, a window at the far end of it, and he made for this on cautious feet, reminding himself that until the moment of the shift, there was nothing for anyone to see which he could not explain away. Nevertheless his heart was hammering in his throat by the time he reached the window, having safely passed two dozen doorways and as many slumbering mages, and discovered it to be shut and locked.

The lock was not a difficult one – no more than a latch, in truth – but it was stiff and recalcitrant, and oh, gods, the *noise*! *O Janus, master of openings and closings, guide my hand* . . .

It was done at last, however, and with no worse effect than a bass-baritone growl of *Great Mithras, not rats* again*!* and a heavy boot tossed in his general direction, which he easily dodged. The window fortunately was just large enough for his human body to squeeze through, so that he might perch on the roof-peak and nudge the two heavy panels inwards with his heels. Of course he could not do much about the latch without magick, and if he were to fly all the way to Ivry-sur-Eure he would need every last iota for that task.

Gray untied his blanket-toga, crouched low along the roof-peak, and draped the blanket over himself once more. Beneath its concealing darkness, the shift went swiftly – he had done almost nothing else for most of a se'nnight, after all – and after a brief struggle with the suffocating folds of wool, he was aloft, setting his face to the north, and home.

'Do I understand correctly, sir,' said Gray incredulously, around a large mouthful of bread and ham, 'that you are ordering me back to Orléans?'

404

Colonel Dubois regarded his civilian attaché – tousle-haired and heavy-eyed, wrapped in several rough woollen blankets and eating as though he had not seen food for months – with steady patience. 'I have not the power to order you anywhere,' he said. 'I am *asking* you to return to Orléans, observe what the Duc is about with his saltpetre-cannon and his sorcerer-century, and learn what more you can. You are not under my command, Mr Marshall; you are of course entirely free to refuse my request.'

'How should I convey to you whatever else I might discover?' Gray enquired. 'Supposing that I did consent to return?'

If he were honest, half of him wished very much to do just that. The self-styled Emperor both unsettled and intrigued him, and those brief glimpses of Appius Callender, looking contented but strangely oblivious, and of Amelia . . .

'Both Mr Lécuyer and Mr Ollivier, of Captain Tremblay's company, have volunteered to act as your liaisons.' Colonel Dubois produced a small, sardonic smile. 'The distance involved does suggest a relay arrangement, though I should of course have preferred to send a night-scout and a day-scout together.'

Gray frowned, drained his tankard of ale, and frowned again. 'But,' he said, 'you should then have no night-scouts at all.'

'To a man with a hammer,' said Colonel Dubois dryly, 'every circumstance may come to resemble a nail. I, however, have no hammer, and am therefore free to make use of whatever tools are to hand. Ollivier and Lécuyer may be the best night-scouts in this regiment, Mr Marshall, but they are not the only ones. We shall make shift with human scouts by night, as many another regiment of His Majesty's army must.'

Gray was not altogether persuaded; but if the Colonel did not know his business . . .

* * *

Gray must be in Orléans again before morning if his flight was not to be discovered, and was therefore in the air again long before prudence dictated – though at any rate his escort consisted of persons experienced in all manner of magickal emergencies. With several stops for rest and refreshment, the three of them reached the wood outside the castle as dawn was lightening the eastern horizon.

'But how will you feed yourselves?' Gray had asked them, in the night-scouts' tent at Ivry-sur-Eure. 'And—'

Ollivier and Lécuyer had looked at one another. 'We are soldiers, Marshall,' said Ollivier. 'We have lived rough in the woods before.'

Gray, having fled with no intention to return, now had no real choice but to return to the barracks as he had left them. To his immense relief, the blanket he had left on the roof-peak was there yet – though damp with dew – and the window had blown open wide in the course of the night; he had only to grasp the blanket in his talons, drag it along the roof-peak until it overhung the window-frame, then dive through the window, shifting as he went, and pull it through after him into the deserted corridor.

How fortunate I am, he reflected, *that not one man in a hundred, when patrolling a battlement, will ever think to look up as well as down.*

He crept down the corridor and into his warm, dry bed, and there lay exhausted but awake until the morning's bugle-call sounded, thinking guiltily of Ollivier and Lécuyer making the best of things in the woods.

CHAPTER XXX

In Which Further Complications Arise

Gray was returning to his sleeping-quarters after a morning spent drilling with the sorcerer-century, so exhausted that he could think of nothing but reaching his bed and collapsing into it, when a pageboy stopped him, executed a bouncing half bow, thrust a folded paper into his hands, and bounced away again across the courtyard.

From a general impulse to conceal his private affairs from potentially hostile observers, Gray pocketed the note and resumed his interrupted trajectory. When he reached his quarters, after pulling off his boots but before collapsing face first into bed, he extracted it from his pocket and, curled on his side with his back to the door, read it through.

Written in a lady's careful, elegant hand, the note contained no salutation and no valediction, but read in full:

> *I must speak privately with you on a matter of urgency. Can you contrive to wait by the fountain in the south courtyard at dusk? If the answer is no, send word by the bearer.*

Gray frowned at it. But he was here to discover all he could, and here, perhaps, was an opportunity. It might equally be a trap of some sort, of course — but in any case it was now too late to refuse.

Dusk found him, therefore, by the fountain in the little-used south courtyard as instructed – more precisely, seated somewhat precariously upon its edge, with his nose in a book of Roman military history. He waited, pulse skittering with nerves, for what seemed an age, though it could not really have been more than a quarter-hour, until at last light, cautious footsteps heralded the arrival of his mysterious correspondent.

Gray looked up and tried to determine whether he was surprised or entirely the reverse. 'Amelia!' he said.

'Mr Marshall,' said Amelia.

She sounded . . . not *pleased* to have found him here, but relieved – as though she had not altogether expected him; at the same time, however, she wore an air of deep chagrin, almost of humiliation. At the necessity of asking Gray, of all persons in the world, for help?

He lifted both hands in a gesture of appeasement and, rather than standing to loom over her, kept his seat on the wide lip of the fountain, looking up at her expectantly. 'I am come as you requested,' he said, 'to hear of your urgent trouble. What is it?'

Ameila gritted her teeth.

'I should not have approached you, if I were not desperate,' she said. 'As it is, I can only throw myself upon your mercy and trust that you will not use my desperation against me, as no doubt you believe I deserve.'

Gray scarcely knew how to reply; he was saved the necessity of doing so, however, by Amelia's immediately going on: 'I came to this place of my own will, but now I wish to leave it again, and cannot. Will you help me?'

To this, on the other hand, there was only one possible answer. 'Of course,' said Gray. 'If I am able. I have . . . trusted friends nearby, by whom I can send a message—'

'And will you help me rescue my father?'

Gray blinked. Not because her request surprised him, exactly – as a devoted daughter, Amelia Callender had no peer, whatever might be Gray's opinions on the object of her devotion – but because he had not the least notion how to reply. To help Amelia – a glorified camp-follower – to escape Castle Orléans was one thing; to extricate Appius Callender from the very centre of the soi-disant Emperor's operations, quite another.

'Does your father wish to be rescued?' he temporised. 'Is he unhappy with his present situation?'

'*I* am unhappy with his present situation,' said Amelia. She was worrying at a hangnail with her teeth, a most uncharacteristic gesture. 'The Emperor made promises to him, which he is very far from having fulfilled.'

'I must tell you frankly, Amelia,' Gray said, 'that your father's welfare is not my chief concern. Not that I wish him ill, but as he has more than once tried to arrange my death—'

'Do you know what they are, the *reserve* mages?' Amelia demanded. 'They are fodder for the rest, feeding them magick – all they have, if need be – they are tied together, and cannot escape.'

Gray swallowed against rising nausea. Surely even Appius Callender did not deserve such a fate?

'You are a mage, Mr Marshall,' Amelia continued, in a sort of furious hiss. 'What do you imagine becomes of a mage whose magick is all drained out of him by another?'

Indeed, Gray could imagine all too well what would become of them. But he hardened his heart in spite of it, for the lives of many thousands of men, women, and children – and, most immediately, those of Lécuyer and Ollivier, fending for themselves in the wood north of Castle Orléans – might well depend on the intelligence he could gather here, and, much as he disliked the thought, Amelia's desperation gave him an unexpectedly valuable lever to pull.

'I do not know what I may be able to do for your father,' Gray said at last. 'I have not yet sufficient understanding of Orléans' mage-work to gauge what is best, or even what is possible. But I shall try my best. In return, however, I shall expect payment in information. And,' he added, 'a pair of bedrolls, two sets of infantrymen's clothing and kit, and rations of some sort – whatever you can most easily liberate from the kitchens.'

Amelia gaped at him. 'You promised to help me,' she said after a moment, 'not a quarter-hour ago, and now you demand payment?'

'Not at all,' said Gray. The more he thought of Appius Callender, he found, the steadier grew his resolve. 'I promised to aid your escape in any way I can, and that promise stands. The payment is for aiding your father, to whom I have made no such promise, nor ever shall.'

The tension-taut silence which followed was perhaps the longest in Gray's memory. Amelia glared at him – clenching her fingers in the folds of her skirts, as he had seen her do years ago – then hugged her elbows and stared down at her feet. At last she said, low and bitterly defeated, 'I will pay your price.'

Gray had not, in truth, any very great expectations from the bargain he had made with Amelia; it did not seem to him that, placed as she was, and with no knowledge of magick or of military strategy, she was at all likely to run across information of use to Colonel Dubois or Lord Kergabet. At any rate, however, it had bought Ollivier and Lécuyer a reprieve from starving in the woods; once supplied with infantrymen's clothing and gear, they could slip into one or another of the myriad companies encamped outside the castle and feed themselves from the common cookpot.

Once again, however, Amelia surprised him. They had agreed that, as he had the greater freedom of movement and was known to be a scholar, Gray should make a habit of studying in the quiet of the south courtyard every evening at dusk, so that Amelia might meet him there whenever she had news to convey. For nearly a se'nnight of this second sojourn at Orléans, he waited out the appointed hour, reading by magelight, and saw Amelia not at all. But on the seventh night she emerged from the shadows and crossed the courtyard swiftly to perch beside him on the fountain's stone lip.

'The King's spies in the Duchies have been disappearing, did you not say?' she began, without preamble. 'I have discovered what became of them.'

Gray sat up straighter. 'Tell me,' he said.

'Your *p'tite amie* must have got her facts mixed,' Lécuyer declared, leaning his broad back against the boot of an oak-tree. 'Or she is inventing tales to force you to keep your end of the bargain.'

Gray glared at *p'tite amie*, and Ollivier gave Lécuyer a mighty shove in the shoulder and said, 'The young lady is Marshall's sister-in-law, you lout.'

Lécuyer righted himself and waved a dismissive hand, as though the distinction between sweetheart and sister-in-law were quite immaterial. 'The *point* is, that what she told you cannot possibly be true.' He stretched his long legs out before him, displacing Ollivier, who growled at him with no real heat. 'A spell to replenish one's magick by drawing power from talentless folk? How could such a thing possibly work?'

'I have not the least idea,' said Gray grimly, 'but I have known Amelia five years, and if she has the imagination to invent such a tale, I will eat not only my hat but my coat and boots along with it. And there are certainly tales enough circulating about Orléans that I should not be surprised at his proving to be a great deal more like the emperor Nero than like Julius Caesar.'

Ollivier sat up, cross-legged on his folded bedroll, and frowned at Gray. 'Mad, you mean?'

'Well,' said Gray, 'that also, very likely. I meant, however, what the natural philosopher Pliny said of Nero – that no one could be certain whether his madness was cause or consequence of his taking what did not belong to him. It is not known just what Pliny meant by that turn of phrase – there are so many possibilities! – but my friend Evans-Hughes – he is an historian, at Merlin College – believes it to imply that Nero achieved the godlike power he boasted of by stealing it from other mages.'

Lécuyer grimaced, and Ollivier blanched and clapped a hand over his mouth.

'But,' Lécuyer objected, 'even if that were true – which, meaning no disrespect to your friend, I do not see how it can be – it is still not at all the same thing as taking magick from folk who have none!'

Gray – who could not be absent indefinitely without its being remarked upon – was beginning to lose patience. 'You may convey my report to Colonel Dubois with as much commentary as seems good to you,' he said, 'provided that you do convey it to him, and at once.'

'It is my turn, in any case,' said Ollivier, unfolding himself and climbing to his feet. He still looked a little green. 'Have you anything else to report?'

'Only that three more men have joined the second sorcerer-century,' said Gray. 'I have not been up on the battlements for some days; what have you seen, out in the camps?'

'Another company of cavalry rode in yesterday evening,' said Lécuyer, 'but two companies of infantry marched out early this morning, with two of those great saltpetre-cannon on siege-waggons.'

Ollivier by now had stripped down to his drawers; he now stepped out of these, then efficiently shook out and folded his borrowed clothing and stacked it on his bedroll. Finally, he crouched down, toes curled round a protruding tree-root, and between one eye-blink and the next, was looking up at Gray with the heart-shaped face of a barn owl.

Lécuyer bent and scooped him up – Ollivier squawked at the indignity, but again it seemed quite without heat – and muttered, 'The gods go with you, Kannig,' as he tossed the barn owl into the air.

'The gods go with you,' Gray echoed, under his breath.

Two mornings hence, the Emperor assembled his sorcerer-centuries in the castle courtyard for the unveiling of his grand strategy; by the time he had finished, Gray was thankful for the press of bodies all about him, which might conceal the violence of his reaction. Nor was he, he was relieved to discover, the only one who did not much like what he had heard; when after some unguessable period of frozen horror he became able once more to interpret the evidence of his senses, he heard mutterings all about him, low and wary and worried.

It was the remembrance of these mutterings which upheld him through the rousing speeches, the obligatory cheering, the parade round the courtyard and back to the barracks, and which – together with Amelia's tale of dozens of men imprisoned below Castle Orléans, dying breath by breath as their spirits fed the Emperor's magick – gave him the courage, when all these things were done, to return to the castle keep and approach the door of Orléans' private chambers.

His way was barred by not two but four burly men-at-arms who eyed him with a familiar distrust; Gray had remarked how little enthusiasm the common soldiers had for the men of the sorcerer-centuries.

'I would speak privately with the Emperor,' he said, 'if he is not presently occupied with some urgent matter.'

The tallest of the men-at-arms said, 'Wait here,' and paced down the short corridor to rap at the door.

Gray could discern nothing from the brief conversation that ensued, but upon turning away from the door, the guardsman held it open and with his other hand beckoned Gray towards it. Gray followed, concealing his trepidation as best he could, and waited for the door to close behind him before looking up to meet the Emperor's gaze.

'Marais,' said Orléans, his tone curious, but unalarmed. 'You wished to see me?'

'My lord Emperor,' Gray said. His throat was dry – this man could have him killed on a whim, could, in fact, carry out the act himself, if the humour took him. 'May I have your permission to speak freely?'

Orléans smiled at him. 'Certainly, my boy,' he said.

'Concerning the . . . battle plan which we were told of this morning,' Gray began – then stalled, and with great effort gathered his courage to continue. 'If the men of those garrisons can be so easily slaughtered, then surely they can as easily be subdued and taken prisoner.'

'Oh! Certainly,' said Orléans, with a wave of his hand, 'for a given value of *easily*, which, I fear, betrays your lack of experience in the field, Marais.' He leant forward in his chair, forearms braced on the surface of his desk. 'Tell me, how then shall we feed and house these thousands of prisoners, and how guard them to prevent uprisings and escapes, without materially weakening our own forces?'

'And how shall we,' Gray swallowed hard, 'dispose of thousands of bodies, without fouling our new nest? This is not a battlefield from which we can march onward, leaving the fallen for the looters and the carrion-crows; you propose to march *into* a fortress already littered with enemy dead, and then – what, my lord? There are not enough trees in all the forests of Breizh to build so many pyres, and the burning would choke the skies for days. Or had you thought to cast the dead into pits, like refuse? How shall men be chosen for that duty, and what will they think of their glorious new empire after they have carried it out?'

Orléans might be mad, but he was not a fool; surely he must have thought all of these ramifications through. But sometimes, as Gray knew from experience, to hear one's ugliest thoughts spoken aloud by some other person made them too real and too ugly to be waved away.

'You have not lived among the people of Britain, my lord,' said Gray, pressing his advantage, if such it was, 'but I have travelled there, and speak some of their languages, and have come to know them well.

'You suppose that they will be cowed by such a display of savagery as you mean us to inflict upon them, but it is no such thing – we shall only raise their ire, and spur them to more vehement resistance, by making martyrs of their brave-hearted young men. Not to speak of the women and children who will inevitably be caught up in the slaughter.'

He stopped, willing his pulse back to steadiness, when he recognised that his voice had risen almost to a shout – and in the sudden quiet, he heard the sounds of shuffling feet and muttering voices from behind him. Half turning, he beheld all four sentries poised in the doorway – how had he failed to hear the door opening?

Orléans rose from his seat to stare them down. 'Back to your posts, gentlemen, if you please,' he said, icily calm; as he spoke, Gray felt a faint, chill shiver of magick, and the hairs on his neck rose.

The four men turned and retreated, like puppets on one

string, and the door fell shut behind them. Orléans sank back into his chair – but the skin-prickling feeling of magick in the air did not abate.

'If you cannot moderate your tone, Monsieur Marais,' he said, 'perhaps you may in future have the foresight to set a ward beforehand. My personal guards are inclined to be protective.'

'My apologies, m'lord,' Gray choked.

With a gesture like a child spinning a top, Orléans muttered something under his breath; Gray nearly stumbled from the force of the warding-spell that shuddered through him, stronger than the most powerful ward he had ever felt Sophie cast.

Orléans regarded him thoughtfully. 'You are a scholar, are you not?' he said.

'I am,' said Gray.

'Ordinarily, scholars do not consider it their métier to give unsolicited advice to military commanders,' he said, 'and still less to kings and emperors.'

'As you have remarked yourself, sir,' he said, 'I am not altogether an ordinary scholar.'

To his astonishment, Orléans laughed. 'That is certainly so,' he said. He waved Gray to a chair, and Gray, bemused but relieved, sank into it. His skin buzzed with the aftershocks of the warding-spell. 'I must tell you, Marais,' Orléans continued, 'that I expected an appeal to sentiment. It is fortunate for you that I was mistaken.'

'There seemed no need to appeal to sentiment,' said Gray, now very glad indeed that he had not done so, 'with such a wealth of pragmatical arguments to be made.'

'Indeed. Nevertheless, it bears mentioning: men of sentiment, I have no use for; men apt in the arts of strategy, on the other hand, may go far in my service.

'I shall think on what you have said,' Orléans continued, 'and in return, think on this: when the first sorcerer-century has taken Ivry-sur-Eure, Château-du-Loir, Klison, Vernon-sur-Seine, and the rest, it will fall to the second to take and hold the keystones at Karnag, and you and your fellows must be ready.'

Gray now had intelligence which, so far as he knew, none of the others had – but he could make no sense of it. The second sorcerer-century, so called, as yet numbered only eighty men; but what in Hades was at Karnag that Orléans should send eighty mages after it? *Take and hold the keystones* – the keystones of what? Take them how, from whom, for what possible purpose?

He did not ask any of these highly suspect questions, however; it was a firm rule among the Emperor's people, from his generals to the boys who fetched and carried for the crews of the great saltpetre-cannon, that whatsoever they might need to know, the Emperor would tell them.

Everything he had heard in the course of this day, he should soon be repeating to Ollivier and Lécuyer, to one of whom – it was Lécuyer's turn, if he did not mistake – would fall the task of conveying it to Colonel Dubois. *And perhaps he may make some sense of it.*

'I understand, sir,' he said, therefore.

'So I hope, Marais. So I hope. You are dismissed.' Orléans snapped his fingers negligently to release his ward, and Gray fled the room with as much dignity as he could manage.

We are to be sent to Breizh; I am bound for home at last! From Karnag, it would not be beyond him to disappear into the Breizhek countryside – Gray spoke the local language, as the officers of the sorcerer-century did not – and a few days' travel would take him to An Alre or even Gwened, where he might decant any further discoveries to the garrison commander and then find passage home.

417

Amelia presented a more difficult problem, to be sure – but if Orléans meant to take the battle elsewhere, was she not safest where she was? And Appius Callender . . .

Appius Callender is my concern only insofar as his fate affects Amelia's.

It was only much later that the implication of Orléans' words dawned upon him: to be ready for battle, in terms of the Emperor's soldier-mages, was to be linked to the mages of the reserves. The realisation woke him, gasping and sweating, in the middle of the night, and not until he had calmed his breathing and reached through the aether to find his connexion to Sophie – still stable and persistent across a kingdom and a half, though, in the terms of the peculiar sight-metaphor in which their magicks chose to represent themselves, finer than a single thread – could he even begin to attempt sleep once more.

CHAPTER XXXI

In Which Sophie Attends to Her Geography, and Roland to His Books

The news reached London across the final days of August that armies under a banner which no one in the field could identify, except in its resemblance to the arms of Orléans, had overrun three British garrisons: first Ivry-sur-Eure in Normandie; then Klison, on the River Sèvre in Breizh; and finally the long-disputed Mainois fortress town of Château-du-Loir.

There had been no formal declaration of war, no negotiating for terms – and, for that matter, no battles to speak of, for the attacks had come in the dead of night, and the British forces, felled by some powerful sleeping-spell, woke in the morning to find their arms and fortifications in the hands of the enemy, and themselves prisoners. After the first such assault, it was said, garrison commanders all along Britain's borders with the Duchies – forewarned of the fate of Ivry – had mustered both mundane and magickal defences as best they could; but Klison and then Château-du-Loir had fallen just the same. Whether the intervening positions had fended off the enemy, or whether there had been no assaults there to fend off, was as yet impossible to say – but thus far all the available evidence pointed, bafflingly, to the latter.

Joanna, Sophie, and Gwendolen, who had taken possession of the Kergabets' library and filled it with crates of rescued books and documents, abandoned their (mostly) systematic study thereof, whenever some new piece of news arrived, in favour of an assault upon Sieur Germain's unfortunately small collection of up-to-date maps.

They knew a great deal about present circumstances on the continent which the general public did not – to begin with, the likely identity of the man behind that mysterious banner, and, if the evidence of Taylor and Merton were to be believed, the Duchies' new foray into magickal weaponry – but the choice of targets remained a source of bafflement.

'Why *those* garrisons?' Joanna wondered aloud, not for the first time, when the news reached them of the fall of Château-du-Loir.

They stood round the large table in the library, studying a map of the Duchies with rivers and lakes picked out in blue ink and borders, so far as they were known, in red. Sophie's fingertip was pressed so hard to the words *Ivry-sur-Eure* that the flesh beneath her fingernail had gone white – Ivry, whence Gray had last reported in before vanishing into the Duchies – but seeing Joanna's gaze upon her, she snatched it away and clasped her hands behind her back.

'There are so many others between,' Joanna continued, circling the table to study the map from a different angle, 'and some a great deal less difficult of access – though I suppose,' she added, 'if the work of subduing our garrisons is being all done by mages, and not by ordinary soldiers, the terrain of the approach does not much signify. But it is very odd tactics, it seems to me, for an invading army to take so few positions, so widely separated.'

Sophie frowned, turned away from the map altogether, and began rummaging through a crate at the far end of the room. She had been skittish and strange since Derrien Robic's death, immersing herself in her centuries-old rescued documents as though she might thus keep the horrors of the present at bay.

'If Mr Taylor is to be believed,' said Gwendolen instead, 'this army is commanded by a madman. Perhaps we ought not to seek logic in his tactics.'

Joanna shook her head. 'A madman he may be,' she said, 'but not a fool, or he could not have accomplished so much. There is some method here, if only we could discover it.'

Farther down the table was a second map on which, by means of pins and coloured wool, Joanna had been tracing the movements of the various armies arrayed against Britain's eastern borders, according to the reports which Lord Kergabet and Mr Fowler, yielding to her pleas not to be left entirely out of their counsels, had been daily bringing home for her. They had given her to understand, most lately, that they now had an agent in the field in Orléans; she was quite certain in her mind that the agent was Gray, though Lord Kergabet refused to confirm or deny this hypothesis.

She itched to be back in the centre of things – but as this was not at present feasible, she should take what she could, and endeavour to be grateful for it.

Leaning close, she studied the line of red wool stretching from pin to pin, following rivers and, where rivers and borders diverged, the borders maintained over the centuries since the last Angevin conflict – except where the taking of Ivry, Klison, and Château-du-Loir pulled the wool into sharply pointed salients. The red shapes reminded her of something, but what . . . ?

In Sophie's corner, the rustling ceased. 'Jo,' said Sophie, in a tone which instantly made Joanna straighten up and wheel away from the table to face her. 'Jo, look at this.'

She was holding in her hands – was it? Yes – the old field-map Joanna had found in the library. Three strides, four, and she was laying it out on the table beside the one Joanna and Gwendolen had been studying.

'There,' she said, pointing with her right forefinger to the salient at Ivry-sur-Eure, 'and there.' Her left forefinger stabbed at one of the mysterious red markings on the field-map – also at Ivry. 'And look—'

'Mother Goddess,' said Joanna.

Gwendolen, peering over her shoulder, breathed, 'Oh, no.'

There were red marks at Klison and at Château-du-Loir, too.

'That cannot possibly be coincidence,' said Sophie. 'Can it? Surely not.' She sounded shaken and uncertain. 'But if it is not . . . the question is, what does Orléans know, that we do not – and *how?*'

'No,' said Joanna positively. 'That is, I should very much like to know what he knows, and how – but for the moment we are strategists, not scholars, and so the question is, *where next?*'

Sophie blinked. 'Yes,' she said, after a moment. 'Yes, of course.'

They bent once more over the two maps, gazes flitting from one to the other. The red markers, if strung together like the pins on Sieur Germain's map, would have made a wobbling, irregular outline of Britain's continental provinces, from the northernmost at Haudricourt-sur-Seine, marching southward along the frontiers of Normandie and Maine, then striking north and west to Martigné-Ferchaud where Maine and Breizh met the lost province of Anjou, then south again to Klison and finally to the unexplained grouping at Karnag, on the Breizhek coast.

'There, perhaps,' said Gwendolen, touching a fingertip gently to the marker at Valennes, 'as it is so near Château-du-Loir and might be taken without spreading his forces too thin. Or perhaps at Martigné-Ferchaud, by sending troops north from Klison and west from Château-du-Loir at once.'

In the event, however, it was neither; the guardsman bearing their urgent missive to Sieur Germain at the Royal Palace crossed with the one he had himself dispatched to tell them of an assault upon Vernon-sur-Seine by ships from l'Île-des-Francs, which now were continuing northward towards Rouen.

* * *

His Majesty's Privy Council, in the aggregate, received the theories of the ladies of Grosvenor Square with a degree of scepticism which was not ameliorated by the revelation of their being premised upon a centuries-old document unearthed from the library of Lady Morgan College. Undeniably, however, dispatches from the border garrisons and from the regiments newly deployed to reinforce them did suggest that the Duc d'Orléans appeared – for reasons at present unfathomable – to be working from the same mysterious map.

Alas, none of this brought either His Majesty or the commanders of his troops any nearer to discovering how Orléans might be defeated, or to identifying the spies or turncoats whose intelligence, and perhaps even direct connivance, had facilitated his successes to date.

'The Princesses Regent were in the secret of this *magick of blood and stone*,' said Sophie positively, 'and we know from the Library's records that their papers were given to the College at the end of their regency; and so it follows – does it not? – that *somewhere* amongst this . . . collection of materials' – she gestured comprehensively at the crates and shelves and untidy heaps which presently surrounded her – 'we shall find the things they knew, and which they meant someone to find one day.'

'Unless whoever ransacked the library succeeded in destroying them,' said Gwendolen, at the same time that Joanna said, 'But if they *did* mean us to find them, why in Hades were they not in the box with the other papers?'

'We are strategists, not scholars.' Sophie's face, as she threw Joanna's words back at her, wore a sort of bright-eyed, frantic glee that boded very ill indeed for someone; Joanna hoped the someone might prove to be Henri-François d'Orléans, and not Sophie herself.

Joanna had not fully understood before how much they had all of them been going through the motions. Now they plunged back into their researches with renewed enthusiasm – not to say manic energy – not merely cataloguing and categorising but searching with purpose. Each morning she awoke eager to get through breakfast and begin, and Sophie fairly hummed with the urgency of the search.

'What do you hear from Gray, Sophie?' Joanna enquired, one morning after breakfast, as they bent together over a stack of tattered manuscript pages.

'Hear?' Sophie repeated. She looked up, brows drawn together in bafflement, and Joanna nearly rolled her eyes: *Never expect sensible conversation from Sophie when she is reading something*, she reminded herself.

'Feel, then,' she said. 'See – sense – you do not suppose me to understand anything about magick, I know,' she went on in a rush, at Sophie's deepening frown, 'but I am not a fool, Sophie.'

Sophie's face cleared – not in relief or understanding, but in that terribly familiar way which meant *I cannot bear anyone to guess what I am feeling* – and she said, low and even, 'He is well. Or, at any rate, he is . . . not ill. Not hurt, not . . .'

'I am glad to hear it,' said Joanna. She laid her hand over Sophie's, where it rested on the table between them, and pressed it briefly. 'And . . . and you?'

In one sense, Sophie's quick recourse to her concealing magick, a moment ago, had already given her the answer. But Sophie's magick was not Sophie's heart – or not entirely – and Joanna and Sophie had been guarding one another's hearts too long to change the habit now.

Instead of deflecting the question, Sophie looked Joanna in the eyes, produced a small, grave smile, and said, 'Yes.'

Then, much less astonishingly, she rolled her shoulders and tapped one forefinger against the manuscript page before her. 'Now – where were we?'

* * *

424

'I shall go mad, Sìleas,' said Lucia positively.

'Now, Lucia—'

Lucia was genuinely fond of her cousin, but at present nothing could have been more calculated to increase her irritation than Sìleas Barra MacNeill's soothing tone.

'Why must *I* be placed under house arrest,' she said, 'when the fault was not mine, and the threat is past?'

The threat, she reminded herself with a carefully hidden wince, being that unfortunate young man, whose death Lucia should forever have upon her conscience, whatever anyone else might say about it.

'Lucia, put yourself in Henry Tudor's place,' said Sìleas. She had abandoned *soothing*, the gods be thanked, in favour of *brisk and practical* – never her strong suit, but a thousand times more welcome. 'It is a perfectly sensible precaution.'

'My guardsmen,' said Lucia, 'are a perfectly sensible precaution; *this* is absurd.'

'The Royal Palace is hardly a prison, dear heart.'

'Any house becomes a prison when one is forbidden to leave it.'

Lucia paced two circuits of her sitting-room, walking as quickly as she could manage without knocking into any of the furniture. Then she stopped, drew in a deep breath and let it out in an explosive sigh, and clenched and relaxed her hands.

'My apologies,' she said. 'I shall endeavour to be grateful to Roland's papa for his care of me, instead of resenting it. And I shall go and see whether Delphine may be induced to take a turn about the Fountain Court, I think.'

The Princess Delphine, who expected her first confinement in October, was overheated and out of sorts, but was eventually persuaded to try whether a breath of fresh air might improve her spirits. If so, the change was not very evident to Lucia; on the other hand, however, half an hour's concentrated exposure to Delphine's fears for her husband, now somewhere on the Mainois frontier with his regiment, had a salutary effect on Lucia, by reminding her how small and petty were some of her own complaints.

Thus fortified and chastened, she returned Delphine to her ladies-in-waiting and her comfortable settee, and went in search of her betrothed.

Roland opened the door to her himself, looking as cross as Delphine if less fatigued and overheated.

'Lucia!' he said.

He was only half dressed, and upon seeing Lucia he blushed, gathering his dressing-gown more tightly about him as he stood aside to let her precede him into his sitting-room.

'I . . . apologise for receiving you in such a state of disarray,' said Roland, looking at the floor. 'I did not expect—well.'

The circumstances were sufficiently unusual that Lucia stared at him for some time, forgetful of what she had intended to say to him. The spell was broken, however, when Roland pushed the door to and crossed the room to peer into her face.

'Lucia,' he repeated, 'what—'

'Can you not make your father see reason, Roland?' said Lucia, cutting him off before the earnest, bewildered worry in his eyes could spill over into awkward sentiment of some sort.

'Not notably, to judge by past experience.' Roland pulled a face.

'But will you try?' Lucia persisted. 'I fear I shall run mad if I am mewed up here much longer.'

Roland sighed. 'I have scarcely seen my father since Ned's regiment left England,' he said. 'Talking of *mewed up* – he is always closeted with Lord Kergabet and the rest, and it seems I am not welcome in their counsels; certainly I am not welcome to interrupt them to talk of . . . of other matters.'

Another grimace. Lucia was reminded that Roland and Harry and Delphine and their mother, too, were confined to the Palace until further notice – though Delphine and Queen Edwina had at least their ladies-in-waiting to bear them company, while Roland seemed to have no one at all. Not even – she looked about her curiously – his valet or any of his usual guardsmen.

'Have you sent all your minions away?' she enquired.

Roland's flush deepened, and he thrust his hands deep in the pockets of his dressing-gown. 'Yes,' he said, hanging his head. 'I had rather they did not see me sulking like a little boy.'

In spite of everything, Lucia laughed. 'If you will not negotiate my release from captivity, Your Royal Highness,' she said, 'perhaps you will at least give me a game of chess?'

Roland returned her a sheepish, lopsided smile. 'Certainly, m'lady,' he said.

The crucial document, when at last they discovered it, was an unprepossessing assemblage of foxed and tattered pages, scattered more or less at random throughout the strata of unsorted and uncatalogued detritus in a crate labelled *Miscellaneous manuscript*. For two days Sophie, Joanna, and Gwendolen, with occasional assistance from Jenny and once, briefly and after much cajoling, from Lady Maëlle, painstakingly sorted through the lot, with a relatively innocuous section from the Princesses' Regent account of their brother's illness pinned to the edge of the reading-stand for reference, and perhaps for inspiration. Their first find – not obviously relevant or useful, but undeniably written in the same hand, and therefore at any rate worth remarking upon – came in the afternoon of the first day; it was not until the following morning, however, that Joanna ran across a second, in which appeared the tantalising words *pierres de Carnac*, and by the time the sixth and, so far as they could deduce, final page surfaced – in fact, it was the beginning of the sequence, for they had located what appeared to be its end some time before – Treveur had rung the bell warning the household to begin dressing for dinner, a foot-high stack of miscellaneous papers plausibly attributable to one or other of the Princesses Regent had been assembled in the centre of the table, and the crate was nearly empty. Jenny had long quit the field, for the paper-dust made her sneeze, and Lady Maëlle, pleading fatigue (in Sophie's opinion, it was less fatigue than melancholy), had retired for a rest before dinner.

Sophie was all for ignoring the bell, and dinner itself, in favour of sitting down at once to the reconstruction of the document which mentioned the Karnag stones; how could she, how could anyone, think of food or conversation at such a time? Joanna and Gwendolen, however, flat refused to have anything to do with the enterprise until dinner had been served and eaten. When Sophie attempted to argue the point, they took her by the elbows and marched her up the stairs to her bedroom, then watched her dress for dinner, herded her into Gwendolen's room, and required her to sit on the edge of the bed whilst they did the same.

For a wonder, there were to be no guests for dinner, and Kergabet and Mr Fowler were not expected to return until late in the evening from their latest council of war. They sat down therefore only five at table for what passed in Grosvenor Square for a simple family dinner, and the conversation, except when Treveur and Harry the footman were actually bringing in the dishes, consisted almost entirely in speculation as to the progress of events across the Manche, on the one hand, and the possible contents of Princess Edith's and Princess Julia's papers, on the other.

'I wish we might be assured that should we find some manner

of help therein, the Privy Council may be amenable to accepting it,' said Joanna. 'But experience suggests—'

'There is no sense in planning to lose your battles before you have fought them, Jo,' said Gwendolen bracingly.

Jenny raised an eyebrow at this military turn of phrase but made no comment aloud.

And besides, Sophie thought, *if the Privy Council will not do what is needful, why should not we do it ourselves?*

For obvious reasons, she said none of this where Jenny or Lady Maëlle might hear.

Assembling the fragments of their find into the correct order took more than half an hour, for two of the pages had been torn in half, one crossed in two different hands, and several covered on both sides; on the verso side of one of the latter Gwendolen found what appeared to be notes for an essay on the theory of spells of concealment, in yet a third hand quite different from the other two, which muddied the waters for a few moments. At last, however, they were satisfied with their reconstruction, and Sophie carefully shuffled the pages into a stack and began to read aloud.

Since the days of Ahez ar Breizh, the queens of England have held the secrets of the magick of blood and stone, have taught those secrets to their daughters-in-law so that the kingdom might be shielded from the assaults of its enemies. In the reign of our father, the eighth Henry, this chain was broken; for though Queen Elinor did her duty by the Princess Catherine when she married our father's elder brother, Prince Arthur – then heir to the throne – Arthur did not outlive his father, and all know what became of poor Catherine thereafter.

But if Queen Catherine, as she for some years was, was
fated never to have a daughter-in-law to whom she might
bequeath her knowledge, she did have a daughter; and it was
to the Princess Julia – not to her successor, Queen Adwen, or
any of King Henry's subsequent wives – that she taught Queen
Elinor's secrets. The Princess Julia, whose love of her kingdom
exceeded her resentment of her father, had every intention of
guarding the knowledge for the sake of her brother's wife, when
he should be of an age to marry; young Edward took the throne
at the tender age of nine, however, and but a few years later,
Mathilda Julia of Britain was called upon to use the magick of
blood and stone in a manner which no prior keeper of its secrets
could have foreseen.

'Why do they write of themselves as if they were strangers?' said
Joanna. 'What a very irritating affectation.'

'Hush,' said Gwendolen; very quietly in Joanna's ear, she added,
'You are quite right, love, but if we are forever interrupting, we shall
never come to the point.'

Joanna subsided; she leant her shoulder against Gwendolen's
arm, and let her head tilt down to rest on Gwendolen's shoulder, as
Sophie read on:

Thus did Edith Augusta of Britain also become a sharer in
the magick of blood and stone, and thus was the chain broken in
truth, for Edward rewarded his sisters' love and loyalty by exiling
them from his Court and—

Sophie stopped. 'We have had this part of the tale already,' she
said, running her eyes down the page; 'I think we need not hear it
again. Ah! Here we are.'

As we cannot fulfil our duty by bequeathing our knowledge to our brother's queen, we set it down here, in defiance of long custom and in the hope that it may one day come to the hand of her successors, and thus be ready at need in defence of Britain's eastern frontiers.

Joanna and Gwendolen exchanged a look.

She who would wield the magick of blood and stone need not be Queen, but she must be a loyal subject of the Kingdom of Britain, and a mage of some talent and skill. She must possess the map of the keystones, and the spell that wakes their power to rouse the kingdom to its own defence.

'And here is the spell,' said Sophie, holding up the page, the remainder of which appeared to be written in verse. 'The *map of the keystones*, I suppose, is the one we have already – at any rate, I hope it may be so.'

But it falls to the kings of Britain to ensure that the magick of the stones is replenished, at the turning of the year, by that of the kingdom which it protects from harm.

'Mother Goddess!' Joanna exclaimed. 'What in Hades does *that* mean?'

Sophie looked up from the manuscript, frowning. 'I have not the least idea,' she said. 'And I suspect that my father has not either.'

'By which you mean that no one has replenished the magick of the stones since the time of Henry the Great,' said Joanna, her heart sinking, 'and there is no use in our having found the map, or in your learning the spell, because no power remains to be called upon.'

431

'Wait,' said Sophie. She held up a hand, frowning now *at* the page before her, rather than over it.

> *In the reign of Edward Longshanks, whose obsession with conquering Alba led him to neglect the defence of his territories across the Manche, the magick of the stones was not replenished for some years. Following the final defeat of Edward Longshanks at the Roman Wall, it fell to his sole surviving son and heir to repair the damage wrought by his father's neglect. Though a misfortunate monarch in most ways, Edward II did succeed in this one task, for which he is to be commended. Posterity may well record as a noble deed his enterprise in setting down in his private diary the method by which the task was accomplished, for it may be that at some future date another King of Britain shall find himself in need of it.*
>
> *A copy of his account, dating from the tenth year of his reign, is appended—*

'But it is not here,' Sophie concluded, sounding defeated, as she raised her eyes from the page. 'Gods and priestesses! Of all the ill luck—'

Joanna and Gwendolen were already shuffling through the larger stack of royal papers, armed now with a greater certainty of their goal, when Sophie said, in an entirely different tone, 'Oh! Listen – under this blot on the verso: *made from the original in the Royal Archives.* If we cannot find the copy, why should the original not still be where the Princesses found it?'

Joanna looked up. 'Why indeed? But how are we to go to the Archives and look for it, when both Lord Kergabet and your father have decreed that we are none of us to leave this house?'

For what seemed the first time in months, or possibly years, Sophie's face lit in a broad, genuine smile. '*We* cannot go looking for it, but Roland and Lucia can.'

Lucia was kicking her heels in Delphine's sitting-room, amongst a gaggle of young ladies whose laudable attempts to divert Delphine from her melancholy thoughts about Prince Edward by talking very cheerfully of gowns and shoes and millinery had, after more than two hours, begun to set her teeth on edge, when a knock at the door heralded the arrival of a page bearing a message from Roland.

> *I am in the Archives*, it read, *on a commission for Sophie, and should be grateful for your assistance.*
> — *R*

Even had the words *Archives* and *Sophie* not set her heart beating faster, Lucia had been longing for escape this hour and more; she retained self-control enough to rise from her seat and beg Delphine's pardon with grace and dignity, rather than leaping up and running out of the room without explanation, but only just.

'Lucia!' said Roland, his face lighting in pleased surprise, when at last she ran him to earth in a poorly lit back corner of the Palace Archives – not at all his natural habitat. He was halfway up a library-stair, using both hands to wrangle a box off a shelf at about the level of his shoulders; his hair was dusty and more than usually rumpled.

'I thank you for that timely rescue,' she said. 'What are we seeking for Sophie in all this dust?'

Roland smiled sunnily down at her. 'The private diaries of King Edward the Second,' he said.

Lucia perched on the edge of the long, narrow table that ran

433

down the middle of the long, narrow aisle. 'Whatever for?'

'That,' said Roland, puffing a little as the box finally came free, 'Sophie was not willing to entrust to the eyes of the guardsman who brought her letter to me; she knows as well as I do that nearly all of her correspondence is opened and read at present, for my father still fears that she will run off after her husband, with or without his consent. And I daresay she should do,' he added, 'if she knew where to find him.'

He was descending the ladder now, slowly and carefully, the box tucked under one arm.

'If *my* husband were missing in enemy territory in time of war,' said Lucia, 'I hope I should not wait for anyone's consent to see him found and rescued.'

Then she remembered to whom she was speaking, and flushed hotly with embarrassment.

'I am happy to hear you say so,' said Roland gravely – was he laughing at her, beneath that solemn expression? It irked Lucia that she could not tell – as he set the box on the table. 'But of course your position and Sophie's are quite different.'

And that – as she ought not to have needed Roland to remind her – was perfectly true: whatever privilege and indulgence Sophie might enjoy by virtue of being her father's daughter, Lucia had real power in her father's kingdom, and would have more hereafter. *But then, Sophie also possesses other sorts of power which I can only dream of.*

'Have you found them, the diaries of . . . Edward the Second, did you say?' she enquired, nodding at the dusty box, in lieu of pursuing this line of thought. 'He was the son of Edward Longshanks, the would-be conqueror of Alba, was he not?'

'He was,' said Roland, 'and wisely did not attempt to follow in his father's footsteps – not in that respect, at any rate. These are some of the diaries, or so I hope; the archivist who labelled the boxes was apparently not a believer in writing a clear hand.'

He levered the box open with an alarming creak of the hinges, and they peered into its interior, which indeed was packed tight with ledgers bound in faded red calfskin.

'Sophie wishes us to find the entries from the tenth year of Edward's reign,' said Roland. 'There are a dozen boxes at least marked *Edwardus II Rex*; he reigned twenty years, so I have begun somewhere in the middle.'

It was a sensible approach, assuming that the long-dead archivist had been more skilled in organising his materials than in labelling them.

'You are not such a bad scholar as you believe yourself to be, you know,' said Lucia.

Roland shifted uncomfortably from foot to foot. 'I ought to be with Ned in the field,' he said at last, with the air of one airing a long-held grievance. 'Or in the field in Ned's place. He is the heir; he ought not to be risking himself so.'

'I am sure he will not be put into unnecessary danger,' Lucia ventured.

Roland's expression made clear, however, that his objection was at least as much to being left behind himself, as to his brother's being sent into battle. 'Shall we begin with this box?' he said, producing a falsely bright smile that defied her to either commiserate or advise. 'Or will I fetch down another now, to save time later?'

They fetched down the two boxes on either side of the first and went through them methodically from either end; the contents proved frustratingly disorganised, and eight boxes were open upon the table before at last records from the tenth year of Edward II's reign began to turn up. Roland would have packed the unwanted volumes back into their original boxes, but Lucia insisted upon sorting them into chronological order, insofar as was possible, and fetched pen and ink and labels and paste-pot from the archivist on duty – to the latter's great bafflement – in order to do the thing properly.

The real fruits of their labours – the box now labelled *anno x Edw. II R.*, containing fourteen ledgers dated to that year, which they had found scattered amongst half a dozen boxes – they took away with them, which occasioned further baffled looks from the archivist on duty but, Roland being who he was, no outright protest.

At the door to Lucia's rooms, they were relieved of their prize by a disapproving Conall Barra MacNeill, presently on duty there.

'Your cousin Sìleas is in a terrible fret over you, Lucia MacNeill,' he said.

'Why should she be?' said Lucia, startled. 'What harm does Sìleas imagine could befall me, when I am not permitted even to walk in the outer gardens?'

Conall shrugged eloquently. 'Not for me to say,' he said. 'But when next you take it into your head to disappear, perhaps you may think to tell someone where you are going.'

Lucia sighed. 'My apologies,' she said. 'And I shall apologise to Sìleas also, never fear. I have a task for you, however.'

Roland and she had agreed, in the course of their journey from the Archives, that they could not in good conscience ask any of King Henry's household guard to smuggle a box of purloined diaries from the Palace to Grosvenor Square.

'Brìghde's tears, Lucia MacNeill!' said Conall, when she had explained the matter to him. 'What tangle have you got yourself into now?'

Roland was looking from one of them to the other with eyebrows raised, but, Lucia was pleased to see, more amusement than offence in his expression at Conall's less-than-subservient tone.

'No tangle at all,' she said bracingly. 'Sophie Marshall requested Roland's help and mine with a foray she is making into historical enquiry, as she is also presently under house arrest' – she could not resist giving Conall a hard stare, for his wholehearted connivance at her own imprisonment – 'and therefore cannot come here to search the Archives herself.'

'An innocent bit of scholarship, is it?' said Conall. Lucia thought she had never seen a man look so disbelieving.

'What else should it be?' Lucia demanded.

'Considering the source,' said Conall Barra MacNeill, who had stood with Lucia and Ceana MacGregor in the shambles of Cormac MacAlpine's yew-grove whilst Sophie worked epic and invisible magicks all about them, 'I should not be surprised if it were any sort of mad enterprise, up to and including armed insurrection.'

'There is certainly no question of armed insurrection,' said Lucia firmly; shifting into English, she said, 'Roland, open the box and find me something very dull to show him.'

Roland, concealing a smile, opened the box and took out the first volume that came to his hand; Conall frowned at him, and then at Lucia.

'Here you are,' said Roland, handing over the open codex.

Lucia took it from him and read – slowly, translating from Latin into Gaelic as she went – '*Luneday, the fourth of April, in the tenth year of King Edward the Second. Court remains at Gloucester. Weather very unsettled. Faucher has sent report that,* er, *Lightning has been delivered of a healthy foal. The entertainment this evening consisted in a troupe of players from Shrewsbury, or so Gloucester said, who gave us the tale of—*'

'Very well,' said Conall Barra MacNeill, waving a hand at her. 'I shall see your dusty old books delivered to Sophie Marshall.'

'You are a treasure among guard lieutenants,' said Lucia, and startled Roland by standing on tiptoe to kiss Conall's grizzled cheek.

437

CHAPTER XXXII

In Which Joanna Counsels Prudence, and Sophie Receives a Gift

The diaries of King Edward II arrived in Grosvenor Square in a crate whose nominal purpose was to convey to Sophie a gift from her friend Lucia MacNeill: to wit, a large and impressively hideous statuette depicting Lady Minerva with an owl. Sophie stared at this astonishing object for some little time before her eye was caught by the corner of a folded sheet of notepaper, protruding from the statuette's base.

> *Sophie*, it read, *we have found you something we hope you shall like, and with it a few books to help you pass the time.*
> *— L & R*

There were fourteen leather-bound ledgers in all, all of them heavy and some a trifle damp, and all – as requested – dated to the tenth year of Edward's reign. Stacked on the library table, they made rather a daunting sight: a full year's worth of his cramped, crabbed hand to pore through, perhaps, before they found what they sought.

If we do find it, which is by no means certain.

Having summoned Joanna and Gwendolen – she had decided already that neither Jenny nor Lady Maëlle could be permitted to assist in this stage of the project, nor to understand its urgent character, for they were neither of them fools and must very quickly have discovered what she was about – she set a ward upon the library to prevent interruptions and then arranged the diaries in order and divided them into three.

'Research,' she said vaguely, when Jenny enquired over dinner as to what the young people presently had in train. 'I may perhaps write something for the *Proceedings of the Society for the History of Magick*.'

'That *you* should bury your head in a stack of books for days at a time does not at all surprise me,' said Lady Maëlle, 'but Joanna?'

'Gwendolen and I have nothing else to do at present,' said Joanna – more gently than Sophie might have expected, but after all, Lady Maëlle had Amelia on her conscience, or thought she had – 'as you may remember; and research makes a change from needlework.'

'And it is quite interesting, by times,' Gwendolen chimed in, then added, as though regretting her small burst of enthusiasm, 'though *very* dusty.'

By design or fortunate happenstance, she sneezed.

Jenny grimaced. 'I shall leave you to it, then, I think.'

It was Gwendolen who found the first clue, about the second hour before noon on the third day, in the diary covering the month of September.

'Jo,' she said sharply. 'Sophie. I think—'

They looked up – Joanna from the second volume of January, Sophie from May – and left their own researches to peer around Gwendolen's shoulders.

x September
Roazhon, en Petite-Bretagne

*Expect to be at Karnag before the Equinox, and am assured
that all shall be in readiness there. It remains to pray that the
gods may forgive me my father's neglect of this duty, and smile on
my efforts to rebuild what he allowed to fall to ruin.*

'Oh, well spotted!' cried Sophie. 'Now, you must read forward
from the tenth of September, and I shall read backwards from the
end of August, for he may have set down something of his plans;
and, Jo, here is July—'

Three hours later, they had assembled a précis of King Edward's
expedition to the Stones of Karnag, and Sophie was aquiver with
ideas and plans.

'We shall need half a dozen mages, according to Edward,' she said,
scribbling shorthand notes on a scrap of notepaper, 'to replenish the
magick of the stones; and if we are to reach Karnag before it is too
late to do any good, we shall have to go by ship – shall not we, Jo?'

'Sophie, you cannot be seriously considering—'

'How long have you known me, Joanna Callender?' Sophie
demanded, low and fierce. At Joanna's shoulder, Gwendolen
shivered – perhaps sensing some magickal exudation which Joanna
herself could not. 'What did you imagine we were about, in
searching through this rubbish-heap, if not to use whatever treasure
we found for some good purpose?'

'And haring off into the midst of a pitched battle between the
armies of two kingdoms, entirely without support of any kind, is
your notion of *some good purpose?*'

'Certainly not,' said Sophie indignantly.

Joanna exhaled relief, but too soon, of course, for Sophie
continued, 'Our *purpose* is to defend Britain against Orléans, and
to rescue Amelia, and to find Gray and bring him home. Haring off
into the midst of a pitched battle is merely the means to that end.'

'And is there truly no other means available?' said Joanna, after a moment of gobsmacked silence. 'None which does not require you to risk your own life, break your sworn word to your father, deceive Jenny and Kergabet—'

'Suppose,' said Gwendolen, arresting Joanna's increasingly manic momentum with gentle hands on her shoulders, 'suppose that we took the results of our researches to Lord Kergabet, or to His Majesty, and explained what is needed?'

'Yes,' said Joanna, with more confidence than she felt. 'Lord Kergabet has great faith in your judgement in magickal matters, Sophie.'

'But Lord de Vaucourt does not,' said Sophie bitterly. 'And it is Vaucourt who must be persuaded – Vaucourt and my father – if the Crown is to dispatch so many Court mages to Karnag on such a mission. And the Court mages themselves, of course, who are nearly all in Vaucourt's pocket.'

'But Lord de Vaucourt and his fellows could work the spell?' Gwendolen persisted. 'If they could be persuaded?'

'I – I do not see why not,' said Sophie. 'But—' She fell silent, biting her lip; after a moment, she continued, 'but if they cannot be persuaded, they will know – or must suspect – what we are about, and will be the more able to prevent us from doing what they refuse to do.'

Which, Joanna conceded, was entirely true. Nevertheless—

'Nevertheless,' she said aloud, 'we are not irresponsible children, Sophie; we must try, at the least, to do as we ought. There is a name for persons who withhold vital military intelligence from those who have most need of it, and it is not a pleasant one.'

Sophie's face twisted into a thunderous scowl. Sophie was in general disposed to be truthful, however, and Joanna was therefore unsurprised when she made no effort to disagree.

* * *

'What a fascinating theory,' said Lord de Vaucourt, leaning his chin upon his folded hands. He turned from Sophie to Lord Kergabet and continued: 'Such imaginations as these young people have! I am all admiration.'

The Sophie who had arrived in London all those years ago at the age of seventeen might well have incinerated Vaucourt's study and everyone in it with the force of her outrage and indignation. The Sophie of the present moment possessed a hard-won level of self-control which permitted her instead – though not without effort – to smile thinly at her antagonist and say, 'I assure you, my lord, that no admiration is necessary – unless, that is, you meant to express admiration of our investigative efforts. There has been no imagination in the case.'

Vaucourt had turned back to her when she spoke to him – according her that show of respect, at any rate, if he could not bring himself to do more – and now returned her edged smile with one of his own. 'You must not think, ma'am, that your desire to assist in the defence of the kingdom is unappreciated,' he said. 'I am sure, however, that you must be aware how much your enthusiasm outstrips your practical experience.'

'Must I?' said Sophie. Vaucourt, who did not know her well, returned her gaze impassively; Joanna, who did, laid a restraining hand on Sophie's, clenched in her skirts beneath the table. 'Tell me, Maître Vaucourt—'

Lord Kergabet, also well acquainted with his sister-in-law, chose this moment to intervene: 'My lord,' he said, touching Sophie's shoulder in silent apology, 'it is a grave mistake, I assure you, to underestimate Magistra Marshall's practical experience in matters of . . . unusual magick.'

'You will forgive me, my lord, I am sure,' Vaucourt returned, 'if I decline to take your word upon it.' He smiled, half apology, half superior smirk. 'It has been my duty to advise His Majesty on all such matters these ten years and more; and I do not presume to usurp *your* authority in matters political.'

The worst of it was, thought Joanna bitterly, that Vaucourt scarcely even *tried* to veil his insults, even when speaking to Lord Kergabet – as His Majesty's chief Privy Councillor, arguably the most powerful man in Britain, save one.

But nearly as bad was the recognition that, in fact, Vaucourt was not altogether wrong; very likely Kergabet's support was based as much on his own faith in Sophie *qua* Sophie as on any sober and rational assessment of the process by which she had drawn her conclusions, and undeniably he was as ill qualified to opine on any magickal question as Joanna was herself.

'My lord,' said Sophie, her hand shaking under Joanna's but her voice admirably even, 'what is your own theory as to the Duc d'Orléans' choice of military targets?'

'The man calls himself Imperator Gallia and has forbidden the worship of any but the gods of Rome in the territories under his control,' said Vaucourt at once. 'He is mad, or at any rate is in the grip of some idée fixe, and his military strategy is that of a madman. We should be foolish to seek reason or logic in it.'

Gwendolen had said something very like this, not so long ago – she remembered it too, Joanna guessed from her guilty half glance at Sophie – but it had not stung as Vaucourt's easy dismissal did.

'I disagree,' said Sophie. 'His logic may be that of some particular madness, yet logic all the same, capable of being reasoned through by a sufficiently patient opponent, and circumvented before its worst conclusions can be reached. I have seen it before.'

The logic of some particular madness – she has Cormac MacAlpine of Alba in mind, yes.

443

Joanna and Gwendolen exchanged a brief but meaning look.

'You refer, I suppose, to that scuffle in Alba three years ago?' said Vaucourt.

The three ladies bridled at *scuffle* – could an incident be called a mere scuffle, in which so many persons had so nearly lost their lives? – but when Sophie spoke, her voice remained calm and even: 'I do. Cormac MacAlpine's attempt to claim the chieftain's seat of Alba relied on his belief that his clan alone could restore the spell-net which his distant ancestor had created to unite the warring clans, and that any action which might further that aim could be justified by reference to it. Considered in that light, his behaviour was logical from first to last, though no person who had not fallen prey to the same, as you say, idée fixe could have dreamt of acting in such a way.'

She paused, looking expectantly at Vaucourt.

'Unless I have been very much misinformed,' he said slowly, 'the resolution of that . . . tangle was a matter more of luck than of logic.'

Sophie grimaced a little. 'That is true,' she conceded. 'But only because we lacked the information necessary to draw the correct conclusions. Whereas in *this* case—'

'In this case,' said Vaucourt, impatient now, 'you have drawn conclusions on the basis of information whose accuracy cannot be verified, and you propose to risk the lives of half a dozen trained and powerful mages – men of incalculable value to the kingdom – in hopes of demonstrating your own cleverness. I call that self-serving and cowardly, *Magistra*.'

'Lord Vaucourt!' said Kergabet, frowning dangerously.

Down the table, Gwendolen gasped.

'I do not ask anything of any other mage which I should not be prepared to undertake myself,' said Sophie tightly, 'were I permitted to do so. If you know anything at all of the Cormac MacAlpine affair, my lord, surely you must know *that*.'

'With respect, ma'am,' said Vaucourt, 'the lesson of your . . . *adventures* in Alba is, rather, that what you lack in judgement, you make up in reckless disregard for the good judgement of others.'

'Were it not for my *reckless disregard for the good judgement of others,*' Sophie retorted – Joanna could feel her trembling, now, with the effort of remaining calm – 'my father would be dead, and my brother reigning under the influence of a conspiracy of regicides; and the gods alone know what Cormac MacAlpine might by now have done to Alba. Do you tell me, Maître Vaucourt, that I was wrong to take those bulls by the horns, wrong to give my help where it was needed?'

'What I tell you, Your Royal Highness, is that you owe your past successes to sheer good fortune; and Dame Fortune's wheel turns. You must understand—'

'Vaucourt.' Kergabet rose furiously to his feet. 'You forget yourself.'

But Vaucourt stared unflinchingly back at him and said, 'His Majesty will not thank you for encouraging his precious child in her dangerous fancies.'

'That may be so,' replied Kergabet, low, 'but it is not I who have committed that error today.' He straightened to his full height and gathered up Sophie, Joanna, and Gwendolen with a gesture; they collected their documentary evidence – for all the good it had done them – and followed him out of the conference-room without a backward glance, all, Joanna was quite certain, equally seething within.

The ladies of Grosvenor Square were leaving the breakfast table, several days later, when the next blow fell.

At first Sophie thought she had put a foot wrong, turned an ankle, stumbled over her own feet as she occasionally did when lost in thought. But the momentary disorientation persisted, and catching the back of a chair as she passed it failed to arrest her dizzy downward momentum. When next she blinked her eyes open, the view was of Joanna's and Gwendolen's faces, wide-eyed with alarm; behind them, Lady Maëlle's, bending closer; behind her, the ceiling of the breakfast-room. Some great invisible weight pressed down upon her lungs; her pulse thrummed in her throat, in her ears; the room dimmed, brightened, dimmed again; an oppressive silence closed in about her, broken only by a sharp shock of distress which, after a frozen moment, she recognised as Gray's rather than her own.

The pain was vicious but short-lived, but the relief of its going was entirely eclipsed, for with it went her faint but ever-present sense of her own magick.

Panicked, she sank deeper, forgetting such mundane concerns as sight and sound and breath in the frantic search for this one quintessential thing. At last, farther down and farther in and smaller and fainter than ever before, but still unmistakably *there*, she found what she sought, and the relief of it nearly shattered her concentration. But Sophie's experience of magickal catastrophe had heavily featured not only her own magick but Gray's, too; and so, having reassured herself that the one remained intact, if strangely subdued, she could not help also seeking after the other.

This took longer – or so it seemed; she had no real sense of how much time might be passing, or how little, whilst she swam these half-familiar depths – but by narrowing her focus again, again, again, she at last perceived the faint, fragile thread of Gray's magick, thrumming the same reassuring deep blue-green. But even this was not quite as it ought to be; shivering up the fine-drawn link, as she listened, there came a note of some altogether alien magick.

No: not one note, one magick, but *many.*

Gray, I thank all the gods that you are alive and well; but what in Hades are you about?

'Sophie, thank all the gods!'

Sophie let her eyes close briefly, then opened them again, confused and assessing: her own bed in Jenny's house; Joanna at her bedside, hollow-eyed with lack of sleep; a bright stripe of morning light through the narrow gap in the window-curtains. *Tomorrow morning, then.*

Her head ached, and the rest of her felt limp and worn out, but her vision was undimmed, Joanna's voice came clearly to her ears, and best of all, when she felt for her magick, she found it near at hand and burning brightly. The link to Gray's magick, too, was easily found and tested, and seemed to have regained its former strength.

But the sense of some other persons' presence was undiminished, and the jarring note spoilt the otherwise perfectly expected harmony between Gray's magick and her own.

'Sophie!' Joanna's tone of real alarm disturbed the fragile equilibrium Sophie had only just succeeded in re-establishing.

'What is it?' she said, wallowing up from the pillows to look her sister in the eyes.

Joanna blinked. 'You . . . were not answering me,' she said, after a moment, sounding a trifle sheepish. 'For a *very* long time, Sophie. I did not know where you had gone.'

'I was looking inwards,' said Sophie, 'and looking for Gray. I am sorry to have alarmed you.'

Reaching out, she caught Joanna's hands in hers.

'Looking for Gray?' Joanna said. 'Looking, how?'

How to explain it to Joanna, who could experience magick only from the outside – and not always then?

But Joanna waved an impatient hand. 'Never mind! You found him, I must suppose – where is he?'

'If I were capable of discovering his whereabouts from this distance,' said Sophie, 'even very approximately, I should have said so long before this. But something has happened, Jo – something happened yesterday; it *was* yesterday?' Joanna nodded. 'What it was, exactly, I cannot tell, but there is something else – someone else – woven in with Gray's magick now, which was not there before. Like—'

'Like Lucia MacNeill's spell for sharing her magick!' Joanna exclaimed.

'Yes,' said Sophie, 'and . . . no – for Lucia's magick was a welcome relief to me, and this . . .' She shivered, remembering the phantom weight on her chest, the dimming of her eyes – the sharp distress sizzling along the link between Gray's magick and her own. 'This was not.'

'Sophie—'

'I may be able to gain some better notion of where Gray is – in what direction, at any rate – once we are across the Manche,' Sophie continued. 'And of course then it will be worth our while to begin trying a finding-spell – from here it would be useless, for the distance aside, open water is a dreadful dampener of finding-spells. And—'

'*Sophie*—'

'Whatever the Duc d'Orléans is about, it is gathering speed.' Sophie pushed back the bedclothes, swung her legs over the edge of the bed, and cautiously stood.

'But how can you know—'

Sophie could not explain, in rational terms, how she knew, and therefore did not try. 'We have wasted too much time already in trying to persuade Lord Vaucourt and my father to act,' she said instead. 'I do not intend to wait any longer. We know what is needed.'

* * *

A frankly enormous breakfast and a nearly scalding bath, undertaken at Joanna's stern insistence, made Sophie feel much more herself, but produced no change in her opinion on the necessity for swift action.

'Then we shall act,' said Joanna simply. 'But *not* by creeping away the moment the night is dark enough. You may be incapable of learning from past experience, but *I* am not; this expedition will be properly planned and provisioned, or we shall none of us have anything to do with it.'

Sophie sighed, but could scarcely argue with this eminently sensible pronouncement.

Their planning was made more difficult by Lady Maëlle's solicitous care of Sophie, and by the fact that Lord Kergabet and Jenny plainly anticipated some attempt at escape; having largely left them to their own devices whilst they sorted and catalogued the voluminous results of their expedition to Oxford, and even during their furious interrogation of the diaries of Edward II, Jenny now seemed cheerfully determined to keep them under her eye, or busy about some other business, at all times.

They were forced at last to enlist the help of Katell, once more sworn to secrecy – all of which smote Sophie's conscience to a degree which might have been insupportable, had there been less at stake – and to pool their coin for the hire of a carriage to take them to Oxford, which must be the first halt on their journey.

More delicate still was the problem of communicating their intentions to Lucia and Roland, as all written correspondence was liable to be opened and read – for their own safety, naturally. But the first thing necessary to their present mission was a sufficient complement of mages; and Roland and Lucia, surely, were among the least likely to reject their proposal out of hand.

Sophie had made a list of likely candidates at Merlin –

headed, of course, by Gareth Evans-Hughes; she did not like to involve Master Alcuin, whose age and health militated against his participation in such an uncertain venture even as his skill and knowledge recommended it – but quailed inwardly at the thought of the time that would be spent, and perhaps wasted, in explanation and persuasion, all because the thing could not be done openly and officially, by the issuing of royal commands.

All the same, a small party of travellers could move more quickly than an army.

The next piece of news was that a fleet of ships flying the banner of the pretended Emperor had been seen departing Tours, sailing down the Loire towards the city of Naoned and, ultimately, the Breizhek coast – directly south and east of Karnag.

Sophie set aside her dignity, therefore, and wrote a pleading letter to her father, asking his permission to make a visit to the Palace, both to escape the four walls of Lord Kergabet's house and to speak with him and with Lucia. His reply arrived sooner than she had dared hope – together with a carriage and a quartet of Royal Guardsmen for her safe conveyance thither.

'I hope you are not come with some idea of further badgering Lord Vaucourt with wild tales culled from the ravings of Edward the Dishonourable, my dear,' said His Majesty, when Sophie and he were settled on opposing sofas in his private study. 'You know, I hope, that if there is any need for a rescue mission, you have only to tell me so?'

Things had gone so far beyond the need for Gray to be rescued that Sophie scarcely knew what to say to this. 'I have no intention of importuning Lord Vaucourt, Father,' she said at last. *Though only because I know very well it would do no one any good.*

She had, it was true, had some hopes that her father might be a more receptive audience than Lord Vaucourt; but clearly they were not to be fulfilled.

'I have no reason to fear for my own health,' she said instead, 'nor to believe that Gray is in more danger now than at any time since he left England.' He had, after all, been in grave danger all along, in one way or another. 'My meeting with Lord Vaucourt was unrelated to either possibility, I assure you.'

His Majesty smiled. 'I am glad of it.'

Sophie drew a deep breath. 'I do have a favour to beg of you, however,' she said carefully. 'If I may not – if I cannot be of any use to Maître de Vaucourt, or to Lord Kergabet, then I should wish to return to Oxford, and continue the work already begun there. If I may be permitted to go, I mean to ask Roland and Lucia to go with me, for I know that they are as weary of confinement as I am myself.'

The King considered her proposal at such length, and in such an imposing silence, that Sophie began to despair of success.

'The Lady Lucia has certainly made her displeasure plain,' he said at last, 'and so, as a result, has your stepmother. I expect that Lucia should be glad of some practical employment, and Roland ought not to be moping about as he has been doing.' He regarded Sophie intently, as though searching her face for some sign of subterfuge; Sophie breathed very steadily, and prayed very hard to wise Minerva, and schooled her features into an expression of hopeful patience.

'Provided that you are adequately guarded,' said the King, 'I suppose there can be no harm in it.' His lips twisted in a rueful not-quite-smile. 'Indeed, on present evidence London would appear the greater danger, for the Lady Lucia at any rate. I must tell you, my dear – for I know you shall not repeat it – that I was astonished at her choosing to remain here, having been subjected to such a gross violation of the laws of hospitality. She certainly does not lack for pluck.'

Pluck, thought Sophie wonderingly, did not come even vaguely near to the truth of Lucia, but for present purposes, it would do well enough.

'I thank you, Father, very much indeed,' she said, rising from her sofa and bending to kiss his cheek. She straightened. 'May I go now to deliver my invitation to Lucia and Roland?'

He waved her away with a kindly smile.

In the corridor outside her father's private study, Sophie ran against Lord de Vaucourt – almost, but not quite, literally – striding purposefully in the opposite direction to herself, with a stack of dispatches in his arms.

It was the work of a moment to decide to listen at the door, and a journey of less than half a dozen steps to put her decision into practice, against both her conscience and her better judgement.

Alas, however, the door was very thick, and Maître Vaucourt highly skilled in the working of warding-spells; and so all that came to her pricked ears, before the two circumstances combined to muffle all sound from withinpast distinguishing, was the single word *Haudricourt*.

It was enough.

CHAPTER XXXIII

In Which Sophie Breaks Her Word

Sophie ran Lucia to earth in the Fountain Court, reading an historical account of Edward Longshanks' defeat at Berwick with great determination and very little success, and Roland in the music-room, irritably picking out a melancholy tune upon his mother's pianoforte.

'I am come to dragoon you into another expedition to Oxford,' she said, with determined cheerfulness, for the benefit of anyone who might happen to overhear their conversation.

Then she herded them both into Lucia's sitting-room, set the strongest ward she could upon it, and, over the ensuing hour, explained all that had been going forward in Grosvenor Square since their last meeting.

'And the answer – the method of renewing the spell-stones – it was in those old diaries?' said Lucia eagerly, when Sophie related the disappointing discovery that the defensive magick they had hoped to wield had almost certainly fallen prey to two centuries' neglect.

Sophie blinked in surprise – but they were neither of them fools, and they must of course already have concluded that her request for those specific volumes had not been an arbitrary one.

'Yes,' she said. 'And that is why I need your help – both of you. Not to go to Oxford – that is, Oxford *first*, but after that, by ship to Karnag.'

She described her conversations with Lord Kergabet, with Maître de Vaucourt, with her father; described the bizarre experience of feeling some other person's magick invade her link with Gray, and her conviction that Orléans' plan was coming to a head (Roland made to object to this reliance on gut instinct; Lucia said firmly, 'If Sophie says it is so, then that is enough for me,' and he subsided); and concluded with her attempt at eavesdropping on the King and his chief mage, which, they all agreed, might plausibly be taken to support their theory as to Orléans' intentions.

'And King Edward's method requires half a dozen mages,' she said at last. 'Gwendolen Pryce and I are two, but her talent is modest and she is largely untrained. You two, on the other hand—'

Sophie fell silent, gazing determinedly at her toes and chewing her lip in nervous anticipation. From the corner of her eye, she could perceive Roland and Lucia muttering together.

Lucia, who owed no allegiance to anyone on either side of this conflict, save Roland and her own friends, was very ready to be persuaded to quit the increasingly stifling confines of the Royal Palace for a highly unauthorised jaunt across the Manche to Breizh.

'And it is not as though we shall even be going near the fighting,' she pointed out, tracing possible routes on the map – an ordinary map of Britain, this time – which Sophie had prudently brought with her from Grosvenor Square. 'Or . . . not *very* near, at any rate.'

'Not yet,' said Sophie. 'But I think it is only a matter of time, if we go to Karnag, before the fighting comes to us.'

Roland, as Sophie had expected, was a more difficult undertaking; for him as for herself, what she proposed to do was a matter not only of genuine risk to life and limb but of defying both father and King – if the bones so tossed fell wrongly, in fact, a matter of treason.

But Roland had already been stinging from being made to stay safe at home when fell the dual blows of Derrien Robic's attempt on Lucia's life and successful taking of his own; he was, it seemed, feeling sufficiently useless, reckless, and unjustly stymied that his thoughts made more fertile soil for Sophie's ideas than she had at all allowed herself to hope.

This is only the barest beginning, she reminded herself sternly, when euphoria threatened. *And we may already be too late.*

But Roland and Lucia were looking at her expectantly, and begining to talk of logistics and supply, and she could not help a very small smile.

The chief difficulty to be overcome, Lucia recognised early on, was not that of slipping away from the escort of Royal Guardsmen told off to accompany them to Oxford – no very difficult matter, when one travelled in company with Sophie Marshall – but, rather, that of ensuring that the said guardsmen, once evaded, should neither come to harm as a result of Sophie's deception nor immediately raise the alarm and thus put the expedition at risk.

The offer of a solution came, to Lucia's surprise, from little Master Alcuin – Sophie's former tutor, it transpired, and before that, Gray's – who, though he did not look it, proved to have been a mage-officer in His Majesty's army in his youth, and to be adept at spells of illusion and misdirection.

'If we could have a se'nnight's start on whatever pursuit my father may choose to send after us,' said Sophie eagerly, 'it would be enough, I think; we ought to be able to reach the coast in three days – I shall not tell you where, Magister; you understand? – and once we are aboard ship we shall not be quite so easily found.'

'A se'nnight,' the little don mused. There was a faraway look in his pale-blue eyes, and he tugged absent-mindedly at the end of his beard. 'Yes, it might be done, I think, with a little ingenuity.'

There followed a moment's thoughtful silence before he rose abruptly from his chair, muttering unintelligibly into his beard, and began searching his bookshelves. After some unsuccessful attempts to recapture his attention, Sophie rose also, and tugged Lucia up by the hand. 'Come along,' she said. 'We have other fish to fry.'

The rest of these fish were also Fellows of Merlin College – young men all, though none so young as Sophie herself – with the exception of one graduate student. The field was necessarily limited by its being still, for some weeks more, the Long Vacation; but the Marshalls' particular friends, it appeared, were as fond of their books and their comfortable quarters as the Marshalls themselves.

Their first call was to Gareth Evans-Hughes, who had been of such material assistance on their previous visit to Oxford, and by whose gifts as a scry-mage Sophie set such store. They had not asked permission to wander about Merlin College; instead, disconcertingly, Sophie had simply caused the Porter on the gate to find them unremarkable, and they had walked in on the heels of a fair-headed young man in a blue coat (who took no more notice of them than the Porter had done) and made directly for Master Alcuin's staircase. Lucia had never before seen this power of Sophie's so clearly on display, and in a way it was more terrifying than any of her more dramatic magickal undertakings: the effortlessness of it, as though to make herself and Lucia essentially invisible were a matter of no more account than calling light!

'Gareth is not the most powerful of mages, in the ordinary way,' Sophie explained, low-voiced and in Gaelic, as they crossed a grassy quadrangle. 'But he is sensible and clever, and has been one of our most loyal friends, and I *hope* that he may be persuaded to forgo common sense for the sake of that friendship, if for no other.'

'And,' said Lucia, with a sidelong look, 'we may perhaps have need of a scry-mage?'

'Yes,' said Sophie. 'That, also.'

If Gareth Evans-Hughes proved astonishingly persuadable, Guillaume d'Allaire, Reader in Magickal Theory, was not.

'*This* is your plan,' he said flatly, when Sophie had finished explaining herself. His pale eyebrows had vanished entirely under his untidy, straw-coloured curls. 'This . . . this hodgepodge of legends and speculation. I must tell you, Magistra, I expected better of you.'

Lucia was struck speechless by the man's effrontery, but Sophie – who had named him a friend! – merely pressed her lips together briefly before returning to the fray.

'It seems absurd to you, I know,' she said patiently, 'and I cannot altogether disagree. But it is by no means the strangest defensive magick I have seen at first hand; if it works as it ought to do, we shall be doing a great service to the kingdom, and perhaps saving a great many lives which must otherwise have been laid down in defence of it.'

Guillaume d'Allaire sighed. 'And how, precisely, do I figure into your scheme?'

He looked reluctant and sounded put-upon, but for all that, there was a certain look in his slate-blue eyes which Lucia – her father's apprentice in matters political since her childhood – had seen before. Unlike Sophie, therefore, she was entirely unsurprised when, at last, d'Allaire agreed to join their clandestine expedition to Karnag.

By the time their party set sail – by night, aboard a smuggler's craft, from the unlovely fishing village of Bognor, upon the Sussex coast – it numbered fully a dozen persons: not only d'Allaire and Evans-Hughes but two more Fellows of Merlin, Henry Crowther and Séverin Proulx, and Gray's former student Rhein Bevan – and (at their own insistence) Ceana MacGregor and Conall Barra MacNeill. It was thus far larger than Lucia considered either necessary or advisable, but she could not deny that the effect on everyone's spirits of travelling with eight mages of some power (and it would not do to discount Gwendolen Pryce, either, she reminded herself) was a cheering one. Of course this was largely an illusion; in fact, it was Sophie's magick which protected all of them at present, and the more persons Sophie must conceal, the greater the drain upon her magick and, thus, the greater the danger to them all.

The company of Royal Guardsmen dispatched to Oxford along with Sophie, they had left to the care of Master Alcuin. His promise to procure Sophie's party a se'nnight's start, to ensure that no harm came to any of the guardsmen, and to pay their tariff at the Dragon and Lion from the purse of coin Sophie had left with him for the purpose, was less reassuring than it ought to have been, from the circumstance of his having refused to tell any of them precisely how he meant to carry out the first of these undertakings.

'I trust Master Alcuin,' Sophie had said, very firmly, but Lucia had wondered whom, exactly, she had been hoping to persuade.

'Lucia?' said Roland, hushed and tentative, at her left shoulder.

Half turning from the taffrail, Lucia saw that Roland had brought her a shawl and was preparing to drape it round her shoulders.

'I thank you,' she said, low.

Roland ducked his head. 'You were shivering.' He shifted into halting Gaelic to say, 'Do you think that Sophie's . . . plan has any chance to succeed, truly?'

Lucia did Roland the courtesy of considering this question

458

seriously. 'If I thought we had no chance at all,' she said, after a moment, 'I should not have agreed to be a party to it. It seems . . . a bow drawn at a venture, I will concede, but I have seen Sophie do some very astonishing things.'

In the darkness, Roland nodded. 'And so have I,' he said. 'It is not that I lack faith in Sophie! It is only that . . . well . . .'

Lucia chuckled. 'That her plan has all the hallmarks of madness, and is founded entirely upon instructions found in the diaries of a mad king whose funeral pyre was cold ashes centuries before any of us were born?'

'Well,' Roland repeated, scuffing at a knot in the decking with the toe of his boot. 'Since you ask me, yes.'

'And that this Duke of Orléans has a very large army at his command, and we have not.'

'That, also.'

Roland shivered, and Lucia, greatly daring, unwound the shawl from the left half of her body and wrapped it, and her left arm, about his waist. He tensed briefly; then, perhaps deciding that the proprieties of his father's court need not be scrupulously observed on the deck of a smuggler's craft, drew the shawl up over his left shoulder and settled closer to Lucia at the rail.

'The last time I followed Sophie halfway across a kingdom,' she said pensively, 'I had an army at my back – though only a very small one. I should have reached her much sooner without it, but I was glad of my little troop when we arrived.'

'Did you . . . Did your father . . .' Roland's voice trailed off uncertainly.

'I made off with a detachment of my father's household troops without asking his leave, yes,' said Lucia, taking pity on him. 'On the principle of its being easier to beg his pardon than to persuade him. He was *very* angry with me, I am told, but he had regained his temper by the time we next met face-to-face, and only subjected me to a detailed and scathing critique of my conduct – from a military perspective, you understand.'

Roland produced a disbelieving chuckle.

'Should you think less of me,' he said, looking resolutely away from her, 'if I confessed to being a little afraid of your father?'

'If closer acquaintance does not alter your opinion,' said Lucia, 'I shall be very much surprised.'

And if Duncan is not frightened of him, how on earth should you be?

'*My* father will say I ought to have stopped her,' Roland continued unhappily. 'As though I *could.*'

'Roland, your father himself tried to stop Sophie from leaving England, and could not; three years ago, he attempted to stop her from remaining in Din Edin, and could not do that either. And he is not only her father but the *King of Britain*! You surely do not imagine that he expects more of you then he can accomplish himself?'

Roland shrugged, his shoulders hunching.

'Roland.' Lucia inched closer, so that they were pressed together from shoulder to hip, and spoke in Latin, near his ear: 'You may not have seen your father's face – or perhaps you may not remember it – after our adventure in the maze, when he was frightened for you, and declared himself in my debt; but I saw it, and I swear to you on the bones of my mother that you are as much beloved as your sister.'

He did not speak, nor turn to look at her, but his stiff posture gradually relaxed, and they stood shoulder to shoulder at the taffrail until the sun began to warm the eastern horizon.

Breakfast was followed by a council of war to discuss the latest intelligence – not so very recent now, but better than none at all.

'If it were only the troop-ships moving down the Loire,' said Lucia, 'that would be one thing; he might only be aiming at Naoned, which would be perfectly rational – a bid to control the provincial seat, if I understand correctly, and the whole of the river from Orléans down to the sea.' She peered at the map, head tilted, and measured the distance with her spread fingers from the Loire to Naoned. 'But he has a force at Klison already, which is far better placed to besiege Naoned.'

'Exactly,' said Joanna. 'If the reports received thus far are accurate, there are more than enough men at Klison to hold it and march on Naoned besides. But if he can sail *past* Naoned—'

'My uncle's troops will stop him if they can,' said Sophie loyally.

Roland glanced sideways at her. 'Of course they will,' he said, 'but we must allow for the possibility that they cannot – as the garrisons at Klison and elsewhere could not.'

CHAPTER XXXIV

In Which Edward the Dishonourable Disappoints, and Gray Reflects upon the Recent Past

Sophie's party were landed at dawn on a wide-curved beach on the Bay of Kiberon, almost due south of Karnag. They splashed through the surf barefoot, with trouser-legs rolled and skirts tucked up, and collapsed all up and down the empty shingle, with bag and baggage, to wait for the sun to rise.

Then, having set their clothing to rights as best they could, they reassembled themselves as a party of travellers visiting the sights and the holy places of Breizh, located the road to Karnag, and walked the two miles to the village of Le Ménec, on the far side thereof, and its one inn, the Ship at Rest.

The innkeeper beamed when Sophie and Joanna spoke to her in Brezhoneg. Yes, she had good, soft beds to offer them – they should find the rooms small, but bright and clean, never fear! – but such a large party, she hoped they should not object to share their rooms? – no, there had been no Orléanais soldiers hereabouts, no soldiers at all in fact, and glad enough she was of it, for there is nothing like a troop of soldiers for eating a person out of house and home! Well, if there was to be war, she only hoped that whichever side was fated to win it might do so quickly, and not drag the frontier to and fro a dozen times, to the harassment (and worse) of ordinary folk on both sides of it.

Joanna and Sophie looked at one another and refrained from translating this last for the others.

That evening, for the first time, Sophie's finding-spell produced the faintest tug of awareness of Gray's location – almost due south, at the very edge of her perceptive range – and she went to bed in good spirits, for all that the Duke of Orléans was advancing on their position, also, and from two directions at once.

After breakfast the next morning, they trooped out of the inn-yard and through the tiny hamlet of Le Ménec. All but Joanna and the two Alban guards were bleary-eyed and yawning; Sophie herself had scarcely slept.

The bleary eyes opened wide when at length they reached their goal, and stood at the westward end of a vast field planted with massive stones, gazing east along the long, almost mathematically straight rows at the rising sun.

'Apollo, Pan, and Hecate!' breathed Bevan.

Sophie felt very much the same herself; it was one thing to know of the existence of this ancient wonder, and another thing entirely to stand in its presence, feeling the vast aetheric echoes of its past.

'But there are hundreds of stones,' said Joanna, her voice oddly strangled. '*Thousands.* How are we to know which of them are important to the spell?'

'Hush, Jo,' said Sophie absently. She closed her eyes and pressed her palms flat over her ears, the better to hear the thing just beginning to tug at the edge of her perception.

Was this what had kept her awake last night? It seemed the most likely explanation. And if the sounds were not aural but aetheric, then *that* would explain both Joanna's easy energy and her own ill temper, for Joanna might very well have slept like a top.

Sophie moved through the rows of stones with her eyes and ears still stopped, hearing their outlines in her mind as faint, shimmering shapes of dull crimson – not radiating magick, but . . . *soaking it in*; and there, *there*—

'That one,' she said, pointing at the stone to her immediate left, which shimmered sluggishly in a shade of scarlet so intense that it hurt her ears. 'There are six, and that is the first.'

A line of . . . *something* . . . ran between that first stone and the next in the sequence, faint and stuttering but unmistakably *there*. It had a scent like wet limestone and old blood and the air after lightning, and Sophie was growing dizzy with the strangeness of it, which at the same time did not feel nearly so strange as it ought.

There had been rain in the night, and the turf beneath her feet was soft and yielding.

She followed the tugging trail to the next stone – laid both palms against its rough-smooth surface – felt something buzz distantly under her hands and beneath her feet.

It was not like riding the blue-fire magick of Ailpín Drostan's ancient spell-net – to begin with, it was still perfectly clear to her where her own body ended and the rest of the world began – but perhaps, perhaps, the long-dead mage-queen who devised this spell had drawn inspiration from Alba.

As the map had suggested, there were six scarlet stones among the dull crimson ones, straggling vaguely southeastward – in, that is, the approximate direction of Klison, the first link in the chain. Upon opening her eyes, Sophie discovered that each now had a human attendant.

'Yes,' she called, cupping her hands to either side of her face to amplify her voice. 'One mage to every stone.'

There was a brief-scuffle just out of sight amongst the stones.

'Do you mean to begin at once?' d'Allaire called back, from halfway along the chain.

'Have you some better notion?' This from Gareth, farther off still. 'We have not come all this way for a picnic luncheon.'

Sophie rolled her eyes (for none of them could see her, after all), then stood very straight and drew a deep breath, for optimal volume. 'Who has the first stone?'

'I have,' called Lucia MacNeill.

'Then you must begin,' said Sophie. 'Jo, where are you?'

Joanna emerged from beyond the northernmost row of stones, trotted towards Sophie, and said, 'Here.'

'Will you go back to Lucia now,' said Sophie, lowering her voice, 'and give the signal to Gareth when she has finished, and so on? I did not think the keystones would be so far apart.'

Joanna nodded eagerly, and trotted away.

And now there was nothing to do but wait in silence for Lucia – then Gareth, then d'Allaire, then Roland, then Bevan – to take their turns, so that she might cap the spell. *And then we shall have nothing left to do but hope we have succeeded.*

She could hear nothing, and could see very little, of how the others went on, but that did not stop her from imagining each of them in turn pricking one finger with a pen-knife or paper-knife, smearing a drop of blood on the stone, and speaking the invocation, so that by the time her own turn came, every muscle ached with tension.

The little knife was so sharp that she did not feel the sting of the wound until her thumb was pressed against the stone's rough face, and then she nearly jerked it away in surprise at the sudden sensation of *pulling.*

'*O gods great and small,*' she recited, '*O gods above and gods below, gods who made the bones and flesh of my kingdom and made men of bone and flesh and blood to walk upon its beloved soil, protect us. O gods who bring the seasons in their proper time, protect us. O gods who gave magick to mankind, defend us. O gods who wear many guises, defend us. With my blood, with my magick, for the sake of my kingdom and all who dwell there, be renewed.* Do ut des.'

She brought her hand away from the stone, staring at the smear of blood where her thumb had been.

She closed her eyes, stopped her ears, reached for her magick – and found everything precisely as it had been before.

Exhaustion and disappointment rolled heavily over her, and she turned her back to the stone and sagged against it.

'We must have done something wrong,' Sophie sighed, as they made their dispirited way back to the inn. 'Perhaps the spell truly cannot be worked except "at the turning of the year", and we ought to have waited for the Equinox—'

'And the arrival of enemy troops?' said Joanna. 'If that is so, then there is nothing to be done about it, Sophie.'

'Or perhaps the words of the invocation – perhaps I was not careful enough in transcribing it – did I misunderstand Edward's instructions? Not that they were instructions, as such—'

'Perhaps at a different time of day,' said Henry Crowther, clapping her encouragingly upon the shoulder. 'Noon, perhaps. Or midnight? Some spells are more efficacious at midnight, you know, or can be worked only then . . .'

It was kindly meant, but surely if the time of day had been a vital component of the spell, the diary must have said so? Sophie sighed and managed a smile at Crowther.

'I move we make another attempt after dinner,' said d'Allaire.

'Seconded!' said Bevan. 'All in favour of dinner?'

There was a good-naturedly derisive chorus of *Ayes*.

They returned to the stones towards dusk, some of their confidence restored by the inn's simple but excellent dinner, and Evans-Hughes, d'Allaire, Crowther, Proulx, Bevan, and Sophie took up positions at the six stones. At first, either the alteration in the choice and sequence of mages or the time of day appeared to be making the difference, for Sophie, at the end of the chain, could feel the stones farther upstream gathering in magick and beginning to radiate it outwards, as they had not done before. But the momentum died with Bevan, and when Sophie herself nicked her thumb and spoke the invocation, it was with the sinking feeling that nothing she now did, or did not do, would have the slightest effect upon the outcome.

Weary and dispirited, they collected themselves, called a flock of magelights, and began to make their way back to the inn.

'Sophie,' said Evans-Hughes quietly, falling into step beside her as they turned into the inn-yard, 'may I see the diary?'

'Of course,' said Sophie. 'I shall fetch it down for you.'

The next two hours were spent by Gareth in close study of Edward II's diary, and by Sophie and Gwendolen in attempting to repair the damage inflicted upon everyone's clothing by most of a day spent tramping about what was essentially a muddy field.

Sophie was mending a rent in Lucia's petticoat, and Gwendolen progressing steadily through a heap of stockings in want of darning, when there came a knock at the door of Sophie and Lucia's bedchamber.

'The answer is in the names,' said Gareth, quite without preamble, the moment Gwendolen opened the door. 'The names of the mages. Edward did not think to be more explicit, I suppose, because he thought it clear enough. Look—' He thrust the diary almost under Sophie's nose, and Sophie, perforce, did look. His broad forefinger touched each name as he spoke it, moving along the line of cramped, faded script; did he hear in his mind's ear the voice of a king five centuries dead? 'Arzhur of Dinan. Guillaume Forestier of Bayeux. Guy d'Ernée. Melyor Penrose of Lamorna. Richard of Lincoln, called Blythe. And Edward himself, of course. Do you see?'

467

Sophie did not see, at first. She read the names over again, however, and a pattern began to emerge. A Breizhek name, then two which were more Français than English; Bayeux was in Normandie, of course, and Ernée . . . yes, in Maine. A Kernowek name, and a very English one, from an English town. But—

She shook her head. 'I thought I saw the pattern,' she said, 'but I was mistaken; there is a second English mage, here' – she tapped Edward's name – 'where I expected a Cymric one.'

'Oh, but Sophie, you forget your history,' said Gareth reproachfully, and Gwendolen exclaimed, 'Of course! Edward of Caernarfon!'

'Of . . . ? *Oh!*' Yes, Edward Longshanks' fourth son had been born in Caernarfon Castle. But did that make him, this long-dead Plantagenet king, a man of Cymru? Surely not – or did it?

It was an absurd method; it was dreadfully impractical; it was . . .

It was, thought Sophie with an inward sigh, just exactly the sort of fail-safe which a mage might conceive of, in an attempt to control some very powerful working otherwise apt to grow dangerously out of hand.

She revolved the matter in her head, surveying the resources at her command. Two English mages – Roland and Crowther – and three Cymric ones – Gareth, Bevan, and Gwendolen. Lucia, whose magick she had been relying upon as the most powerful after her own, was suddenly removed from the equation altogether. Guillaume d'Allaire was Normand and Séverin Proulx Mainois, entirely by luck, and she herself was Breizhek enough for this purpose, surely?

But the pattern had a gap in the shape of Melyor Penrose of Lamorna, Edward's Kernowek mage, and how was Sophie to fill it?

Had she dragged all these men and women across the Manche – and into something very like treason – to no good purpose, after all? *Minerva, Lady of Wisdom, how am I to untangle this knot?*

Before settling down to sleep, she worked the usual finding-spell, ignoring – or attempting to ignore – Lucia's silent sympathetic gaze. To her surprise, the result this time was strong and immediate: Gray had grown closer since yesterday, much closer, and the direction of the pull had altered.

If Gray is coming here . . .

Was Gray, whose parents were English but who had been born at Glascoombe, near Dowr Carrek, sufficiently a man of Kernow to stand in the place of Melyor Penrose of Lamorna?

The small fleet of ships bearing the second sorcerer-century – such as it was – down the River Loire and across the Bay of Kiberon had sailed all day and all night, whenever possible, to cover the distance more quickly. When they came in sight of the long, shallow curve of the beach where they were to go ashore – standing afar off, to be on the safe side, for though the passengers might trust to the Emperor's spells of concealment, the crew did not – the sun was hanging low in the western sky, and Gray watched as the crew prepared to lower the boats over the side of the *Coulèvre* with a strange tight thrumming in his chest.

All through the journey, the signs had been there which told him that he was growing nearer to Sophie (or she to him). He had done his best not to dwell on what this must mean, for knowing Sophie to be safe and well and, above all, out of danger from Orléans' armies had been a comfort to him, but so unmistakable were the sensations of proximity now that there was no denying it: She had, in fact, somehow put herself directly in their path. Why should she do so? And, by all the gods, how had she managed it?

This is British soil we are landing on, he reminded himself; *it is she who has every right to be here, and Orléans' troops who have not.*

In the ordinary way, there was no reason why Sophie should not come to Breizh whenever she liked. But nothing about the present circumstances was ordinary, and so . . .

So, then: Sophie was very near. Sophie had given her father her word not to attempt to follow Gray to Normandie, and her presence in Breizh certainly violated the spirit, if not the letter, of that promise. Sophie could be impetuous, true, but she would not lightly break her word to her father.

Certainly there were few enough things he could trust at present, and few enough people. The other mages treated Gray with a more or less friendly condescension, except when actually engaged in some manner of drill or rehearsal of joint manoeuvres. Only twice – in silent shared horror on the occasion of Orléans' original announcement of his campaign plan, and poorly concealed relief at its subsequent revision from hingeing on wholesale slaughter to making use of spells for deep sleep, immobility, and concealment – had any real fellow-feeling subsisted between the others and himself. How odd that after half a day's acquaintance he had been prepared to trust Ollivier and Lécuyer with his life, yet here . . .

'Marais!' Bertrand jostled Gray's shoulder. '*T'es encore dans la lune, hein? Allons, on descend.*'

Gray mumbled an apology for his inattention, and followed Bertrand and Girard over the starboard rail and into the next boat.

Two young crewmen rowed in near silence by the faint light of magelight lanterns. Crammed in beside Gray in the stern of the boat, Girard tilted up his head and murmured, 'What do you suppose the Emperor wants with this godsforsaken place?'

Gray liked Girard well enough, most of the time – he was not much given to cruelty, and had once helped Gray rescue one of the kitchen-maids from the unwanted attentions of a drunken comrade – but confiding in him was quite impossible. And, in any case, what did Gray know? *Take and hold the keystones at Karnag,* Orléans had said; though it was more than any of the others –

save, presumably, their commander – had been told, it did not answer the questions *why*, or *how*, or *to what purpose*.

'I suppose that we shall be told what his purpose is when he deems it necessary,' said Gray, therefore – but not reprovingly. Girard was very young, and it was perfectly natural to be curious, and even apprehensive, in the circumstances.

Girard sighed. 'Yes,' he said. 'I suppose so.'

He subsided, leaning gently against Gray's arm and shoulder, and Gray sank back into thought.

When word had come that the sorcerer-century was to sail from Orléans in three days' time, Gray had come near to pleading with Amelia to allow Ollivier and Lécuyer to engineer her escape, but to no avail, for she refused categorically to abandon her beloved papa. Gray could appreciate the integrity of her position – but the problem of the reserve mages' mysterious compulsion, which ebbed and flowed with the strength of their connexion to the field-mages, was a more complex task even than he had anticipated, and a solution unlikely to materialise in the time remaining to him. He bore Amelia's recriminations on this point without protest but equally without concession, until at last she said, 'Even if I were to leave Papa, what would become of me then? I followed him here because, for all his faults, he loved me and needed me; but now he is fallen under the Emperor's spell, and I have nowhere else to go – no one else to go to.'

'How can you say so?' Gray exclaimed. 'Your sisters and your cousin Maëlle were half sick with worry for you, when last I saw them in London, and dreading what might have befallen you in Taylor's company. Why else should I so readily promise to help you?'

Amelia blinked at him, tears beading on her long lashes, and caught back an emerging sob. 'Truly?' she said, in a very small voice.

'Of course,' said Gray, nonplussed.

Amelia sat down heavily – and with an uncharacteristic lack of grace – on the lip of the fountain. 'But why?' she demanded. 'Why should they take me in, any of them? I have been rude to Joanna, and cruel to Sophie – I am a burden to Lady Maëlle, and likely to remain so—'

'I do not pretend to understand even Sophie, let alone Joanna or Lady Maëlle,' said Gray, by now rather desperate to stem this tide of self-recrimination, 'but love need not be rational. Your sisters, I dare say, remember a time when you were better friends; and as for Lady Maëlle . . . well, she has no children of her own . . .'

'And – and she would take me back, after . . . all of this?' An expressive wave of her hands indicated their surroundings.

'I have not the slightest doubt of it,' said Gray truthfully.

Gray had seen many things, but he would not soon forget the sight of Miss Amelia Callender, erstwhile chatelaine of Callender Hall, weeping into her hands in a moonlit courtyard in Orléans. He reflected, not for the first time, that nearly all of Amelia's behaviour in Grosvenor Square, and most of Sophie's and Joanna's, could be explained very tidily as a means of self-defence – each attempting to wound the other before she could be fatally wounded herself.

The storm of weeping was intense, but mercifully brief; and when its aftermath had been assuaged by means of first Amelia's own handkerchief, then Gray's, she had sat up straight on the fountain's edge, folded her hands in her lap, and said quietly, 'Very well, Mr Marshall—Gray. I am at your disposal.'

Ollivier had smuggled her out of the castle courtyard the following evening, dressed in yet another purloined infantryman's uniform, and by now she might already be safely over the Mainois border, or so Gray hoped.

The boats deposited their passengers on the fine shingle, then at once put out again towards the *Coulèvre*, now nearly invisible in the gathering dusk. The sorcerer-century formed up into small, relatively inconspicuous groups for the brief march inland — the stone-fields of Karnag were only a few miles distant – and Gray, one of very few speakers of Brezhoneg present, found himself in the first group to depart, together with Bertrand, Guillemeau, Dolet, and Decurion Rousseau's particular crony, Antoine Martel.

The high, sweet thrum of Sophie's magick sang louder and louder in his blood as they climbed up from the beach and strode along the road. The strength and the nearness of it both comforted and alarmed him: *Sophie is here!* sang one part of his mind, triumphant, joyful, whilst another gibbered, *Sophie is in terrible danger!*

As the link between his magick and Sophie's tugged him in one direction, his links with the mages of the reserves in Orléans tugged resolutely the other way – each in itself a small and fragile thing, but collectively a weight upon his spirits.

For his own sanity, he had still to avoid recalling too closely the process of forging those links. What Rousseau and Girard had described as mildly unpleasant, on the order of a mild headache or a case of indigestion, Gray – whether because of his existing link to Sophie or because of his violent, if unexpressed, objection to Orléans' modus operandi – had experienced as excruciating pain. He had lost consciousness only briefly (or so he was afterwards assured), but the feeling of disorientation, the skin-crawling sensation of something *wrong*, had taken days to fade, and even then had not vanished but merely subsided.

Worse than all of this was knowing what the links were *for*. Talk amongst the sorcerer-century confirmed Amelia's claim that nothing in the linking-spell prevented a reserve-mage's magick from being entirely drained, should the field-mage's need be sufficiently great. Some drew confidence from this notion; a few had confessed, though quietly and obliquely, that the implications troubled them;

but the majority expressed no opinion in either direction. Did they simply take the reserves for granted as insurance against difficulty or disaster, or did they harbour objections which they were too afraid to voice even to one another?

And if, as it was said, only Orléans himself could forge those links between a mage of the sorcerer-century and his reserves, was the reverse also true? Must Gray now pass the rest of his days with half a dozen strangers' magicks uncomfortably twisted up with his own – and, worse, with Sophie's?

Gray wrenched his thoughts away from this distressing tangent, focusing as narrowly as he was able upon the here and now: the sounds and scents of the night air, already hinting at autumn's chill as the Equinox approached; his companions' footfalls, their quiet voices, all about him; the silver glint of moonlight on Martel's dark hair, on the buttons of Bertrand's coat; the precise spot where his own boot was rubbing a blister on his left heel.

When he was calm again, within as well as without, he allowed himself to consider once more how to go on from here. The easiest and least risky choice was to slip away once the first few groups of men had reached the rendezvous point between Karnag and Le Ménec and settled in for the night; if he volunteered to take the first watch, then he should have only one sentry to subdue or outwit, rather than two. By awaiting the next morning's promised briefing, on the other hand, he should have more precise intelligence to carry to Sophie, or to the nearest British garrison, if he should stumble across the latter before finding the former. But what if that small delay should make the difference in his ability to escape, or if it should mean that the intelligence came too late to do any good?

And what in Hades does it mean, *that Sophie is here?*

CHAPTER XXXV

In Which Gray Seizes His Opportunity

The following morning, the whole of the party followed up their breakfast with a largely undirected ramble about Le Ménec, so that they might speak more freely without setting wards. They paused for a quarter-hour's rest in a coppice-wood on the far side of the stone-fields, and at Sophie's insistence she, Gareth, and Lucia worked yet another set of finding-spells. This time, they were pulled so strongly towards Gray that Sophie had to be physically restrained from following her finding at once.

'He may not be alone, or free,' Lucia pointed out reasonably. 'He went into the Duchies to investigate this Imperator Gallia, as well as to search for your sister; we cannot know what schemes he may have in train, and we should do no one any good by interrupting them.'

Sophie, now resting with her back against the trunk of a tree, bounced one knee in suppressed frustration. 'I can go to him without being seen,' she said. 'I have done such things before, as you may remember' – here a pointed look at Lucia, as though Lucia might perhaps have failed to remark how entirely their journey from London to Karnag had depended on Sophie's particular talents – 'and if Gray is in need of rescuing—'

'If he were in need of rescuing,' said Joanna, 'should you not have known it already, now he is so nearby?'

'Well,' said Sophie, looking at her feet. 'Yes, very probably I should. But—'

'And if you can find him,' Joanna continued, 'then *he* ought also to be able to find *you*? He must know already that you are here, just as you have known for some time that he was travelling towards us?'

'Yes,' said Sophie. 'But—'

For a long moment the sisters faced one another in silence, conversing, it appeared, in some language made up entirely of pointed looks.

At last the contest, whatever its precise nature, was resolved in Joanna's favour; Sophie turned away, clasping her elbows and curling in her shoulders, and said, 'Very well.'

Joanna sighed, looking not at all satisfied with her victory.

'I know how eager you must be to see Gray, Sophie,' said Lucia, clasping her shoulder. 'I should be frantic, in your place. But if he is not in any danger . . .'

'It is not only that,' said Sophie.

Lucia mentally chalked up a point to herself, for provoking her friend into speech. *It is a fact of human nature*, her father was fond of saying, *that we are loath to let a wrong statement go unchallenged.*

'This is what Gareth and I wished to explain,' said Sophie, 'here, away from the inn and whoever else may be in it. We need a Kernowek mage, in order to renew the magick of the stones; and Gray is . . . the nearest available approximation.'

'Why?' said d'Allaire blankly.

'Because he was born in Kernow,' said Sophie. She frowned at him.

'Not—' d'Allaire scrubbed a hand across the back of his neck. 'I meant – why do we need a mage from Kernow?'

'The diary,' said Gareth. His sideways glance at Sophie held some exasperation; he himself, Lucia suspected, would have begun at the beginning. 'Edward the Second was born in Cymru, and when he came to Karnag to replenish the magick his father had neglected, he brought with him mages from each of Britain's other provinces. If Sophie and I are correct, we shall not succeed unless we do the same.'

'What an odd requirement!' said Crowther. 'You are certain of this, are you? It seems . . .'

'We can be certain that both of our previous attempts failed,' said Evans-Hughes.

'And the first, I think, failed almost straight away,' said Sophie, 'but the second . . . the magick *was* settling in the stones, as it ought to do, until we reached Bevan's stone, and then the . . . the flow reversed itself. Which suits Gareth's theory perfectly, because Gareth had the first stone in the chain, and so you, Rhein, represented a doubling-back to Cymru.'

Bevan nodded thoughtfully.

'I agree with Lucia and Joanna, that we ought to wait for Marshall to seek us out,' said Roland. 'In case he may be occupied with something which ought not be interrupted. But if you had rather not wait, Sophie, could you not use a drawing-spell to bring him here? He is very near now, you said?'

'Very near,' Sophie agreed, 'and to the south. Roland, have you ever *felt* a drawing-spell? Or seen one?'

'No,' said Roland, a little defensive. 'It is not a very common magick.'

'At this distance,' said Sophie, 'it would be very difficult to resist, and quite impossible to explain.'

'A last resort, then,' said d'Allaire, with a wry smile.

The light drizzle which had begun whilst they were debating Evans-Hughes's theory was now thickening into rain of the sort which demanded to be taken notice of.

'If our plan at present is to wait quietly for Marshall to grace us with his presence,' said Crowther plaintively, 'let us at least wait within doors, and out of the damp.'

The slow and stealthly reassembly of the Emperor's troops in a fallow field a few hundred yards from the stones of Le Ménec was accomplished a little before midnight; and when the tents had all been pitched, the latrines and fire-pits dug, and the ring of concealment-spells, wards and shielding-spells set in place, the sorcerer-century retired to its bedrolls. From the tent he shared with Bertrand and Girard, Gray could hear the occasional low murmur of voices from the men standing the first watch, the chirping of crickets, the wind singing through the lines of stones. Soon Girard and Bertrand were snoring to either side of him; Gray lay long awake, however, contemplating the bizarre turn his life had lately taken.

By the time the watch changed, he had dozed and awoken several times, and was forced to concede that Morpheus had chosen not to favour him with restful sleep tonight. Very well, then; he was not likely to find anything more like privacy than this. He closed his eyes, settled his thoughts as best he could, then reached deep for his magick and, holding in his mind's eye an image of Sophie's face, sent it out on the quiet words of a finding-spell: *O amisse reperiaris! Verba oris mei ad te eant. Remitte ea ut me ad te adducant.*

The returning flow of magick was immediate and almost overwhelming – Sophie was very near now, and he had failed to compensate for the proximity of her magick. He had not been aware of any ebbing of his own power, but now it strained towards hers, clamouring in tandem with the finding-spell to pull him up out of his bedroll and southward towards the village proper. He could follow it – could nudge aside the tent-flaps and crawl out from under the canvas, tug on his boots and creep between the tents and out of the camp – but tomorrow, tomorrow he should discover what Orléans was about with this manoeuvre, and then he should not have spent all this time and effort to no purpose.

Tomorrow.

He rose at dawn having slept scarcely at all, performed his morning ablutions, fell in with the others, and waited for their commanding officer to speak. Beyond their wards and shields, and beyond the woods ringing the field in which they had pitched their camp, some heavy cart or waggon rumbled past along the road from Le Ménec. The Centurion, so called, was ordinarily a man of terse orders and brief but rousing extempore speeches; when instead he drew from his uniform coat several folded pages of writing-paper, a murmur passed through the ranks of mages. It subsided as he began to speak, but rose again, baffled, when he said, 'Once we have taken possession of the stone-fields of Karnag, our empire will hold the reins of a great and ancient magick, older by far than the Kingdom of Britain from whose grasp we must reclaim the remaining lands of Gallia Romana.

'Our brothers of the first sorcerer-century now hold all of the line of fortress-stones, but the wellspring of the magick is here: three thousand stones, three thousand repositories of power, sleeping since the days of Divus Iulius. When we possess the stones, we shall wield unimaginable power. Our task now is to secure the stones – no great matter, as the local people are ignorant of their power, and suppose them no more than a historical curiosity – and then to wake them.'

'To *wake* them?' muttered someone, close enough for Gray to hear. '*Three thousand* stones?'

And how, exactly, does one wake a stone?

Gray did not have long to ponder this question; the answer went some way towards explaining why the half-trained and undermanned second sorcerer-century, and not any of the large, well-equipped infantry regiments presently mustered at Orléans, had been sent to Karnag: to wake the power that slept within the stones, it appeared, required an infusion of magick from without. But how much magick? There were three thousand stones, so said the Centurion, and but eighty mages; how long could each of them keep feeding their own magick into stone after stone after stone, before – reserves or no reserves – they came to the end of themselves?

But he had what he needed now, more or less; there was little to be gained by staying longer.

'When our task is done, the Emperor himself will come to take possession of the legacy of Divus Iulius. All hail the Emperor of Gaul!'

'All hail,' Gray muttered along with the others.

They departed their camp as they had entered it, in twos and threes, and as they filtered into the long field of standing stones, he cast about for some opportunity of escape, placing himself deliberately on the right edge of the field.

From afar, the stones in their long straight rows had looked more or less uniform; close to, however, they varied in size from the height of Gray's knee to well above his head, and were far more irregular in shape than he had supposed. Here and there one had fallen on its side; Gray wondered whether it would be part of the mages' task to right these deviants from the regimented pattern, and, if so, how the Centurion proposed that they do so. Moss and lichen patched their surfaces, particularly on the north faces and in the deep clefts that marked some of the larger oblong stones, bright and pale and deep greens, brown and gold and rust-red. Around their feet, grasses still green or autumn-gold stirred gently in the breeze.

Towards the middle of the sea of stones, a particularly large specimen, just barely taller than Gray and three times as wide at waist height, offered him temporary cover, and whilst the men to his left advanced, he slipped away into the trees to the south. Once out of sight amongst the trees, he moved more quickly – sometimes, when the way was relatively clear, breaking into a run – and when he judged he had got clear, he settled down with his back to a large tree-trunk and repeated his finding-spell.

Sophie was away to the west, now – not because she had moved much, Gray judged, but because he had come so far east since the previous night's attempt. His possessions were scattered across three separate military camps in two kingdoms; he owned, at present, absolutely nothing but the clothes on his back and the meagre contents of his pockets; but the relief of simply following where the finding-spell led him, as he had done hundreds of times in his life (though seldom for so high a stake), was indescribable, and a weight seemed to lift from his shoulders as he strode along the lanes towards Le Ménec.

'A gentleman to see you, ma'am,' said the innkeeper to Sophie, not a quarter-hour after Sophie had left the breakfast-table and retreated to her bedchamber. Sophie's heart leapt; she quashed the feeling firmly. *But who else could it be?*

'Please show him up,' she said, and folded her trembling hands in her lap. She chanced to be quite alone at present, for Lucia and Roland and Joanna and Gwendolen had developed an unexpected passion for long, exploratory walks about the village and the countryside, which they were presently indulging, and none of the Oxford men had yet emerged from their rooms. When the door opened again and Gray walked through it, she thanked all the gods for the blisters on her heels.

'Thank you, Mrs Cariou,' she managed to say. 'You may leave us, if you please.' At the innkeeper's frankly dubious expression, she added, 'It is most irregular, I know; but this gentleman is my husband, who is just come from England to join me and our friends.' *Without bag or baggage, and looking as though he has been sleeping under a hedge.*

'Very good, ma'am,' said the innkeeper, with the air of one who has many questions which she has decided not to ask, and finally, *finally* went away.

'Sophie,' said Gray, in a voice thick with exhaustion and relief.

He held out his arms, and she ran the length of the room on her blistered feet to fling herself in to them, clinging as tight as though she had suspected him of wishing to escape.

By the time Lucia, returning from her walk, pushed open the door of their shared chamber, Sophie had subjected Gray to a hot bath, two helpings of breakfast, and other things not for public consumption; had demanded an accounting in the matter of Amelia, and attempted to come to terms with the revelation that his 'rescue' thereof had apparently consisted in sending her off into the Orléanais countryside with a pair of Breizhek mage-officers; and was well along in explaining how she, her brother and sister, her sister's intimate friend, the heiress of Alba, and five Merlin men had come to be filling up all the guest-rooms of the Ship at Rest in Le Ménec.

'Gray Marshall!' cried Lucia, grinning widely. 'Brìghde's tears, you are a sight to see!'

Footsteps thumped along the corridor, and Joanna, Gwendolen, and Roland crowded in behind her. After the barest greetings, Sophie shushed all of them, in order to carry on with her tale.

'And so,' she concluded, 'now that you are come, we ought to be able to make the spell work, and renew the keystones, so that the magick of blood and stone can help my father's armies to repel Orléans.'

'But, Sophie, I have been thinking,' said Joanna. 'We have not got a mage from Breizh, either.'

'We have got Sophie,' Gwendolen objected. After a further moment's thought, however, she exclaimed, 'Herne's horns! What if Jo is right?'

Sophie felt very cold, suddenly, though a moment since she had been warm and contented, pressed against Gray's side with his arm wrapped firm about her shoulders.

'Sophie is more Breizhek than I am Kernowek,' said Gray. 'I shall go and round up the others for another attempt, before—well.' He was on his feet now, and crossing to the door. 'I shall have to explain as we go. But, Sophie, it will not overtax your strength, to conceal all of us at once?'

'No,' said Sophie firmly; of that, at least, she was quite certain. 'Not now.'

Navigating the standing stones and the seventy-odd mages now wandering about in them – thank all the gods, and Ceana MacGregor's plea to see *something besides those gods-accursèd stones*, that their morning's walk had taken them in the opposite direction! – was a new and nerve-stretching undertaking. It was not, of course, that Lucia did not trust Sophie's magick to conceal them from unwelcome notice; there was always the danger of running against someone emerging from behind a stone, however, not to mention the unknowable consequences of success, or of failure, with upwards of half a hundred hostile mages all about them who might well be able to detect the effects of the spell they were presently attempting.

Sophie arrayed her forces – Bevan, then Roland, d'Allaire, Proulx, Gray, and last of all herself – and told off Joanna, Gwendolen, and Evans-Hughes as signalmen between them, and Lucia to make sure that Gray spoke the invocation correctly. Then she paced out an irregular sort of ellipse encompassing all six keystones and set a ward around it, so powerful that when the magick rippled through Lucia's consciousness, she staggered with the force of it.

For all of them but Gray, the spell was by now tiresomely familiar, and they were not so long about it as they had been the first time, or even the second. Unfortunately, however, the results were more or less the same.

'It *was* working,' Sophie insisted, near tears with exasperation. 'Better than the second trial; all of the stones but mine responded, this time.'

'Which means, I fear,' said Gareth Evans-Hughes, 'that birth and not descent is the deciding factor, and we are still short one mage born in Breizh.'

Joanna was listening intently to this exchange, her expression growing increasingly grim.

'Your spell, the one you worked on Sophie in Din Edin,' she said, low, edging closer to Lucia. She caught Lucia's wrist and held it; her grip was surprisingly strong, for all that her hand was scarcely bigger than a child's, and Lucia was reminded that Roland had described her as *a thorough horsewoman.* 'You cannot give your magick to the stones, but if you will share it with me, then—'

'*No,*' said Lucia, almost simultaneously with every other person present.

'But do you not see? If birth is the criterion,' Joanna insisted, 'then we have no other choice. Sophie was born in London, but *I* was born in Breizh, and the only obstacle is—'

'Joanna, the spell does not work that way,' said Lucia, helplessly. 'It is meant for one mage to share magick with another, not—'

'Has it ever been tried?' Joanna demanded.

'I—'

'*Has* it? And, more importantly, can we afford not to make the trial now?'

'The danger is—'

'We are *all* in danger already – we are, quite literally, surrounded by the enemy! – and the kingdom, and everyone in it – and all of those "reserve mages" held prisoner at Orléans, and Kergabet's spies—'

Lucia tried to pull away, but Joanna held fast; her grey eyes had gone a little wild, an impression not hindered by the mad tangle of chestnut-coloured curls about her face, and Lucia suspected that she looked rather wild herself.

'What makes you suppose that the magick will answer to you?' she said. 'How shall you know how to wield it? Joanna, no one has ever done what you ask of me, that I know of. I do not know whether it *can* be done, or, if it could, what the consequences might be. We cannot properly control the parameters of the experiment, and—'

'Whatever the consequences,' said Joanna, 'they cannot be worse than allowing the Duc d'Orléans to march the armies of the Duchies over Britain's borders and declare war upon our gods.'

She was not wrong; but nor was Lucia.

Lucia tried again to wrench her arm away; this time, Joanna let her go. She resisted the urge to cast a beseeching look at Sophie, at Gray, at Roland – in the course of her debate with Joanna, the rest of the party had surrounded them, and giving the choice over to someone, anyone, else would be all too easy. *When you sit the chieftain's seat of Alba, Lucia MacNeill,* she told herself sternly, *it will be your task to make difficult decisions. Had you not better begin as you mean to go on?*

But this did not feel like a decision that ought to be made by one person alone.

'I am willing to try the spell,' she said at last, slowly, making sure to meet each person's eyes as she looked about her, 'but only on condition that all of us agree.'

Sophie's betrayed expression — there and gone in the instant before the blank bland mask descended — was terrible to see. Gray interposed himself between them and drew her into his arms, bending his head to speak into her ear; Joanna, wisely, kept clear of this conversation.

'I should not ask this of you — of anyone — if I thought there were any other choice,' she said, looking up at Lucia with both defiance and apology in her wide grey eyes.

'We are *in Breizh*,' said Lucia. 'Surely we ought to be able to find a Breizhek mage?'

The five Oxford mages exchanged a look.

'What have I said?' Lucia tried to make her voice flat, uncompromising, but did not altogether succeed.

There was another exchange of looks, the upshot of which, it appeared, was to elect Guillaume d'Allaire as spokesman.

'The stones,' he said, with a vague one-armed gesture, 'are a sort of sink for magick; it is a matter of record — though the local people naturally do not like to advertise the fact — that no mage has been born within thirty miles of them these past two hundred years.'

'And that those who come from elsewhere tend to go away again after no more than a year or two,' Evans-Hughes added. He ducked his head and scratched absently at the back of his neck. 'Now, I suppose, we know why.'

'Do we?' This from Bevan, the young graduate student. He looked both horrified and fascinated by the notion of a magick-sink, and stared at Gareth as though expecting him to produce a physical artefact of some sort to demonstrate.

Lucia was about to echo him when at last the pieces fell into place in her mind. 'You mean,' she said, 'that the stones became a magick-sink only when their own magick was allowed to decay.'

'Yes,' said Gareth, smiling at her in spite of everything, like the patient tutor he undoubtedly was, pleased with a student's acuity. 'Exactly. Of course, it is a theory that may take generations to test—'

Crowther jostled his shoulder and said in an exasperated tone, 'Do shut up, Gareth, there's a good chap. The point is, Lady Lucia, that there are likely to be no Breizhek mages within anything like a reasonable distance.'

Lucia sighed. 'I have truly not the least notion whether Joanna's proposal will work,' she said. 'I should not be at all surprised if it did not. But if it were only that—'

'This spell of yours,' said Rhein Bevan. 'How long do its effects persist?'

'It depends,' said Lucia, 'or, rather – for *depends* implies a cause, and I know of none – it *varies*, for no apparent reason; but I have never heard of its lasting longer than a se'nnight.' She glanced about her anxiously, then lowered her voice still further: 'This magick has been used in my clan for a dozen generations at the least, but only ever between one mage and another; I have truly no means of predicting—'

'But,' said Henry, 'how can any field of enquiry advance, except by experiment?'

487

'I am a great believer in the value of experiment,' said Lucia tightly. 'That is, of controlled experimental trials. What you propose is – is not that.'

'*I* do not see,' said Joanna, evidently deciding that she had kept her prudent silence long enough, 'why, if the risk is mine, the decision should not be mine also, if Lucia is willing.'

'Do you not?'

Joanna turned sharply at the sound of Gwendolen Pryce's voice, tight with some barely contained emotion. The Oxford men regarded them curiously – all but Gareth, whose mouth crimped tight in sympathy.

'Oh,' said Joanna, in a very small voice.

Gareth turned to Lucia and said, a little more loudly than strictly necessary, 'How does the spell work, if I may ask? Professional curiosity, you know.'

This drew the others' attention as perhaps nothing else could have done, and Lucia – watching from the corner of one eye as Joanna and Gwendolen slipped away from the group to the shadow of the nearest great stone – was grateful for it, though already bracing for their inevitable disappointment.

'It is Clan MacNeill magick,' she said. 'I should never be forgiven for revealing its secrets outside the clan, and still less to – my apologies – Sasunnach mages. That is' – she held up a hand to forestall the inevitable objections – '*British* mages.'

'And no other clan has ever devised a similar spell?' Crowther enquired.

Lucia shrugged. 'Not to my knowledge – though they would scarcely advertise the fact, if they had. We may be a united kingdom now, but the clans and clan-lands still keep their own counsel on some matters, and clan magicks are one such.'

Gwendolen, towing Joanna by the hand, strode back to the

488

circle, followed after another moment by Sophie and Gray, both wearing expressions of grim resignation.

'Well?' said Lucia, looking round the circle of faces. 'What say you all?'

Though none of them looked happy at the prospect, none objected, and almost before she had time to regret her rash promises, Lucia was seating herself against a hip-high stone and calling fire to a candle-stub to heat her knife.

CHAPTER XXXVI

In Which Joanna Rises to a Challenge

Though her arguments in favour of this course of action had – of course – all been entirely rational ones, that part of Joanna's mind which was always unflinchingly honest could not deny that the prospect of *knowing*, once and for all, what it was to have magick was part of its appeal. She put out her hand for Lucia's knife willingly enough, and watched with interest as Lucia, after wiping the tiny blade and passing it through the candle-flame once more, nicked her own thumb and pressed the two bleeding digits together.

Then hot sharp fizzing panic swept through her, and the world glowed red and gold and upended itself, and for some indeterminable time she was entirely incapable of observation, analysis, or even coherent thought.

When next she opened her eyes on an intelligible vision of stones, long grass, sky, and anxious faces, everything was rimmed with the same faintly glowing aura of crimson and gold.

'Jo,' said Sophie anxiously. 'Jo, are you all right?'

'Yes,' said Joanna at once, though she was not at all certain that she was telling the truth. She had the bizarre impression of feeling her blood flowing through her veins, even the smallest of them; her body felt much too large for the skin meant to contain it; and her head seemed to vary in size according to some pattern of its own devising.

Clutching Gwendolen's left hand and Roland's right, she struggled to her feet, then leant heavily on Gwendolen's arm, panting, until the horizon steadied again. Walking was a frustratingly strenuous exercise, for her feet seemed at once larger than usual and farther from the ground; but at last Gwendolen and the hovering Roland delivered her to what had until now been Sophie's stone, and she sank to her knees beside it.

Her thumb was still bleeding sluggishly; she had the invocation by heart, having heard it several dozen times in the past two days, but how in Hades did one persuade magick to flow out of oneself and into an inanimate object, or, indeed, to do anything whatsoever?

Sophie and Gwendolen knelt on either side of Joanna, each clasping one of her hands; she was pathetically grateful for these tethers to the world of solid and observable things.

'You have only to do one thing,' said Sophie, 'and I shall tell you how to go on.'

Joanna nodded, then at once wished she had not.

'Keep your eyes shut,' Sophie said. Her voice was low, soothing, as though Joanna had been a child waking from a nightmare. 'Breathe deeply and slowly, and listen for the beating of your heart.'

Breathing slowly was an effort, but Joanna's heartbeat was already thudding in her ears. She forced herself to focus on it, however, and felt it slow and steady as she brought her rapid breathing under control.

'Now,' said Sophie, 'go deeper — imagine you are diving to the bottom of a pond, and rising out of the muck and weed is something beautiful — in your case, I should imagine, something shining in gold and scarlet—'

All of these instructions were entirely incomprehensible, and impossible to carry out, until, quite suddenly, the black nothingness behind Joanna's eyelids was interrupted by a gleam of gold. The gleam grew – slowly, then by rapid bursts – into a maelstrom of fire, scarlet and gold and almost too bright to look upon.

'Yes,' she breathed, clutching Sophie's hand. 'I see it, like a fiery whirlpool.'

'Well done,' said Sophie, her voice warm with relief. 'We are nearly there, Jo. Now, can you reach into the whirlpool – gently, now – and pull out a thread from it – wrap it about your wrist, I think, so as not to lose hold of it – and now back up through the water—'

Joanna's metaphorical hand was wrapped about with shining streamers of magick; her physical hands – indeed, the whole of her body – thrummed with a weird amalgam of nervous and magickal energy. What might be happening in the world around her, she could not begin to imagine, so strange and vast and inexplicable was the terrain of her own spirit.

Her left hand was moving – Gwendolen was lifting it – her thumb pressing against rough lichen-covered stone.

'*O gods great and small*,' Sophie prompted gently, and Joanna repeated the words, ran through the whole of the invocation without pausing for breath. The magick flowed out into the stone – was *pulled* out, spiralling down into a yawning chasm which, she saw at once, would take and take and never be filled; and then, in an eyeblink, it *was* filled, was overflowing, was not a chasm but a wellspring, and the air was humming with a sound like bees in a clover-field in summer, and there were arms about her and the laughter of relief, and the ground fell away and her face was pressed into the smells of wool and sweat and woodsmoke and sea air.

'I shall go to sleep, I think,' said Joanna.

Sophie could never afterwards recall the details of their journey back to the inn on the afternoon of the Autumn Equinox; the whole of it was a blur of triumph, terror, and a determined focus on evading the notice of Orléans' legions of mages. She walked beside Gray, clutching the tail of his coat, so that she should not have to look where she was going; Joanna hung limp in Gray's arms, her sturdy boots and one plump little hand swinging with the rhythm of his stride.

They had succeeded this time, that was the important thing; the magick of the keystones had been replenished, and so the spell could now be used as its makers had intended. But what, precisely, were they to do with a defensive boundary, now that the enemy was on the wrong side of it?

They deposited Joanna in her bed, leaving her to the care of a pale and grim-faced Miss Pryce, and foregathered with the remainder of the party in the cramped private dining-room which Mrs Cariou, the innkeeper, had provided for their use. Lucia had taken the precaution of ordering a substantial meal, in case of magick shock, and they applied themselves to their bread, hard cheese, ham, and apple-tart with cautious enthusiasm.

'Well,' said Roland at last. 'We have brought the spell back to life – the magick of blood and stone – and now what are we to do with it?'

There was a general chorus of *what, indeed?* around the table, and a ring of expectant stares in Sophie's direction.

'*She who would wield the magick of blood and stone need not be Queen,*' Sophie recited, '*but she must be a loyal subject of the Kingdom of Britain, and a mage of some talent and skill. She must possess the map of the keystones, and the spell that wakes their power to rouse the kingdom to its own defence.* That is what we are to do with it – to rouse the kingdom to its own defence.'

They looked at her doubtfully, as though she had not told them all exactly this, not so very long ago in Oxford.

Bevan and Roland (who appeared to have forgotten for the time being that he was a prince) cleared away the remains of the meal and stacked the dishes on the sideboard, and Sophie spread out the map on which the magickal stones were marked in red and the manuscript page containing the relevant spell. The writings of the Princesses Regent on the subject of the magick of blood and stone were frustratingly cryptic – or, more probably, relied on the context of the time to convey their meaning – but both map and spell were mentioned as requirements. A spell, as Sophie had been told often and often, is merely an *aide-mémoire,* a means of focusing mind and magick on the desired working or its outcome; the difficulty here was that they had no real notion of the nature of the spell, or of what it was meant to do.

'Perhaps,' Roland suggested, oddly diffident, 'the spell will do whatever you wish it to do. Within the limits of its capacity, that is.'

'That would be a very useful spell,' said Gareth.

'And unimaginably complex to design,' said Proulx, frowning thoughtfully. 'But more easily worked than a collection of simpler spells designed to produce the same outcomes, and less prone to error.'

'Queen Ahez knew what she was about, I am sure,' said Sophie, with some asperity.

'If *I* were designing such a spell,' said Lucia, 'if I knew how, which alas I do not, I should give the land and the people the power to resist invasion, and leave to them the choice of means to do so. After all, the same tactics are unlikely to be equally useful against longship raiders and siege-engines.'

'And sorcerer-centuries,' added Roland. Lucia smiled at him, and laced their fingers together atop the tablecloth.

'Indeed,' said Sophie. 'But—'

'It seems to me,' said Gray, leaning forward with his chin in his hands, 'that as the stones are now all in the hands of Orléans, the most important thing is to prevent him from making use of them. He supposes, apparently, that waking all the stones of Karnag – there are three thousand altogether – will give him dominion over the whole of Roman Gaul.'

'How?' said d'Allaire, bewildered. 'And . . . how?'

'That information,' said Gray, 'was not conveyed to the rank and file, alas. For myself, I do not greatly care, so long as he is stopped. It is any ruler's right to seek to expand his territory by conquest, of course, but to declare war on the gods who were worshipped here before the Roman Conquest, and to enslave men, not to mention mages, by compulsion to risk their lives for the sake of victory in battle – *no*.'

There was a general shudder around the table; Sophie, who (with Roland, Lucia, and Joanna) had heard all of this in more detail already, flinched and swallowed back nausea at the thought of those mages linked to Gray who, in the wrong circumstances, could be drained of their magick without warning and through no will of his.

'In any case, it scarcely signifies what his foul purpose may be,' said Lucia, 'if we can prevent whatever it is by invoking Queen Ahez's spell. Sophie, you are the only one who can wield the magick, or so the Princesses Regent tell us; you need not wait for the rest of us to conclude our debate before acting as you see fit.'

Sophie glanced round the table again, and was heartened to see no censure or disapproval of this last remark. 'Very well,' she said. 'I shall do my best.'

They fell silent, waiting – they were all of them mages, after all, and knew the value of a quiet room. Sophie read over the spell again, twice more, so as not to stumble, and focused her mind on what seemed to her the desired outcome: the absence of the Duc d'Orléans, his mages, and his troops from all of Britain's provinces; peaceable borders between Britain and the Duchies; and peaceful coexistence amongst the old gods and the new.

She found Gray's hand and clasped it, skin to skin, and felt their magicks well up to meet one another.

Then she closed her eyes, let her magick flow out into the aether, and spoke the spell.

The magic of the stones raged through Sophie like a river in flood through an opened sluice-gate, vast and old and terrible – but there and gone in the space of two heartbeats.

'Sophie?' Gray's voice by her ear; Gray's large warm hand curling over her shoulder.

Somewhere, the sound of a door slamming.

Sophie peeled the side of her face from the table and sat up as straight as she could.

'Hallo the house!' came a voice from the inn-yard below the window, calling loudly in Français.

Roland jumped up to peer through the window, followed in short order by every other person in the room, apart from Sophie herself. Gray went last of all and was back almost at once, cursing under his breath.

'He is *here*,' he said, low and urgent in Sophie's ear. 'He was to come in triumph when we had awakened the stones – all three thousand of them – but surely—'

'Who?' said Sophie, in hopes of making him explain. She felt slow and stupid, as though her thoughts were swimming through treacle.

'Orléans,' said Gray, as though it had been obvious. 'Come and see.'

She levered herself upright, with one arm wrapped tightly about Gray's waist, then made her way to the window and peered down into the forecourt.

496

Sure enough, there stood in the forecourt of the Ship at Rest an elegantly caparisoned black horse and, holding its reins, a small man, resplendent in a blue coat trimmed with gold braid and positively radiating power.

Sophie straightened away from Gray's side; half turned, grasping the windowsill for balance; and beckoned to Roland to stand beside her. 'We are the generals of this little army, I think,' she said, low, in her brother's ear. 'We stand on the battlefield, face-to-face with the enemy. What say you – will we challenge him?'

Roland's hand caught hers and squeezed it tightly. She glanced aside at him and found him wearing a broad, exultant grin. Lucia stood at his other side, her hand on his shoulder, and Evans-Hughes and Crowther behind him; Joanna clasped hands with Sophie on one side, and Gwendolen Pryce on the other; behind the three of them stood Gray, Bevan, d'Allaire, and Proulx.

Sophie gently detached her hand from Joanna's, flung open the windows, and let go her mother's magick before reaching for her sister's hand once more.

'Monsieur le Duc d'Orléans!' she called. 'We are the Kingdom of Britain, and we and our gods defy you.'

He looked up at their first-floor window and stared at them in outrage; his voice boomed out so loud that Sophie repressed a yelp: 'I am Imperator Gallia. I command legions such as the world has not seen since the great days of Rome; I wield the power of two sorcerer-centuries and of Divus Iulius himself. You, it appears, command an army of eleven. You are a brave and noble band of warriors, I have no doubt, but I need hardly cast the auguries to predict the outcome of this contest.'

'I urge you to reconsider your plan of campaign,' said Roland. His shoulder trembled against Sophie's, but his voice was steady. 'We are not alone; we have the whole of Britain at our backs, and she is waking in anger at the threat to her sons and daughters, and to her gods.'

Orléans stared up at them, frowning – not in anger, if Sophie read his face aright, but in bafflement at this bizarre and inexplicable turn of events.

Then he shook his head, half turned from the window, and began to speak some spell; a spell it was, Sophie felt quite certain, for the very air shivered with the force of his magick drawing in. The air darkened – or were Sophie's eyes failing under the onslaught? – she swayed and staggered against Roland's shoulder, and Joanna's stumbling threatened to pull her off balance from the other side – the air grew thin and hot, and bruised Sophie's throat as she gasped for breath—

—until, between one breath and the next, the cobbles of the forecourt cracked across, with a sound like thunder, and Orléans' horse stumbled and slid, its hind legs sinking hock-deep into the resulting chasm. Orléans himself, stumbling too, backed away from the struggling horse, and the buzz and burn of his gathering magick abruptly ceased as he sat down hard upon the cobbles.

'Oh,' Sophie gasped, her stomach churning. Had her spell done *that*? And not even to the enemy she had meant it for, but to a beast which had no choice in the matter? Or was this the effect of whatever magick Orléans had himself been working?

'Lady Epona,' she whispered, 'let not the blow fall on the innocent.'

It occurred to her then – whether in answer to this prayer, or by sheer happenstance, she could not have said – that here was a use for the drawing-spell she had feared to use yesterday. She drew a deep breath, fixed her gaze on the foundering horse, and began quietly to hum a jaunty march.

The horse's hindquarters rose very slightly; it found its feet just long enough to scramble out of the crack in the cobbles, and stood for a long moment on trembling legs before lifting its head and walking towards the front door – no, the front *window*. Sophie abruptly ceased humming and let the magick go, sighing with relief when the horse lost interest and wandered away to browse in Mrs Cariou's herb beds.

'We have Orléans at our mercy here,' said Lucia quietly, gesturing at him; he was picking himself up, dusting off his elaborate coat. 'This war, the ugly means of prosecuting it, his mad notions about the gods of Rome – cut off the monster's head, and the body will fall to pieces of itself.'

Sophie recoiled in horror.

'Lucia is not suggesting cold-blooded murder, Sophie,' said Roland hastily.

'Well,' said Lucia, 'I—'

Roland gave her a meaning look, and she swallowed, then went on: 'Could not the spell which drew that poor horse out of the crevice in the courtyard also draw our uninvited guest into, for example, the inn's root cellar? And hold him there until further reinforcements can be summoned?'

Sophie blinked at her, considering this, and at last smiled a little. 'Yes, that is a very good notion,' she said.

She was still reaching for a suitable melody, and wondering how to overcome the problem of the locked door, when Orléans got his second wind. His brush with the abyss had not diminished either his power or his determination to use it against his opponents, it appeared, for he was snarling as he spread his hands and began chanting another spell. The magick seemed to come at them from everywhere at once – pressing in upon Sophie's skin, her eardrums, the top of her head – the air like treacle, thick and clinging – *Arachne's Web*, thought Sophie, for she had felt something like it before, but surely Arachne's Web could not be cast on such a scale?

Gray's hands descended on her shoulders, thumbs pressed to the bare skin at the nape of her neck; magick thrummed between them. Sophie straightened her spine, clutched Roland's hand and Joanna's, and held on.

'Mother Goddess, bountiful and kind,' she said aloud. The roaring air swallowed her prayer, but the words came tumbling past her lips, faster and louder: 'Gods above and gods below, gods of the rivers and woods and stones, gods of the Britons and gods of the Gauls, gods who made this land and gods who guard it, hear me!'

'You have no dominion here!' Orléans roared. 'Take your petty gods and your hangers-on and begone!'

The floor trembled beneath Sophie's feet with the force of his spell, whatever it was; the rafters groaned; before her eyes, the window-frame sagged out of true. The floor tilted, the shutters began to splinter and crack.

'Hear me!' cried Roland.

'Hear me! Hear us!' the others echoed, over and over as the staggering heat and pressure of Orléans' spell built up around them, driving them one by one to their knees.

Sharp pain exploded through Sophie's head as her ears gave in to the onslaught; she swallowed back a shriek, and with it the warm iron tang of blood running down over her lips. Her back bowing over, she struggled to regain her feet – fell to her knees again – cracked her chin against the window-sill.

If I am to die here, she thought defiantly, *at any rate I shall not die alone.*

She opened her mouth – it was an effort, by now – and repeated the words of the spell, the Brezhoneg and English and Cymric and Français and Kernowek phrases tumbling over one another (she could not hear her own voice over the tumult of noise and pressure and pain) as her magick and Gray's, Roland's and Lucia's, Gareth's and all the others', rose up to meet the magick of the stones.

Sophie spoke the last word of the spell, and the gathered magicks erupted.

Another teeth-rattling thunder-crack resounded through the house, and another chasm opened in the forecourt – this one immediately behind Orléans' heels, so that he stumbled and nearly fell headlong into it.

From the middle distance – northward, in the direction of the stone-fields – came a series of what sounded like small explosions, accompanied by the occasional pained yelp or howl.

On her knees on the floorboards, Sophie peered over the warped and splintered window-sill. 'Mother Goddess,' she breathed, as the implications began to dawn upon her: the enemy was not only at this particular gate, and therefore Queen Ahez's spell would not be so restricted, either. 'Mother Goddess, what have we done?'

CHAPTER XXXVII

In Which the Fellows
of Merlin Change Their Mind

The death toll, in the end, was so low as to beggar belief, and His Majesty declared a feast day throughout the kingdom in thanksgiving to the gods for the carnage spared. The third and last of the minor earthquakes at Karnag claimed the life of Henri-François, Duc d'Orléans, before Sophie could carry out Lucia's scheme to lock him in the cellar of the Ship at Rest; at Klison, the flood that swept away the invaders' weaponry and siege-engines also killed two men of His Majesty's army who had been taken prisoner; and a similar flood at Ivry-sur-Eure carried off two men and their mounts who happened to be crossing the bridge.

The suspicion of many in Britain that Orléans' followers had been under the influence of some magickal compulsion, though never unequivocally verified, was borne out by the startlingly high proportion of soldiers and officers who deserted or surrendered in the aftermath of the earthquakes, fires, floods, lightning-strikes, rock slides, and sinkholes which Sophie had called forth by invoking the magick of blood and stone. Many claimed to remember nothing of what they had done, thought, or said during the previous year – for most a safely unverifiable claim, but not without a kernel of truth. As a result, the men who had first conspired to murder King Henry, and later provided aid and intelligence to the enemy, were not condemned to death, but only returned to a more secure imprisonment.

Joanna recovered without incident from her encounter with magick, rather pleased to have had the experience of seeing magick use from the inside but infinitely grateful to be spared repeating it in the foreseeable future. Amelia, whose journey across Orléanais and Maine had resulted in a thorough change of heart on several points, returned to London to make her peace with her sisters and her guardian, and was invited, together with Lady Maëlle, to continue in Grosvenor Square at least until after the royal wedding. Over the course of that autumn and winter, her quiet beauty caught the eyes of many a young man, but her heart was won, in the end, by a gentleman of five-and-thirty who confessed that he had heard her playing upon Lady Lisle's pianoforte, and singing a Breizhek love-song, some time before he ever saw her face (for he was rather short-sighted), and been inspired by the sincerity of her performance to seek an acquaintance with her.

Some two months after what the public insisted on calling the Battle of Le Ménec – though there had been no battle in the ordinary sense – the Princess Royal and her father received identical copies of a letter from the Fellows of Merlin College, which after the usual salutations read as follows:

> *Whereas trustworthy reports from the scene of the battle indicate that the actions of female mages, though appearing at the time to be ill-advised and based in pure speculation, in fact spared the kingdom much of the expense of prosecuting a costly war and saved countless lives on both sides;*
>
> *Whereas the contributions of the said female mages are reliably reported to have been integral and even*

indispensable to the strategy which accomplished these feats;

Whereas the female members of the expedition to Karnag are reliably reported to have conducted themselves with bravery, resourcefulness, intelligence, fortitude, moral courage, and a spirit of enquiry in the course of the said expedition, equal to those of their male counterparts; and

Whereas, in light of these and other facts, it seems high time to revisit the policies and attitudes of the past several centuries with respect to higher education for young ladies,

We, the undersigned Fellows of Merlin College, Oxon, do hereby endorse and support the re-establishment of a college for women on the site of the former Lady Morgan College, Oxon.

The signatures of some half-dozen Fellows remained conspicuously absent from this missive, but these absences were very effectively overshadowed by the signatures of every other Fellow of Merlin and several Fellows of other Colleges.

The marriage of Prince Roland of Britain and Lucia MacNeill, heiress of Alba, was celebrated in London in October, and in Din Edin in December, of the year of the Hundred Days' War. It was rumoured in Britain that they had been secretly handfasted at some time during their unauthorised journey to Breizh; the rumours were never confirmed or denied, and speculation continued for some time. The royal couple's first child, a daughter, was born in the following October, and was named Maeve Edwina Sophia Joanna MacNeill, for her two grandmothers and her aunts.

In the autumn of that same year, the newly established Regents' College opened its doors to its first matriculating students.

CHAPTER XXXVIII

Thereafter

Joanna was well accustomed by now to being among the oldest in her year – second only to Gwendolen and to Mathilde de Courcy – but the feeling was magnified, somehow, by the experience of seeing young ladies several years her junior shake hands with the College Mistress and receive degrees exactly equivalent to her own.

'To Mademoiselle Joanna Claudia Callender,' declared the Mistress of Regents' College, 'is awarded the degree of *Artium Baccalaureus, cum laude.*'

Polite applause from the assembled guests was drowned out entirely by the cheering and, not to put too fine a point on it, hooting of Joanna's particular friends; and, diploma in hand and flushed with both triumph and embarrassment, Joanna retreated to her seat beside Justine Beauvois to watch Mathilde, next in the queue, take her turn before the multitude.

This first matriculating class had been a small one, and had grown smaller as the years progressed, so that by now only one-and-twenty young women remained to receive their degrees; no more than another quarter-hour had passed, therefore, before Mademoiselle Gwendolen Cornelia Pryce was awarded the degree of *Magicēs Baccalaureus, summa cum laude*, together with the prize (established by the Fellows of the College) for coming first in the practical examinations for the said degree. Joanna beamed up at the stage, and at Gwendolen blushing prettily at the centre of it whilst Mór MacRury stepped forward from the ranks of Fellows to ambush her with a congratulatory embrace, until she felt her face would split in two from the joy of it.

At dinner in Hall, the atmosphere was buoyantly triumphant, the hum of conversation almost painfully loud, and the hall itself packed to the rafters with Fellows, students, and their families and friends. Joanna, so tightly wedged between Sophie and young Agatha that she could scarcely manage her knife and fork, had almost no attention to spare for missing Gwendolen: Agatha was ecstatic to be granted the honour of sitting down to dinner with the grown-up ladies and gentlemen, and expressed her elation by chattering nineteen to the dozen all through dinner; Sophie was full of plans for her summer in Alba, and was attempting once more to persuade Joanna to make one of the party ('Should you not like to meet Roland and Lucia's little daughter, before she grows taller than either of us?'), before she should return to London to take up her official post as Secretary to the Chief Privy Councillor; Amelia was anxiously seeking advice from Jenny on the rearing of little boys. Joanna had only to look up and along the table to her right, however, to see Gwendolen sitting between her father and her sister Branwen, quietly glowing with pride in her own accomplishments and, more unusually, with pleasure in her family's being by to share them. It was odd, after all these years, to see her in such company – and her father, at least, could not have looked more awkward and ill at ease had he set out to be so – but in a way that warmed Joanna's heart and made her smile.

After dinner they walked about the grounds with their guests, and at last saw them off at the College gate, whither they should return to their lodgings at the Dragon and Lion.

'I could not be prouder of either of you, if you were my own children,' said Sophie, not for the first time, embracing first Joanna and then Gwendolen with undiminished enthusiasm. Gray shook their hands solemnly in the Alban manner; then the two of them strolled away towards their own rooms in the Senior Fellows' wing, hand in hand and heads bent together.

Joanna watched them go, and smiled.

'Jo,' said Gwendolen softly, 'what are you thinking of?'

Joanna turned a little and looked up at her. 'I hardly know,' she said honestly. 'We are come to the end of something, today; but I cannot regret it, for I hope it may be the beginning of something better still.'

Gwendolen, laughing, tangled her long fingers with Joanna's amongst the mingled folds of their skirts. 'From your lips to the gods' ears,' she said.

ACKNOWLEDGEMENTS

This is the last book of a trilogy whose first book I began writing a decade ago, and thanking everyone who has contributed to its (and my) success would require a whole 'nother book. Still, I'll give it a go!

Many, many thanks to my fantabulous family (immediate and extended) and friends, my terrific day-job colleagues, and the lovely and supportive members of Kol Rina Women's Choir, the Orpheus Choir of Toronto, and Congregation Darchei Noam for general and particular cheerleading and encouragement; to Anne Marie Corrigan, Alex Hunter, Tawnie Olson, Luisa Petroianu, Antonia Pop, and Kim Solga for walks, plot talks, and milkshake summits; to Jeannie Scarfe for late-night text conversations and beta reading; to Stephanie Sedgwick for equestrian consulting (and the owl colouring book!); and to Michael Appleby for emergency Latin support. All remaining errors are my own. For much of the writing of this book I was digging my way out of a not-so-nice brain-space, and I appreciate every. single. person. who offered hugs, tissues, encouragement, chocolate, and/or a listening ear when I needed it.

Thanks to my amazing agent, Eddie Schneider, and his colleagues at JABberwocky Literary Agency for everything they do and for a delicious Indian dinner in a pub in London this spring, as well as to John Berlyne of Zeno Literary Agency in the UK. Thanks to my equally amazing and very patient editor, Jessica Wade (without whom this book would be much longer and nothing like as good), and her able assistant, Miranda Hill; to Amy J. Schneider for helpful copy-editing, and Christina Griffiths for the hat trick of gorgeous covers; to Cortney Skinner for mapping the world of the series so beautifully; and to Michelle Kasper, Jennifer Myers, Kayleigh Webb, and Kim Burns for shepherding the book the rest of the way into your hands. A huge thanks also to the team at Allison & Busby for bringing the trilogy to readers in the UK! And a shoutout to the fabulous Toronto Public Library system, and particularly to the North York Central Library, where at least half of the words in this book were written. Writing was fuelled by Kicking Horse Coffee, the Second Cup Coffee Co., DAVIDsTEA, and Adagio Teas.

It's not easy living with someone who's writing a book while also holding down a full-time job! So all the thanks to Alex and Shaina Hunter, who have been putting up with me (and all the weirdos who live in my head) for twenty-four and fourteen years respectively; and to my mum, Luisa Petroianu, my baby brother, Dan Izzo, and the rest of the mishpacha (and mishpacha-of-choice), who have been putting up with me for even longer. *I love you all so much!*

The necklace and earrings Joanna lends to Gwendolen are modelled on a set made for me by Anne Marie Corrigan; Amelia's silver-and-garnet eardrops, on a pair given to me by Deborah and Sam Appel. The Kergabets' bigger, fancier house in Grosvenor Square has many sofas, chairs, and chaises longues, but the green-and-gold-striped sofa in the morning-room is a close cousin of the silk-upholstered one which my mother inherited from her parents, on which (unlike the rest of the furniture) many generations of cats have been forbidden to sleep.

Although 'Duc d'Orléans' was a real title in pre-revolutionary France (a title reserved for members of the French royal family, rather like 'Prince of Wales' in the UK), Henri-François, Duc d'Orléans, is an invention of my own. Similarly, Nevenoe (in French, Nominoë) and his wife, Argentaela, are real historical people, and Nevenoe really is considered the first king/duke of Brittany, but almost everything else this book states or suggests about either of them is completely 100 per cent made up.

I have also, of course, played fast and loose with the history and geography of France and its neighbours. The territories and places mentioned are, or at some point in history were, real ones; most of their alliances and allegiances, however, are fictional. Exceptions to the former are Ivry-la-Bataille, which I have renamed Ivry-sur-Eure (not to be confused with Ivry-sur-Seine); and the territory around Paris, historically known as l'Île-de-France, which, because no kingdom of France exists in the world of this book, I have renamed l'Île-des-Francs.

Most of the songs in this book echo those in the two previous books. The exceptions are 'The Oak and the Ash' in Chapter IV and the two Welsh songs ('Suo Gan' and 'Llywn On', known in English as 'The Ash Grove') and the Scots song 'O Whistle and I'll Come to Ye' in Chapter XI. 'The Oak and the Ash' is the contemplations of a young woman from the north of England who wishes she weren't living in London; 'Suo Gan' is a lullaby; and the others are both love songs, though they could not be more different in character. The story mentioned in Chapters XV and XXIII is, of course, the French fairy tale 'La Belle au bois dormant' by Charles Perrault (1628–1703), better known to English speakers as 'Sleeping Beauty' – judiciously adjusted for congruence with the Midnight-verse.